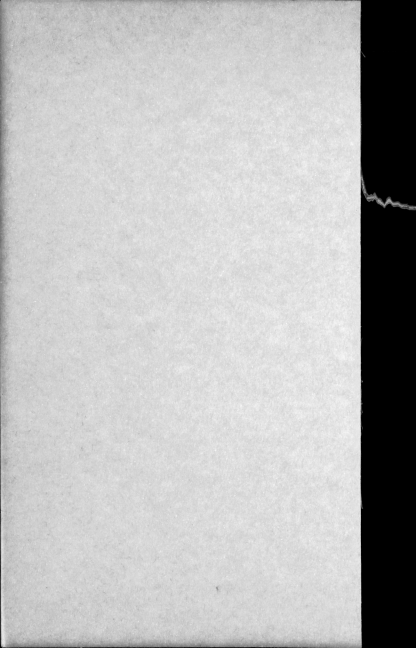

Critics rave about Miranda Jarrett and her marvelous tales of sea-swept romance . . .

CRANBERRY POINT

Named Amazon.com's #1 Best New Romance Paperback for June 1998 and a "Pick of the Month" for July 1998 by barnesandnoble.com

"This delightful spin-off from *The Captain's Bride* sweeps readers to colonial Cape Cod and the home of the Fairbourne family. . . . As always, Ms. Jarrett paints a vivid and exciting portrait of colonial America. With a delightful and charming cast of characters, *Cranberry Point* is a memorable tale of trust and love, of healing and passion, and most of all the magic of romance."

—Kathe Robin, *Romantic Times*

"Ms. Jarrett has written another passionate love story rich in history and characterization. She takes the reader back in time and place to an era where men are strong and caring and extremely possessive and defensive of their women. . . . This is an award-winning saga from a sensational author."

—*Rendezvous*

"No author . . . brings to life the early eighteenth century better than Miranda Jarrett. . . . [The] fast-paced story line is exciting and the lead protagonists are thrilling and real. . . . Everything Jarrett does is magic."

—Harriet Klausner, *Affaire de Coeur*

"*Cranberry Point* warms the heart, challenges the mind, and fills the soul with characters to treasure. Miranda Jarrett brings humor, empathy, and romance to her story by showing growth and compassion. The universal appeal of Cinderella finding her Prince goes straight to the heart of every romance reader. In this book, Serena finds not only her prince in Gerald, but that he is charming. Tears, passion, and joy make this a golden chest of memories."

—Kathee D. Card, *Romancing the Web*

"Five stars. Charming, witty, and oh-so-tender—a great book!"

—Amazon Books

. . . And so do the booksellers!

"Ms. Jarrett is in a class alone when she takes you to Colonial America. Her writing is bright, beautiful, and bold."

—Bell, Book and Candle

"[Cranberry Point] was a treat to read, the characters are so animated you feel as if you are living alongside of them. Miranda [Jarrett] . . . has a rare gift of telling a heart-warming story and making her characters so believable."

—Janice Pentecost, Dreamweaver Books

"Ms. Jarrett creates the most wonderful families, so that you are always waiting for the next book. Readers need to know what happens to everyone!"

—Anita Schmitt, B. Dalton

"[Miranda Jarrett] writes great entertainment."

—Ruth Collette, The Bookery

"Miranda, you've outdone yourself. *Cranberry Point* is undeniably your best to date."

—Merry Cutler, Annie's Book Stop

THE CAPTAIN'S BRIDE

"As always, Ms. Jarrett takes the high seas by storm, creating one of her liveliest heroines and a hero to be her match. Readers are sure to delight in Anabelle's some-times outrageous schemes and fall in love with Joshua, hoping to see them return in another book in the Fair-bourne chronicles. Hurrah for a new series!"

—*Romantic Times*

"The queen of colonial romances has another winner. . . . Miranda Jarrett is the admiral of the historical sailing romance and *The Captain's Bride* is at her usual level of excellence. The story line is superb and filled with nonstop action, and the lead protagonists are a delightful, intrepid couple. The surprise ending is simply a pleasure to read. Another great tale that is on an even keel with the top of the Sparhawk series."

—Harriet Klausner, Amazon Books

"The Captain's Bride" is a fabulous colonial sailing romance that is loaded with action and high-seas adventure. The lead characters make a classy couple as they passionately duel with each other and fight to survive their ruthless enemies. Miranda Jarrett continues to be top sea dog of the historical romance."

—*Affaire de Coeur*

"A delightful look at Georgian England and the expectations of the *ton,* as well as an excellent voyage through the dangerous waters of the Atlantic and the even more dangerous activity of smuggling. Anabelle is . . . a daring and definitely entertaining departure from the heroines we often see in historical romance. I . . . look forward to seeing more of Ms. Jarrett's offerings."

—*CompuServe Romance Reviews*

"A well-written book that is a joy to read. I'm all set to settle in with the founding of another dynasty of unforgettable, sparkling characters created by the marvelous Miranda Jarrett. As usual, Ms. Jarrett's heroes raise your blood pressure and make you want to claim them for your very own!"

—Suzanne Coleburn, *The Belles and Beaux of Romance*

Books by Miranda Jarrett

The Captain's Bride
Cranberry Point
Wishing

Published by POCKET BOOKS

MIRANDA JARRETT

Wishing

SONNET BOOKS

New York London Toronto Sydney Tokyo Singapore

This book is a work of fiction. Names, characters, places and incidents are products of the author's imagination or are used fictitiously. Any resemblance to actual events or locales or persons, living or dead, is entirely coincidental.

An *Original* Publication of POCKET BOOKS

 A Sonnet Book published by
POCKET BOOKS, a division of Simon & Schuster Inc.
1230 Avenue of the Americas, New York, NY 10020

Copyright © 1999 by Miranda Jarrett

ISBN: 0-671-00341-0

First Sonnet Books printing January 1999

10 9 8 7 6 5 4 3 2 1

SONNET BOOKS and colophon are trademarks of Simon & Schuster Inc.

Front cover illustration by Fredericka Ribes
Tip-in illustration by Harry Burman

Printed in the U.S.A.

For my parents,
who gave me the love
to make my wishes come true
Happy Fiftieth Anniversary!

Wishing

One

Island of Barbadoes
1721

*T*he sky over the bay of Bridgetown was close to black, dark with night and the clouds that hid the stars and moon, and a near match for the black mood that bedeviled Samson Fairbourne.

"So help me, Zach," he growled at the younger man beside him in the ship's longboat, "if you were not kin, I would hurl your sorry carcass over the side for how you've shamed me this night."

For once his cousin had sense enough not to answer, instead steadfastly staring over the shoulders of the men at the oars to avoid meeting Samson's eye. That was fine with Samson; if Zach had tried to argue with him now, when his temper was still roiling so furiously, he might very well have tossed his cousin into the waves, blood kin or not.

It was bad enough for the *Morning Star's* bosun to have to drag befuddled seamen from the rumshops, but for the captain himself to go brawling in the street to rescue his own first mate—and over some silly strumpet, too—was beyond bearing. Samson grumbled another oath to himself, tugging his cloak over the sleeve of his best superfine coat. The *torn* sleeve, thanks to Zach, torn and spotted with the same street filth that dabbed his back and breeches and likely even his hat as well.

"I never meant to shame you, Sam," ventured Zach with an unfortunately accurate prescience of his cousin's thoughts. "All I did was bring Ma'm'selle Lambert a cup of punch and dance one dance with her when the fiddler began. One tiny dance, Sam, I swear that was all. How could I know her brother and his friends would take such offense?"

"Her brother, hah." Samson glared at his cousin. "More likely her pack of bully boys. That's the last time I take you ashore for supper, Zach. Next time we're in port you'll stay on board, and the time after that, too. You won't set one wretched foot on land for the next year if I've anything to say about it."

"Aye-aye, sir," agreed Zach forlornly, hanging his head so that his long dark hair fell across the blossoming bruise on his forehead. After losing both his hat and the ribbon that had bound his queue in the scuffle, he looked to Samson more like some disreputable stableboy than a ship's officer, and exactly the kind of charming, worthless rogue that drew low women like flies to honey cakes.

Samson sighed again. "It's for your own good, Zach. To keep the strumpets from getting their greedy little hands on you."

"But begging pardon, Sam, you're mistaken about Marie—I mean Ma'm'selle Lambert. She was a lady through and through, and—"

"And from the veryest moment she clapped eyes upon you, she felt only the purest love for your own dear person," said Samson wearily. Not a single man in the tavern had missed the little French chit, trying to outdo every other woman in the room in the amount of lace, furbelows, and breasts prodigiously displayed, but only his young cousin had been foolish enough to fall under her spell. "How much did you tell her, Zach? Did you brag about our profits for this voyage, or how you were the first mate of the finest vessel in the harbor? Did you jingle the gold in your pocket loud enough for her to hear?"

"I did no such thing," said Zach with all the wounded dignity his nineteen years could muster. "I didn't have to. She liked me for what I was, Sam, and that's God's own truth."

Samson regarded his cousin with sorrow, his anger now tempered with despair. Jesus, had he himself ever been this pathetically innocent where women were concerned? He was fond of the boy. He truly was. But though he was only seven years older than Zach, there were times when he felt as if a whole lifetime of experience stretched between them instead.

"You listen to me, Zach, and you listen well," he said sternly. "I don't care if that lass tonight was the granddaughter of the king himself. It makes no difference, mind? None at all! She'd still be a female, rich or poor, lady or otherwise. And as entertaining as females can be, in their place, there are still no more taxing, troublesome distractions on this earth to a sailing man. The sooner you learn to keep clear of them, Zach—*all* of them—the happier your life will be."

Zach stared down into the bottom of the boat, his shoulders hunched in misery. "I don't believe it, Sam," he muttered, and pulled a small rum bottle from inside his coat for solace. "Not even from you."

"Give me that!" Samson snatched the bottle away and poured its contents into the water for emphasis.

"What the Devil's gotten into you tonight, anyway? Whoring and fighting and drinking—"

"What about your sister?" demanded Zach. "She's a woman, isn't she? Are you saying that Serena's naught but trouble, too?"

"You leave off Serena, Zach," warned Samson. No man said ill of Serena in his hearing, not even Zach. "Besides, I don't mean sisters. Sisters are different."

"Well then, how do you find the different ones if you keep clear of them all?"

"You don't," said Samson decisively. "You can't. You'd sooner find a drop of fresh water in an ocean of salt than one good woman in the great sea of doxies in a port, all of them set to prey upon luckless sailors."

"But why can't I wish—"

"Wishing means nothing with women, Zach. Less than nothing, else I'd . . . I'd—" He broke off abruptly, aware of how close he'd come to telling more of himself than he'd ever want Zach or the other four men at the oars to know. His fingers tightened around the empty bottle in his hand, and impulsively he reached into his coat for the pencil he always carried for calculations. The only paper he had with him was the innkeeper's reckoning from their supper, and he drew that from his coat now, too, smoothing the strip across his knee to hold it flat against the breeze.

"I'll show you how much wishes are worth," he said, determined to make his point with his head-strong cousin as he began pressing the words into the paper. "I'll wish to Neptune himself for the perfect woman. Look here, I'm putting it all proper in writing: 'I, Samson Fairbourne, with the ocean as my witness, do wish for a young woman sweet in temper and without vanity, modest and truthful in words and manner, obedient and honorable, to take as my lawful wife.' Is that a grand enough wish for you, Zach?''

But as he waited for his cousin's reply, the young man's startled face was suddenly washed with light, and Samson turned to look for the source. The full moon had at last shown herself, the dark clouds tearing into little wisps across the brilliant silver circle that now seemed to fill the night sky. As if awed by the moon, the waves went instantly, strangely still, as even and smooth as a mirror to reflect the skies overhead.

Mere coincidence, Samson told himself fiercely, coincidence and no more. How could one foolish oath have power over the sea? Yet still he felt the uneasiness prickle beneath the collar of his shirt, an uneasiness that was perilously close to fear.

"A most grand wish, Zach," he said again, though even to his own ears the brash words now sounded hollow. "Grand enough not to have a prayer of coming true, eh?"

"Nay, Sam, stop," said Zach quickly, his eyes wide as he, too, stared up at the moon. Behind him one of the men at the oars raised a hand to cross himself. "Don't do this. 'Tis wrong to make such vows, even in jest, and you know it."

But Samson shook his head, determinedly turning his back on that glowing witch of a moon. Damnation, he was a rational Englishman, a Massachusetts-man, his own master, not some superstitious heathen who'd cower and quake before a pack of wayward clouds. With a great effort, he forced himself to laugh.

"You are right, cousin, right to stop me," he declared. "This perfect woman I wish for must be a rare beauty in the bargain. I'll mark that down here on my list, after 'honorable'."

He twisted the paper into a tight little scroll and stuffed it down the neck of the empty rum bottle, wedging the cork in tight to seal it. As he did, the tall, dark shadow of the *Morning Star* loomed beside them, the boat bumping gently against the brig's side. Samson seized the guide-rope that hung from the rail, braced his feet, and clambered easily up the side to the deck. In three long strides he'd crossed to the bow, ignoring the startled looks of the handful of crewmen on watch.

"Here, Zach, here," he ordered, his voice booming effortlessly over the water as his cousin hurried to join him. He was master now, master of his ship and the lives of those who sailed with him, and the knowledge renewed his confidence. Moon, hah! This was the Caribbean, with weather as changeable as a whim. Besides, all he really wanted to do was set his cousin on a steadier course, with a dramatic gesture the boy wouldn't soon forget. Where was the sin in that?

He swept the bottle through the air, encompassing the harbor, the sleeping town, even that infernal moon. "There! Even with all this as my witness, you'll see how empty such wishes for women will be!"

Before Zach could protest again, Samson hurled the bottle as far as he could, far out over the bowsprit and into the water. It bobbed there for a moment, the neck spinning gently in the moonlight, then vanished down below the glassy surface so abruptly that it seemed almost to have been pulled from beneath by an unseen hand.

Samson frowned. A corked and empty bottle should float, not sink.

"Oh, hell," he muttered, all too aware of how every other man on the deck was holding his breath in anticipation, or dread, or fear, or maybe all three. "It's not natural for a bottle to—"

But his words were torn away by a gust of wind so strong and so sudden that he had to grab at the foremast to keep from being swept over the side. Even with all her sails still furled tight for port, the *Morning Star* heeled before the wind's force, her timbers groaning in protest as she tugged hard against her anchor.

He squinted back over the water, struggling vainly one last time to spot the bottle in the wind-whipped waves. Yet the churning waves were empty, the brilliant moon still there to taunt him for his rash words.

Damnation, he would *not* be cowed! He would claim this wind as his, and tame it for his own purposes. None had ever dared question his courage or his wisdom before this. He'd no intention of letting them start now. He'd give orders for the *Morning Star* to sail at once, and with such a wind to carry them they'd be clear of Barbadoes by daybreak. He'd prove to his men once and for all that he wouldn't quiver before superstition and a wayward moon.

And that idle, fool's wish of his could just as soon go to the Devil where it belonged.

Two

~⟐~

*P*atience and grace were most pleasing virtues in a woman, or so Polly Bray had heard the minister preach from the high pulpit in the Marblehead meetinghouse. But if what that wise man preached was true, then on this cold gray morning Polly knew she must be the most soundly unvirtuous woman in all of New England.

She braced the heels of her sea boots against the low side of the *Dove* and, with a deep breath, pulled as hard as she could on the heavy nets. Despite the bright October sun, her fingers in their mittens were clumsy with the cold, and her back ached from the hours she'd already toiled, ached so much she longed for the freedom to weep from exhaustion and loneliness.

Not that she would. She hadn't cried since the fever had taken Father last spring, and she wasn't about to begin now, especially not over a net full of codfish. Wasn't this the reason she'd sailed this early anyway? There'd be little use shedding tears over a bounty like this, or feeling sorry for herself because Enos and Abe, the *Dove's* usual two crewmen, had been still too befuddled with rum to sail with her this dawn. All the more profit that needn't be shared: that was what Father would have said, and laughed merrily as he figured how rich they'd be one day, rich enough for Polly to be a lady in a silk gown instead of cut-down homespun breeches and an old knitted cap.

But the tears threatened anyway, brought there by remembering poor Father and his endless dreams. Furiously she blinked them back, wiping her jacket's rough sleeve across her eyes for good measure. Pretty wishes and memories wouldn't pay the debts her father had left behind. Only hard work and luck could do that, and with fresh resolve she threw herself against the weight of the nets and pulled as hard as she could.

And this time the nets gave way, the lines rushing over the side of the boat and onto the deck with the wriggling, glistening mass of cod trapped within. With a gasp of surprise Polly tumbled backward, sprawling across the deck beside the fish. Breathing hard, she slowly rolled over onto her knees and surveyed her catch.

"I've won this time, you little noddies," she said to the fish with satisfaction. "You're mine now, and I—"

She stopped and frowned. Tangled in the middle of the squirming, silvery fish and netting lay a long-necked rum bottle. Not only did she despise strong drink for what it did to men, she also hated what the very bottles themselves could do to her nets. Holes and snags and knots aplenty, she muttered crossly to herself as she worked to free the empty bottle, and all because of some careless, wastrel drunkard of a *man*.

But the bottle wasn't empty, not entirely, though through the dark green glass she couldn't quite make out what lay curled inside. A paper of great importance to be so carefully rolled and sealed, thought Polly, her imagination bounding headlong as she remembered Father's whispered tales of pirates' maps and hidden treasures. She sat back eagerly on her heels, easing the cork out with her thumbs. If not a pirate's map, then perhaps the paper would be the lost deed to a great estate, or some nobleman's will, or . . .

Or a water-stained tavern reckoning. Glumly Polly stared at the blurry words: a roasted chicken, three made dishes, a cheese, two pipkins of ale, and a bottle of Madeira. So much for dreams, indeed. Even the gulls that wheeled and danced in the sky overhead seemed determined to taunt her, their raucous cries like mocking laughter to her ears.

"So much for a fool's dreams, Poll, my girl," she murmured as the paper fluttered between her fingertips. "Next you'll be fancifying you're the Queen of Sheba her own self, and off you'll ship for Bedlam."

The wind folded the paper backward, enough for her to see the smudged words on the other side. Polly turned the paper over carefully, holding it up to the sunlight as she studied the scrawling penmanship, blotched here and there with seawater.

Her brows came together as she concentrated, sounding the words aloud as she made them out. " 'I . . . I' something, or someone, 'with all' . . . oh, bother . . . 'a young woman sweet in temper . . . truthful in words and manner' . . . what nonsense *this* is! . . . 'obedient and honorable, beautiful'—oh, bah!"

She wrinkled her nose in disgust. Whatever man had written such clod-pate drivel had most likely first emptied the bottle of its rum. Her fancies after pirates' gold were nothing besides this mooncalf's

longings for a lady too perfect to exist outside of his
own muddled head.

"'To take as my lawful wife'—his *wife!* As if any
woman with half her wits about her would take *him,*
the pompous, puffed-up scrod! 'To take as my—'"

The gust of wind caught her by surprise, catching
and filling the *Dove's* single half-furled sail so suddenly that for the second time that morning Polly
tumbled backward, this time onto the pile of wriggling fish. *Careless!* she scolded herself as she scrambled back to her feet, careless to be so taken with the
foolish note that she hadn't seen the weather changing. The morning sun had vanished behind a bank of
black clouds, the water ruffling uneasily into white-
caps before the rising wind.

Swiftly Polly stuffed the bottle and the note into
her pocket and made her way aft across the slanting
deck, toward the *Dove's* tiller. All she had to do was
turn the boat into the wind to steady her, a task she'd
done a thousand times before.

But as she reached for the tiller, another rush of
wind caught the *Dove* broadside, filling the sail so
abruptly that the lashed stay on the boom snapped
beneath the force. Freed of the stay, the heavy timber
of the boom swept wildly across the deck. Instinctively Polly ducked, but not fast enough. The boom
struck her shoulder, lifting her off her feet, off the
deck, and then, to her infinite surprise, clear over the
side. For one instant she felt as if she were flying with
the same grace as the gulls, hanging in the air where
she could see the *Dove* and the angry clouds and dark
waves draped with froth as white and delicate as lace.

Then she hit the water, sinking fast, and there was
nothing delicate, nothing lacy, about it. Her boots
and clothes were pulling at her, dragging her deeper

into the icy darkness, her limbs already numbing with the cold even as she struggled, and she could not breathe from the weight of the water, and from the shock of her fear and the certainty of her fate. There would be no one to help her, no one to miss her, no one to mourn her when she didn't return.

But, God help her, why did she have to die like this?

"You found him, then," said Samson as the two crewmen lifted the lifeless body over the *Morning Star*'s side. "Poor bastard. Leastways we saved him from being gobbled by the fishes, eh?"

It was all Samson had hoped for when he'd ordered the boat lowered after the lookout had spotted the body in the ocean. No one survived long in the open sea, especially not after the storm they'd suffered through since leaving Martinique, but this way they'd at least be able to give the poor fellow a decent, Christian burial. Though drowning was a common enough death among sailors, it would never be an easy way to go, and Samson watched with genuine sympathy as his men laid the body carefully upon the deck. A small fellow, scarcely more than a boy from the look of him. Samson himself had gone to sea when he was younger than this, and only God and good luck had kept him from a similar fate.

"Not long in the water," he said as he looked down at the forlorn, waterlogged figure curled on its side, its face mercifully turned away from him and further masked behind a tangle of wet hair and a shapeless knitted cap. The clothes were worn and homespun, clearly cut down from those of a larger man, though the patches on the coat and breeches were neatly made. Somewhere, thought Samson sadly, there'd be a grieving mama for sure. "Any notion of his ship or port?"

"Nay, Cap'n." Plunkett, the man who'd led the rescue boat, uneasily shifted his shoulders and stared down at the deck. "No notion, sir."

Samson sighed. Sailors were often leery of their dead fellows, and he guessed Plunkett was no better than the others who were keeping an overly respectful distance. "Ah well, perhaps there's something on his person to tell us."

He knelt beside the body himself, reaching for the first of the horn buttons that held the coat closed.

"Wait, Cap'n, wait!" said Plunkett quickly. "There's something . . . something you should know about that one."

Samson paused, his hand stilled, and waited expectantly for Plunkett to continue. But the man decided to think better of his interruption, only shaking his head as again he stared shame-faced at the deck.

"Very well, Plunkett," said Samson curtly, and he began to unfasten the dead man's coat. "I expect I'll find out your mystery soon enough for myself."

He slid his hand inside the sodden woolen coat, searching for a clue to the young man's identity. A letter from home, perhaps, or a purse marked with his name.

But instead Samson jerked back his hand as if he'd been burned. What he'd just discovered might not have told him the dead sailor's name, but it certainly explained Plunkett's distress.

"Damnation, man!" he swore. "Why didn't you tell me outright he was a *woman?*"

He rolled the body onto her back, tugging the heavy cap from her head and smoothing the hair

from her face. When his hand had felt the soft
rounded curve of a breast beneath the rough linen
shirt, he'd thought he'd lost his wits. But the lifeless
face now bared to him proved he hadn't been mistak-
en: a round little face with full cheeks and a small
plump chin, dark brows still arched in perpetual
surprise over a fringe of sooty lashes. It wasn't a face
that would make men stop and stare, but even in
death there remained a certain intangible charm,
enough to make Samson wonder how she'd smiled,
what her laughter had sounded like, and what color
were the eyes now closed forever; and he caught
himself wondering, too, what he might have done to
save her.

"Poor little lass," said Zach softly beside him.
"What a pity for her to end like this."

"Aye." Samson rose, striving to put aside the
feelings the dead woman had roused in him. It wasn't
like him, turning soft like this over something that
couldn't be helped. "The Devil only knows what she
was doing out on the water dressed like some
wretched ragamuffin."

"Maybe she was hiding from someone," said Zach,
his blue eyes so filled with sympathetic grief Samson
half feared he'd weep on the spot. "Maybe she'd run
away from a cruel father, or from some man who'd
treated her ill."

Samson groaned. "Or maybe she'd run away from
some honest man who'd made the mistake of marrying her. Maybe what she did instead was to play at
being some rogue's pretty cabin boy. Look at her,
dressed all against nature! Who'd trust a woman like
that?"

"I'd wager she had a good reason for doing it,

Sam," said the younger man staunchly. "She doesn't have the look of a liar."

"Ah, Zach, you are beyond redemption." Samson shook his head with a sigh. But it was better this way, he reasoned, far better, to worry over the living who mattered to him. "May the Lord deliver *you* from a faithless wife, for you're as ripe for picking as a plum from the lowest branch."

A wife, thought Polly, the word drifting to her through the fog in her head, a fog worse than any she'd known. *A faithless wife . . . no, a lawful wife . . . Oh, her whole body hurt so very much!*

She heard the man laugh, deep and rich, a sound that cut through the fog. She liked the sound of that laugh. Laughter was something she heard precious little of, and the warmth that came with it reminded her all too much of Father. Maybe it *was* Father, come here to find her in the fog and take her back with him to Heaven, and with a great effort she forced herself to open her eyes.

The sun overhead was blindingly bright, piercing through the fog in her head like a razor, bright enough to make her catch her breath with a little yelp of pain that rippled through her entire body. Then the sun was gone, blocked out by the tall man leaning over her.

And he wasn't Father. Not at all. Not with those blue eyes that were studying her with distasteful curiosity, and not with brows so thick and black they seemed joined into one stern line over a nose that had surely been broken at least once. His jaw was unshaven, with a small white scar on his stubbled chin, his hair long and as black as his brows.

"High holy hell," he muttered, as much to himself as to her. "You're alive."

She couldn't deny that he was handsome, in a wickedly blackguardish way. But she also knew he could not possibly be the man whose warm laughter had brought her back from the fog in her head, not speaking to her like this. No man talked like that to Polly Bray, at least not more than once.

"Aye, I'm alive," she said, her voice raspy from thirst as she propped herself up on her elbows, "and so are you, more's the greater pity."

The man's black brows seemed to darken more, as if such a thing were possible, and from behind him came a quickly stifled guffaw. For the first time Polly noticed the other men, a ring of curious faces peering down at her. She was sprawled on a deck that most decidedly didn't belong to the *Dove,* her clothes were soaking wet and she'd no memory of how they'd come to be that way, and she lay surrounded by a pack of wolfish, gawking sailors like a bedraggled lamb in their hungry midst.

Wherever she was, she decided, it did not seem a very good place for her to be.

As quickly as she could she pulled her knife from the sheath at her waist and scrambled to her feet. With the long-bladed knife she used for fish-gutting in her hand, she immediately felt better.

"Now, you great rogue, you just tell me where I am," she said, as firmly as she could with a tongue that tasted like salty straw. "And no more swearing, mind? I'm not one of your rumshop strumpets, and I expect men to be more respectful of me than to go hell-ing this and that and every other little thing in my hearing."

But the tall, black-browed man didn't flinch, nor did he seem much inclined toward respectfulness. "I'll speak however I damn well please, you silly chit.

I'm Captain Samson Fairbourne and I'm master of this vessel, and if you'd any wits at all you'd be bowing down and thanking me for saving your life instead of acting like some infernal little queen in breeches.''

Polly blushed, something she thought she'd long ago forgotten how to do. But why, then, must she remember it *now*?

"If you'd ever tried wearing petticoats while you climbed the rigging,'' she said, ''then you'd know why I don't.''

This time the smothered laughter came from two different men. Polly wasn't sure if it was the image of the fierce black-browed captain in petticoats that had made them laugh or her own wretched, blushing appearance. With the knife still outstretched in her hand, she lifted her head higher and tossed back the flopping weight of her trailing wet hair for good, defiant measure.

But in return Captain Fairbourne merely glared back at her. "Do you truly believe I give a tinker's dam for why you dress yourself against the laws of God and man and nature combined?''

" 'Tis not unlawful,'' said Polly warmly. '' 'Tis practical.''

" 'Tis wrong,'' he declared flatly, ''and may that be an end to it. Now come, what the Devil is your name?''

Polly paused, making him wait. Was it anger that turned his eyes so blue, or were they always the brilliant color of an evening sky? And what foolishness made her care, anyway?

"I'm Poll Bray,'' she finally said, ''as any noddy along this coast could tell you.''

"Paul?'' His voice rumbled deep and ominous.

"Don't toy with me, girl. I found out for myself that you're female, before you woke."

Her blush deepened as she considered all the awful possibilities of his claim, and her fingers tightened reflexively around the hilt of the knife. It didn't matter that he was the most handsome man she'd ever seen; he'd no right taking liberties when she'd been unable to defend herself, and she folded her free hand protectively across her chest.

"My name is Poll Bray—Polly Ann, if you must know all: Polly Ann Bray of Ninnishibutt River."

"Ninnishibutt?" He tipped his head to one side, studying her curiously. "That's clear beyond Boston, a tiny flyspeck north of Marblehead. How the Devil does Miss Polly Ann Bray come to be bobbing like a cork in the waters off Bridgetown?"

"Now you are toying with me," she said crossly. "We could not possibly be off Bridgetown, because I have never once sailed more southerly than New London."

"No?" He swept his arm through the air, the white linen at his shirtcuff ruffling back in the wind. "Look at this water, Miss Polly Ann Bray. Have you ever seen its like in Massachusetts Bay, or even as southerly as New London?"

And to her great sorrow, she hadn't. She'd never seen water like this at all, a bright, translucent blue as clear as colored glass. The sky above was a match for the sea, without a single cloud to mar its cheerful purity. Even the wind felt different, a soft and gentle breeze that seemed to caress more than to blow, and warmer than even the hottest of August days in Massachusetts.

"But this cannot be," she said slowly, fighting the panic rising within her. "It cannot! I tell you I cleared the cove this very morning, before dawn, by myself in my father's boat. Yet now you say I am here, hundreds of miles away from my home, and I say it cannot *be*!"

"Hush now, miss," said another man's voice beside her. "Be calm, and drink this."

He was smaller and younger than Captain Fairbourne, with the same blue eyes and black hair but none of the captain's arrogance, and in his hand he offered a battered pewter tankard.

"It's only water, Miss Bray, I swear," he said, taking a sip himself as proof before he held it out to her again. "Here. You must be thirsty, aren't you?"

She was, and the sight of him drinking made her thirstier still. But she would take nothing more from any of these men, not even a drop of water, and she shook her head defiantly.

"Perhaps she is what she says, Sam," said the younger man slowly, still watching her over the top of the rejected tankard. "Who's to say she's not?"

"Oh, aye," scoffed Captain Fairbourne, his expression now one of skeptical bemusement, "and next we'll all sprout wings to fly to Gibraltar. You're just as daft as she is, Zach."

"But I'm not daft," said Polly, striving hard to keep the shrill fear from her voice. "I don't know how you've managed to trick me this way, but if you don't take me back to Ninnishibutt at once, I'll lose the *Dove*—that's my father's boat—and my catch and— and it won't matter if I'm daft or not. Most likely they're already gone, and I've nothing left to my name. Nothing, mind?"

She swallowed hard, blinking back the tears that were making Captain Fairbourne's face muddle and swim before her. Even if she did somehow escape these men and return home, what could she hope to find waiting for her? She said she'd have nothing, and in a way she'd have less than that. She'd still be carrying Father's debts, with no way to begin to pay them off with the *Dove* lost. No other cod boat would take a female into their crew, but she'd none of the usual womanly skills—spinning or weaving or sewing or cooking or caring for children—with which to make her living on land.

She sniffed furiously. "I know to you this is one big foolish jest, but so help me, I'm not daft, and I'm telling you the *truth!*"

"I never said you weren't, lass," said Captain Fairbourne. "You're only a whit confused, that's all. No sin to that. You were so close to drowning, we thought you'd passed over already, and that's bound to have left you, ah, shaken. Aye, perhaps that's it."

He smiled then, and to Polly's dismay his expression softened to something horribly close to pity. His arrogance, his bluster, his overbearing contempt—these she could accept, but not his pity. Dear Lord, she'd never taken that from anyone, and she looked down at the deck to hide the fresh tears she felt welling up.

"And perhaps, Sam," said the younger man called Zach, speaking softly, as if he scarcely dared speak at all, "perhaps Miss Bray's that perfect woman you were wishing into the sea for last night. The one you said would make such a fine wife."

Polly gasped and looked at once to Captain Fairbourne, who looked every bit as mortified as she did herself. In all her twenty years, she'd yet to hear any man mention her name and marriage in the same breath, and certainly not a man like Samson Fairbourne. Not that she was complaining. Not at all. The last thing she wanted was some foolish man ordering her about, and this particular man seemed monstrously in love with order-giving.

Yet still there was something disconcertingly familiar about that word *wife,* used the way Zach was using it now, and other words, too: *obedient, modest, sweettempered;* words half remembered as if she'd been awakened too soon from a dream.

"That's stuff and rubbish," said the captain brusquely, locking his hands behind his waist as the circle of crewmen around him and Polly abruptly backed away. "I didn't mean Miss Bray."

"And why not, Sam?" said Zach, his confidence growing. "You told me most all women were alike, nothing but wasteful distractions to a seafaring man. Well, here's one that seems different enough. *Very* different."

Captain Fairbourne shrugged carelessly, his gaze taking in every bedraggled inch of Polly's appearance. "Oh, aye, I'll grant you that, on the outside, she looks powerfully different from her sisters, but in her heart I'll wager she's the same."

Zach grinned. "And I'll wager she is better. A real wager, Sam, not just words."

Polly's chin rose like a shot. "I'm better enough to know when I've been insulted," she retorted. They were all treating her as bad luck, as if they hadn't been the ones to bring bad luck to her, and she didn't like it at all. "Better than *you,* anyways."

Samson looked from Zach to Polly Bray to the rest of his crewmen, and then back again to the girl he'd fished from the water. How the Devil had he gotten himself into this particular mare's nest, anyway? If he backed down now, Zach would never learn his lesson—and worse, he'd gloat over it the rest of their mortal days.

But how could Samson seriously consider proving anything with an odd little creature like Polly Bray? True, with skin as nearly sun-browned as his own, a lingering smell of codfish, and a tendency to sharp speaking, she was different from other women, as Zach had said, though these were hardly the qualities to tempt him or any other man into matrimony. The insistent memory of how sweetly curved her breast had been was entirely beside the point. And, of course, she was mad as a hare, with all that talk of sailing from Ninnishibutt this dawn. Samson felt sorry for her—who would not?—but to consider her that perfect, wished-for wife, even in jest, was ridiculous.

Yet the more he considered her stubborn face, the more he realized that this could be the easiest wager he'd ever won. Nonexistent perfect wives had nothing to do with it. The instant he waved a trinket or two before a girl like this, she'd trade her dirty breeches for silk petticoats and be eager for more.

"Very well, Zach," he said expansively. "I'll accept your challenge. Twenty guineas says that by the time we make Boston and this voyage is done, we'll see Polly Bray become the perfect twin to that yellow-haired chit you left behind in Bridgetown."

He saw how the girl's eyes widened with shock. So twenty guineas was a fortune to her, a ransom fit for kings. Twenty guineas could most likely buy her wretched little boat three times over, with spare to jingle in the market. Jesus, this wager could be done before it had started.

Yet his cousin only nodded. "Done. My guineas say

the girl doesn't change, and stays the virtuous female you say does not exist."

"Nay, I will not do it!" cried Polly anxiously. "'Tis not decent for you to do this, wagering against one another over my—my virtue. I'm no twin to any 'yellow-haired chit,' and I won't have you saying it. You put me ashore directly, do you hear? Directly, this very day!"

Samson smiled, noticing how becomingly she blushed. He hadn't expected her capable of it. With that glow to her cheeks and the bright, innocent confusion in her gray eyes, she was almost pretty.

Almost.

"Your virtue's safe enough, lass," he said gallantly and, he believed with confidence, truthfully as well. "As long as you stay here with us, that is. I cannot vouch for what would become of you if we put you ashore now, on one of these islands, among the Dutch or French."

"Dutchmen?" she repeated weakly. "But I don't speak their heathen tongue, nor French, neither!"

He shook his head solemnly. "Now that would be a trial, wouldn't it? Best you stay with us. Besides, this wager's not about, ah, sullying your good name, not even in Ninnishibutt. All that's wanted of you, Miss Polly Ann Bray, is for you to be your own self, and if you agree, then you'll be rewarded."

Her eyes narrowed with suspicion. "You would reward me? After I've done nothing? Faith, I will never take a farthing that I haven't earned."

"Then earn it by being my guest on this voyage." *And be spoiled,* he added mentally, *and cosseted and petted until your true greedy nature shows itself.* Thoroughly pleased with himself, he smiled the smile guaranteed to dissolve all female hearts.

All, that is, except this one.

"I won't share your bunk," she said warily, fingering the hilt of her knife. "I'm a good woman, Captain Fairbourne, and I won't be your trollop, not for a hundred of your guineas."

"You have my word on it, Polly," he said, wondering if she'd ever used that knife of hers on some poor male. "No bunk-sharing, and no trolloping, and I'll see you home safe in the bargain."

She considered this for a long moment, far longer than was comfortable for Samson. She looked very young and very vulnerable, and very much like someone who had no choices left in her miserable excuse for a life. It was an idea he instantly tried to shake off, but not before his conscience had given him a quick mental shake first. Even for the brusque captain of the *Morning Star*, badgering witless, castaway females was hardly the kind of behavior to boast of with pride.

But at last she nodded and shoved her knife back into its sheath. Then to Samson's surprise she seized his hand and shook it, her small, rough fingers squeezing around his. Her round, upturned face was glowing with determination, and he realized one more unsettling way she differed from other women: mad or not, Polly Bray liked a challenge, perhaps nearly as much as he did himself.

"You can say what you please, Captain," she said firmly. "But your cousin will win, because *I* will not change."

Samson tried to smile and couldn't. High holy Hell. What *had* he done to deserve this?

Three

"And this," announced Joseph the cabin boy as he pushed open the door, "this be where Cap'n says you're to sleep."

Polly blinked, letting her eyes accustom themselves to the murky half-light between decks. The little cabin was tucked into the side of the ship, the bulkhead curving up toward their heads. Snugged in between the beams was a narrow bunk, the invitingly plump wool-stuffed pillow and mattress covered by a checkered coverlet, and hooked into the rough-hewn oak was a wrought-iron candlestick in a gimbal, waiting to shed its cozy light across the tiny space. A square mirror, framed in black, hung over the stone-ware bowl in a bracketed shelf that would serve for washing.

But what caught Polly's eye first was the linen washing cloth folded neatly on the coverlet, with a lady's tortoiseshell comb, a small, round hand mirror, and, laid on top, a pale green ball of soap so sweetly scented that Polly could smell it clear from the doorway.

"This be Mr. Fairbourne's cabin," explained Joseph, already edging down the companionway. He'd made it clear enough he'd wanted none of this errand, and even less to do with Polly herself. "But he give it up for you, so you must take it."

Polly shook her head with bewilderment. "The captain gave up his quarters to me?"

"Nay, nay!" exclaimed the boy hurriedly. "Mr. Fairbourne's the mate. Mr. *Zachariah* Fairbourne. Mr. *Samson* Fairbourne's cap'n and the master, and don't you never confuse them. Your quarters is here because the cap'n told the mate he had to give them up to you. Cap'n Fairbourne, well, he'd never share *his* cabin with anyone."

"Nay," she said softly, remembering Captain Fairbourne's forbidding severity. "He would not."

She took a single step into the cabin. As gingerly as if she feared being burned, she touched her fingers to the little round mirror on the bunk, tracing the pattern of leaves and flowers twined around its polished pewter rim. As she bent over, she caught sight of her own reflection set inside the elegant frame, her cheeks too plump, her hair straggling down from beneath her cap, her skin dull with dried saltwater.

She jerked upright and bundled the comb, mirror, and soap inside the cloth, clutching them together in one hand. "Where is he now?"

"The cap'n?" asked the startled boy. "Why, in his cabin, I 'spect."

"I must speak to him." She squeezed her way past Joseph and hurried down the companionway herself. Though the *Morning Star* was by far the largest, grandest ship she'd ever been aboard, there was still a certain nautical logic that made all ships and boats the same. The captain's cabin would always be in the stern, and so Polly headed aft, toward the imposing paneled door at the end of the companionway that must surely open into Captain Fairbourne's private sanctuary.

"You cannot go there, miss, indeed you cannot," sputtered Joseph as he scurried after her. "No one goes there 'gainst orders!"

"Orders are for crew," said Polly as she rapped her knuckles against the door. "And I'm not crew. You heard him, didn't you? I'm his guest, and guests don't heed orders."

"Ah, but miss, that don't mean you can—"

"I'm not sure he's even in there," said Polly, pressing her ear close to the door to listen. "He's not answering, is he? Else he's just being a sight more quiet than I ever dreamed he could."

She jiggled the latch until it gave way, and before the boy could stop her, she pushed the door open.

And gasped.

The entire stern of the cabin was windows: a sweep of curving glass that framed the ripe colors—orange, red, pink, red, shading to deep violet—of the sun sinking into the turquoise tropical sea. The entire cabin glowed with a warm, rosy light, reflecting up off the water and down from the whitewashed beams overhead, a light so beautiful that Polly smiled unconsciously with delight. It was almost as if she'd tumbled inside a wild rose on a sunny day, one of the brambled roses that grew on the south side of Westerly Hill at home, near the river, where—

"What in blazes are you doing here?"

Polly gasped again, this time not from delight but from dismay. How could she have managed to overlook someone as large as Captain Fairbourne, there in the middle of all this blissful rosiness? He lay sprawled across his bunk, propped up on his elbows the better to glare at her, and he wore nothing whatsoever beyond his breeches.

"Damnation, I asked you a question," he growled as he swung his legs over the side of the bunk to sit upright. "What the Devil are you doing here, in my cabin? Am I to have no peace from you?"

"Your peace has nothing to do with it." Nor, she realized belatedly, did it have anything to do with *hers*. To her an undressed man meant one in his shirtsleeves and without a waistcoat or a hat, the most a decent man would ever remove even in the mild warmth of a Massachusetts summer. She'd no experience with a man baring more than he covered, especially not a man built on the unsettling scale of this one.

"My peace has everything to do with everything," he said, running one hand through his untied hair. "Leastways it did before you came aboard."

"I didn't come aboard," she said defensively. "You brought me here, and there's a world of difference between the two."

"And I don't give a damn about either one." He sighed, halfway to a groan, and rubbed the back of his neck. "I am tired, dead tired, thanks to that storm last night, and all I wanted was to sleep before the next watch. Not much for a captain to wish, is it? But not from you. Nay, not from you, *Miss* Polly Ann Bray, who has still not told me what was so all-fired important enough for you to force your way into my cabin."

He didn't look weary to her so much as wicked, sitting there mostly naked upon the rumpled sheets, with his great muscled thighs straining the linen of his breeches, his black hair slipping across his broad, bare shoulders, and the complete lack of modesty with which he was waiting for her answer.

Very, *very* wicked.

Not that she had any more experience with wicked men than with undressed ones—Father had made sure of that—but she felt fairly sure she could identify one, and Captain Fairbourne at present seemed to be exactly that. If she'd any sense at all she'd turn on her heel and leave now. She could speak to him just as well later, when he was once again dressed. But he'd take her leaving for running away, and even for propriety's sake she refused to let him believe he'd scared her off. At least she could be thankful for the sunset's glow, masking the fiery embarrassment that surely must be coloring her entire face.

And—dear Lord help her—the cabin seemed to be growing warmer by the second. And smaller. How could she have ever thought that the snug little bunk in the other cabin would accommodate *him?*

She raised her chin and tried to focus upon his face alone. "I wish to speak to you about the quarters you've given me."

He frowned, storm clouds in the making. "The cabin doesn't suit? Didn't Zach tidy it as I ordered? By God, if he didn't—"

"Nay, not that at all," she said quickly. " 'Tis—'tis too grand for me, too grand by half."

" 'Too grand'?" He laughed, and the black clouds vanished before a grin full of large white teeth. "That tiny little nest of a cabin's too grand? Grand— hah. Perhaps for a hen accustomed to her roost in the chicken house, aye, but not for any guest of mine."

Polly didn't answer. Her home on shore wasn't exactly a chicken house, but as homes went it wasn't far removed. Since Father had died, all she'd been able to afford was a tiny, windowless lean-to room off Widow Marton's house. Because the lean-to backed up to the chimney wall in the widow's kitchen, Polly had no fireplace of her own but instead stole what heat she could from the brick wall. Her bed was a wobbly, orphaned trundle stuffed with old rushes, her carefully hoarded candles made of smoky tallow, and the single ladder-back chair served as much for propping against the door as a makeshift lock as for seating. No wonder she'd spent so much time aboard the *Dove.* The accommodations weren't much better, but they were hers alone, and without Widow Marton and her son quarreling over religion each night in the kitchen, too.

But how could she explain all that to someone like Captain Fairbourne? Helplessly she gazed around his cabin. The tall desk with the polished brass, the armchair, and even the bunk were all simply fashioned but elegantly expensive, made from fine imported mahogany. There was a handsome long looking glass, a rack of leatherbound books— *books!*—an elaborate hanging lantern with the finest spermaceti candles. Even the buttons on the coat he'd so carelessly tossed over the chair were well-polished pewter, and all of it together meant only one thing.

He was rich. She wasn't.

And he wouldn't understand.

She stared down at the small bundle in her hands, striving for the right words. " 'Tis not so fine a cabin as this, I'll grant you that much," she said with a stubborn little shake of her head, "but 'tis far too grand to take as my own, with me giving nothing in return."

"And I say that's where you're staying. Where the

Devil else could you go? Down to the fo'c'sle, to sling a hammock among the men?"

"But it don't seem proper!"

"It's not," he said evenly, though his half-closed eyes glinted in a way that made her uneasy. "None of this is, not the way you mean it. But I gave you my word I'd not harm you, and neither will anyone else aboard, which is a sight more proper than you'd get from most ships in this part of the sea."

Samson had meant to tease her, to make a jest from the unlikeliness of her situation. Didn't she realize how utterly safe her peculiar arrival had made her among a crew full of superstitious sailors?

But instead of snapping back at Samson the way he'd expected, the girl wilted, her shoulders sagging and her head drooping, and in that instant she robbed him of whatever pleasure he'd found in their banter. Worse yet, she'd made him feel mean and small, almost a bully, and he didn't like that at all.

He stood up, then grabbed his shirt from the end of the bunk and yanked it over his head. No woman, especially not a homely one with scrambled wits, was going to make him feel like that.

"Besides," he said gruffly as he jerked the shirt down over his chest, "if you're so blessèd concerned about what's proper, you'd best think twice before you come rushing in here again like the chimney's afire. Who knows what you might find, eh?"

But again she didn't answer, and he looked at her sharply. When she'd first awakened him, yammering about Zach's cabin, he'd have wagered a guinea that she'd been after his quarters as a replacement. He'd heard that often enough from other women, the way they'd begun rearranging his things and measuring for fringed damask curtains the minute they stepped through the door. No wonder he'd stopped bringing them here. In fact Polly Bray was probably the first female to see the inside of the *Morning Star*'s main cabin in at least two years. But she didn't understand the honor, any more than she seemed to covet his cabin for her own.

So what the Devil was the matter with her, anyway?

He sighed, rolling his cuffs up over his forearms. Even though the sun was nearly down, the afternoon's heat still clung to the cabin; she was damned lucky he'd kept his breeches on when he'd laid down to rest. But if he wanted to win his wager, he'd have to forget such quibbles and borrow a bit of Zach's cheerful gallantry for his own.

"If you've some genuine complaint," he began again, forcing himself to smile, "well then, Miss Bray, I want to hear it. Welcome it, even."

At last she raised her face to meet his gaze. In the fading light her eyes looked more silvery than gray, a striking contrast to her sun-browned skin. Her lashes weren't thick as much as spiked, little rays of surprise to frame her eyes like stars, and once again he caught himself wondering the color of her hair beneath that grimy knit cap. If he hadn't made a private vow against tossing anything more into the sea after that last misfortune with the bottle, he'd rip that wretched, misshapen hat from her head now and send it out the open window.

"I'd left orders for you to be made as comfortable as possible," he said. "Wasn't there anything for washing up in your cabin?"

"Aye." She raised the bundled cloth in her hands, holding it open so he could see the mirror, soap, and comb, her silver eyes suddenly sparking with defiance. "These were on the bunk. Such rubbishy trinkets as you'd give to your harlot."

"More as like I'd give to my sister." He must remember not to be lulled again by her silences. "Or my guest. All from London, those are, and dear they'd come in a shop. Hardly the sort of things I'd squander upon a harlot, even if I kept one. Which I don't, not that it is any of your affair."

"Then how *did* you come by them?" she demanded. "New like this, and here on a ship full of men?"

"Because it's my trade, you suspicious little creature," he explained impatiently. "Mostly I carry molasses to the north and rum to the south, but like all captains I'll fill in the odd spaces in the ship's hold with whatever London fancy goods—your 'rubbishy trinkets'—I can find for cheap here, to sell to the shopkeepers in Boston."

"Oh." She looked down at the things in her hands. "Then I must keep them?"

"You *must* do nothing," he said firmly. "I thought I'd made that clear enough. But it's ill manners to refuse a gift, even one you deem 'rubbishy,' and particularly gifts that you could damned well use yourself."

She sighed, a soft breath of what he realized was concession. "They are not really rubbishy. They're—they're nice."

"Then go ahead and put them to use." He'd accept that sigh of concession graciously, and accept it, too, as thanks. He might as well. He doubted he'd get anything better. "You'll find water in the pitcher there. Go ahead, no ceremony. I'll light the candles so you can see."

With another sigh, she nodded, and Samson

turned away toward the lantern to hide his own smile of satisfaction and to give her a bit of privacy. He could hear the water as she poured it into the washbowl, and the cabin was soon filled with the fragrant scent of lathered soap. At heart she truly was like all the others, he decided as he struck a spark for the candles in the lantern. She'd accepted this first gift, albeit grudgingly. But Samson had no doubt that the rest would follow soon enough, and he could already feel Zach's wager jingling in his own pocket.

"Do you really have a sister?" she asked, her words muffled by splashing water.

"I do," said Samson, his satisfied smile widening into outright smugness. What woman could resist measuring herself against another in men's eyes, even if the other were a mere sister? "Her name's Serena Fairbourne Crosbie, and she's hands down the prettiest, cleverest woman in Appledore. And that's not just me talking, either. Her husband's a true gentleman, an Irish lord who came clear across the ocean to woo and wed her."

The water stopped splashing. "Jupiter, an Irish lord," she murmured, obviously every bit as impressed as Samson had intended. "She must be very beautiful."

"She is," said Samson fondly. He hadn't seen his younger sister in three years, but he'd had letters aplenty from her in Appledore, and from them he was sure Serena hadn't changed in that time, despite the new husband that Samson had yet to meet. She'd still be the beauty he remembered, with their mother's blue eyes and fair hair, and she'd still cook the best cornbread and quahog chowder he'd ever eaten, there on her hearth in the shingled house on Cranberry Point. "There's not another woman alive like Serena."

"How could she be otherwise, given such a name as that?" the girl said wistfully. "Serena Fairbourne. Aye, she'd have to be born fair, wouldn't she? Not like plain Polly Bray."

She tried to laugh, but the sound that came out was so much more forlorn than happy that Samson turned around toward her.

"Polly's a good enough name for any lass," he began heartily, then stopped. It wasn't the name that made him unable to continue but the sight of the woman before him.

And for the second time since she'd been hauled onto his deck, there was no question at all that Polly Bray *was* female. She stood with her back to him, bending slightly forward over the washbowl as she peered unhappily into the looking glass. She'd shed her oversized coat while she washed, and this first view of her in boy's breeches—the drawstrings pulled tight in a neat bow at her narrow waist, the gathers below stretched snugly in a decidedly unboy-ish fashion, the curves of her hips and thighs clear through the worn, still-damp linen and emphasized by the low-slung belt with her knife—was enough to make Samson forget his own name, let alone hers. No wonder decent women dressed in petticoats, he thought with despair; if instead they all donned breeches like this, then men would be too busy gawking to accomplish a blessèd thing, and the entire world would thump to a libidinous halt.

To make matters worse—or better—the misshap-en knitted cap had disappeared, and her fresh-washed and combed hair slipped over her shoulders, the water from it again dampening the white linen of her shirt to make the fabric cling here and there over her arms and back with fascinating imprecision. Thank God she'd kept her waistcoat, for at least its coarse homespun covered her where she most needed covering. But even so, Samson's unredeemed memory filled in the rest, reminding him of that finely round breast he'd inadvertently discovered earlier.

"Oh, aye, Polly's a good enough name," she said without much conviction, addressing his reflection behind her own in the mirror. "Leastways good enough for such as me."

"One name's as good as another," he said carefully, "so far as I can see." He could see more than that. Even slick as her hair was with water, the ends were beginning to curl, corkscrewing over her shoulderblades toward her waist with such determined waywardness that he wondered how she'd ever contained it beneath her knitted cap.

How and, more provokingly, *why?* Any other woman would have made a preening display of such hair, not hidden it away like a secret shame. It made no sense, and he didn't like things that didn't make sense. And why couldn't she stand upright so he didn't have to keep studying her nether side in those infernal breeches?

"One name's as good as another only if it suits the bearer," she mused, unaware of his thoughts. "A Samson must be strong. What if you'd turned out poorly, a spavined clerk named Samson?"

He smiled at the ludicrous image. Fairbournes were always large, and never, ever landlocked clerks, let alone ones with crooked legs. "My mother read her Scripture, that was all. She chose a name she liked."

She caught his smile, reflected in the mirror, and narowed her eyes at the amusement in it. "Then your mother was a most fortunate woman, to choose a name she liked *and* that suited you."

His smile faded, his expression growing guarded, the way it always did when anyone mentioned his mother. No one could ever call his poor Mam fortunate, may God keep her safe in Heaven: widowed at twenty-five, with four small children and no means to feed them save the charity of the parish, and dead herself the year after.

Not fortunate at all, and neither was he, for foolishly bringing her name into such a conversation. There was already enough ill luck surrounding this voyage without him speaking of the dead, even of his own dead mother, and he reached surreptitiously beneath the heavy oak table and tapped his knuckles three times, just to be sure.

"It's a fine-sounding name," he said, feeling marginally better, "and I've made it my own. But then you've done that yourself, too, haven't you, Miss Polly Ann Bray of Ninnishibutt River?"

She turned around to look at him, absently running her thumb along the horn hilt of her knife while she considered what he'd said. Her hair fell in waving curtains on either side of her face, shading and softening her features in a way he wouldn't have expected. The candles in the lantern burnished her damp hair to dark copper, and he wondered what color it would be when it was finally dry. Dark chestnut, he guessed, though he wanted to see it in sunlight to be sure. Of course, the pleasing sight of all that magnificent hair tossing in the wind would have nothing whatsoever to do with it.

"You are right, Captain Fairbourne," she said finally. "Plain Polly Bray I may be, but I'm also the only Polly Bray from my county, leastways that I know of."

"The only one in the entire blessèd colony," agreed Samson. "Maybe in all New England."

She nodded gravely. "That could be, aye. I've never heard of another of me."

"No," he said truthfully, tallying the lushly curling hair and the close-fitting breeches against that horn-handled knife. "There isn't one."

She nodded again, and with a sinuous twist of her neck she flipped all her hair over one shoulder. Deftly she began to braid it, the budding curls disappearing into a single tight rope.

"Don't," he said softly. "Leave it loose."

"What, and have you tell me again I'm not proper?" She wrinkled her nose and kept on braiding. "Besides, 'tis a terrible nuisance unbound, and tangles wicked in the wind. But I do thank you for the use of your comb for the snarls, I do indeed."

She smiled, a smile far too guileless for him to deserve, even with the knife at her waist. Carefully, she refolded the washing cloth and laid it over the edge of the bowl with the comb and hand-mirror on top; neatly, precisely, more like a well-trained seaman than a woman. She found a thin leather strip in her pocket to tie the ends of her hair, flipped the finished braid over her shoulder, and reached for her coat.

She'd finished, she'd thanked him, and now she was leaving—and, damnation, he didn't want her to go.

"Stay," he said impulsively. "Dine with me here. Supper will come soon, and I promise my cook will make it a good one."

She shook her head, still smiling. "Nay, I cannot. Mind, Captain, I will be proper, even with you."

Especially with you might have been closer to the mark, and he ran his fingers back through his hair as he tried to sort out his own misguided inclinations. "Supper is proper."

Her smile vanished and her eyes turned wary, proof that he wasn't being nearly as circumspect as he'd hoped. "Supper can be proper, aye," she said slowly. "But not tonight."

"Blast it all, I gave you my word you'd be safe, didn't I?"

She nodded again, a quick, reluctant jerk. "You did. But you never said why."

He scowled down at her, using his height to reaffirm his position over her. He was the captain of this ship, and he owed explanations to no one, especially not when he couldn't make a decent one to himself. "Because you're my guest, that's why. It suits us both to be friends for this voyage, and friends dine together."

Her whole body tensed. "I must go."

He stepped forward to block her way, seizing her by the wrist for good measure. The sleeve of her linen shirt was still damp, her skin warm and soft, her heartbeat racing beneath his fingers.

"Stay," he said again, low, an unconscious, implicit order instead of a request. "Here, now, with me. Stay."

"You said I was safe," she said, her words as rapid as her heartbeat. "You said I needn't be your trollop. You said I'd have a *choice*."

She would not meet his eyes, instead staring down at his hand on her arm. Yet this way he could see the sweep of her lashes over her cheek, the freckles that dotted the sunburned bridge of her nose, the tiny, wayward curls that had escaped from the severely braided hair, hair that was redolent of the lavender soap and her own woman's scent mingled together and everything so close he'd scarcely have to bend at all to kiss her.

Kiss her: God in Heaven, what was he thinking?

"Of course you have a choice," he said, easing a step away, though he could not bring himself to release her arm just yet. "I wouldn't have it otherwise."

"Then let me go," she whispered, so softly he could scarcely hear her. "Please."

That whisper shamed him more than any accusation ever could, and he followed her downward gaze to where his fingers still held her arm. Finger by finger, he watched his grasp uncoil and gentle, almost as if his hand belonged to another. He was wrong to hold her against her will like this, and knowing he was wrong only made it worse.

"Ah, Miss Bray," he began, meaning to apologize, "I didn't—"

But what he did or didn't intend didn't matter as he felt his feet kicked out from beneath him and he fell, hard, over a chair and crashed to the deck. With an oath he tried to twist his way back up, but she'd already dropped onto his chest, pinning his arms to his sides with her legs as she pressed the blade of that infernal knife to his throat.

"You great ill-bred scrod," she said with disgust and, he thought, a certain amount of disappointment, as she leaned her face over his. "I'd thought better of you, I did, but you're no better than the rest of mankind. I told you I wanted to be treated respectful, and I meant it."

She'd caught him carelessly off-balance and unawares, but she'd also caught him in the wrong, which
was why he lay there as her contrite prisoner a
moment or two longer than was necessary. It had, he
told himself, absolutely nothing to do with having
her straddling his chest in such an interesting position, or the feel of her thighs against his chest, or the
wild, fierce light in her eyes as she hung over him,
breathing hard.

But even contrition, however well earned, had its
limits. He quickly rolled to one side, reversing their
positions and trapping her beneath him with his full
weight and size as he freed his hand to grasp her
wrist again. This time he gently forced her hand to
one side, pressing his thumb to her wrist until the
knife slipped from her hand and clattered to the deck.

"Ah, Miss Bray," he said softly. "You wanted my
respect, lass, and by God, you've earned it. But if you
ever try such a trick again, I swear I'll put you ashore
on the first landfall I find, and you'll never see your
dear Ninnishibutt again."

She didn't struggle or fight him, the way he'd
expected, nor did she wail or weep like other women.
Instead she lay quiet beneath him, soft and almost
yielding, with all the fight drained from her body. He
wished she *would* fight him, at least a bit, so that he'd
have something else to concentrate on instead of how
her breasts were pushing into his chest and her round
little belly into his groin. He'd already learned she
didn't wear stays, but until now he'd tried not to give
much thought to exactly how unprotected she was
without the usual female layers of whalebone and
quilting and petticoats and hoops. Now he could
think of nothing else. At most three layers of linen lay
between them, and that was damnably scanty protec-

tion for keeping thoughts, and the rest of him, where they honorably belonged.

Not that he trusted her stillness, either, or mistook it for any sort of acquiescence. He'd learned that much from the way she wielded that knife. He'd never trust her again.

"Worthless, bullying scrod," she hissed from beneath him, their faces so close he felt the force of the words on his nose. "Pea-brained, tin-plated, heaving, retching excuse for a *scrod*."

"And a good evening to you, too, Miss Bray." He pushed himself away from her and sat back on his heels, letting her scramble to her feet. "You were right. There's not another woman like you, not in all the world."

Furiously she snatched her coat from where she'd dropped it, thrusting her arms into the sleeves, and jammed the knitted cap back over her hair, clear down to her brows. She looked at her knife, still on the deck beside Samson, hesitated, then glared at him.

He slid it across the deck toward her. "Take it," he said. Strange how the angrier she grew, the more magnanimous he felt. As captain, he was generally the one who was angry, not the other way around, like this, and it was an intriguing experience. "I wouldn't want you wandering about unarmed."

"I should gut you instead," she muttered as she tucked the knife back into its sheath. "I could do it, you know."

He smiled and shook his hair back from his face. "I've no doubt that you could. But I'd believe it better for us both if you didn't try."

She turned away from him, muttering something he could not hear but guessed had much to do with his parentage. But at the doorway she stopped and rushed back to the washbowl. Hurriedly, as if she feared he'd stop her, she stuffed the soap, mirror, and comb into her coat pockets. Then she glanced back at him with an undisguised look of triumph beneath the woolen brim of her cap and fled.

Yet he'd won. She'd kept his first little gifts. It hadn't happened exactly the way Samson had planned, but he'd still have something to hold over Zach.

But the rest of it—how, since sunset, in some mysterious, unfathomable way, plain Polly Bray had ceased to be plain, or homely, or waifish—that he'd keep as a troubling secret to his grave.

Four

❧

*P*olly leaned back and rested her head against the mast, letting the warmth of the early sun sink deep into her joints. If only all her other woes could as easily be soothed, then she'd never leave this perch again.

The *Morning Star* rolled gently beneath her, the clear blue sea so far below making the ship's passage an easy one. She'd never been much for numbers, and she couldn't guess exactly how far below that might be—was it forty feet, or maybe fifty?—but she did know she'd climbed infinitely higher than she'd ever gone along the *Dove*'s single stubby mast, and higher, too, than the tallest tree she'd climbed as a girl. It had been high enough to make her arms and legs ache and the sweat prickle along her back, and more than high enough that halfway to the top she'd wondered at her own foolhardy recklessness for accepting Zach Fairbourne's invitation to come aloft.

But now her fear had vanished, and if, as she'd suspected, the first mate's offer had been more of a dare than an invitation, then she'd passed his challenge. And he'd been right about one thing: this was the most peaceful spot on the entire ship.

She leaned forward to look down, taking care to keep her hands gripping tight to the furled sail and her legs curled around the spar for safety's sake. As much as she'd hate to admit it (and she wouldn't, not to Captain Fairbourne), the *Morning Star* was a well-run ship, a profitable joy to whichever fat Boston merchant owned her. From this height Polly could see how precisely every line was pulled taut or coiled into tidy bundles, and how the long planks of the deck had been holystoned until the wood gleamed like old silver in the sunlight. Even the barrels of the long guns the ship carried for protection, six to a side, had been buffed and polished, each pointing precisely in readiness at its gunport. Every sailor moved about with easy confidence and purpose, almost as if they'd already anticipated their orders. The only thing out of place in all this order was Polly herself, and with an unhappy sigh she leaned back against the mast.

"Here now, I asked you here to cheer you," said Zach Fairbourne, his own cheerfulness a match for the bright red waistcoat worn open over a checkered shirt. "No long faces permitted. I'll make that an order if you don't agree directly."

She glanced over at him, sitting on the other side of the crosstrees, lounging there with his long legs dangling with the same ease as a landsman would in his favorite chair before the fire. No one could miss the resemblance between him and the captain. Their coloring was the same, as was the shape of their jaws and mouth, and Lord only knew they were both built on the same oversized scale.

But to Polly's eye, the younger man seemed sweeter and happier by nature, more inclined to smile than frown, and therefore infinitely better company than his cross-tempered cousin. Oh, Zach Fairbourne could bark orders and swear a blue streak like any other good mate—she'd heard him with her own ears—but he had none of the captain's self-centered haughtiness, and for that, given her own ill humor on this particular morning, she was most heartily grateful.

"I do not wish to be sad, Mr. Fairbourne," she said with another sigh. "But I'd say I have a powerful lot to be sad about."

"No more 'Mr. Fairbourne,'" he said firmly. "I'm Zach to you, mind?"

She considered this for a moment, trying to decide whether using his given name would be proper or not. She suspected it wasn't. Little to do with men this handsome and close to her own age was. Yet, like her father, she'd always called the other Ninnishibutt fishermen by their given names unless they were very old and venerable, and no harm had come to her.

"Zach, that's all," he coaxed. "It's far easier to say than 'Mr. Fairbourne.'"

She sighed again, this time with resignation. "Very well then: Zach. I don't have much to be cheerful about, Zach. I've lost my boat and my catch and all my belongings with it, and I'm hundreds of miles from my home, and while I'm grateful that you saved me from drowning, I know that every last man on board thinks I'm a witless idiot."

"There now, lass, there, there," he said gently, and with the patience reserved for witless idiots. "It's not so bad as all that, is it?"

She swung one leg back and forth through the air. "Nay, it's worse," she said gloomily, brushing a stray strand of hair from her face. " 'Twould be bad enough alone being a witless idiot, but I'm a Jonah, too. Nay, don't deny it. I know what men think of women on a ship, especially castaway women, and I've seen how they all avoid me, crossing their fingers against bad luck whenever I pass. I'm a Jonah, plain and simple. You might as well have sailed on a Friday—a Friday that's the thirteenth of the month—for all the misfortune I'm bound to bring."

Zach's mouth screwed up as if he'd bitten a sour lime, his eyes so studiously serious that Polly knew she'd guessed right. She was sailor enough to understand the sorry significance of being a Jonah, that baddest of bad-luck harbingers at sea, and her spirits sank even lower.

"I don't know why Captain Fairbourne doesn't just heave me over the side right now," she said dolefully. "Not even that wager of yours is worth the sorrow I'll cause his ship. He's made it clear enough he hates me. What would he care if I were to disappear the same way as I came?"

"Don't say such things," said Zach urgently. "There's no point in tempting luck, bad or good, with that manner of talk."

"Can you look me in the eye and tell me it's not true?"

"I can tell you that Sam doesn't hate you," he said, so patently avoiding Polly's question that she might have laughed if that same truth hadn't hurt. "He wants everything arranged particular for you, from what Cook fixes for your meals to the proper coverlet for your bunk. Now, would he do all that if he hated you?"

"He would," she retorted. "Jupiter, Zach, if you'd seen how he carried on last night, you'd be calling *him* mad, too. Raging on and on about how I must do this and I must do that, and how undutiful I'd be unless I used his blessèd comb and soap, there and then before his eyes like a wicked child that needs watching, and *then* how I must stay and eat with him, as if I'd no will or wish of my own!''

The sad truth was that, deep down inside, Polly *did* feel as if she'd lost both will and wish together. She'd scarcely slept at all after the previous evening's humiliating encounter with Captain Fairbourne.

And with good reason, too: she'd let herself be overwhelmed by him, swallowed up as completely as a minnow by a shark. She'd been so busy gawking at the sunset, and his cabin, even his wretched *chairs*, that she'd had to concentrate all her wits upon not gawking at him, parading about fine as a lord in royal near nakedness, that she'd nothing left to spare for guarding herself. She'd let him lure her into believing his crocodile trust, with hideous results. Even when she'd trapped him with her knife to his throat—a tactic that had succeeded with every other man foolish enough to cross her—she'd turned weak and flustered, focusing instead on how sitting on his chest was like riding a tiger, all coiled danger waiting beneath her, and how the hard muscles of his arms were pressing against her open thighs and his blue eyes hooded so close to hers, his breath so warm upon her cheek, and—

Lord help her, the memory was wicked enough without it returning now to torture her again!

She shook her head, determined to shake away such dangerous thoughts that made her grow hot with shame. No man had ever made her feel that way. And if she'd anything to say about it, no man—

particularly Captain Fairbourne—would ever do it again.

But through all this Zach had merely listened and nodded, his expression turning thoughtful. "Sam wished you to stay? To dine with him?"

She nodded, adding what she intended to be a ladylike sniff of disdain. "Likely it's the same invitation he offers to the first doxie he sees in any port."

"Likely, no," said Zach. "Sam doesn't much fancy doxies—or decent women, either. He says he hasn't the time to bother with females. His humor might be improved if he did, but he doesn't and never has, more's a pity."

"But he didn't treat *me* the way I ought to be treated, Zach, supper or no supper," said Polly with as much dignity as possible while swaying so high in the air. "Aye, that's it in a nutshell. He behaved ill mannerly and hateful toward me, the way he has from the beginning, which is scarcely the way to make me change for the sake of his wager. Not that *that* bothers me. No. I wouldn't care if he lost every last farthing from his own foolishness."

"I told you before that he doesn't hate you," said Zach firmly. "You're wronging him to believe otherwise."

Yet Polly's little laugh was hollow and unconvincing. "Oh, aye, he does. He does, and near every other man on board does, too. You're the only one who's been halfway nice to me."

"Poor Miss Polly." He reached out to rest his hand on her sleeve, giving her arm a sympathetic pat. "You deserve better than this, I know, but I do believe things will turn out—"

"*Mr.* Fairbourne!"

The voice came roaring upward from the quarter-deck, and while Polly stared at Zach with surprise and a certain degree of guilt, neither had to guess the identity of the voice's owner. There square in the middle of his own quarterdeck stood Captain Fair-bourne, his legs angled wide against the ship's motion, his hands clasped behind his waist, and his entire person radiating intense displeasure—displeasure that was unquestionably directed toward her and Zach.

"I must go," said Zach, already sliding from the spar to begin his hasty descent to the deck.

"Wait!" called Polly, twisting to watch him go. "I'm coming with you!"

She couldn't let Zach face the captain's wrath alone, especially since she was undoubtedly the cause of it. But as she began to follow the way Zach had taken, hand over hand down one of the thick rope lines instead of using the ladderlike shrouds, she realized too late that if climbing up to such a height had been hard, then going down from it would be easy—far *too* easy. As she slid down the rope, the momentum from her own weight made her go faster and faster without any way to stop. Racing before her she saw sails and clouds, a hovering white-winged gull, the flat line of the horizon, all of it in a breakneck blur that matched the thumping of her own heart.

She could not stop, she thought wildly—she would not stop—and then, with terrifying sudden-ness, she had, her feet slamming hard against the deck. Her knees buckled beneath her, and only the rope that she still grasped tight in her hands saved her from melting into a clumsy heap on the deck.

She took a deep breath to calm herself, and then

another. She slowly unwrapped her trembling hands from the line and winced with pain. The rough hemp and friction had combined to rub her palms raw, her calluses from hauling nets still no match for those of a blue-water sailor. But she wasn't going to let anyone else know that, least of all Captain Fairbourne. Determinedly she thrust her stinging hands into her pockets to hide them, and as quickly as her unsteady legs would let her, she made her way to the two men on the quarterdeck.

"The hell you will," the captain was saying. More precisely, he was roaring, while Zach stood so straight before him that his spine nearly arched backward. "I won't have you putting at risk anyone or anything on board this vessel and I—how the Devil did you come to be here, Miss Bray?"

"Dropped clear from the heavens, and the Devil had nothing to do with it." She met his gaze evenly, or at least as evenly as she could given the difference in their heights. "Though to hear you talk, the Devil does seem to have a precious lot of influence on this ship."

"If that were true," he said, "then I'd invite him to take your tongue and save me the trouble."

He glared down at her, shifting his ire from Zach. She was surprised to see the care he'd taken with his dress this morning. While even Zach as mate had left off his coat and rolled back his shirtsleeves for comfort in the warm sun, Captain Fairbourne wore an elegantly cut coat of royal blue linen with a buttercolored waistcoat glittering with buttons as well polished as the buckles on his shoes. His hair was tied back with a blue silk bow, and his head was crowned by a black cocked hat edged with silver lacing and worthy of the King himself. The captain might not know how to behave like a gentleman, thought Polly, but she'd grudgingly admit that he knew how to trick himself out like one when he tried, and she wondered what might be the occasion.

Could they in fact be putting into port? And if so, would she be left behind? It was bad enough to be a Jonah here on the *Morning Star*, but at least she was a Jonah who was being fed and given a place to sleep and promised a handsome reward for her inconvenience at journey's end. There'd be no such guarantees if she were put ashore in a strange place, without money or friends.

"I didn't mean Miss Bray harm, sir," said Zach, falling into the respectful shipboard formality that, even between cousins, was appropriate for being dressed down by a captain. "I only took her aloft so she could see the view."

The captain swung around to face Zach again. "You 'took her aloft,'" he repeated scornfully. "You 'took' her? And how exactly did you accomplish that? In an egg basket looped over your wrist?"

"He did no such thing!" said Polly indignantly. "I climbed up—and down, too—by myself! Whatever else could you think?"

What Samson had thought first when he'd seen the two of them in the foretop was fear, plain and simple, fear that she'd slip and crash like a broken-winged bird to the deck. He'd seen others fall like that, and he could imagine it with sickening clarity. She had seemed so tiny up there in the rigging, and so innocently unaware of the danger, that it had taken all of Samson's will not to race up the mast to save her.

That first thought, then, had been noble enough, but the one that followed it was base and low, so low that Samson hated himself for thinking it. He'd looked up at his cousin, the young man he regarded as another brother, and hated him for being there with Polly Bray, there with his hand on her arm as if he'd every right to do so, their heads and bodies bent together in a wordless understanding and sympathy that excluded the rest of the world. Most of all, it had excluded Samson himself.

But damnation, wasn't the point of this whole foolish wager to teach Zach a lesson about women? It certainly wasn't supposed to be letting him make another conquest out of Polly Bray. And, more important, who the Devil was meant to be doing the teaching?

He cleared his throat as he frowned down at the pair of them now, feeling like some ancient, finger-wagging schoolmaster. "We will discuss this further, Mr. Fairbourne. Now return to your duties directly."

"Aye-aye, sir," said Zach promptly, relieved to escape so easily. He flashed one last quick smile at Polly, a smile that she returned with a readiness that deepened Samson's frown even further.

Not that he'd conceded the battle yet. Far from it.

"Oh, and Mr. Fairbourne," he said, making the younger man pause. "We'll be making a change of course. West by northwest, for St. Pierre."

Zach's mouth fell open with surprise, exactly as Samson had hoped it would. "St. Pierre, sir?"

"St. Pierre." Samson allowed himself to smile expansively. "Given this wind, we should be there by nightfall. I'll thank you to give the word to the men directly."

Zach ducked his head and gave the only acceptable reply before he hurried to obey: "Aye-aye, sir."

Samson's smile widened. There'd be no question

now as to who was in charge, or who was going to win this infernal wager, either. He hadn't put on his shore-going clothes for nothing.

"St. Pierre, Captain Fairbourne?" asked Polly anxiously, her hands twisting deep in her pockets. "I may not know much of this part of the sea, but I do know that Boston, and Ninnishibutt, are not to be reached on a westerly course."

"True enough." He let his smile beam her way, anticipating her reaction when she understood his surprise. Women generally liked his smile, almost as much as they liked gifts. Perhaps she'd throw her arms around his neck with excitement, and he remembered how pleasantly soft her body could be against his own. Perhaps she'd even kiss him, by way of thanks. "You are right, Miss Bray. St. Pierre is not ordinarily on our course north. Yet on your account, I have decided to put in there briefly."

"For *me?*" Her voice squeaked upward and she began to blink her eyes very rapidly, as if she'd caught a piece of grit. "St. Pierre is a French place, isn't it? Oh, faith, I told you, I cannot even speak their tongue!"

Hell, she was going to cry, and he hadn't the faintest clue why.

"You won't have to say a word," he said swiftly. "I'll tell them whatever needs telling. But as I recall, the *mesdames* speak English proper enough once they see your purse."

"But I have no purse," she said wretchedly. "I haven't a farthing, either, and now you're going to put me ashore and abandon me among Papist Frenchmen, just as I asked, and I'll never, ever, see home again."

He stared at her for a long, mystified minute.

"Where in blazes did you get an idea like that? I mean to take you to a mantua-maker's shop and have you rigged out like a decent woman, that is all. I'd hardly maroon you after I'd spent that kind of coin, would I?"

"I—I—don't know," she said, hiccuping the words as she struggled to hold back her tears. "All I know for sure is that I'm a—a Jonah, and bad luck, and—and everyone on board hates me because of it, you most of all."

Now it was his turn to stare open-mouthed. "That is the greatest stinking crock of offal I've ever heard. There's no such fanciful creature as a Jonah outside of the Testaments, and there's certainly not one aboard any ship of mine! A *Jonah!* If I ever find out which rascal put that idea into your head I'll flay him alive with my own hand!"

"No—no one told me," she said. "I figured it for my—myself."

"Well then, just unfigure it, because it's not true. A Jonah, for God's sake." He shook his head with disgust, then stopped abruptly. No one had dared call her bad luck to her face, but what if she'd overheard talk, talk about that wretched bottle and the message he'd heaved into the harbor at Bridgetown? The wager with Zach was idiotic enough, but if she put the two together he'd look like the greatest horse's ass in creation.

"Then you're not going to cast me away again?" she asked. "You'll take me back to New England?"

Samson studied her uneasily, clasping and unclasping his hands behind his waist where he hoped she wouldn't notice. The tears were still there, making her silver eyes glisten, but now, thank God, she seemed reassured enough to be able to keep them unshed: a rare and agreeable talent in a woman. She wasn't acting as if she'd heard any tales about him. Perhaps that Jonah-nonsense was the end of it. "I gave you my word I'd take you back home, didn't I?"

She nodded. "Then I thank you. I thank you indeed."

"You are welcome," he said, studying her closely as she blinked away the last hint of her tears. Her mouth was twisting curiously to one side while her hands still fussed inside her coat pockets, almost as if she'd a pair of squirrels hidden inside. It was distracting, and he wished she'd stop it. Besides, he kept wondering whether she'd tucked her knife in there this morning for safekeeping, and if all this fidgeting was her trying to decide whether to use it on him again or not. For both their sakes, he hoped not.

But fidgeting was nothing compared to what came next.

"You might as well turn about back north, Captain Fairbourne," she said with a deliberateness he hadn't expected after the near tears, "because you can also forget that notion about the mantua-maker. I told you before I'm already a decent woman, and I don't need petticoats to prove it. Especially not petticoats paid for by you."

"Damnation, Miss Bray, I didn't intend it that way," he said defensively. No giddy, thankful embraces, then, and certainly no kisses. "I'll be buying the petticoats, not you in them."

The brows lowered beneath that wretched woolen hat. "I should hope not."

"It's part of the blasted wager, that is all," he said, struggling to keep his voice low enough so that the entire crew wouldn't overhear. "I'll pay for the wretched frippery, and you'll wear it so that my bullheaded cousin can see you."

She made a little snorting noise of disgust. "Oh, aye, you're a right generous one, aren't you, Captain Fairbourne?"

"I would be if you let me." He glared at her murderously, wishing she hadn't goaded him into being so rudely truthful. "For the sake of the wager, that is."

She smiled shrewdly. "I didn't mistake it for Christian charity."

"Then don't mistake this, either," he said warmly. "The entire point of this is to teach my jackass of a cousin a lesson that he sorely needs to learn."

"A lesson?" she asked curiously. "What sort of lesson?"

"Never mind that," he said hurriedly. "What matters to you is this: that I do not give a tinker's dam whether you keep a single scrap of ribbon I give you. You can burn it, or give it to the poor, or make a donkey's silk-satin bed of it for all I care."

He had never been forced to persuade a woman to accept a gift, let alone something as generous as he was offering now, but even without the experience, he was certain he was doing it badly. *Persuasion* wasn't even the word, anyway. He doubted there was a man on this earth who could *persuade* Polly Bray to perform even the simplest request if she wasn't already inclined to it.

Now she was looking up at him suspiciously from beneath half-closed lashes—a look that somehow, at the same time, managed to be damnably, unintentionally seductive, blast her wicked little hide.

"So you fear that unless I am willing to let you

dress me as you please," she mused, "as if I were your own wooden doll-baby, you'll lose your wager?"

"That's the sum of it, aye," said Samson, his imagination too quick to picture undressing her as well. "He needs to see the difference decent clothes will make in you."

"Ha," she scoffed. "I should like to see the pile of rags that could do that."

"In St. Pierre, Miss Bray, you will. I'll warrant you'll be outright astounded." He smiled half-heartedly, praying that Madame LaFontaine's seam-stresses were equal to such a challenge. But when Polly didn't answer beyond a wry half smile, he decided to seize that as her agreement.

"Until St. Pierre, then," he said. "Good morning, Miss Bray."

He touched the front of his hat to her and, with a bow to excuse himself, turned on his heel to begin his customary walk back and forth on the quarterdeck. He breathed deeply, hoping to clear her from both his thoughts and his conscience. The quarterdeck was the proper place for such activity. By long tradition it was the captain's exclusive domain, visited by lesser mortals only by invitation, and Samson cherished this undisturbed time alone each fair morning. Everyone on board knew it, and respected it.

Everyone, that is, excepting Polly Bray.

At first he didn't notice she hadn't left. She hadn't spoken or otherwise called attention to herself to disturb his thoughts, but when he reached the starboard rail and turned back, she was *there*, her face turned expectantly toward his. Perhaps, he thought with faint hope, if he didn't speak, she'd leave on her own, and he purposefully ignored her as he crossed the deck twice in silence. But still she followed close at his side like a homeless puppy, stretching her legs to match her stride to his and spoiling his peace in the process.

He stopped abruptly. "Miss Bray," he said, "surely you have somewhere else on board you'd prefer to be."

But she only shook her head, the little curls that had escaped from beneath her cap dancing over her forehead in the breeze.

"Wherever else would I go, Captain?" she asked disingenuously. "I might as well stay here with you. Leastways if you do not mind."

"No," he lied, unable to make himself tell her and her dancing curls the disagreeable truth. "Not at all."

He began to walk again with her as his shadow, and his despair grew with every step. He liked being alone; on a crowded ship, it was a rare and hard-earned luxury. But simply by being here on his quarterdeck, she had turned his time for solitary reflection into a social exercise, and he felt the weight of that responsibility settling upon his shoulders like a yoke. However unwillingly, he'd agreed to keep her company, and now he must supply the required conversation.

But conversation meant speaking, and to his horror he could think of nothing more to say. On the rare times he'd gone walking with women before—on land, of course—the women had always been the ones to talk, able to spin the thinnest topic into endless speculation and chatter. But it was a feminine gift that, along with petticoats and stays, Polly Bray didn't seem to possess. He'd never had to fill such a silence himself, and this particular silence between him and Polly was becoming as vast and unbreachable as the Atlantic.

"The day is warm," he began in desperation.

"Aye," she said solemnly. "But tolerable."

He cleared his throat, hoping to free the words. "And fair."

"Aye." She nodded. "Aye, 'tis that, too."

And that *was* that, as far as Samson was concerned. Lord, what he would give now for a dollop of Zach's ease with women! His cousin had certainly not been at a loss for things to say to Polly Bray when they'd been aloft together. And she'd spoken to him, too, the pair of them with their heads together, chattering away like magpies in the rigging. So why the Devil couldn't she talk to him now?

"Was it my cousin who called you a Jonah?" he blurted out suddenly. "Was he the one?"

She looked up at him, startled by his abruptness, her silver eyes wide in the bright sunlight. "Oh, nay, not at all," she said instantly, without a thought or hesitation. "Zach would never be so cruel as that."

Zach would never be so cruel. But he had become "Zach" instead of "Mr. Fairbourne," while Samson seemed forever entombed as stern old "Captain Fairbourne," and doubtless as cruel as the day was long. Clearly there'd been no wakeful night for her, none of the tortuous half dreams of regret and desire that had plagued him.

Unless she'd dreamed of his cousin instead.

Samson bowed his head in the shadow of his hat's brim. He was surprised that he should care about the judgment of a Polly Bray, and even more surprised by how much it stung.

She had turned away from him, instead squinting intently out across the turquoise water. Despite his unhappiness, he caught himself smiling fondly as he studied her. She almost looked like a real sailor, the ends of the faded kerchief she wore around her throat fluttering behind her as she turned her face into the breeze. Of course, a Massachusetts girl would never have seen water of such a jewel-like color, and for her to see such a pretty sight would—

"There's a sail," she said matter-of-factly. "No, at least two. Another ship, then. There, off your larboard bow."

Samson squinted in the direction she was pointing and saw nothing beyond the usual slight haze on the horizon where the water met the sky. "No, Miss Bray," he said indulgently. "There's nothing but—"

"Ship ahoy!" bawled the lookout from his post far overhead. "Three points off th'larboard bow!"

Samson cocked one brow suspiciously at Polly, who merely smiled. "However'd you see that, eh? Are your eyes that keen?"

"Aye, they are," she said proudly. "If you put me in the top in place of that blind almsman you call a lookout, I'd have spotted that ship a good ten minutes ago."

Samson glanced once again out to sea, a sea that, to his chagrined eyes, still remained empty.

"Then here," he said, taking the long spyglass from the boy who'd fetched it automatically as soon as they'd heard the lookout's cry. He pulled the glass open to its full length and handed it out to Polly. "Tell me what you see with this."

Her face lit with eager anticipation and a bit of awe.

"I've never used a glass so fine," she said as her

hands finally came from her pockets to take the glass from him. Carefully she lifted the polished brass and mahogany tube to her eye, adjusting it with experienced ease, and gazed at the white speck that was only now visible to Samson.

"Two sails—so I was right!—but only one mast," she said, concentrating. "That great spanker sail aft fooled me. But not quite a schooner rig. Nay, not with that foretopgallant. I'd vow she's a cutter, then."

"A cutter, you say." Samson was impressed—deeply impressed—though he couldn't begin to fathom how she'd be so knowledgeable. "What manner of cutter?"

"Folkstone or Dunkirk," she answered promptly. "Though what either would be doing in these waters is beyond me."

"Up to mischief, same as the rest of us." He smiled broadly, unable to help himself. He'd never heard a woman make half this much sense, and it amused him mightily. "But can you make out her colors yet? What port's she sailing from, eh?"

She hesitated, considering. "Spanish, I think, but I am not certain. Could that be possible?"

"Possible, and likely, too." Strange how he'd no trouble thinking of what to say to her now. "There's every sort of flag to be found in the Caribbean these days."

The lookout, breathless following his belated descent from the top, rushed across the deck toward them to report what he'd seen, and Samson waved him away. The man had already lost his ration of rum for the day for being so slow to notice the other ship. Besides, right now Samson trusted Polly's eyes more.

"Anything else, lass?" he asked. He liked watching

her even more than listening to her, her small, slender body gracefully arched as she steadied the glass in her outstretched hands. It was a moment he didn't want to end.

"I cannot quite—oh, blast, she's going!" cried Polly in frustration. "She's tacking away from us!"

"Or running. The effect will be the same, eh?" She might be disappointed, but Samson wasn't. Though he carried guns enough for a fight, he didn't seek one, and the tidy twin rows of cannon were as much for show as anything. He'd had his fill of gunfire and bloodshed for honor's sake when he'd sailed on his oldest brother's privateer in the last war. Peacetime seemed considerably more agreeable.

Nor did he wish for any sort of danger that could put Polly at risk while she was in his safekeeping. It was strangely the same way he'd felt when he'd seen her swaying in the rigging.

Exactly the same.

"So tell me, Miss Bray," he said, unwilling to share such thoughts with her, "how did a little lass like you learn to tell a cutter from a cornstalk?"

With the cutter now vanished below the horizon, she reluctantly lowered the glass. "One summer on our boat, Father took on a share-man who'd been pressed as a boy. He'd no use for the King's navy, but with it he'd sailed the world, and he'd point out all the Boston-bound vessels we'd see afar." She shrugged self-consciously. "I guess it passed his time to teach me."

"You must have been an apt student," he said softly.

She heard the change in his voice, her eyes full of question. Did she feel it, too, he wondered, that strange, fleeting, intangible bond that had, for a moment, drawn them together? Or was she simply more wary of him after they'd tussled the night before?

"He was a good teacher, that was all. I only saw what he showed me." Skittishly she broke her gaze away from his. "Here, you'll be wanting this back."

Eager to escape, she thrust the spyglass back into his hands. But as she did, Samson caught a glimpse of what the rope had done to her palms. He tucked the glass beneath his arm and gently, so as not to hurt her anymore, he took her hands and turned them palms-up. With a little cry she tried to pull away, and when he held fast she curled her fingers protectively inward to hide the raw, torn skin, blotched with blood and already swelling.

"Steady now, lass, I've no wish to harm you." He recognized at once what had happened—he'd suffered worse himself, his first hapless time at sea as a boy—but he also knew it would take more than sympathy to ease her discomfort. "There's nary a man aboard who hasn't hashed his hands this way one time or another."

"But I should have known better." She hung her head in miserable shame. "First you judge me daft, then I become a Jonah, and now I'm a goose-brained landlubber."

"Hush now, I'll hear no more of that talk." From his pocket he pulled his pair of clean handkerchiefs—he always carried two, one for his personal use and one to clean saltspray from the spyglass lens—and carefully wiped her wounds clean before he began to swaddle the soft linen around her hands to cushion them.

"You should not be doing this," she said as he

worked, her voice firm as she tried to convince herself as well as him. "I'll be well enough on my own."

"You will if you do as you're told," he said sternly. Even before she'd burned her palms on the rope, her work-roughened little hands were among the least feminine examples to be found, yet he found he was reluctant to let them go, cradling them in his own as gently as if they'd been made from porcelain. "You go below and rest now, mind?"

"Why should I need to rest?" she protested. "I've done nothing to grow tired from!"

"Well then, you must go and soak your hands in a basin of sea water," said Samson, "and then I'll have Cook send you some softened lard to use as a salve for healing."

She shook her head, though this time she didn't pull away. In the bright sunlight he could see for the first time the tiny, charming freckles, nearly lost in her tan, that were scattered across the bridge of her nose and over her cheeks. "I do not wish to be a bother, or cause you more trouble."

"You haven't caused me any trouble at all," he said warmly, and to his surprise he realized he meant it. "In a day or two your hands will be right as rain again. But no more skylarking aloft, mind?"

She did not agree but pulled her bandaged hands away from his and slipped them back into hiding in her pockets. "If I tumbled into the sea and drowned, you would lose your wager, wouldn't you?"

"I would, yes. But I would also lose you, which would be far worse."

Polly searched his face, uncertain whether he was teasing her or not. He seemed serious enough, and there was no telltale twinkle in his blue eyes to betray him, no hint of mockery in his voice, the way there'd been last night.

But why should a man like Samson Fairbourne care what became of her? She thought she'd understood him, and then he'd gone and bandaged her hands as gently as her father might have, with such care and concern that she'd wanted to weep like a grateful baby. It made no sense. No, *he* made no sense, and the uncertainty of her own position on board the ship only made things more confusing.

"Truly? You would care that much what became of me?" she asked, half expecting him to laugh. "You are not jesting?"

"Truly," he said firmly, without even a smile. "Zach will tell you I'm not much given to jesting. All you need do is ask him his opinion of me."

"Faith, I would never ask Zach such a thing!" she said, unhappy that he'd think she would.

A shadow seemed to fall across his eyes, almost as if their blue had shaded to a colder gray. "I misremember," he said, biting his words with a strange, unfathomable moodiness. "You believe my delightful cousin is not sufficiently *cruel* to hold unflattering opinions of others."

"I'm sure he does, but it is of no matter to me," she said uneasily. She might have been born among the lowest fisher-folk, but she still had pride, and honor, too. "My father taught me 'tis better to judge people for my own self, and I've never found reason to do otherwise."

But the moodiness didn't leave him, his expression dark and guarded. "Then tell me, Miss Bray," he said softly. "How do you judge me?"

She stared at him, her discomfort growing. She might be proud and honest, but she knew nothing of the one-sided games that he was playing with her, all in the name of that dreadful wager. In her village, people didn't ask questions that had no polite replies. For how could she give him an answer when she hadn't decided one for herself, when he was standing so near that she couldn't make herself think?

"I must go," she said abruptly, turning away from him to flee.

"A moment more, Miss Bray," he called after her. *"If* you please."

She paused reluctantly, her clumsy hand on the guide-rail rope at the top of the companionway. They were far enough apart now that whatever they said would be public, overheard by sailors eager to repeat such a conversation to their friends. Did he believe that such an audience would make her temper her words in his favor, or did he simply not care?

"I wish to know, Miss Bray," he called, his voice carrying effortlessly across the deck to her. "If you reckon yourself such a proper judge of people, then how do you judge me?"

The sun was so much brighter here than at home, glancing off the water with a glittering brilliance that gilded the tall man before her with such intensity that it hurt her eyes.

When he'd given her his spyglass, she'd dared to forget the misfortunes that had brought her here, and to hope that she and Captain Fairbourne could be friends. But how misguided those hopes had been! In less than a day, he had saved her life, and he had damned it; he'd made her laugh, and made tears sting in her eyes; he'd showed her both the greatest disdain, and more kindness, more generosity, than she could remember from any other man; but he still could not make her give an answer she did not have, not before a hundred witnesses, or deceive her again unless she let him.

"Miss Bray!" he called again across the deck. "I have not heard your answer!"

"Nor will you, Captain Fairbourne," she shouted into the wind, her fingers twisting inside the fine linen that he'd tied with such surpassing—and surpassingly false—gentleness. "Not now, not ever. And if you wish to win your blasted wager, you will never, never, never ask me again!"

And then, miserable coward that she knew she was, she fled.

Five

Five minutes, the boy had said. Five minutes until she would be expected on deck, ready to join the *Morning Star*'s boat when it cleared for shore. Already she could hear the preparations overhead, the rhythmic squeak of the boat being lowered to the water, the bosun's barked orders to keep the ropes pulled in unison, the hurried footsteps of men eager to leave the ship for the amusements of land.

Polly glumly dragged the comb through her hair, avoiding her reflection in the little mirror on the bulkhead. If she looked even half as worn as she felt, then the sight would have been grim indeed, and this day was going to be difficult enough without beginning it in such a depressing fashion.

She did not want to go ashore. She didn't want to see the rare sights of St. Pierre, or visit the market for flowers, or dine in the best inn, or choose whatever she pleased at the mantua-maker's shop—all of which, according to the boy who'd brought her breakfast, were activities planned for her day.

She didn't want to do any of them because, most of all, she didn't want to see Captain Fairbourne. Already she'd managed to avoid him for nearly two entire nights and a day in between, and if she could have her way she'd never see him again at all. But she also wished to return to Ninnishibutt, and when she'd refused the captain's second invitation to supper last night, he'd made it clear enough in a tersely worded note that her homeward journey could well hinge on her accompanying him into St. Pierre this morning. She didn't entirely believe he'd abandon her—she'd come to suspect that he was a good deal more kindhearted than he wished the world to know—but she wasn't certain enough to risk refusing him. He *was* the captain, while on board the *Morning Star* she—she wasn't much of anything. Not knowing how she'd come here, or where she'd go next, had robbed her of her sense of herself as well as what little seemed to remain of her sanity.

She had no choice, no choice at all. And so much, she thought bitterly, for the value of his sainted *word*. The best she could say of his behavior was that it would make her own part of this fool's wager—to remain as she always had been, plain Polly Ann Bray—so much easier to accomplish.

Awkwardly she began braiding her hair, her hands and fingers still stiff as they healed. She'd sent back the captain's handkerchiefs as soon as she'd rinsed them clean, preferring to use the torn rags that the cook had sent along with the salve. There was no use in ruining such costly gentleman's linen for her sake, or so she'd told the cabin boy, Joseph, who'd returned the handkerchiefs for her. Practicality, that was all. So why wasn't it as easy to put aside the memory of Captain Fairbourne wrapping those same handkerchiefs so gently, so tenderly, around her hands?

With a sigh at her own foolishness, Polly reached into her pocket for the leather strip to bind the end of her braid. Instead her fingers touched something smooth and round, and she pulled out a small, corked bottle. She squinted at it curiously, holding it up to the candle's light.

How had *that* come to be there, she wondered, and when? A rum bottle, though long ago drained of rum, but why would she have bothered to preserve such rubbish in her pocket? Like so much else, that reason, too, seemed to be one more lost wisp of her memory, and the water-dappled scrap of paper that she found rolled inside the bottle offered no clues either. Whatever had once been written on it was now smudged and blotted into impossible illegibility, and if she'd ever been able to read it once, she certainly couldn't now.

The knock on the cabin door came sharp as a gunshot, loud and sudden enough to make her gasp. Had five minutes really passed already? She undid the latch on the door to let Joseph in, then turned to tuck the little bottle under her bunk pillow for safekeeping until her memory returned.

"Good morning to you, Miss Bray," said Captain Fairbourne behind her. "Hiding sprigs of rosemary beneath your pillow bier?"

Polly spun around to face him, her cheeks flaming. She didn't know which was worse: that he'd caught her unawares, which would mark her as careless, or that he'd seen her squirreling away the inexplicable bottle, another sign that she truly was as mad as he thought.

"I recall my sister doing that," he continued. "She

claimed it would make her dream of her own true love, whoever the lucky wretch might be. Have you the same maiden's hopes, Miss Bray?"

It was a foolish question, and insulting enough to make Polly recover her tongue. Just because she wore breeches didn't mean she wasn't entitled to the same hopes and dreams as other girls. She'd heard that kind of cruel assumption too many times before, and it stung.

"And wherever would I come by rosemary in the middle of the Caribbean Sea, as if I needed such trumpery?" she asked tartly. "Rosemary for sweetheart dreams! Faith, Captain, if you believe in that, then I don't know why you refuse to accept me as a Jonah."

He stood in the murky half light of the companionway, his expression so masked by shadow that she could not read it. Yet by the length of time it took for him to reply and the uneasy way in which he cleared his throat first, she realized with a little leap of triumph that she'd managed to unsettle him exactly as he had her.

"True enough," he admitted grudgingly. "There is precious little rosemary to be found in these waters, and fewer sweethearts, from what I've heard."

"True enough, aye," said Polly with a righteous sniff. She'd had two long days alone to convince herself of his iniquity, and she was sure she was entitled to that sniff. "On both counts."

But to her great surprise, he seemed for once unwilling to argue. "I'll choose to believe instead that you were tidying your quarters, and no more."

"Well you should, especially since that's the truth, too." She nodded, mollified except for the nagging suspicion that she might—just might—be overreacting, and that perhaps she'd misjudged both him and his rosemary dreams. "Where's Joseph?"

"Wherever he should be, I trust."

"But I was expecting Joseph," she said, her misgivings making her voice edgy and defensive. "To fetch me for the boat, that is."

"He's not coming." The captain cleared his throat and took one step forward, into her cabin without invitation and into the light of her single candle. "I fear you must make do with me instead."

If in the harsh, bright tropical sun he was a golden gentleman, here between decks his face seemed to gather the darkness into it, accentuating his features with broad strokes the way an artist would in a charcoal sketch. He was as well dressed as he'd been the day before, ready once again to play the prosperous shipmaster on shore, but now her eyes were drawn instead to the flaws in his face: the nose with the bump from a long-ago break, the little lines that fanned from his eyes, the old scars that proved how hard a sailor's life could be. This close to her, his face became too marred and too complicated for him to be called handsome, the way she'd first judged. But instead, in some strange way, those same imperfections made him infinitely more attractive to her, and infinitely more dangerous because of it.

He was watching her closely, too, his brows drawn together in a slight frown of concentration, or perhaps concern. "After your message last evening, I wished to see for myself how truly ill you were."

"I'm not," she said quickly, too quickly to be anything but caught in the little lie she'd told to escape his invitation. "That is, I was ill as can be last night, but I'm not now. I'm all to rights."

"And your hands?"

"My hands?" She glanced down at them as if they, too, had somehow caught her in another lie, and tucked them away into hiding behind her back.

"I told you, I'm all to rights," she said in a rush, "though the good Lord knows why you should care."

His expression didn't change. "Because, Miss Bray, I do," he said gravely. "I do."

There was no flippant answer to be made to that, nor, if she were honest, did Polly truly wish to give one. She wanted to believe that his concern was as false as crocodile tears, just as it had been before, but the serious, respectful way he was waiting for her now wouldn't let her.

He held his arm out to her, crooked at the elbow, the way gentlemen did for real ladies. "You are ready?"

She stared at that offered arm, strong and sturdy beneath its genteel sleeve, unsure what she should do with it. She was perfectly capable of running up the narrow steps to the deck by herself, and she knew he knew it, too. But she'd never had the chance to feel like a dainty, well-bred creature in this way, and the temptation to pretend, even if for the sake of this fool's wager, was powerful indeed.

"Damnation, lass, it's not such a quandary," he grumbled as she hesitated. "It's not as if I am asking you to put your hand in a bramble bush, am I?"

"Nay," she said firmly, his little slip of ill temper deciding her. "You are not."

But most likely she would have shown less trepidation with the bramble bush. She rested her fingers so gingerly upon his arm that not even the soft linen of his sleeve gave way beneath her touch.

He grumbled again, a wordless grumble this time, and settled his hand heavily over hers.

"There," he said firmly. "No butterfly wings, mind? Clap on as if you mean it, lass."

She ducked her head with sudden, bewildering shyness, unable to meet his gaze, but she didn't pull her hand free. It felt strangely . . . *secure*, something rare indeed in her life. No wonder so many women let themselves be led about by men like this. Once in a great while, such as this, it would be rather nice.

But only once in a great, great while.

She forced herself to raise her chin. "Do you order all the other women to 'clap on,' too, as if they were your crew, or is that order only for me?"

"I don't know." Puzzled, he frowned for a moment while he considered, then smiled sheepishly. "If I do, then likely you are the first and only one who understood what I meant. Not that there have been that many women, either."

She glanced at him suspiciously, her eyes narrowed. "I believe the part about the women not understanding your sailor talk, but not the other. Not many women, hah! Not a man like *you*."

"Then believe me when I say that not a one of them has been anything like *you* either." He patted her hand. "Now come along, lass, topsides, cheerily, cheerily."

"There, you've done it again!" she crowed, but still she did as he'd asked, letting him guide her toward the companionway. But when they reached the doorway, she didn't know to give way with ladylike demureness, instead pressing herself without a thought against his side—his warm and very large side—as together they awkwardly squeezed through the narrow space. She sprung away from him as soon as she could, but he pulled her to a halt.

"Ordinarily the gentleman goes first through the

doorway," he said mildly. "To lure away the catamounts and wolves that might prey upon the weaker
sex."

"I know that," said Polly immediately, though
until that moment she'd known nothing of the sort.
"But you said to go cheerily, and so I did."

He raised one skeptical brow but didn't argue, and
when they reached the narrow steps to the deck Polly
gave up his arm to let him go first. Though it seemed
a foolish sort of rule to her, especially since there'd be
no threat of catamounts or wolves on board the
Morning Star, she didn't wish to appear ignorant and
ill bred to him, either.

She shielded her eyes against the brilliant sunshine
as she reached the deck, and after the two days in her
close little cabin, she breathed gratefully of the clean,
fresh breeze.

"I cannot fathom how every morning in these
waters is so fair," she said as she gazed up with
delight at the cloudless sky. " 'Tis like midsummer
every day. Faith, I wonder that you'd ever wish to
leave!"

"Oh, the first good blow from a hurricane would
convince you soon enough." He took her hand again,
turning her around toward the shore. "There now,
lass, if you've an eye for pretty sights. That's St.
Pierre."

If ever there were a town, decided Polly, that had
been created as a match for the Caribbean's turquoise
waters and skies, then it must be St. Pierre. Unlike the
gray shingles and faded, whitewashed clapboarding
that marked a Massachusetts town from the sea, St.
Pierre was cloaked in sunny shades of pale rose and
yellow, with nearly every window framed with shut-

ters as blue as the sky overhead. Lush vines and bushes surrounded the buildings like plump green cushions, and curious trees with tall, straight trunks and nodding crowns of broad leaves shaded the streets and gardens. In the distance stood darker green hills and mountains, the crest of the tallest wrapped in a gossamer mist. The whole town seemed nestled in the bosom of the harbor itself, set in the center of two long, protecting arms that shielded scores of ships and boats of every size and country as well. It was, as Captain Fairbourne had said, a pretty sight, cheerful and gay and vibrant, and as far away as Polly could imagine from the poor, drab, cheerless Ninnishibutt she'd left.

"It doesn't seem real," she said slowly. "None of this does."

Captain Fairbourne laughed, obviously pleased with her reaction. "Oh, aye, it's real enough, and full of magpie Frenchmen to prove it, as you'll see for yourself. But first we must get there, eh?"

He began across the deck, drawing her to the side with her hand still firmly in his. "You have a choice, lass: you may clamber over the side to the boat with the rest of us jacks, or you may spare your hands and take the lady's way."

He waved his hand grandly toward a strange contraption dangling over the deck, a kind of crude swing with a plank seat suspended from the yardarm between two ropes and steadied by a pair of grinning seamen. To one side stood Zach, his face carefully noncommittal, and that, for Polly, was warning enough. Even though she hadn't seen him to speak to since they'd gone aloft together, she still regarded him as an ally.

"I've ordered a bosun's chair jury-rigged for you, you see," explained Samson proudly. "You have a seat there, and we'll see you swung over and lowered down to the boat as neat and pretty as ever you please. No lady could wish for an easier journey."

Polly's gaze slid from the dangling swing to the waiting boat below. It didn't matter now that the sea was so clear that she could see the fish and other creatures frolicking beneath the ship; it was water still, capable of both soaking and drowning any trusting, incompetent fool of a lady who tumbled from that silly bench as she swung from the yardarm.

Bosun's *chair*, hah, thought Polly with disgust. A bosun's noose would seem more accurate. Without a word she freed her hand from the captain's grasp, turned at the boarding port in the rail, and slipped over the side, her feet easily finding the toeholds carved into the ship's curving planks. She winced as she grasped the twin guidelines, her still-tender hands protesting at the rough rope, but she forced herself to concentrate on finding the next foothold instead of the discomfort. It wasn't that far to the boat, anyway, only fifteen or—

"What the Devil are you doing?" demanded Captain Fairbourne as he seized her arm to stop her. "Have you lost your wits completely?"

She scowled up at him, his face only a little above hers, since he'd thumped upon his stomach on the deck with his arm over the side to stop her descent. It wasn't a very dignified position for a ship's captain, particularly one in his best shore-going clothes, and her own wasn't much better, snagged like an old stocking on the thorn of his presumption.

"You've precious few of your own wits showing,

Captain!" she said warmly. "You gave me my choice, and I made it!"

"I didn't give you a choice to kill yourself!"

"And I didn't make one!" she said furiously, trying to wrench her arm free. Not that such a thing would be possible, not the way his fingers were holding on as tightly as if they'd been forged from iron, and she'd only to remember back to that first night in his cabin to know how impossibly strong he was. She twisted her head around and away from him, trying to see how far she still was from the boat. As she did her old knitted cap slipped off the back of her head and dropped to the water.

"Now look what you've done!" she cried out with frustration as she peered around to watch the hat already growing sodden in the water. "You could at least offer to fetch it for me, especially since I was only trying to go to the boat the way *you* wanted! Leastways I would have if you'd let me!"

"Damnation, don't try to put this upon me!"

"I don't know why not, when you're the one being so—so blasted contrary!" For emphasis she gave her trapped arm an extra tug backward. But as she did, she felt one foot slip from the toehold, and as she scrambled to find it again, her weight shifted and the other foot, too, was suddenly scraping helplessly without purchase against the curving planks. For a single, endless moment, she fell, then stopped with a jerk as his grasp pulled her up short. Though her own fingers tightened convulsively on the guidelines, they were still too weak to support her body alone, without his help.

"Hold now, lass," he ordered. "I'm coming."

She wanted to shout that he should stay exactly

where he was, that she would do much better without any more of his humiliating so-called help, but her heart was pounding so loudly in her ears that she couldn't think of the right words for shouting. Another pair of strong male hands seized her arms, steadying her enough that her scrambling feet could, at last, find the toeholds again.

But before she could make use of them, Captain Fairbourne himself was suddenly there behind her, plucking her from the side of the ship with one arm circling around her waist to hold her close to his chest. With his other hand on the guide rope, he worked his way down the side of the ship to the boat with maddening ease, keeping her close against his chest as if she were some tiny, helpless kitten that he'd rescued from a too-tall tree.

Rescued: that was the worst of it. It was one thing to pretend to be a dainty lady, with one hand upon his arm, but quite another to be *rescued* like a quivering, useless ninny, cradled there against Captain Fairbourne's great muscled wall of a chest. As much as she wished to, she couldn't fight him, or they'd both end up in the water, which would mean he'd have to rescue her all over again.

It was awful, shameful, and mortally unfair, and the instant he set her down upon the bench in the stern sheets of the boat, she flew from him to sit as far away as she possibly could. She stared determinedly over the side and across the water, her arms folded tight and her back rigid with angry disapproval, and she said not one word of thanks for being rescued.

Rescued, hah. She'd rather have taken her chances in the water with her poor lost hat.

With a sigh of pleased relief, Samson dropped onto

the bench beside her. He nodded, and the men used their oars to push the boat away from the ship and began to row in perfect, practiced unison. It was a simple, graceful maneuver that usually gave Samson enormous satisfaction, reflecting so well as it did on his ship and crew, but this morning he scarcely noticed. Instead he resettled his hat upon his head, rested his palms upon his bent knees, and frowned at the straight little back presented to him.

Once again Polly Bray was angry with him, and once again he wasn't really sure why.

He cleared his throat, hoping that would be enough to make her look his way.

It wasn't.

"A ship can be a dangerous place for a woman, Miss Bray," he began, woefully conscious of the men at the oars, their faces impassive and their ears wide open. "Given how you'd hurt your hands the other day, and how you've been so, ah, indisposed, I thought that the bosun's chair would suit."

Her head snapped around, her face every inch a chilly match to that rigid back. "Then you thought wrong, Captain Fairbourne. *And* you have lost my only hat."

He refused to be made to feel guilty over the loss of that wretched hat of hers. "I shall buy you another in St. Pierre. I shall buy you a dozen, if you wish."

"Oh, blast, the hat has nothing to do with anything, and you know it! You were the one risking my life by that great blundering show of saving me. *Saving* me, sweet Jupiter, when I didn't need saving in the first place!"

"Then you damn well put on a show of it yourself, flailing your arms and legs about like a spider in a head wind," he said, struggling to keep his voice even before the others. "About the only thing you didn't do was scream your fool head off."

Her brows came together. "I never scream," she said primly. "Never. It frightens the fishes."

"Well, I am thankful of that," he said, "because you surely frightened the hell out of me."

She had, too. She could talk spit and courage now, but he'd seen the terrified look in her eyes when she'd lost her footing. Likely she did know her way around ships enough to realize the danger she'd been in: the fall itself wouldn't have been far, but she could still have crashed headlong into the waiting boat, or been crushed between it and the *Morning Star*, or dragged and trapped beneath the ship's broad hull. But if she knew that much, then why didn't she have the sense to see how he'd saved her?

She lifted her chin, high enough that the reflections from the water played along her throat. "I am sorry if I scared you," she conceded. "I didn't mean to be vexatious like that. All I wanted to do was to reach the boat, and the ladder seemed the better way."

This wasn't the heartfelt thanks Samson had hoped for, but it was probably the best he was going to get. And at least she didn't seem angry any longer. He should be grateful for that much alone. "Most ladies would have chosen the bosun's chair."

She sighed deeply and brushed a stray lock of that lovely coppery hair away from her throat. He was heartily glad that the cap had been lost, glad indeed.

"I am not most ladies, Captain Fairbourne," she said. "I am not even one single lady, because I'm not a lady at all, which is most likely why I have been running up and down the sides of vessels my entire life. I'm good at it, too, when I'm not meddled with."

He heard the swell of pride in her voice and felt too unsettled to answer. He, too, was good at running up and down the sides of ships. Hadn't he just proved that to her? He was also good at climbing up masts and around sails and dancing along spars, and he was hands down the best there was at marking another ship on the horizon with a spyglass. Or at least he had been, until she'd come on board.

In other words, he was proud of exactly the same things as Polly Bray, and it was enough to make chills shiver up his spine. Despite her breeches and not screaming, she was a woman, a rather pleasingly arranged woman at that, and women were supposed to be like his sister Serena, taking pleasure in incomprehensible female mysteries like preserving cranberry quiddanies and sewing fine seams on a husband's shirt. It didn't seem right for Polly to be bragging about the same things he'd brag about himself. To Samson, the whole notion seemed—well, *unnatural*, and the most unnatural part about it was how much of her feelings he could actually understand and, worse, share. He'd never done that with any other woman, and it worried him sick. What was happening to him, anyway?

"I *am* good at it," said Polly again, misinterpreting his silence as disbelief. "I'd be willing to prove it, too, once my hands heal all the way. I'll race you down the side of the *Morning Star* to the water and back."

He stared at her, just stared. However could she conceive of such a horrifyingly wrongheaded idea? A race, for God's sake, a race between a shipmaster and this sweet-faced chit of a girl!

"Damnation," he growled, and said the first notion that came into his head: "Do you want to lose this wager outright?"

"This wager?" she repeated, blinking with confusion. "You misremember that I've no money for a wager, though I vow I'd give you a good run without one."

"No, no, no, you ninny," he said, keeping his voice low against the others' listening. "The wager that's already in place. The one that says you can tidy yourself into a regular lady if you set your mind to it, and if you quit all this yammering about races and such."

"Oh," said Polly. "Zach's wager."

Why the Devil did her eyes have to go all soft whenever she mentioned his cousin? For that matter, why did she have to mention him at all?

"Aye," he said, "call it that if you must. Zach's wager with *me.*"

"Oh, aye, the wager that's worth twenty guineas to you," she said, her expression turning guarded in a way he wished it wouldn't. "To see if you can turn a sow's ear like me into a silken purse. Oh, aye, *that* wager."

Though she gave her shoulders a careless shrug to prove how little it all meant to her, he wasn't fooled. Somehow he'd managed to say the wrong thing yet again, and he didn't miss the bewildered, wounded look on her face as she turned away from him to study the town ahead.

At least that was what she wanted him to think she was doing. She could stare ahead all she wanted, but he'd be willing to swear she wasn't seeing a single thing before her. He should know: he wasn't seeing much more himself.

And, God help them both, it wasn't even noon.

Six

"St. Pierre, sir," said the coxswain as he used the long boathook to pull them close to the wharf. In unison the rest of the crew tipped their dripping oars skyward before they shipped them, letting the boat bump gently against the weed-covered pilings. Bobbing on the water around them were narrow, flat-bottomed skiffs, loaded with baskets of fresh fruits, vegetables, and flowers, that were bound for the ships moored in the deeper water of the harbor. Impulsively Samson whistled to the nearest as it glided close by.

"Here," he said as he flipped a coin to one of the young brothers at the skiff's oars. "Those roses, the red ones."

Grinning, the first boy let his oars drop in their locks as he reached for the bundled flowers and held them up for Samson's inspection. "*Merci, oui, m'sieur, merci. Ici très belle, non?*"

"Very *belle*, and all the rest," said Samson, wishing his French were better. "Now, ah, *passez-vous ici, pour la jeune mademoiselle.*"

"*Pour la mademoiselle, m'sieur?*" Confused, the boy

held the flowers raised, ready to toss them across the water to Samson. *"Et où est la dame, m'sieur?"*

Samson frowned, annoyed by the insult to Polly. Couldn't the fool see her with his own eyes?

"Oh, he's going to throw them away!" cried Polly anxiously, unable to understand any more than that the boy in the skiff seemed poised to hurl the flowers into the water. "Don't let him waste them, Captain, please don't!"

At the sound of her voice, the boy laughed, the hoops in his ears dancing in the sunlight.

"Ah, regardez-vous," he said with a smirk, *"le beau jeune garçon est la belle jeune mademoiselle!"*

He giggled to himself as he bowed gaily from the waist, then tossed the flowers to Polly as the skiff slid away into more open water. *"Bonjour, mademoiselle!"*

"Impudent little bastard," fumed Samson. "I'd *beau garçon* him proper if he—"

But abruptly he stopped there, forgetting the boy and his insult and everything else save the sight of Polly. She sat by herself in the now near-empty boat, the bunch of roses nestled in her hands and her eyes closed in oblivious bliss as she buried her nose in the soft petals and heady fragrance. Her pleasure in the ha'-penny bouquet was so open and unfeigned that it shamed him. She seemed to have a way of doing that.

"There now, lass, you've a proper welcome to Martinique," he said gruffly. "Nothing like the French for flowers."

She nodded, and though she smiled, dazzling him over the flowers, he could have sworn there were tears glittering in the corners of her eyes. Hell, hadn't she ever been given a posey before this? Hadn't there been at least one fisher-boy in Ninnishibutt eager to

cut a ragged bundle of daisies and Queen Anne's lace
for her?

He cleared his throat self-consciously. "Well now,
along with you then."

"Cheerily, cheerily?" she said, and he was relieved
to see the threat of tears fading.

"Aye, cheerily it is," he said, both cheerily and
heartily, too, as he held out his hand to help her from
the boat. "We cannot keep Madame LaFontaine waiting, can we?"

Yet to his surprise she hung back, holding the roses
tightly in both arms. "You needn't do this. Truly. The
flowers are enough, aye, more than enough."

"And I say they're not," he declared gallantly. "I
have to tempt you properly, else Zach will cry foul.
Besides, I've heard there's not a lady alive who can
resist Madame's wares."

But still she shook her head. "I told you before: I'm
not like your other ladies. We'd do better to return to
the ship now and save us both the trouble."

"I'm not like other captains, either. What of it?" He
took her hand, drawing her gently forward from the
boat to the wharf. "Don't be selfish, lass. Consider
the pleasure I'll take in rigging you out like this."

"But you won't, not when you see—that is, when
I—oh, blast!" She hung her head unhappily over the
roses. "I'm going to shame you, I know it. I'll make
you wish you'd left me in the ocean to rot like an old
timber, see if I don't."

"And I say there's no such thing as a Jonah in a
mantua-maker's shop." Once he would have said,
too, that there was no such thing as a woman who'd
refuse such generosity, but no matter. He patted her
hand to reassure her. "You'll see. Before this morn-

ing's done, you'll have all manner of pretty reasons to be grateful you're not a rotten old timber."

But she remained unconvinced. Though she barely spoke as they walked through the narrow streets, he could feel her agitation growing with each step, and by the time they finally reached the shop, she was nearly trembling with it.

He glanced up at the signboard hanging overhead, a painting of a plum-colored lady's hat with three curling yellow plumes. He remembered that sign from the one other time he'd been here, with his older brother, Joshua, and he was secretly relieved that he'd managed to find the place again. He pushed the door open and afterward practically pushed Polly inside.

The door tripped the little shop bell overhead, tinkling cheerfully to announce their arrival to the women in the rear workshop. After the bright morning sunshine, it took a moment for Samson's eyes to grow accustomed to the cool, perfumed shadows of the shop's interior, lit only by the single, cluttered display window. Rows of narrow shelves lined the walls, each filled with precisely folded lengths of cloth of every color imaginable, from the palest peach summer muslins to silvery blue lutestrings to gold-struck brocades waiting to gleam beneath ballroom candles. Harateens and damasks, cherry-derrys and starrets, kerseymeres and blondines: as a seagoing merchant, Samson recognized the fabrics and their exotic names, just as he knew which would sell best in Boston.

Other shelves held cards of laces and ribbons and fancy trimmings, and in a Canton bowl on the single counter a selection of curled feathers, much like the painted ones on the shop sign, had been loosely arranged like exotic, long-stemmed flowers. Beside the bowl stood a fine example of the shop's workmanship in miniature, a solemn, cross-eyed doll dressed in the newest of fashions from the French court, correctly elegant from the top of her powdered-horsehair head to the crimson leather heels of her buckled brocaille slippers.

Samson cleared his throat uneasily. Such places seemed designed to make men feel like outsiders, and he heartily wished he were back among the safely familiar, masculine smells and noises of the *Morning Star*. The shop gave him the unsettling feeling that the deepest female secrets were tucked away among the bombazines and velvet ribbons, that he'd somehow stumbled into a woman's mysterious stronghold simply by opening a door.

Being a man, he had a right, almost an obligation, to feel this way. But why in blazes was Polly Bray nearly trembling beside him, her fingers cold and clammy inside his own? This should be a magic place full of pleasurable temptation for her, or at least it would be for every other woman he could name.

"I hate this," she whispered vehemently, tugging on his sleeve. "I hate it all, and I don't want to be here, wager or no. Can't we go now, before anyone sees us?"

But before he could answer, Madame LaFontaine herself swept through the curtained doorway to the shop, her hands clasped elegantly at her waist, one on top of the other, as she made her graceful curtsy.

"*Ah, bonjour, Monsieur le Capitaine!*" she said warmly. "It is my dear handsome Captain Fairbourne, come back to us at last!"

"Most likely you mistake me for my older brother," said Samson with an uneasy smile. Joshua had a new young wife whom he doted upon extravagantly and showered with gifts to sweeten every voyage he was away from her; Samson, to his ever-thankful relief, had no such expensive habit to maintain. "Captain Joshua Fairbourne. He's the one who's brought you all the custom."

"*Non, non,* I never would confuse such handsome men!" The woman wagged her finger playfully at Samson. Though she was old enough to be his mother, she was still a handsome woman in her rich, dark silks, with clear blue eyes and a figure many girls would envy. She pursed her lips in a sly moue of interest as her gaze shifted toward Polly. "But who might this be, *mon cher capitaine?* Is this how you New Englanders pass your long voyages, with a pretty cabin boy for amusement?"

Samson could feel Polly's indignation prickle beside him, and though he couldn't really blame her, he'd have to try a different tack. She wouldn't like it at first, but in the end she'd thank him.

He hoped she would, anyway.

"No cabin boy, Madame," he said hastily, answering before she could. "This is Miss Polly Ann Bray. Miss Bray has suffered the most grievous misfortune. She is a castaway, ma'am, lost in the ocean without a decent stitch to her name. We covered her as best we could from our own sea chests, though you can see that for yourself."

"Oh, *mademoiselle, quelle horreur!*" murmured Madame with a commiserative clucking of her tongue, though Samson wondered if her sympathy was for Polly or her lost wardrobe. "How tragic for you, *ma petite!*"

Again Samson rushed in before Polly could answer for herself. He was working this out as he went along, and he'd rather Polly didn't begin volunteering too many embarrassing variations just yet.

"Christian charity demanded I bring her to you, ma'am," he said soberly. "After all she'd suffered, it seemed only right."

Polly gasped with sputtering indignation. "All *I* suffered! Oh, aye, you evil-tongued scrod, I'll suffer *you* next!"

"*Mais oui, mademoiselle,* you have suffered enough," agreed Madame LaFontaine with sympathy, and evidently without any knowledge of what a scrod might be. She squinted her eyes and tapped her forefinger against her cheek, already appraising Polly for size and form. "But how fortunate that this generous gentleman has brought you here to me! We shall make you a lady once again, *ma petite*, and you will forget everything else but your own beauty, eh?"

"But I do not wish to forget who I am!" protested Polly. "I am well enough without being a beauty, which I will never be anyways!"

Madame smiled coyly, beckoning to the assistant who'd joined them from the workroom. "You are mistaken, *mademoiselle*. Every woman is a beauty if only she is properly guided."

"There now, Madame, I knew you'd be up to the task!" Samson beamed, delighted that his plan was working. Madame LaFontaine was right: he *was* being a generous gentleman, more grandly generous than he'd ever been before, and to his surprise it didn't really have that much to do with Zach's wager any longer. He wanted to see Polly in the pretty gown and petticoats she deserved, but even more he wanted to see the joy on her face when she stepped in front of the mirror for the first time. He wanted to be able to give her that rare pleasure in herself, and she was welcome to every last thread of lace in the shop if that was what it would take.

"Whatever Miss Bray wants," he said decisively, "whatever she needs, as long as it's all ready for me to make my tide in the morning."

"Your tide, *Monsieur le Capitaine?* In the morning?" Madame gazed heavenward—or, rather, ceiling-ward—with an emphatic shrug of dismay. "What of the cutting, the stitching, the fittings? *C'est impossible!*"

"There, you see how foolish all this is!" declared Polly, already edging away toward the door. "Impossible, she said, and rightly, too!"

"Impossible for another," said the Frenchwoman with a triumphant twitch of her starched linen cap, "but not for this house. We shall do what you wish, *monsieur*, and do it to beautiful perfection, but you must understand that the impossible will come very dear."

"Hang the cost," said Samson, feeling more expansively generous by the moment. "I told you Miss Bray's to have whatever she pleases."

"What would please me is to leave!" cried Polly, wild-eyed, as the seamstress took her by the arm to show her to the dressing room. There was a frantic edge to her voice that Samson hadn't heard earlier, or expected to hear at all. What had become of the brave, bold little creature willing to scamper over his ship as if it were her own?

Gently he reached out to brush the back of his fingers over her cheek and felt her quiver beneath his touch.

"I told you before, lass, that you don't have to do anything you truly don't want to, and I mean that still," he said. "But I thought this would be a treat for you."

She swallowed hard, her gaze fixed on his with the same silent desperation of the gallows-bound. "For Zach's sake, then?"

"For you, Polly," he said softly, not realizing he'd used her given name for the first time until he'd done it. "A gift from me, to give you pleasure."

Her eyes filled with luminous wonder, the fear sliding away into something close to trust. Unconsciously she ran her hand along the side of her well-worn boy's breeches, almost a gesture of sad farewell, and suddenly Samson understood how much of her own odd little self she would have to abandon to be able to accept what he was offering.

Swathed in Madame LaFontaine's new petticoats, she'd have no choice but to use the bosun's chair. There'd be no more running races, or climbing high to the masthead, or even using two hands to steady a spyglass when at least one would be needed to control a swirl of skirts against the wind. The more he considered her sacrifice, the less he felt she should make it, and the more selfish his own grand "generosity" became.

He cleared his throat, determined to tell her so, but she'd made up her own mind first.

"For you, then, I shall do it," she whispered. "But only for you alone."

They were going to laugh at her.

Here she stood, half dressed before them, balanced precariously on the tiny stool in the center of the workroom. Any moment the three women fluttering around her would step back and laugh and jeer and point at her for what she was, plain Polly Bray, aping her betters and pretending to be a lady.

She shut her eyes for a moment, closing out this perfumed world where she was such a hopeless misfit. Her back ached from standing still for so long and her toes pinched from her new heeled slippers, her ribs hurt from tight lacing, and her head spun from overhearing so much incomprehensible French.

Samson had promised to return to fetch her for supper. It must be nearly time by now; she felt as if she'd been here for hours and hours and *hours*.

"Only a short while more, mademoiselle," murmured Madame LaFontaine as she smoothed a pleat in the sleeve over Polly's shoulder, jabbing in yet another pin to hold it in place. *"Vraiment,* you are nearly complete."

But Polly had heard the same words from the older woman too many times this day to believe them. Who would have guessed the trouble it took to become a lady, or at least the trouble it seemed to take to transform her? Surely the three Frenchwomen with their ruffled linen caps would have been finished long ago if she hadn't been such an impossible challenge. Impossible: that was one word that seemed almost the same in both French and English, and Polly could think of no other that was more apt.

Her trials had begun as soon as Samson had left her, when the women stripped her of her own familiar clothes and dressed her in a white linen shift that billowed down below her knees. The shift was not so very different from her usual shirt, but then came the stays, the first she'd ever worn—and the last, too, if she had anything to say about it: an unyielding cage of buckram, crash, and endless strips of whalebone, covered with a deceitfully pretty pink brocade and ribbons on the shoulder straps, that squeezed and crushed her poor body inward and upward with each pull of the laces until she protested that she couldn't breathe.

But the Frenchwomen only winked at each other and gave the laces one final tug. With shock Polly stared down at her unfamiliar new shape, her ribs and middle compressed into a flat, straight front that tapered to an impossibly narrow waist. Most bewildering of all was what had happened to her breasts— her small, rather insignificant breasts, Polly had always believed, best hidden modestly beneath her waistcoat and jacket. But now when she looked downward she saw two high, round pillows of her own flesh presented wantonly on a whalebone shelf, and when she flushed and tried to pull the shift higher to cover herself, Madame simply moved Polly's hands away, clucking her tongue with disapproval.

Next came three gowns with the petticoats to match. Clearly these had been bespoken by another woman, shorter and heavier than Polly, whose order the shop would have to re-create later, when the tide—and the opportunity to charge double—were not at issue.

The bodice was fitted close to the stays, the neckline low and squared, the sleeves fitted above deep, flounced cuffs at the elbow, and the skirts rustling with enough yardage to make a sail. The fabric was silk—French silk, for a Bray woman!—of the palest golden yellow, patterned all over with sprigs of rosy apples and green twining leaves. It was the most beautiful single thing that Polly had ever seen, and as the seamstresses settled it over her, gathering here, tucking there, she couldn't quite believe this fairy-queen gown was real at all, let alone drifting around herself.

But magic was a rare substance in Ninnishibutt, and rarer still for Polly. The moment she dared touch the silk, reality returned, her rough, scarred hands in their makeshift bandages snagging on the delicate fabric.

"*Non, non, non, mademoiselle!*" scolded Madame crossly. "*Soie de Lyon* is very dear, very fragile! You would not wish to displease *Monsieur le Capitaine* by ruining it before he has even paid his reckoning, do you?"

Immediately Polly's hand flew away, as swiftly as if her fingers had been held to a flame. Of course she didn't want to displease Samson. It was his whims that were being satisfied here, not hers, for he was the gentleman, the one who was paying the bill for yellow silk.

To these women she was nothing, merely another homely fashion doll to be dressed like the wooden one on the counter in the front. Doubtless they were convinced she'd already shared Samson's bed for him to have squandered so much upon her. They would never understand the wager. For that matter, Polly wasn't sure she understood it herself any longer, and if it weren't for Samson, she would have already marched from the shop and these sly, worldly women.

Samson. How easily he'd become transformed from "Captain Fairbourne" to "Samson," and in one startling moment, too, the instant he'd called her "Polly." She'd never heard her name sound like that, the way he'd spoken it in his rough whisper, and when she remembered again, now, she couldn't help but smile. He'd said the gowns were the purest kind of gift, with no thought to the wager. The only pleasure he'd find would be in pleasing her. Her wary sense of survival warned her not to believe him, but another, more headstrong part of her refused to be so reasonable. How could she turn away a gift so nobly offered?

"C'est bonne, mademoiselle," said Madame, stepping back with a generous nod of satisfaction. "You may look."

Automatically, the two assistants brought a tall mirror forward, tipping it up between them, so that for the first time that day, Polly could see her reflection.

And when she did, she gasped. Not with delight, or pleasure, or amazement, but with bewildered shock.

The reflection staring open-mouthed back at her *was* her, but at the same time it wasn't. This new Polly in the mirror stood so straight and tall on account of the stays that she almost arched backward. Her waist had been made tiny and her breasts lifted high, while the layers of petticoats had turned her lower half into a yellow-silk bell without any legs at all. She was elegant and stylish and almost—*almost* pretty. But most of all, this strange Polly was a woman, a lady in appearance, in all the ways that the world would mean that, and all the same ways that she'd never been one before.

Staring at her reflection, she could feel the panic rising up around her, the same as if she'd been tossed into water over her head. She'd sworn that no mere clothing could change who she was, but here in the mirror was the proof to the contrary. How was she supposed to act, dressed like this? She didn't know the first thing about being a lady. She wasn't even sure she could *walk*.

"A final *folie, mademoiselle,*" purred Madame as she snaked a narrow scarf of black lace around Polly's neck and over her bosom, weaving the ends into the front of her bodice. "The sea, the sun, have been so cruel to you! But we shall hide the unhappy evidence, *oui?*"

Polly flushed, belatedly recognizing the "unhappy evidence." Not only was her face golden brown from all the days she'd spent in the summer sun, but her throat and chest were colored as well with a darker V from her open-necked shirt, a mark that was ludicrous above the gown's fashionably low neckline. Without Madame's artful black lace to soften the piebald contrast, she might have been two women pieced together.

Two women, or one wretched Polly. Dear Lord, did Samson truly believe this would make her happy?

"Your hair now, *mademoiselle,*" continued the Frenchwoman, already unraveling Polly's single braid over her shoulders. "*Vraiment,* I do not dress heads as a rule, but we might manage a simple chignon beneath a cap, a ribbon or two."

"No."

The single word came as a command, a captain's order expecting obedience. *Her* captain, thought Polly as her heart thumped wildly, and instantly she turned toward the doorway where he stood. Her unaccustomed skirts swung around her and she nearly toppled from her perch on the stool, but she didn't care. She could see he'd spent at least part of his day at the barber—his jaw gleaming and ruddy from the razor and his hair drawn back in a neat, sleek queue—but she would have greeted him with the same joy if he'd returned in his stocking feet. What mattered now was that Samson had come back, and he'd come back for her.

And please—oh, please—let him call her "Polly" again!

"*Bonjour, Monsieur le Capitaine,*" said Madame, sinking into a businesslike curtsy with the comb still raised in her hand. "You take us by surprise! One more moment for *mademoiselle*'s hair, and—"

"I said no." Samson frowned, wondering why the woman refused to understand. "Miss Bray's hair is fine as it is. Quite fine. Quite fine, same as all the rest of her."

He cleared his throat uneasily. "Fine"—even "quite fine"—didn't begin to describe how Polly looked. He wasn't even sure he'd recognize her if he'd come across her somewhere else, she'd changed that much. In the space of a few hours she'd been transformed into the kind of fair creature that turned men's heads and made them sing foolish, lovelorn songs in taverns before, finally, she broke their hearts. How much of that teasing black lace and yellow silk had been Polly's own choice? His first reason for bringing her here was to give her the opportunity to show her true female colors, in whatever flirtatious plumage she wished, but he hadn't expected the change to be so overwhelming.

And he *was* overwhelmed. That display of newfound bosom alone made Samson want to stare nearly as much as he wanted to look away, embarrassed by his own instant, shameful response. Blast it all, he hadn't wanted to win the wager this way, not if it meant losing the girl somewhere beneath the trappings.

"But *monsieur*, she cannot go about with her hair trailing so!" protested the Frenchwoman. "It is not proper, not seemly, even for *l'Anglaise!*"

"English or French or Guinea hen, makes no difference to me," said Samson firmly. He needed to see her hair loose, to remind himself of the way it had been that night when she'd washed it in his cabin. God only knew, her hair was about the only familiar thing left. "Her hair stays down."

"And am I to have no say?" said Polly, setting her hands indignantly at her waist—a waist that seemed to have shrunk to a most provocative size. "You're not the one who'll have to comb out the knots, nor will you have to live with it blowing about in your eyes and into your mouth. But if it matters that much to you, I shall do it, *Mon-stair lee Ca-pee-tin*. I shall—but mind, only this once."

Then she grinned at him, her whole face lighting with wicked delight as she mangled the French version of his title. She did it so badly that he wondered if she'd made such a royal mess intentionally. Most likely she had, given it was Polly who was doing the messing.

"I like your hair the way it is," he said. "Your hair is very handsome, and I don't see the reason in hiding it away."

"Madame and I have given you a bushel full, if you'd cared to listen." She sighed, self-consciously tugging at the front of her bodice. "And after all the money you've squandered in this shop this day, I'd hoped you'd have more to say for your investment than 'quite fine.'"

He would have liked very much to say more, if only he could think of the right words. "If you wish to be a fine lady," he said gruffly, "you'll have to learn not to fish for praise."

"But I don't want to be a fine lady," she protested plaintively. "I never have. And I can't help fishing, even if . . . if . . . oh, you don't like this gown at all, do you?"

"I didn't say that now, did I?" he exclaimed hastily, but too late. Already her shoulders were sagging forlornly, and she looked as dejected as a woman in a froth of pale yellow silk possibly could. He hated to see her like this, and on an impulse he reached for her hand, curling his fingers around hers.

"I like the gown, lass," he said, his voice dropping lower. "It's as pretty a piece of work as ever I've seen. Aye, it is. But it can't hold a candle to you inside, Polly, and I mean that, too."

Her shoulders stayed bowed but her gaze shifted upward, looking up at him through her lashes with a curious mixture of hope and outright suspicion. "You don't, Samson. You can't."

"I do, and I can," he said, taking it as a favorable sign that she'd used his Christian name again. "I wouldn't say it otherwise. You should know that much of me by now."

"That is true," she agreed slowly. "You do not seem to lie, leastways that I've discovered."

Yet she turned away skittishly, glancing back over her shoulder at her reflection in the mirror.

"Father always told me that one day I'd wear a silk gown like a gentleman's daughter," she said wistfully. "I wonder what he'd say to see me now."

"He'd be pleased as pie, and honored to go out walking with you," said Samson. "As will I, if you'll but hop down from your roost."

"But I haven't changed," she said quickly. "Not the way you wagered I would. Underneath all this I'm still Polly Bray."

"More's the pity for my poor pocket." He wished she wouldn't remind him of that foolish wager, and even more he wished she'd stop reminding him of what lay underneath all those fine French clothes, not while he was doing his damnedest to forget. "You say you haven't changed, but my eyes are telling me a different tale, and a mightily pleasing one at that."

"Rubbish," she said automatically, but still she blushed with pleasure as she hopped down from the stool, her smile disingenuous enough to make him catch his breath.

There were things passing between them that he didn't comprehend, with more said in that fleeting smile than could be said in a thousand words. It was the same uncomfortable sensation as being in a foreign land where he didn't speak a language that everyone else did. He wondered if Polly felt it too, if that was the real reason she was blushing, and he wished there was some decent way to ask her. He couldn't, of course; no woman, not even Polly, would understand. But he *would* be honored to walk out with her, and it had nothing to do with all the French fripperies rustling about her.

"If no pins for her hair, *monsieur*, then at least a ribbon," coaxed Madame as she fluttered after Polly, holding a narrow length of rose silk in both hands like a banner. "She cannot go without that little much."

Polly nodded vigorously. "Oh, aye, Samson, one ribbon, else I won't see where I'm going and walk into walls. One tiny, helpful ribbon to save me. There's scarce harm in that, is there?"

But instead of letting the Frenchwoman tie the ribbon into her hair, Polly proudly pulled the little tortoiseshell comb that Samson had given her from the pocket tied around her waist and beneath her skirts. With great care she combed the front of her hair back from her forehead, gathering the sides loosely over her ears before she tied it back with the ribbon and cocked her head to one side for Samson's approval.

"*Mademoiselle* knows what favors her," said Madame dutifully. "I shall send the other articles when they are ready to *Monsieur le Capitaine's* ship this very night. Before the tide, as you wished."

"And my other clothes, too," said Polly promptly. "I want those back. Oh, but I nearly forgot my knife!"

Swiftly she darted across to where her old clothes had been piled unceremoniously into a basket, scrambling through them until she found her knife, still safe in its sheath on her worn leather belt.

"You won't be needing that tonight, lass," said Samson, remembering all too well the last circumstances when she had. He should remember it; the details certainly returned to haunt him often enough. "You'll be with me."

She hesitated, clearly remembering that night in his cabin, too, before she began to thread the belt through the pocket slit in her skirt.

"I can't say if I'll be needing it or not, but 'tis better to have it with me," she said, giving her petticoat a little pat where the knife was hidden beneath it. "There, none will be the wiser."

But Samson himself was, and he couldn't help but be struck by the incongruity of dainty patterned silk over a battered old fishing knife. He should be used to this about Polly by now, but he wasn't. Somehow he doubted he ever would be. With a sigh he plucked the freshest of the roses from the pitcher—most had already begun to wilt and fade in the island's heat since he'd bought them from the vendor this morning—and carefully peeled away the thorns.

"For you, lass," he said as he handed the flower to her. "That is, if you don't mind my disarming it first."

"You should have asked the rose." She held the flower briefly to her nose before she tucked it into the front of her bodice. The red rose, black lace, yellow silk, and white, white skin of her breasts: with a strangled small cough, Samson forced himself to look back at her face.

Blessedly unaware of his thoughts, she slipped her hand into the crook of his elbow. "I hope we don't have to do too much of this walking before supper. I have another sort of contest in mind." Her eyes were bright with gleeful anticipation. "I'll wager I can eat more than you tonight, I'm that hungry."

"*Pardon, monsieur,* but one more question, one more favor before you leave." The Frenchwoman waved her hand toward her assistants and the carefully wrapped bundles they were bringing forward from another room. "Another tide, *mon Dieu,* another wind that must be obeyed, and these were left behind. Surely the lady must wish them now, *oui?* You will take them to her?"

"The lady?" Mystified, Samson frowned at the cherry-colored jacket the assistant was holding. Surely this could not be one of the "articles" meant for Polly. Not only was the brocade too bold for her coloring, the lavishly ruched sleeves far too ornate, but the close-fitting jacket itself had been sewn for a much differently sized woman, small in height but abundant in the front. *Most* abundant.

"Oui, oui, oui," said Madame with a touch of impatience. "For Madame Anabelle."

"Oh, aye. Anabelle." He sighed with resignation. His blissfully besotted brother had likely left gifts for his round little wife bespoken all over the island. Now that Joshua had married, he'd stopped making his twice-a-year voyages to London, trading more in the Caribbean instead so he'd stay closer to home and his bride, a change that Samson had never thought he'd live to see. It simply made no sense. Hadn't Joshua been the one to teach him that trade must always come before pleasure, that women were nothing but a hindrance to any man who wished to make something of himself? Yet now even his mighty brother had become as cowed as any other love-sick mooncalf.

Samson looked at the jacket hanging in Madame's hands. He had yet to meet his sister-in-law, but from Joshua's endless descriptions of Anabelle's charms, he should have recognized her from the astoundingly female outlines of the jacket alone. No wonder Joshua was so befuddled.

He sighed again, this time more uncomfortably. It had been three years—or was it four?—since he'd last sailed into the harbor where he'd been born. He'd never intended to stay away so long. Perhaps it *was* finally time for him to return home. Wasn't the *Morning Star* proof enough that he'd become successful on his own, outside of Joshua's shadow? He'd stay only a day or two, but long enough to see Serena again and meet her new husband, and to pay his respects to the legendary Anabelle. This dunnage of hers would be his excuse, so it wouldn't look like he'd come crawling to Joshua.

"Very well," he said at last. "Send those things

along with the rest. We can't keep Anabelle shivering in the snow, can we?"

Madame winked at him, her smile a shade too familiar for Samson's taste. "Oh, *non, monsieur,* no indeed! But a lady like that—I do not think she is left much alone to shiver, eh?"

"Ah, no," he answered with a shameful stab of disloyalty. "I warrant we cannot."

There wasn't much point in disagreeing with the truth, but Anabelle was now a Fairbourne, and whatever his problems were with Joshua, she didn't deserve personal discussion among Martinique's shopkeepers. As quickly as Samson could, he settled Madame's reckoning—it seemed it cost nearly as much to outfit a young lady as it did a small ship—and managed to volunteer not a single word more about his sister-in-law.

With great relief he led Polly from the shop and into the slanting sunlight of the late afternoon. St. Pierre was turning its other face now, changing from the bright, jostling, jangling island port where all was business, peopled by sailors and merchants from every part of the world, into the more seductive, more French town of the evening, a place for every pleasure. The same wide-leafed palm trees and overhanging porches that sheltered the narrow streets from the tropical sun created deep, velvety shadows after nightfall, just as the shutters that had guarded every house against the heat were now thrown open to welcome both the cooler breezes from the water and the lilting, laughing conversation of passersby.

Everything in St. Pierre seemed to intensify in the twilight: the fragrance of the ever-present flowers— roses, hibiscus, calla lilies, balisier, gardenias—grew richer, deeper, the calls and cries of the wild birds more insistent, and even the people themselves seemed to glow with a renewed vibrancy, their Parisian clothes for evening boldly colored dashes of silk against the moonlit stuccoed walls, their gestures grander and more sensual. If any place could free a woman to follow her true nature, then it must be St. Pierre.

Any woman, apparently, other than Polly. Instead of the excitement that Samson had expected, she'd grown silent and withdrawn, her interest in the town and people around her gone. She trudged along at his side as if it were the grimmest duty imaginable and kept her gaze steadfastly on the pointed toes of her new slippers. She was making it impossible to have the merry evening Samson had planned, and his own spirits began to sink with hers. If this was what new finery did for her, he thought glumly, then he could collect his wager from Zach the minute they returned to the ship.

They soon reached the inn where Samson had arranged for their supper. Though near the waterfront, L'Orient Bleu was a respectable house, one that catered to shipmasters and other gentlemen, and while the French-born cook prepared all the spiciest of local delicacies, the host at the door was a stout, good-humored Hampshire man named Parse, wise enough to offer ale and beer along with burgundy wines and, of course, the finest rum in the Caribbean.

Best of all, as far as Samson was concerned, Mrs. Parse had notoriously little patience with harlots or other low harbor women, and Polly would be spared the insults that lesser tavern company might offer. Nor, for that matter, thought Samson as he remembered the knife hidden in Polly's skirts, would she be tempted to offer any of her own in return.

Yet none of that would be worth a fig unless she could manage to enjoy herself, and at the arched doorway Samson stopped and gently turned Polly toward him.

"Is there something amiss, lass?" he asked. "Are you unwell?"

To his great surprise her eyes filled with sudden tears, even as she shook her head.

"What could be wrong?" she asked fiercely. "Why should anything be wrong? If you *know* of no reason, then faith, neither do I!"

"Polly, sweet," he began carefully. "I, ah, I'm missing your meaning."

"Likely because there was no meaning to begin with." She pulled away from him with a wounded rustle of silk, toward the doorway. "Besides, we've come here to eat, not to yammer away here in the street. Leastways *I* have."

But by the time Mrs. Parse herself had set the first course before her—a savory fish pie redolent of wine and shallots—Polly's appetite seemed to have vanished along with her conversation. She sat silent and stiff-backed in her chair across the table from Samson, poking a pattern of tiny holes into the crust with the twin tines of her fork instead of using it to eat. He hadn't the faintest notion of what he'd done or said to earn such treatment, and even less of an idea of how to stop it—at least to stop it in a manner that would not involve her jabbing that fork into him instead of the pie.

It didn't help that they'd become the center of speculation for the rest of the dining room. He had asked for a table in the common room, wishing to avoid the scandal that came with a private room, but he hadn't expected Parse to seat them at the very best public table, before a tall arched window with its shutters thrown open to the view of the harbor.

And it didn't help either that Polly, unhappy or not, was still the most beautiful woman in the room, the candlelight caressing the soft curves of her lips and—God forgive him for paying such close attention!—that bewitching scrap of black lace across her bosom. Glinting copper twisted through the curls of her hair, and even her downcast eyes took on an air of seductive mystery, her lashes thick and sweeping over her cheeks. The same men who would have laughed and jeered or simply ignored her in her knit cap and worn breeches were now craning their necks for a glimpse of her, and it took all of Samson's willpower not to challenge the lot of them to a wholesale slaughter in the street.

But first, of course, he'd have to challenge Polly.

He took a long swallow of his wine and set the glass down on the table with a self-conscious thump.

She jabbed at the crust again, the pastry disintegrating into the creamy white sauce.

He cleared his throat with a rumble and discovered that if he placed each of his forefingers on either side of the wineglass's stubby stem, he could center the glass precisely above his plate.

Which was accomplishing precisely nothing.

"Miss Bray," he began. "Polly. I wish to know . . . that is, I wish you . . . oh, hell, Polly, what the Devil is wrong here, anyway?"

She had to look at him now. Blast him, he hadn't left her a choice, asking her outright like that. *He* would know exactly what was happening. *He* had probably been in similar situations a score of times before, or even a hundred, while she had never, not once, sat in a fine inn meant for gentry, at a table with a cloth, opposite a handsome, generous gentleman who was as cold and heartless as every other miserable scrod in the entire ocean.

With infinite care she lay down her fork, brushing a crumb off one of the tines with her fingertip. To be fair, none of this was Samson's fault. He was what he was, and he hadn't pretended otherwise, not even for the sake of his horrid wager. She was the one who'd let herself be hurt, who'd wanted to believe so badly that his smile and his little endearments and his awkward, well-meant teasing were for her alone.

You'll be with me, he'd said, and she'd let her hopes soar with her heart. He didn't lie; he was, as he'd said, a truthful man.

You'll be with me. And like the innocent fool that she was, she'd thought he'd meant tonight, and tomorrow, and endless tomorrows after that.

And then, like a rock to shatter all those smooth, endless tomorrows, had come Anabelle.

Of course, she was Samson's mistress. Even an ignorant fisherman's daughter from Ninnishibutt could understand that. Anabelle: even her name was lovely, not common like "Polly." She'd be tiny and beautiful, but with ample breasts that didn't need stays for men to admire, and if she expected lavish gifts like that brocade jacket from Samson, then she paid it back by keeping him warm through the long Massachusetts winter. In his constant honesty, he hadn't denied it when Madame LaFontaine had said so, and how could he, with Anabelle waiting for him at home?

"Are you too willful to answer me then, Polly?" Samson said, his patience at an end and his resentment bubbling over in its place. "Or have you grown too proud and fine for me now?"

His kindness had made her mournful and self-pitying, but for him to accuse her of pridefulness was something else altogether. She might be an over-trusting ninny, but she'd never been wrongly proud, not in her life, and when now she finally raised her gaze to meet his, she tossed her hair back with an extra measure of her own resentment.

"If simple decency makes me too proud, then aye, I'm too proud for you, Captain, too proud by double and double again," she said warmly. "And willful, too, if that means I'll not stand meekly by while you trick me out in your mistress's leavings!"

He stared at her with stunned surprise. "My mistress? My *mistress*? For God's sake, Polly, I do not ha—"

"Nay, hush, I won't hear it!" she cried furiously, shoving back her chair as she rose to her feet. "You've always been honest before this, and I won't have you spoil it with an empty lie now!"

"Damnation, Polly, stop," he ordered, his face rigid from the spectacle she was making. "Sit down so we can talk."

He reached for her arm, but she stepped swiftly backward. She felt the high heel of her unfamiliar slipper hook into the equally unfamiliar hem of her petticoat, and though she barely saved herself from toppling over, she did it while shaking her head in angry refusal.

"You may sit, Samson Fairbourne, and you may talk as long as you please, but you can't make me stay and listen!"

He glared at her. "Where in blazes do you think you're going that's better, anyway?"

"To the women's privy," she said with her chin lifted high. "Where the stench will not be quite so bad as it is here."

This time she bunched her skirts in one hand before she fled, rushing past the open-mouthed host and a score of other faces that melded together in a scandalized blur. She hurried down the steps and through the nearest door, into the inn's square courtyard, open to the night sky and the stars above.

On the far side was the stable, and behind her the open windows, cook smoke, and clatter of the busy kitchen, but to the left was the walkway that led to the inn's private garden, and here she ran to be alone. The walkway was dark, covered by a colonnade of plastered arches and tubs of potted hibiscus, but Polly didn't care. With her sides aching from the whalebone stays, she ran until she reached the farthest arch and the welcoming darkness, rested her cheek against the rough plaster pillar, and gave way to the hot, angry tears of frustration that she'd worked so hard to keep inside.

If only she'd drowned, if only he hadn't saved her, if only she'd never wakened to see his face for that first time and—

She started as she felt his hand on her shoulder, but she refused to turn. She wouldn't give either of them the satisfaction of her falling into his arms with her eyes full of tears.

His touch was warm, his fingers sliding deftly beneath her hair to caress the softest skin beneath her ear, to feel the pulse at the side of her throat. She gasped at the intimate audacity of it, reflexively twisting around to confront him.

"Pretty pigeon," murmured the stranger, his voice neither English nor French but dark and purring as a jungle cat, and as full of coiled danger. His fingers tightened into her hair, pulling her head back and forcing her face toward his. "You must not cry, *dulce*. That bastard is not worth the salt in a single one of your sweet tears. But when you weep for me, when you cry out my name—ah, now that will be the purest joy!"

Seven

With the light from the kitchen door's lantern behind him, Polly could not see the man's face, whether he was young or old, or comely and sleek, or pockmarked and seamed by old scars. The lace from the cuff of his shirt prickled her skin, and when she shoved her hands up against his chest to push him away the fabric beneath her fingers was soft and furred, velvet, wrong for this climate but right for a man who wished to dress like a courtier. To dress like one, but nothing else: his hands were strong as a butcher's, his silhouette against the lantern light broad and thickset, and though he wore a flowery, effeminate scent on his velvet coat, his words were redolent of rum and onions and the pungent self-satisfaction of a man who knew he was powerfully, indisputably in control.

But he didn't know Polly. It was the one thing—the only thing—that she had on her side now. And God help her, it wasn't much. If only she could keep him believing she was the flighty little chit he thought she was, if she could keep him talking instead of acting, at least long enough for her to reach her knife, she

might have a chance. She had run across the courtyard from the inn once, and she figured she could do
it again. But if she couldn't manage to break free, if he
dragged her farther into the shadows, into the garden, then she'd have no chance at all.

"I don't cry for any man," she said as defiantly as
she could, her voice still wobbling with the fear she
was trying so hard not to show. She had to keep him
talking and focused on that instead of how her hand
was inching around to find her knife.

The man laughed. "Brave words, *muchacha*. Too
bad the tears on your face make you lie. But maybe
you do not lie. Maybe it is that Fairbourne is no man,
eh?"

"That is your lie, not mine," she said instantly,
defending Samson without a thought. Yet this man
knew Samson, at least by name. Perhaps, she
thought, Samson had sent him out here to find her,
and then she immediately discarded the idea. Whatever other faults he might have, Samson could not
possibly have such a bully as a friend. More important, though, she doubted sadly that Samson would
be much inclined to care what became of her after the
scene she'd just made at supper. Instead he was likely
wishing she wouldn't return at all.

Which, considering her current situation, was entirely, horribly possible.

The man laughed again, pulling her close to him so
that she felt his belly shaking against her, and her
growing fear mixed with revulsion. She twisted sideways, trying to lessen her contact with him, and as
she did she brushed over something more frightening
still: the hard butt of a pistol beneath his coat. Her
hand stopped behind her back. Merciful heavens,
she'd thought *she'd* be the only one armed!

"I will make you forget Fairbourne," said the man decisively, pressing his body to hers against the pillar. "You are too beautiful to be wasted on that cold, thieving *Inglesa*. I will make you love me instead, *dulce*, my little pigeon."

With a frightened gasp Polly twisted her face away from his mouth, scraping her hand against the rough plaster pillar behind her as she groped desperately for her knife. Where the Devil could it *be*? She'd always kept it there before when she needed it, always there right below her waist.

Always, but not now: too late she remembered tying the strap beneath her petticoat at the mantua-maker's shop, and having to move the sheath to the pocket opening toward the front of her skirt where she could reach it. But she'd never be able to reach it there now, not with the man grinding his lower body against her in this awful, suggestive way.

"Do you—do you know Captain Fairbourne?" she gasped. "He is—is in your acquaintance?"

"*Sí.*" That was all. He'd stopped laughing, his breath was coming harder, and her panic grew as she realized he'd stopped his leaden playfulness as well.

The hand that was tangled in her hair jerked her head back so sharply that she cried out, then cried out again as she felt his palm, moist with excitement, slide across her breasts, exposed above the low-cut neckline. No man had ever touched her like that, not there, and revulsion rose up in her throat with a wave of nausea.

She jerked her knee upward, the one sure way she knew to disable any man. But again she'd forgotten about her unfamiliar clothing, and the crippling blow she'd intended became so muffled and mired in the yards of silk and linen that all she did was tangle herself.

With the man's weight against her, she felt herself begin to sway backward, beside the pillar, and she wildly flailed one arm behind her to keep her balance. Her wrist struck a heavy crockery planter, struck it hard. Any other time she would have cried from the pain of it, but now she silently rejoiced. Here was her chance; not quite a knife, but she'd take it anyway.

She thrust her hand blindly beneath the hibiscus leaves and dug her fingers deep into the damp soil. Impatiently the man pulled her forward, back towards him, and as he did she shoved the fistful of dirt and mud into his eyes.

With a howl of rage and pain he shoved her away, wiping frantically at his eyes instead. Polly didn't wait. At once she turned and began to run, bunching her silk skirts in clumsy bundles over her legs. She ran, her heels clicking on the brick walk, the kitchen lantern before her like a safe harbor's beacon across the courtyard. She ran, her heart pounding, heedless of the man swearing incoherently behind her.

She was almost there, to safety, and if she'd been wearing her old clothes she would have been there already. She wouldn't have felt one high, dainty slipper heel skid on a mossy brick, or heard the rush of a cry as her temple hit the walk while the rest of her landed in a soft rustle of treacherous, tripping silk. Then the man was there again, over her, his hands rough and his voice rougher as he dragged her upward and her hope gone, gone.

But abruptly the man vanished. No, he hadn't vanished; he was swearing again, then staggering backward. She had a glimpse of another man, heard them grunting and scuffling and the sickeningly dull thumps of fists striking flesh. Then the stranger was before her again, his silhouette in the lanternlight turned loose-jointed like a broken puppet before he collapsed into an awkward, lifeless heap.

She pushed herself up onto her hands. Her breath was coming in broken gasps that were close to sobs, torn from deep inside her, and with shaking, dirt-covered fingers she tried to smooth her skirts over her raw, skinned knees. And her head wasn't working quite as it should, as if her skull were packed with soggy wrack and bracken.

"Polly, lass!"

She didn't question that Samson was there, nor did she understand yet what he'd done. "My beautiful new gown," she said, her voice squeaking upward. "Oh, Samson, I didn't mean to—"

"Are you hurt?"

"Faith, no," she said thickly. "But see what I've done to my beautiful—"

"Damn." Carefully he swept her hair back from her forehead. "You're bleeding. Do you think you can walk?"

She gazed up at him mournfully as he took her hands in his. He was breathing hard, too, his shirt pulled from his waistband and his neckcloth all askew, and she frowned. He'd lost the ribbon to his queue, so his hair flopped around his face every which way, and there was a thin dark line of blood trickling from his lower lip. She was a little dizzy, true, but still she'd never dreamed Captain Fairbourne could fall into such disreputable disrepair.

"Samson," she said slowly. "You look like a . . . like a *scrod*."

"And you're the queen of Egypt." He'd pulled his

handkerchief from his pocket and was tying it around her forehead, leaning close to her face as he concentrated on the knot. She had the oddest desire to lean forward and kiss that lovely, stern mouth of his, there so close to her own. He probably wouldn't like it, not at all, and the idea made her giggle.

"Jesus, Polly," muttered Samson. "Are you certain you're not hurt?"

She shook her head, and wished she hadn't. It *did* hurt, hurt like blazes, but even now she'd too much pride to confess it to Samson.

"Then come," he said, pulling her to her reluctant feet, her knees nearly collapsing beneath her. "We can't stay here. We have to return to the ship before Hidaldgo's men find him. Or us, for that matter."

"Hidaldgo?" She followed his glance toward the lumpy, lifeless shadow on the ground. Abruptly the wrack in her skull seemed to disappear, and all the terror and revulsion she'd felt before came rushing back in its place. She pressed her hand to her throat, too late to stifle the odd, strangled cry that forced its way out as she stared at the man's body. Yet suddenly that, too, was gone, as Samson turned her away from the sight, holding her trembling body close against his.

"There now, it's done. It's done." With awkward tenderness he patted her shoulders, an awkwardness that meant more to her than a thousand practiced words of comfort. She didn't want to leave this sanctuary, this warm, safe place that he alone could offer. "You are—you're certain he did not hurt you?"

This time she realized what he meant, just as she understood how hard it must be for him to ask. "Nay," she whispered. "But oh, Samson, he tried. He *tried*."

She felt his arms tighten around her in response. "I'm sorry, lass," he said softly. "Sorry in more ways than I can tell you. But we must go now."

She would go anywhere with him, even at the furious pace he insisted was necessary. By the time they reached the wharf, he was more than half carrying her. Her sides were aching and her shift clung damply to her back beneath all the layers of her clothing, but she didn't care. She could forget the wager that had brought them together, and she could even forget Anabelle. Samson had come after *her*, come when she hadn't deserved it, and for now that was more than enough.

The boat was tied where they'd left it, with one of the sailors, left as a guard, sitting in the sternsheets with his pipe for company. As soon as he saw Samson he was on his feet, his face full of the question he didn't dare ask.

"Hidaldgo," said Samson curtly as he handed Polly into the boat. "Here."

Two words, but enough to make the sailor swear bitterly to himself as he clambered from the boat to the top of a stack of crates on the wharf. With two fingers he whistled, shrill and urgent, and almost instantly his companions came trotting along the wharf to the boat. The Spaniard's name, and the oaths, passed swiftly among them as they settled at their benches, and as they bent their backs over the oars it seemed to Polly that the boat fair flew across the water. She tugged Samson's coat higher over her shoulders, but the chill she felt now had nothing to do with the seaspray.

"You are warm enough?" asked Samson beside her, his shirtsleeves billowing in the wind.

She nodded. "Besides, the wind clears my head."

"I am glad." He adjusted the handkerchief around her head, his smile lopsided. "You cause me a great deal of concern, Polly Bray, and a great number of handkerchiefs, too. I won't have a scrap of linen left to my name by the end of this voyage if I must always be tending to you."

But Polly didn't smile in return. "Tell me, Samson," she said softly. "Who is Hidaldgo?"

He looked away from her, out across the water, a sure sign that he meant to tell her less than the entire truth, a sign that, unhappily, she'd come to recognize all too well. "Didn't you learn enough about him for yourself this evening?"

"Not what he means to you," she said. "Not the reason why every man in this boat swears and spits at his name as if he were the Devil himself."

"He's brother to the Devil, which is close enough kin for me. For any of us." He took her hand in his, running his thumb across her fingertips. Even by moonlight it was easy to see the dirt from the hibiscus pot ground into the skin and the mud still caked in grimy half circles beneath her fingernails.

"You fought him, didn't you?" he asked, the answer as obvious as his question.

Polly jerked back her hand, her attempt at a laugh turning brittle. "Faith, but you're always looking for tales in my hands."

"Perhaps because they have so many to tell," he said evenly. "You did fight back, didn't you?"

"But not very well." She bowed her head with shame and pulled off the bandage around her head. The scrape on her head had long ago stopped bleeding, and besides, she hadn't earned such a sign of valor. "Father wanted me to be able to look after myself. He said it was one of the perils of being a female among men. I'd always thought I could—look after myself, I mean—but I don't seem much good at it any longer."

"Don Diego Hidaldgo is not your ordinary Nin-nishibutt drunkard." He took her hand back, letting her keep her fingers curled tight into themselves. "You were brave to defend yourself, lass. Not wise, no, but very brave."

"It was these foolish clothes," she said quickly. "They may look very fine, but I'm as trussed up as a hen for stewing. If I'd been wearing my old clothes, and if I'd been able to reach my knife, then things would have turned out differently."

"If you'd drawn your knife," said Samson softly, "Hidaldgo would have used it to slit your throat. Ah, we're home."

Polly stared up at the tall, dark side of the *Morning Star*. This wasn't home, not for her, though by now she wasn't sure where exactly her home was. She was shivering inside Samson's coat, unable to stop shaking, despite the warmth of the Martinique night.

She wished he hadn't said that about the Spaniard slitting her throat, for as soon as Samson had spoken, she'd known he was right. The unmistakable edge of cruelty in the man's manner, his desire to see her suffer and cry more for him, confirmed it, and she squeezed her eyes shut for a moment as she tried to close out the memory. If Samson hadn't followed her to the courtyard of the inn, she would have been raped, then killed. It was as horrifyingly simple as that.

The boat bumped against the ship's side, and on the deck above she could hear the voices and bustle of the crew making last-minute preparations for their captain's return. She could not possibly climb up the way she'd begun to come down. This time she'd have to put aside her pride: her hands, her head, her shaking knees, even her petticoats, weren't going to let her do otherwise.

"I believe I shall make use of that bosun's chair after all," she said. "For the sake of the wager, I mean."

Samson shook his head with exasperation. "That damned wager," he muttered. "For God's sake, let's not worry about that now."

"Nay," she said with a weak show of independence. "You've done a great deal for me today, Samson. I can certainly do this much for you now."

She tipped her head back, cupping her hand around her mouth. "Zach! Ahoy, Zach, it's me, Polly!"

"Enough of that," ordered Samson gruffly as he rose to his feet, "and to hell with the bosun's chair. You'll come aboard the same way you left—with me. Now clap on, else you'll end up in the sea again."

Before she could protest he'd slipped his arm behind her knees with a *whoosh* of silk and swept her feet from under her, tipping her against his chest. She no more had the strength to fight him this time than she had to climb the ship's side on her own, and so, with a sigh of resignation, she slipped her arms around his neck and clapped on exactly as she'd been told. She was too tired anyway to do much else, and as Samson slowly climbed up the side of the ship, she dared to rest her cheek against his chest. There was, she thought wistfully, no harm in pretending she was more to him, and when they reached the deck, if he seemed to hold her still a moment longer than was necessary, well then, there was no harm to that, either.

No harm, and no hope.

"We'd no thought of seeing you so soon," said Zach with a grin as he greeted them. "Not before midnight, anyways."

"Then start thinking again," said Samson curtly. "We're clearing the harbor tonight. As fast as we can make ready, mind?"

Dubious, Zach shook his head. "You know as well as I do, Sam, that we'd do better to wait until morning, when the tide turns." His glance slid toward Polly, his eyes widening with undisguised appreciation. "Look at you, Miss Bray! I do not believe I'd recognize you on the high road, the handsome way you are now."

Polly flushed, and she shyly spread the coat from her shoulders so that Zach could see the gown beneath. There were a few smudges and snags in the silk, wrinkles and daubs of mud that would have made Madame LaFontaine exclaim with dismay, but the effect was still surprisingly the same as when Polly had stood perched on the shop stool.

Zach whistled his approval. "Most handsome indeed, Polly, and if Sam wished to settle our wager now, why, I fear I'd—"

"Hidaldgo's here," interrupted Samson, and instantly Polly's gown, and the wager, were forgotten.

"Hidaldgo here?" demanded Zach. "In St. Pierre?"

"Oh, he's here, no mistake," said Samson grimly, and the look that passed between the two men said infinitely more. "And we're clearing St. Pierre tonight even if we have to row."

"Within the hour," answered the younger man. "As soon as the boat's back on board we'll begin hauling in the chain. Sooner if we can."

He turned and immediately began shouting orders

to the few crewmen on deck. But though he never mentioned the Spaniard's name himself as reason for haste, the word had already spread from the men in the boat to the rest of the crew, and every hand raced to his task, even anticipating orders before they were given.

Polly watched, and listened, and her uneasiness grew as she stood beside Samson. "You say I'm not to worry, but how can I not?" she asked anxiously. "Why—how—would this man follow you clear out into the harbor?"

"Because he'd like nothing better," said Samson with a sigh, "and bastards like Don Diego Hidaldgo have a way of getting what they want. But he won't be getting us, not this voyage, anyway, which is why you must not worry."

"You have quarreled with him before?"

"Aye, I suppose we have," said Samson, his answer so deliberately vague that Polly worried all the more. "Sailors being sailors."

"But most sailors' quarrels end in a rumshop, not with a ship running out to deep water as fast as it can!"

Samson shrugged, his gaze so steadfastly directed out to that same deep water that it stung Polly to the quick. She wanted to shout at him that she was a sailor, too, not some dimwitted landsman to be coddled and cosseted with benign platitudes. Hadn't she proved anything to him with the spyglass? As if to mock her, the end of the scarf of black lace drifted up in the breeze to tickle her nose, a black lace scarf that no true sailor would ever wear. But she still didn't need protecting like this; what she wanted was the truth, however unpleasant it might be.

"We're not exactly running away," he conceded at

last. "At least not in a low, cowardly way. But it's your, ah, encounter with Hidaldgo this evening that's put a little extra wind in our sails this night."

Looking up at his profile, sharp against the spread of pale canvas overhead, Polly felt the impact of his words more keenly than any wind. She'd wanted the truth, and there it was. A Jonah didn't have to wait until a ship and her crew were at sea to bring bad luck; misfortune could come from land as well, lured out to the ship on the back of that self-same Jonah. Whatever "quarrel" Samson had with Hidaldgo had been increased a hundredfold by her actions this night. It was her fault alone, and nothing now could change it.

But oh, if she hadn't lost her temper over supper, if she hadn't let herself be so foolishly, wrongly jealous of a woman she'd never met, if she hadn't been so deep in her own selfish misery that she hadn't heard the Spaniard following her into the courtyard, if she hadn't behaved like such a helpless, mewling creature who'd needed Samson to rescue her one more time.

If, if, if. Why was it everything she tried to do with Samson was wrapped up in that single word of possibilities gone wrong?

With the anchor drawn, Polly could feel the ship once again come to life beneath her, the pull and jump as the sails caught the breeze and filled. The bow swung gently around, away from the town and toward the open sea, and beside her Polly could sense Samson coming to life, too, drawn by the water that was, for him, much more than his livelihood. She understood because she felt it herself as well, and as she looked up at him, she longed in silence for some way to share this moment with him.

"I—I am sorry, Samson," she began in a small, hesitant voice, "sorry for all the troubles I've brought you."

He shook back his hair and frowned down at her, almost as if he'd forgotten she stood beside him. "Don't be foolish. If anyone's to begin apologizing, it should be I, for tossing you into Hidaldgo's path."

"But it's my fault for being so wicked about— about Anabelle."

He shrugged again, a gesture that Polly found herself wishing never to see again. "That's not really your fault, either, feeling like that. Anabelle isn't the kind of woman that's easy to ignore."

Polly didn't answer, for there was nothing, really, that she *could* say after an explanation like that. She tried reminding herself that she wasn't often ignored, either, but most likely for far different, less alluring reasons than Anabelle, and as reminders went, it wasn't much consolation.

They were under way now, the ship rapidly picking up speed, and Polly grabbed her skirts in one hand to keep them from fluttering in the wind. To her consternation, she'd learned from Madame LaFontaine that even the most respectable ladies wore nothing save their stockings beneath their petticoats. It was a discovery she'd rather not accidentally share with the men, but as the ship moved faster, her skirts were becoming more and more unmanageable. She should go below to change back into her old clothes. If she'd any sense, she'd go to sleep, too. She had the worst headache of her life from where she'd fallen against the paving stones, and after everything that had befallen her, she was exhausted both in body and in spirit. But she wasn't ready to be alone, and she didn't want to leave Samson's side, not just yet.

"They haven't a prayer of catching us now, Sam," said Zach with satisfaction as he rejoined them on the quarterdeck, giving a quick tap to the front of his hat both to Samson and to Polly. "Not unless Hidaldgo's added wings to the *San Miguel*."

"Don't be so damned cocksure," said Samson with more irritation than Polly thought was necessary. "Just because we didn't see his infernal ship in this harbor doesn't mean it isn't tucked away in some inlet nearby, ready to cut that braggart's tongue right out for you."

"Aye-aye, sir," said Zach, touching the front of his hat again with crestfallen respect. "Leastways we got Pol—I mean, Miss Bray's new things stowed away in time. The boat from the mantua-maker came right before you did. Though we couldn't fit them all into your cabin, miss, I had the men stow the cases as close to the companionway as they could, so you could reach what you needed."

"Damnation, Zach, they're not all Polly's," said Samson crossly. "She has more good sense than to need all that. You could grant me a few more wits, too. There's generosity, and then there's pure, reckless idiocy. Most of that dunnage belongs to Anabelle, or will, once we haul it off to Appledore."

Polly was thankful that neither man was paying enough attention to her to see how she flushed with wounded misery. Good sense, ha. Though she might prefer breeches, she did have pride. But if that was the sort of compliment she inspired, well then, no wonder Anabelle had earned the lioness's share from Madame LaFontaine's shop, and, more important, of Samson's admiration as well.

An admiration that Zach must share, or so it seemed from the enormous, gleeful grin that lit his face. "Anabelle, you say. That's explanation enough, isn't it? Lord, but she has your brother by the—ah, the, ah, *nose*."

But Polly didn't hear how close he'd come to affronting her. "Your brother?" she repeated incredulously as she turned to gaze up at Samson. "You share Anabelle with your brother?"

"*Share* her?" repeated Samson with his own disbelief, while Zach fought a dreadful, strangled guffaw. "If I'd even thought of it, Josh would come thrash me within an inch of my life, and rightly so, too. Where the Devil would you get a notion like that?"

"But if Anabelle is your mistress—"

"Anabelle," said Samson with the kind of severe dignity used by preachers, "is not my mistress. I've never even met the dear woman. For God's sake, Polly, Anabelle is my brother Josh's *wife*."

Polly stared at him, speechless. Faith, she'd been feeling wretched over a woman who was as good as Samson's *sister*. She looked at him, all stern and outraged and more wickedly attractive than any man had a right to be, and then she thought of what a perfect noddy she'd been, and felt the laughter begin to well up inside her. She pressed her hand over her mouth to try to keep it in, but still it bubbled out, laughter born of relief and exhaustion and her aching head and just plain simple foolishness. She was laughing so hard that she couldn't explain, so hard that tears were spilling from her eyes to slide down her cheeks.

"Polly," he said, only her name, and uneasily at that. "Polly?"

He was watching her with the same close wariness that had been in his expression when they'd first met, and he'd judged her witless. She couldn't say she blamed him for feeling the same way now, which made her laugh all the more, and all the more unable to stop herself. She knew she must go below and collect herself, alone, before she found a madwoman's irons on her wrists and ankles, and without another attempt to explain herself, she ran across the deck to the companionway to her cabin, Samson's coat billowing around her shoulders like a cape.

With her feet hidden by the petticoats, she missed the bottom two steps and landed with an ungainly lurch, but by now she was long past caring. She needed to be alone, she told herself as she jiggled the latch on her cabin door, alone to—

"Wait, Polly, stay!" Part of her knew he was there before he'd even spoken, before he'd taken her arm to make him face her. "Damnation, lass, you *will* wait!"

The urgency in his voice shocked the last of the laughter from her, and the desperation she saw in his eyes, visible even there in the half light between decks, made her instant, defensive retort die unspoken in her mouth. Abruptly conscious of his hand on her arm, he let her go, instead bracing himself with his hands flat against the bulkhead on either side of her, his body leaning into hers without touching it, his face so near that she could feel the raggedness of his warm breath on her forehead.

"I should go," she said, her own breath strangely ragged too. "I should sleep."

Yet she made no move to leave him, to escape. No matter how close he stood to her, she did not feel trapped by him the way she had with Hidaldgo. This was Samson, and she was here because, God help her for a fool, she wished to be nowhere else under Heaven.

"Tell me, lass, tell me how I've misled you," he

demanded hoarsely. "What makes you believe I'd do as you say, that I'd keep some slattern as my plaything and then flaunt her like that before you? That I would be such a blasted idiot as that! Do you truly think so little of me? Why do you judge me like this, Polly?"

She felt lightheaded and confused, overwhelmed by his questions and the scent of his skin, the raw uncertainty in his voice, the way his full, untucked shirt brushed against her and her skirts billowed between his wide-spread legs, how his very anguish seemed to fill the narrow passage as much as his body.

"Why, Polly?" he asked again. "Why?"

"Because—because you are rich, and powerful, and a deep-water captain with—with amusements," she whispered, the wager that held her here looming unspoken between them. "Because you are a gentleman."

"Then may God strike me for a fool," he said vehemently, "for I've no wish to be a gentleman such as that."

"I didn't mean it in such a way!" she cried softly. "I didn't mean that you—"

"Hush." His hands came down suddenly to cradle her face, lifting it toward his, his fingers spread wide across her cheeks as he searched her eyes for an answer she did not know herself. "We neither of us know or mean a blessèd thing, mind? Not one! I know nothing true of you, Polly Bray, not who you are or how you've come to plague me or even if you are of this earth or—or—oh, the Devil take it all!"

His mouth came down on hers, his hands still holding her face so she could not turn away, and without thinking her fingers came up to cover his. His lips were at once firm and warm, demanding and gentle, as they moved over hers, and she let her eyes flutter shut to close out everything else. So this was what it was to kiss, she marveled; this was one of the great, wonderful secrets that made other girls whisper, that she'd never known for herself.

Then he slanted his mouth, opening hers to slide inside, and she realized she still knew nothing of kissing—less than nothing. The intimacy of it startled her, this unimaginable kind of touching that had no counterpart in her innocent inexperience. She felt herself tumbling headlong into a new pool of sensation, floating in its warmth as it spread around her whole body. She slid her hands down along his forearms to his shoulders to keep her weak-kneed self from sliding to the deck. Tentatively she began to kiss him in return, following his lead and her own instincts together, and the warmth spread with her own eagerness, driving away any other thought but to let this moment with this man continue. From deep in her throat came a small, unbidden moan of surprised pleasure, a sound she scarcely heard herself.

But he did, and suddenly broke away from her. Slowly, reluctantly, Polly opened her eyes and saw the horrified look on Samson's face. At once the pleasure she'd felt shattered, and with a shameful horror of her own she dropped her hands from his shoulders.

"Oh, Samson, forgive me, pray!" she cried, her voice breaking along with her heart. "You've every right to turn me away for being so—so wanton, and I—"

"No more." His voice was thick with bitterness and regret, his face now bowed so she could not see it in the shadows. Gently, he put his fingers across her lips to silence her, the touch another kind of torture to her newly sensitized mouth. "I'm the one who's sinned, lass, not you. What a bastard I've been, preaching at you one moment, then falling on you the next like a—Jesus, you'll never trust me again."

She slipped her fingers into his, twining them together and taking his hand from her lips and holding it instead. "Nay, Samson, I won't let you say that."

"And why not, when it is the truth? You were too tired and hurting too much to stop me, and I knew it."

" 'Tis not true, not at all," she said fiercely. "I am not some feeble little child, Samson. I am all I have left in this world, and I answer to myself alone. *Myself*. You did not force yourself upon me, the way that man Hidaldgo did. If I did not wish your—your attentions, then I would have fought you, too."

"This is not right, Polly," he began uneasily. "None of it."

"I don't know if it's right or not, Samson. I only know what *is*." She sighed unhappily. "But if kissing me gave you no pleasure, well then, that is another thing entirely."

As he shook his head, a faint shaft of moonlight washed across half his face, grim and moody. "For God's sake, Polly, don't play the fool. You, of all women, must know better than to ask me a question like that."

She sighed again. "I don't. You said yourself that I'm not a wise woman."

"You seem to be a great deal wiser than I this night." He raised their joined hands together, as if it were a sign or symbol to be deciphered. "What course have we set for ourselves here, eh, Polly Bray?"

Footsteps clattered on the companionway steps behind them, then hesitated and stopped. "Sam?" came Zach's uncertain voice. "Are you coming topsides again, Sam? The wind's changed again, round from the west."

"I'll be there directly," called Sam over his shoulder, already beginning to work his fingers free. "I must go, Polly. You sleep now, mind?"

"The Devil with the wind, Samson, and the Devil with my sleep," she whispered rebelliously. "No matter how hard we each might wish it, this will not go away with the moon."

"Did I say I wished it otherwise?" He eased around her to open her cabin and light the single candle in the lantern over her bunk, returning to the passage to pointedly hold the door wide for her to enter.

"It's your doing that I'm on this voyage at all." She touched her fingers to the tender place on her temple. She wished she could blame it for how she felt: edgy, incomplete somehow, and once again close to tears. "I didn't ask to be rescued, you know."

"Oh, aye, as if either of us had any choice in the matter." He made a rumbling noise of resistance or maybe resignation before he bent and kissed her again, hard and fast, and no comfort at all when he turned to leave her.

"Wait." She drew the rose from the front of her bodice, the same rose he'd tucked there himself earlier. The petals were crushed, but the scent had only intensified, and she carefully wove it into the top buttonhole of his waistcoat, letting her fingers linger briefly upon his chest. Then, before he could leave her, she left him instead, slipping inside her cabin with a last flick of her skirts.

She was too tired to undress except to unbuckle and kick off her shoes, and in her clothes she curled on the narrow bunk, drawing the coverlet up high over her shoulders. She closed her eyes and listened to Samson's footsteps fade along the deck, his voice faint as he greeted his cousin. Gently she touched her fingertips to her lips, still swollen from his kiss. His *kiss:* Lord, Lord, she'd never dreamed such a shameful, exquisite, confusing thing could happen to her.

She turned her cheek to the rough pillow, steadfastly tucking her hand beneath it. Her fingers brushed against a hard cylinder, and she remembered the old empty bottle she'd hidden there. Had it really been only this morning? Tomorrow she'd tuck it back into her coat pocket, a better place to hide such rubbish.

One more chance, she wished as she drifted off to sleep, her fingertips drowsily stroking the smooth glass of the bottle beneath the pillow. It didn't seem like so very much to wish for, not really. One more night to make things right between her and Samson, one more supper with him across the table, one more kiss . . .

One more chance.

Eight

"You should have finished Hidaldgo for good, Sam," said Zach firmly, his face determined in the moonlight on the quarterdeck. "Your knife in his ribs, clean and neat. There's not an honest man in this part of the world that would have begrudged you that."

"It's not the honest ones I worry over," answered Samson irritably. He had enough on his mind right now without addle-pated conversations like this. "A scuffle in the dark is one thing to a magistrate, but a murder's a great deal harder to overlook, especially when there'd be plenty of Spanish *pesos* to make sure I'd hang. I trade too much in these waters to risk my neck like that."

Zach shook his head indignantly. "But Hidaldgo's little more than a pirate himself!"

"He's a pirate, true enough, but he's also a *guarda-costa* in the employ of the King of Spain, and kings don't take kindly to having their people killed. Even if, like Hidaldgo, they deserve it."

Zach grumbled, unconvinced, and Samson sighed. At least here in the middle of the night there were few other men on the graveyard watch to overhear Zach's ravings. The history between Hidaldgo and the *Morning Star* was a long, complicated, and dangerous one; Samson couldn't deny that. The Spaniard's name alone had been enough to spark growling and chest-beating among the crew, and it had been part of the reason he'd ordered them out of St. Pierre so fast, before the hotheaded talk about revenge sprouted into more than bluster.

He'd already noted how Zach was now ostentatiously wearing a pistol thrust into his belt, and he wondered if he'd ever been this young and blood-thirsty himself. Perhaps on his first privateering voyage with Josh against the French, when they'd all been so eager to cover themselves with glory and gold. That was the time he'd discovered he'd no real taste for war. The gold had been there, true, but the glory was sadly wanting, and he'd learned to his horror both how easy, and how hard, it was to kill another man—a lesson his young cousin had yet to learn, and wouldn't on this voyage, if Samson had anything to say about it.

"It's better this way, Zach," said Samson, trying to placate him without sounding like a cowardly old schoolmarm. "This ship's been built to outrun anything else in these waters. You know that as well as I, and the reasons for it, too. We'll sail clear of Saint Domingue and Havana, and Hidaldgo will most likely stay clear of us in return."

"But if he don't—"

"Pray that he will."

"Aye, but if he doesn't, we'll have to—"

"We're not armed for that kind of fight, you blasted idiot," snapped Samson, his patience finally at an end, "and you'll damned well remember it before the men. If you want to get your fool head blown off, then join the navy. We're a merchantman, not a warship, and unless the Spanish King up and declares war on our King, that's the way it's bound to stay. Clear enough, *Mr.* Fairbourne?"

The struggle between Zach's emotions and his duty was visible on the younger man's face, but finally, to Samson's relief, duty won.

"Aye-aye, Captain," he said, practically throttling himself in the process. "Clear enough, sir."

"I am glad." Samson glanced up at the sails, giving Zach, and himself, time to recover. "And your mama will be glad, too. She would much prefer to have you return home in your entirety."

"Aye-aye, sir," said Zach again, his expression growing more unhappy by the moment, clearly preferring not to be reminded of his mother when such adventure beckoned.

Which was exactly why Samson had mentioned her, and why now, his absent aunt's work done, he was content to let silence settle between himself and Zach. For the first time since he'd returned to the deck he let himself think of Polly, all she'd said and all he'd done. No, what *they'd* done. That was the way she wanted to describe it, anyway, and he was too tired now to argue over the distinction.

He wondered if she was as confused as he by now, or if she were instead peacefully asleep. By now: no, it could only have been five minutes since she'd shut the door in his face. More likely she was still undressing. Nothing confusing about that. All too easily he could picture her unfastening her gown, tugging the long laces through the eyelets on her bodice so that inch by inch the sides of the front would slip apart, lower and lower over her stays and shift and high, round breasts and—

"He should've died for what he did to Polly," muttered Zach, ostensibly to himself but more than loud enough to reach Samson's ears, and to destroy the charming picture in his mind, too. "After he dishonored her like that, he deserved it."

"Zach," warned Samson softly, "do not push me."

But the first persistent little doubt had been planted into his uneasy conscience. Perhaps Polly, too, believed he'd behaved like a coward. She wouldn't have known all the reasons why he'd reined in his temper and stopped short—barely—of outright murder. Perhaps she had expected him to avenge her more completely than he had. Perhaps this was why she'd been so insistent about taking care of herself, because she thought he'd done such a piss-poor job of it on her behalf.

But worst of all was wondering if she'd rather it had been bold, hot-blooded Zach there doing the rescuing. She'd certainly run to him as soon as they'd returned to the ship, flinging his coat aside—*his* coat, offered in a most chivalrous moment—to display herself in her new finery. Not that Samson could blame her, if he were being honest with himself. She and Zach were closer in age, closer in temperament, and closer in God only knew how many other ways that Samson could only suspect.

"Leastways you're winning the wager," said Zach, fortunately unaware of the black turn that Samson's thoughts had taken. "Faster than lightning, too. One trip to shore, a few baubles, and you've made Polly a winsome new creature, just as you swore you would. She fair took my breath away tonight, Sam, took it as surely as if I'd been the one dropped on the deck. Who'd have thought our Polly could become such a tasty little poppet?"

"She's not changed that much, not yet," snapped Samson quickly—too quickly to be anything but defensive. "And I'll thank you not to be calling her your 'tasty poppet.' She's 'Miss Bray' to you, mind?"

Zach cocked a single brow in surprise. "You were the one swearing that all women were alike, and none too fine at that. If you didn't believe it, then you shouldn't have made the wager. Unless you've changed your mind and wish to call it off."

"Now why the Devil would I do that?" said Samson crossly. He had the uncomfortable feeling he'd just stumbled into a trap, without knowing exactly what form the trap was taking. "It's just that—that I'm not done with Miss Bray yet."

"But if she doesn't change, you know what will come next," said Zach carefully, and the trap yawned wide. "Your oath, Sam, your oath with the bottle. Maybe Pol—ah, Miss Bray truly is your perfect woman, and if she is, you'll have to wed her, won't you?"

"Our wager has nothing to do with the bottle," said Samson quickly, "nothing at all, mind? I want to, ah, tempt Miss Bray more so she'll show her true colors, else you won't learn a blasted thing. Not that you will, anyway, not with a head as thick as yours."

But instead of listening, Zach was looking pointedly at Samson's chest.

"Maybe you're taking lessons from Polly instead, Sam," he said, with undisguised fascination and a decidedly unwise glee. "Maybe you're learning what manner of nosegays do look best tucked beneath your chin, like every other London-bred dandy."

In horror Samson looked down at his chest, at the crumpled rose that Polly had so carefully tucked into the top buttonhole of his waistcoat. If he wished to make his point with Zach, he knew he should rip the flower from his chest and toss it over the side, to prove how little it meant to him.

But he didn't, and he couldn't. What he could do was remember exactly how Polly's fingers had lingered almost tenderly on his chest, how her head had bent over her hand, so close that his head had been filled with her scent. He could no more throw away that wilting rose than he could forget his own name, and though he pulled it from his buttonhole, it went not over the side, but into his pocket for safekeeping.

"Damn your fo'c'sle wit, and your impertinence, too," he growled as he jerked his hand self-consciously from his pocket. "Just because you're my blasted cousin doesn't give you the right to—"

But Zach's rights and Samson's words were suddenly carried away together as a great gust of wind ripped across the deck, catching the ship broadside so hard that she heeled dangerously to port. As if he were little more than a dry oak leaf, Samson felt himself blown backward by the wind, his heels scuffling across the slanting deck as he struggled in vain to find his footing. Desperately he grabbed at the shrouds before he was forced over the side, his fingers clutching at the rope as he caught and braced himself against the ratlines, the wind flailing at him like a wild creature.

Overhead the sky was still clear, the stars and quarter-moon bright in the deep blue of the Caribbean night, but the crazy, inexplicable wind remained, blowing as hard as a winter gale from the west and churning the seas into white-flecked waves as high as houses.

He twisted about, shaking his hair back from his eyes, to squint up at the *Morning Star*'s mainsail. The huge canvas square was stretched as taut as was possible, every line straining to hold it steady. The timbers and the mainmast groaned in protest, but with the chilling certainty of experience, Samson realized they'd sway and give only so much more before they snapped before the wind's force. Dismasted, they'd be easy prey for Hidaldgo. He'd lose his ship, his crew, his freedom at best, his life at worst—the same risks every sailor like him gambled when he put to sea. But the thought of Polly's life in danger, of her tumbling into Hidaldgo's cruel hands again—that was something altogether different.

He craned his neck the other way, aft to where the helmsman, Plunkett, was fighting to hold the wheel steady. That was good; Plunkett was strong as a bull, and he'd be the one man on board that might have a chance of holding the ship on course in this wind. But that great billowing mainsail overhead had to be taken in at once or the wheel wouldn't matter, and he seized the nearest flapping guideline to begin clawing his way, hand over hand, across the lurching, empty deck toward the mainmast.

Damnation, where was Zach?

He roared his cousin's name, raising his voice as loud as he could over the wind. No answer came, and with sickening, hideous clarity Samson remembered how not ten minutes before he'd teased the younger man about returning home. Whether he was lost to a Spaniard's pistol or this Devil's sea would make no difference at all to his poor mother, and, fighting his furious, guilt-ridden helplessness, Samson bellowed his cousin's name again.

Not Zach, not like this . . .

"Sam!" The voice was faint, pulled apart by the wind, but enough for Samson's head to whip around.

The deck was empty still, enough to make him wonder if he'd imagined his cousin's voice.

"Sam, here!" This time he followed the voice upward, into the rigging over his head. Zach had already begun the long climb aloft, following the first half dozen men he'd roused to haul in the dangerous mainsail. Samson's relief was swiftly followed with pride in the younger man's resourcefulness: he could make all the juvenile jests he wished about nosegays if he turned out the men this fast. But the seven of them weren't going to be enough, not in this wind, and without hesitation Samson plunged ahead to join them as the necessary eighth, his hands and feet blindly finding the familiar holds even as they swayed beneath him, higher and higher still.

As last man up, he was last man along the foot-lines, inching along with his belly pressed to the yardarm. Years had passed since he'd hauled in a sail, especially in conditions such as these, and though he labored as part of his four-man team, it was his own strength and balance that would keep him from being blown to the deck far below. The rough canvas was heavy with seawater, scraping his hands raw as he wrestled with it against the wind, a fierce tug of war with an invisible adversary.

He hauled and bunched, hauled and bunched, his back and arms aching from the stress. They were nearly there, the bottom of the huge sail only a few feet below them, when from the far end of the spar came a muffled cry as the last man lost control of his sail, the canvas billowing wildly from his hands. The force pulled the furled sail from the hands of the man next to him, and the one after that, until Samson, too, felt the canvas torn from his hands.

But worse followed: free from both the lines that

had held it taut and the men who had hauled it in, the canvas suddenly split down a seam, a jagged weakening that shredded again until the single huge square was reduced to a twisting tangle of ragged cloth.

And then, as suddenly as the gust had appeared, it vanished. The waves calmed as well, as swiftly as if oil had been poured on their churning surface, leaving the ship to slowly even and settle. The invisible force that they had fought against was gone, the torn sails fluttering benignly like banners in the breeze.

With an oath of frustration, Samson let his exhausted body sag against the yard. They'd have to limp along on short sail until they could put in to port for a new mainsail, praying all the while that Hidaldgo and his compatriots weren't close on their wounded heels. There'd be hours of repairs ahead, time and money to be spent. The best that could be said was that they'd kept their mast and no one had been lost or hurt, but Samson was still left with the uneasy, irrational feeling that the wind had risen somehow to challenge *him*, personally and vindictively, and to cause the greatest damage in the shortest span of time.

Only once before had he seen such a gale come without warning, and he didn't need Zach to remind him of the circumstances.

" 'Twas like the other time, Sam," he said, his voice low and his expression fearful, as they paused side by side at the masthead while the others began the long descent to the deck. "That night in Bridgetown, when you threw the bottle, when you swore that—"

"Don't say it, Zach, because I'm not listening," said Samson, as angry at himself for having thought of the coincidence first as he was at his cousin for daring to put his own misgivings into words. "You know well as I how skittish blows can be in these waters. Nothing mystical or contrary about it. Besides, you were with me the whole time. Did I go saying anything I shouldn't? Was I tempting fate to strike me dead, or begging for woe to make such an infernal mess of all my standing rigging?"

"Nay," said Zach reluctantly. "You didn't. But still and all, coming right after I'd said you'd won the wager about Polly—"

"Hogwash, Zach," said Samson firmly. "Hogwash is all it is, and I'll thank you to tell the rest of the men the same if they ask."

Before his cousin could argue any more, Samson slid over the side of the masthead until his toes found the ratlines. He climbed down the shrouds rapidly and without a thought, his mind still striving to make sense of the strange, vengeful wind and its consequences. He wasn't superstitious, he told himself— no, *ordered* himself—again, and he'd be damned if he began to let himself be swayed by coincidence and sailor's tattle. If he did, he'd be no better than Polly and her foolish Jonah talk, peeking with quaking dread into cupboards and under hammocks for demons and ghosts, even Davy Jones himself.

And bad luck, a Jonah's bad luck, first with Hidaldgo's reappearance and now this ill wind with its bounty of no good.

"Hogwash," he muttered to himself. "Hogwash, every bit of it."

He never saw the block that hit him, the heavy oak piece, as large as a man's head, torn from its place by the wind and left to swing free in a deadly pendulum's arc. He never saw it, but he felt it in a myriad of ways: in the first, sudden blow to his back, high between the shoulder blades; in how the air rushed driven from his lungs; in the way his feet and hands lost all instinctive knowledge of the rope ladder they held; in the haste with which he dropped through the air—not far, but far enough; and in the last, jarring, agonizing pain that ripped through his shoulder as he struck the deck.

"Sam!" There was Zach's pale face over his, centering the whirl of stars and moon and sheer, nameless agony. "Can you tell me where it hurts, Sam?"

As hard as he tried, he could not. Every word he wished to say was swallowed first by the blasphemous fire searing into his shoulder, transformed into the kind of terrible, raw noise that would shame an animal.

"We'll mind you, Sam, you know that we will," said Zach, his urgent reassurances at odds with the taut lines of horror and worry on his young face. No wonder: he was now captain, master of the ship and her crew. "We'll get you below, into your own bunk, and set you to rights, and you'll be fine again soon, Sam, I swear to it!"

Bad luck, more bad luck, more than any living man deserved . . .

"You'll mend fast, Sam, you always do," Zach was saying as the others linked their arms to lift him. "And when you're settled, I'll send for Polly to come and—"

"No!" he gasped, his order reduced to a rasping croak. But no matter how much he wished her at his side, her comfort, her touch, he could not—*would* not—let her see him like this. "Not—not Polly."

Slowly Samson poured the rum from the bottle into the tumbler, letting the liquor trickle in a thin, silvery stream. He did everything slowly now, whether it was pouring yet another tumbler of rum for himself, or working his free arm into the sleeve of a shirt, or simply beginning the convoluted process of rising from his bunk without help. Yet slow or fast or anything in between, the pain was there with him, as inevitable as salt in the sea.

The first day had been the worst, after two of the strongest sailors had had to hold and twist his arm with excruciating imprecision until his dislocated shoulder slipped back into place. The *Morning Star*, like most merchant ships, carried no surgeon on her list; all physicking was done among themselves, and for each other, whether captain or cabin boy. Not even the rum had helped then, and he wasn't sure it was helping now.

With his right arm bound to his side to give his shoulder a chance to recover, he could scarcely feed or dress himself, let alone shave. He walked like an ancient lopsided crab, bent and scuttling, and by the time he made his way to the deck he was sweating from pain and exertion. But he sought no help, nor was anyone foolish enough to offer it, not when they saw the expression in his eyes.

And in the five days since he'd fallen, not once had he seen Polly Bray.

The first few days had been easy, for he hadn't risen from his bunk and she'd been kept away by his orders. Returning to his quarterdeck had taken more stealth, relying on Zach's reluctant complicity to report when she slept or was dining, always alone, in her cabin. She'd been told he'd fallen, but that was all, and he meant to keep it that way until he'd mended, until he could laugh and dismiss his injury as an exaggerated mishap.

To keep away from her was as painful as his

shoulder and back, for her smile, or the way her eyes lit when she challenged him, or—God take him for the greatest fool—how she'd tasted when they'd kissed were in his thoughts all the time. He missed her, and he shouldn't. It was as simple, and as complicated, as that. But for that same reason he would not let her see him as anything other than the man who could protect her from harm; and as a man who could not now comb his own hair, it seemed an impossibly distant goal.

He sipped the rum, wrinkling his nose as it slid down his throat. Jesus, he didn't even like the stuff, a miserable admission for any New England sailor. But rum was the best, and only, physick he had, and in two days, maybe less, the *Morning Star* would limp into the harbor at Charles Towne. He'd no intention of limping into town the same way.

He heard the familiar rattle and clatter from the other side of the cabin door as Joseph wedged the tray with his dinner against the bulkhead long enough to free a hand to knock. There, there came the knock, just as Samson had expected. Most days he took real satisfaction in the order of his life, but other times, like now, it felt as damned predictable as clockwork.

"Come," he called, without bothering to turn. He swirled the rum in the tankard, staring moodily into it. He wasn't thirsty, and he wasn't particularly hungry, either, but he'd have to make some show of eating, for appearance's sake, or the rumors would start in the galley that he was wasting away. "Blast it, boy, I told you to enter!"

"No wonder poor Joseph's terrified of you, with you snarling at him like that," said Polly as she pushed the door open with the edge of the tray. "Who in their right mind would wish to have his head bitten off three times a day, without so much as a by-your-leave?"

"What in blazes are you doing here?" demanded Samson, forgetting his shoulder and twisting about with keenly painful results, and oaths to match.

"Oh, aye, bite my head off, too," said Polly as she set the tray down on the table with a flourishing clatter of silverware. "*I* shall live, which is more than might be said of you this morning."

She'd returned to her old boy's clothing, her hair plaited again in the long, single braid down her back, and if he'd harbored any secret hopes that she'd been pining away with thoughts of him, her rosy, sun-pinked cheeks quickly dashed them. His memory could never quite recapture how vibrant she was, how boundlessly full of energy she could be, and how hopelessly puny and wretched she was making him feel right now by comparison.

She leaned across the table, peering at him as if he were some rare curio. "Let me look at you, Samson. Faith, from what the others say, you should be at death's very door."

"Then look your fill," he growled, "and be gone." He didn't like the sound of those "others," or whatever it was they were saying. He'd made the effort to come topsides and put on a show of being well just to stop talk like that, and he didn't want her adding to the speculation. For that matter, he didn't really want her talking to any of the men at all.

She narrowed her eyes and flung her braid back over her shoulder for emphasis. "Pretty words, those, when I'm the one who's been wronged. I might not be experienced in the world's ways, but I do know that gentlemen who kiss ladies and then run away and hide aren't exactly behaving like gentlemen."

He met her gaze without flinching: an extraordinary feat, he decided, given the way she was studying him. "I thought you were dead against being a lady. Proud of it, almost."

"Then I'd say we're dead equal," she shot back, "for you seem to feel the same way about being a gentleman."

There wasn't much he could venture in his own defense, and so, reflexively, he swung around to another tack. "Mind you, I haven't been exactly hiding either, Polly. I smashed the hell out of my shoulder, and I can tell you that's brought me a deal of suffering."

"Hah!" She tapped her fingers on the table between them. "I didn't believe you'd admit it, you being a man and all. But it was certainly worth coming to hear you say it."

"If that's your only reason for coming, why then—"

"But it's not," she said quickly. "I came to bring you your dinner. I came because I wished to see with my own eyes if you were as poorly as everyone seems to fear. I came because I've heard things—fearsome, lobcocky things—about this voyage that I'd like to hear you deny. And, of course, I wished to prove that you are the one in hiding, and not me."

He glared at her, his uneasiness growing as he realized this would not be a short visit. "Is that the sum of it, then?"

"Nay," she said, then hesitated, just long enough to show how shallow her bravado truly was. That hesitation surprised him—he didn't think she was afraid of anything, least not that she'd want him to know—and it touched him, too.

"Nay, there's one other reason, Samson," she continued softly. "I'm here because I'd nothing left to lose by coming. Now let me see this great grievous wound. Since I'm the Jonah who brought it to you, seems only right that I do my best to help your suffering now."

"Here now, none of your Jonah nonsense," he said gruffly, though without the same indignant fire he'd felt before. Didn't she realize how dangerous it was for her to confess such things? Here, clear as day, was the undeniable, exhilarating proof that she did care what had happened to him. What wasn't clear was what such proof might mean to either of them. This was all uncharted waters to him, too. Besides, even in jest, the notion of her as a Jonah ran too queerly close to his own doubts for comfort. "I've told you before I don't believe in that superstitious tripe, haven't I?"

"Oh, aye, tell me all you wish," she said evenly, "but telling won't change the facts."

She had circled around him, to his side, and was already easing his hand free from the cuff of his shirt. Five minutes before, his reaction would have been to pull away, to shake her off, but after that hesitant admission, he found to his own surprise that he didn't have the heart or the wish to do that to her. She'd revealed a great more of herself than a shirt alone would ever hide of him, and awkwardly he began to help her, wincing as he tugged it over his head.

He did it willingly, without protest, but he was still glad his back was turned to her when she gasped aloud, and that he didn't have to see the pity or horror that must be on her face. Vulnerability had its limits.

"I told you it was not a pretty sight," he said, staring steadfastly ahead. Even brave women could be expected to show disgust over things men took for granted.

But once again he'd read her wrong.

"You great noddy," she scolded. "What matters is how it pains you, not how it appears to anyone else."

She touched him gently, her fingertips first tracing the torn linen strips that bandaged him before moving on to his back. He tensed and braced himself for the sudden pain he was sure was inevitable. Self-protection, that was all it was, he told himself firmly, but he still could not remember the last time he'd trusted a woman enough to let her touch him like this, and he wasn't entirely sure why he was allowing Polly that freedom now.

"Whichever of the men did this for you—Isaac, wasn't it?—he bound you well enough," she continued. "The tighter the frapping, the quicker the healing. Your shoulder's likely feeling better already, isn't it?"

He nodded grudgingly. "Since when do fisher-girls take to chirurgical learning?"

"Since their fathers' spines were fair ruined from hauling nets in the damp, that's when. An old woman in our town taught me what she'd done to ease her husband, who suffered the same ill. But mind, this is the sum of what I know. If you'd broken your leg, I'd be helpless as a new lamb." She fell silent, concentrating. "I'll wager what ails you most now are these deep bruises that make you all tight inside. Knotted up like a rope to your very core, aren't they?"

He nodded again. Though he hadn't thought of it quite that way, the description was apt enough. That old village woman must have been a witch to teach her such sorcery, for the warmth of her touch and the soft singsong of her voice were making him drowsy.

"Damnation, Pol," he muttered contentedly, "where were you when I needed you, eh?"

"In my cabin, by myself," she said, "where you banished me for no particular reason at all."

"I disremember doing any such thing," he said, disinclined to remember, either. "Jesus, but that feels good."

"I can make it better," she said with a little chuckle, "though you must stay with me in the beginning."

How kind of her to warn him, he thought sleepily, especially when her touch was bringing him the kind of bliss that the rum never had.

Then she began using her thumbs and the full strength of the heels of her hands, and he nearly shot from the chair with an oath strong enough to curdle cream in a jug.

"I warned you, didn't I?" she said, pushing him back down with her palms. "But I promise 'twill be better. If you're brave enough to trust me, and to keep a decent tongue in your mouth."

"You wicked, contrary she-devil," he muttered, but still he could not resist a dare like that from her. He clasped the arm of the chair, bowed his head with his eyes squeezed shut, and prepared for the worst.

It came, and it took all his willpower not to bite his tongue clear off from stifling another oath. But then, as she'd promised, the pain seemed to recede and drop away, his aching muscles relaxing beneath her warmly insistent fingers in a way that was nothing short of miraculous.

But for Polly the miracle was of a far different nature.

It had taken more nerve than she thought she possessed to bluff her way into Samson's cabin like this, and only desperation had made her do it. Four days without word from him, except to keep away, had been very hard—especially after she'd learned of his fall during a storm that she'd somehow slept clean through—very hard indeed. She'd gone from hope to loneliness to despair to dread and, finally, to anger. Once she'd decided to confront him, she'd armed herself with reason and bravado, prepared for battle with a man who fell uncomfortably between friend and foe. Given the circumstances, she doubted she knew what a victory might be.

But as soon as she'd shoved open the door to Samson's cabin, she'd forgotten her anger and her battered pride, forgotten everything but her empathy for the sorry-looking man before her. For all the world he'd reminded her of a wounded dog that had strayed from home: bedraggled and hurting and lost, his fur—well, his hair, anyway, and the stubble along his jaw—unkempt, but with too much fight and spark bred deep in his bones to give up.

And neither, she realized, would she. Faith, they were so much alike sometimes it frightened her.

If she'd been secretly stunned when he'd agreed to let her tend to his shoulder, then she'd stunned herself equally by offering in the first place. She was by nature too self-sufficient to be a compassionate nurse, just as he'd never savor the role of needy patient. Of course, she'd taken care of her father, as a good daughter should, rubbing the aches from his knobby spine and wizened flesh. But never had she expected that to lead to where she was now, her hands open and fingers spread across the broad shoulders and powerful muscles and warm, taut, browned skin of Samson Fairbourne.

Heaven help her, was there any greater temptation to sin than this?

She closed her eyes and struggled to regain her thoughts, to find again those weighty reasons that had brought her here. She'd already betrayed far too much of her own feelings. She needed distance, or she'd be lost. She must speak sensibly, and receive her answers, and then be gone, as swiftly as she could.

Aye, that was it. Swiftly, sensibly, and without another thought for how impossibly strong he must be to have survived such an accident, how sleek his skin was beneath her fingers, what it would be like to press her lips to it, there, beneath the linen bandage.

It was then that he groaned, a deep vibration beneath her fingers that was an unmistakable sound, not of pain but of pleasure. Even in her inexperience—inexperience that he was fast educating—she recognized it, and her hands flew away from him as if they'd been burned. In a jumble of vivid memories she recalled kissing him, and the feel of his arms around her, and, worse, the wanton thrill of having him lie upon her, that first night when he'd taken her knife.

All that, she thought wretchedly, had come from that single, low, male groan, and, her cheeks flaming, she scuttled around him and sat on the far side of the table. There, with the safety of oak planks between them, she clasped her wayward hands firmly in front of her before she dared meet his gaze.

And, blast him, he was *smiling.*

"You stopped," he said.

"You were better," she said. "You *are* better."

"Thanks to you." His smile widened, wolfish in his darkly unshaven face. "I could be better still if you'd continue."

"You're better enough." She cleared her throat and reclasped her hands. "Besides, you need to eat your supper."

"Do I now." He glanced down with disinterest at the now-cold roast chicken on the plate before him. "I find I'm not hungry."

"Well, you must eat, or you'll never recover." It was his right shoulder that was injured, his right arm incapacitated by the binding, and she wondered with a little frown of dismay if next he expected her to feed him. "And you shall need your strength to tell me the true nature of this voyage, which is something you've neglected to do before."

"Ah." His expression didn't change, but she sensed the guardedness in that noncommittal reply. "You believe that I've been hiding something from you."

"Aye, because you have." She looked down at her hands, troubled by what she must say. "You are a merchant captain, true enough, but you sell your British goods in Spanish ports, which is wrong, and then you bring back Spanish goods to Boston, which is wronger still, because you're doing it without paying a farthing in custom tariffs. That is smuggling, Samson, and though I am no magistrate, I know what is done to smugglers. They are fined or imprisoned or even hung as pirates, and I do not see that any profit could be worth that."

To her sorrow, he didn't deny a word. "Who told you this?" he asked. "It was my cousin, wasn't it?"

"*You* should have been the one to tell me, Samson," she said, her voice full of the anguish he refused to share. "If you cared for me at all, you should have warned me of the danger of simply being aboard this ship."

He laughed. "Is drowning in the sea any less dangerous? Perhaps I should have left you there to find out for yourself, instead of taking you in and making you my guest."

"Don't try to muddle me, Samson," she warned. "I'm not half the fool you want me to be. This man Hidaldgo, the one you all call such a perfect villain, is instead a costa—a costa—"

"A *guardacosta*, lass," he said offhandedly. "'Tis a Spanish phrase."

"A Spanish phrase for a man who serves his king by catching the rogues who would cheat him!"

"I don't give a damn who he sails for, Polly. Don't you remember what he tried to do to you?"

"He only wanted me as a way of hurting you!" she cried unhappily. "Samson, Hidaldgo has spent years hunting you, and though you have had luck with you before this, it won't always be so. Someday he will catch you, same as he nearly caught me, and oh, dear Lord, what he will do to you! What he will *do!*"

Samson sighed and leaned back in his chair. "Zach—for it must be my hand-wringing cousin— Zach had no right to fill your head with such tales. But if you wish, I shall leave you in Charles Towne, and make arrangements for you to return home in a more respectable vessel."

"Merciful heavens, Samson, that is *not* what I wish!

I wish for you to stop this foolish risk now, and save yourself! You must consider your future, your life! You have two brothers and a sister. What would they say if you were to perish for a cause as sad and vain as this one?"

He looked at her evenly, his smile tight. "Most likely Josh would fault me as careless for being caught."

"I cannot believe your own brother—"

"Pray believe it, Polly, for that much is true," he said sharply, his whole face darkening to match his tone. "I'm but following in Joshua's wake, doing much as he has done, and if I am to prosper as well there is no other course for me to take. How do you think he became a rich enough man to afford a noble wife and a big house to keep her in? Not by being soft and sentimental, I can tell you that."

"Maybe not," said Polly slowly, "but still he must love you enough to care what becomes of you, doesn't he?"

But Samson only shook his head. "Not Joshua," he said. "He's not like that, not at all."

The bitterness in his voice only hinted at long rivalries and old quarrels between the brothers, but it was more than enough to make Polly grieve on his behalf. Though she had no siblings of her own, she'd seen enough of the love in other families to know what she—and Samson—were missing.

"I am sorry, Samson," she said wistfully. "I didn't know that—"

"What else have you heard?" he demanded bluntly, rebuffing her kindness. Clumsily he shoved his chair away from the table and rose to his feet. He began to pace, a lopsided lurch back and forth across the deck. "Perhaps the whispers around the fo'c'sle say that inside my stockings I possess hooves cloven like a goat's, or that I can read the future like a prophet. Come, tell me everything, *Miss* Polly Ann Bray, so that I might know myself."

She hated it when he called her by her full name like that, almost as if it were a low, dirty insult, especially when she'd done nothing to deserve it except to wish he'd save his own life before it was too late. Where was the provocation in that? Had she imagined that moment earlier, when they'd each seemed to trust one another? Or was it that they were simply too stubbornly alike to ever be anything but at each other's throats?

Her whole body was rigid with resentment as she stared at his broad, battered, willful back, and she fought the urge to flip the tray with his dinner at him and stalk from the cabin.

"There's one other thing, aye," she said, anger adding a tremor to her voice. "Zach told me that he'd tried to end the wager, that I'd changed enough for him, the way you'd swore I would. He said that you'd won, all fair, but that you wouldn't let him quit, that you claimed the terms weren't yet met."

His pacing came to an abrupt halt, but he didn't turn to face her. "Do you wish that much to leave us, Polly?"

He wasn't going to get the entire truth from her now, not when things were disintegrating so rapidly between them. "I mean to stay until I've earned my part of this wretched bargain. I want my boat restored to me, but I won't take charity from you or anyone else."

He swung around awkwardly, unbalanced by the bound arm, his gaze flinty, appraising. "You would stay and keep company with a traitorous, smuggling scoundrel like me? You'll risk your own life and honor to throw in your lot with us against Hidaldgo?"

She lifted her chin defiantly. "You won't cheat me out of what I'm due by trying to scare me."

"Ha, what man could?" He smiled, but it was a cold, conspirator's smile, granted only to mark a truce of convenience. "We'll cross the Charles Towne bar by noon tomorrow. Though I'll be occupied refitting the ship during the days we're in port, I'll expect you to accompany me into town in the evenings. For the sake of the wager, mind?"

"For the sake of the wager, aye," echoed Polly as she stood to leave. There seemed little reason for staying any longer, and besides, she wouldn't have him see the tears that she was so perilously close to shedding. "Likely you'd prefer me dressed like a lady again?"

"Put the new finery to use." He was watching her so closely as she paused by the door that she feared he could see those still-unshed tears. "You're a brave little creature, Polly Bray, but I'd warrant we're in no real danger from Hildaldgo this far to the north. I've never known the bastard to venture any farther than New Providence."

"I pray you're right, Samson," she said. "For if you're not, all the bravery in the world won't save my life."

And as she closed the door behind her, she still did not know if she'd won or lost.

Capitán Don Diego Hidaldgo stood at the bow of the *San Miguel*, his gaze fixed on the tiny gray slivers on the northern horizon. Even at this distance he recognized the slivers as the masts of the *Morning Star*, and in a low whisper he thanked all the saints for granting him such joy. For four long days and nights he had prayed for this moment, and he now let himself savor both the pleasure of answered prayers and the anticipation of taking the greatest prize of his career.

This time, the English thief would not escape; this time, at last, the saints would smile on him instead.

"He sails for Charles Towne, Fernando," he said to the bosun standing nearby. "Does he believe I will not follow him there, I wonder?"

"He has no choice, Capitán," said Fernando. "If he was as damaged by the storm as the crew of that pettiauga said, then he must put in for repairs before he heads farther north."

"North, bah," said Hidaldgo, pulling his long velvet coat more closely around his body. The wind had a chill, inhospitable edge this morning. "We are north enough for any Christian, eh?"

"Which Fairbourne is not, Capitán, may Satan claim the bastard's putrid heathen soul," said Fernando as he spat over the side for emphasis. "Better we should catch and take him now, before he hides himself away in the bay, beneath the English guns."

Hidaldgo clucked his tongue, smoothing his fingers along his plush-covered arm. "Patience, Fernando, patience. If we chase him now, he will be warned, alarmed. Another plague of wind like that last one, and he could slip away and be lost to us. This way he will be trapped like a buzzing fly in a bottle, until we choose to draw the cork and tempt him out with a daub of sweet honey."

"Honey?" Fernando furrowed his brow.

"The girl, Nando, the girl," said Hidaldgo with hissing pleasure at his own cleverness. "A prettier little honey pot you shall never see! She left St. Pierre with him, and she is surely with him now. It is the first time in my memory that he has carried a woman with him, and how fortunate for us! All we must do is steal her away, and Fairbourne will follow."

The bosun chuckled and wiped his sleeve across his mouth. "It's been many months since we've taken an Englishwoman, Capitán."

"This one will amuse me," said Hidaldgo, remembering how the girl had fought him. "She has fire, she has spirit. What a rare joy it will be to tame the plump little pigeon! Perhaps I shall make her watch as I end her lover's worthless life, and feel her tremble with need beside me as he suffers and dies by the minutest degrees. Then I will take her, just as I will have taken the Englishman's ship, and his cargo, and his crew for slaves. Fairbourne will have nothing, and I will have all."

Hidaldgo smiled. Truly the saints had spread their blessings upon the just.

Nine

Samson stood at the rail, his hands clasped behind his back, and glanced from the twinkling lights of the Charles Towne waterfront to the companionway and quickly back to the harbor, praying again that no one else would notice. He was sure he'd already looked that way a hundred times in the last five minutes, but all that looking didn't seem to be doing one bit of good.

Furtively he patted his waistcoat pocket, where he'd tucked two treasures inside for safekeeping. The first was a necklace he'd bought the day before, a pretty little piece that had cost him far more than he'd intended to spend. The strand of coral beads was a rare pale color, perfectly matched, and, as the jeweler had been quick to point out, the ideal pink to favor any lady's complexion.

It had been easy enough for Samson to imagine the beads around Polly's throat, the pale coral nestling against her rosy-warm skin, but the necklace's pendant was what had made it irresistible to him. Set in a gleaming band of gold lay an oval Italian cameo of a mermaid, her laughing face turned in profile and her unbound hair cascading down her back to the top of her fish's tail. The carving of the shell was exquisitely done, the tiny mermaid's pale, delicate features in misty relief against a background that was nearly the same pink as the beads. She reminded Samson so much of Polly standing on the deck of the *Morning Star* that he'd paid the jeweler's exorbitant price without dickering.

Samson had told himself, and Zach, that the necklace was the final tempting portion of the wager, the last irresistible trinket calculated to free Polly's hidden wellspring of female greediness. But the explanation had sounded contrived even to Samson's ears, and the expression on his cousin's face as he'd murmured appreciatively had showed he didn't believe such pompous drivel either.

The truth was, of course, that the necklace was a peace offering, a pink coral attempt to restore the fragile bond between them that he'd trampled upon with all the intemperate insensitivity of the village bull. He didn't know why he cared so much that he be back in her good graces, but he did. He cared very much, and with an alarming, shameful desperation, too. While in direct contradiction to his side of the wager, he secretly doubted that Polly would be swayed by such blatant tribute—and doubly secretly he was proud of her for being that way—but still he gave the pocket with the cameo mermaid an extra pat for good luck.

There was a second bulge in that pocket beside the necklace, a bulge whose contents he never intended to share with anyone, least of all with Polly. It was there for luck alone, luck for *him:* wrapped up in a handkerchief, dry and crumbling and inexplicably dear, lay the rose she'd worn and given to him the night they'd kissed.

He tried telling himself that this was the act of a sentimental old spinster, that squirreling away old flowers as mementos and waxing maudlin over cameo mermaids was a disgrace to every stalwart Fairbourne man in the history of the family; but it didn't stop him, and he kept it still, and despaired of what Polly Bray had done to his sorry manhood.

Surely she should be ready by now, but he didn't dare risk looking at the companionway again. He didn't want her to catch him, and so instead he drew his watch and flicked it open, tipping the face toward the binnacle light to read the time.

Half past five. No wonder evening had settled into night. The boat had been ready for a quarter of an hour. Where was she, anyway?

"We'll be ready to clear when the tide shifts during the middle watch," said Zach with satisfaction. Unlike Samson, waiting in his shore-going best clothing, Zach was still dressed for the long day of repairs, in well-worn and mended canvas breeches, with fresh blotches of paint on the sleeves of his gingham shirt. "We're all fresh revictualed with the water casks refilled, too, and we've even had time to brighten up the paintwork to go with the new suit of sails."

Samson nodded absently. He knew all this. He'd spent these last two entire days in port seeing to it that the ship had everything necessary to complete the voyage.

"Aye, we're ready," continued Zach with satisfaction. "If it were up to the men alone, with no say from wind or weather, we'd make record time up the coast."

Samson winced as he slipped the watch back into

his pocket. It was the first time he'd gone without having his shoulder and arm bound together, but he wanted no such shows of weakness before Polly, or reminders of the circumstances in which they'd last parted.

"A record, eh?" He liked speed; in his particular kind of trading, it was a necessity. "Don't see why the men would be in a particular rush on this run, Zach."

"Because we're bound for Appledore afore Boston, Sam, that's why," said Zach. "You know we're mostly Appledore-bred, with a smatter from Yarmouth and the two topmen from Dennis, but all Cape men, with families waiting. Who wouldn't be eager to reach home?"

He wasn't, for one, thought Samson glumly, though likely he was alone in that, too. It wasn't that he'd changed his mind about going back to Appledore, but he still had his misgivings about what kind of welcome he'd find from Joshua. Three days, that was all he meant to stay—less if his brother made things unpleasant. Then with a grateful sigh he'd be off to Boston to sell their cargo and gather a new one. And finally, before he turned toward the south again, he'd keep his promise to Polly and return her to Ninnishibutt.

Ninnishibutt. He wasn't in much of a hurry to go there, either, though his reasons were far more muddled.

"Sam?" asked Zach, uncertain after so long a silence. "You do mean to sail with the morning tide, don't you?"

"Whatever else could he mean?" said Polly, suddenly standing beside his cousin. "You told me yourself, Zach, that I must never doubt a word that the captain says. Isn't that true, Captain?"

She looked at him without any other greeting, her lips curled in a slight smile, waiting for him to reply. But at first all he could do was stare at her, aghast, and swallow his immediate, stunned reaction.

While she'd kept him waiting, he'd imagined her dressing, enjoying herself as she decided among the new clothes from Madame LaFontaine's shop. He'd been anticipating the results. But what he now saw instead was the same familiar Polly in the same wretchedly familiar boy's clothes, made even more disreputable by a dark streak of paint that seemed to match the blotches on Zach's shirt. He did not want to consider how they'd come to be there.

Which of course, however, he immediately did.

It didn't help, either, to see how Zach was watching her, moon-eyed and besotted, with the same mindless devotion he lavished upon every barmaid and strumpet who tumbled into his path. Polly deserved better than that—or, more specifically, she didn't deserve a damned thing from his cousin.

"Are you ready, then?" she asked when Samson didn't answer. She glanced over the rail. "The boat seems to be, anyways."

"The boat has been ready this past half hour," he said, nearly strangled by everything he'd vowed not to say. "And so, Polly, have I."

"Then I suppose we should make use of it," she said cheerfully, ready to sling her leg over the side.

"But you're not ready! You said when we went into port that you'd dress like a—dress in your new clothes."

She paused and frowned, her neatly arched brows coming together. "For the past two nights, Samson, I did just that, and if it was a trial for Madame LaFontaine to push and prod me into a lady's shape, then for me to do it to myself was ten times the effort. But because you'd asked, I did it, and both nights my only reward was a scribble-scrabble chit from you with regrets. Regrets, hah!"

"Polly, I've been mired in drafts and billings and sailmakers, striving to set things to rights so we could sail! I couldn't come, no matter how much I wished it!"

The neat brows rose in unabashed skepticism. "Then I *regret* that I've had my fill of petticoats and stay-bones. Two nights of that was enough, Samson, more than enough, even if I must go against your orders."

"You will not dress yourself properly?"

"Nay," she said, with a smile that warned him she wasn't about to give in, or to quarrel with him about it, either. "If by 'properly' you mean in skirts, then nay, I shall not."

He thought of the coral necklace waiting in his pocket and tried to imagine it sitting ludicrously inside the fraying linen collar of her boy's shirt. He couldn't possibly give it to her now, not with her dressed like this. She'd laugh outright at the inappropriateness of such a gift, and who would blame her?

"Not even for the sake of the wager?"

"Nay," she said firmly. "Though I cannot fathom why one must be dependent upon t'other. What sort of dim-witted noddy would I be if I could change who I am as easily as I change my clothes?"

There was no answer to such a question—at least not one that wouldn't end the night immediately— and Polly knew it as well as Samson did himself. She'd won, without having to stoop to a fight, and he was left feeling both helpless and foolish.

It was not an agreeable feeling, and as the ship's boat made way across the harbor toward land, his sense of indignation grew. He forgot all the pretty speeches he'd prepared to tell her, forgot all the compliments he'd planned to offer to wipe out the unpleasantness of their last meeting. Instead he sat beside her in righteous, morose silence, the necklace like a pound of lead in his pocket.

"The ship looks very well," she ventured. "You've all done wonders to bring her back in such a short time."

He nodded curtly, unable to be gracious. "The damage was not so grievous as it first seemed."

"Mightily grievous enough!" She grinned and shook her head to toss the loose wisps of hair away from her face, and he thought with a certain dull ache of how very much she resembled the cameo mermaid.

"I've seen worse," he said. "We were lucky."

"Then perhaps my luck is changing." She pointed to a splotch of paint on the thigh of her breeches. "I did my Jonah's penance, though. I've a deft hand with a paintbrush, as Zach soon understood as we worked."

"I wish you'd be less—less familiar with my cousin," he said before he could stop himself. "It's not proper, and besides, the whelp needs no such encouragement."

She looked at him strangely. "I've been unproper again, have I? And with poor, sweet Zach?"

"He is not 'poor,' regardless of what he has told you otherwise, and he'd do a sight better keeping his sweetness to himself."

"He is good company," she said warmly, "and he

is not so proud that he won't talk to me, or explain things to me. He treats me like a *friend*, Samson, not like some empty-headed hussy to be ordered about as it suits your whim."

He'd never judged her empty-headed or a hussy, either, but it didn't seem the best time to point that out. "I don't order you about. From the first, I've treated you as my guest."

"Oh, aye," she said, raising her voice with a withering emphasis. "A guest you *kissed*."

Every man at every oar must have heard her. By the time the ship sailed in the morning, every other man in the crew would have heard it, too.

"Are you daft?" demanded Samson in a hoarse, horrified whisper. "For God's sake, keep your voice low! Do you know what will be said about you?"

"And do you believe I truly care?" she said, her voice dropping to a whisper to match his, a sadly urgent whisper that proved she cared very much indeed. "When this voyage is done, I'll never see any of you again. Besides, what could they say now that likely hasn't been said already?"

"Nothing has been said," declared Samson vehemently. "I've forbidden it."

"Oh, aye-aye, Captain," she scoffed. "You order an end to clacking tongues, and all obey."

"You listen to me, Polly—"

"Nay, you listen to me, Samson Fairbourne. You've left me plenty of time alone for thinking, and by Heaven, I've used it. All this madman's voyage I've tried to do my best by you and your blessèd wager, but I still don't know what you truly expect from me. I'm not certain you do yourself."

"You're wrong," he said automatically, without letting himself consider that she might be right. "I've told you before that all I wished of you was to be my guest."

She tipped back her head with a short, scornful laugh. "And what of all that nonsense about teaching Zach about the fickleness of women?"

"I never said that, not in those words."

"Then in words precious close. You should have brought poor Zach with us tonight, instead of banishing him to the ship again. How else is he to see how fickle I can be?"

"Fickle, nothing," he said, ignoring her question. She probably did want Zach—her poor, sweet friend—along with them—or, worse, here in the boat in place of him. "You're the most damned contrary woman I've ever met."

"I am not," she retorted. "Faith, I'm likely the most uncontrary one in all Massachusetts, maybe in all the colonies!"

"Well then, I wish you joy of your un-contrariness, Miss Bray," he said, "and I hope it keeps you warm on long winter nights."

She folded her arms over her chest and glared at him as the boat bumped against the wharf. "If you've so little use for my company this night, then you'd best order this boat around at once."

"Damnation, we're here in Charles Towne, and here we'll stay." He swept the cocked hat from the head of the startled man at the nearest oar and dropped it onto her head. "There, now cover your hair. Wouldn't want you to be *contrary*, or mistaken for the female you were born, or anything else that's *contrary* to your nature."

She shoved back the brim of the oversized hat from her eyes and scowled at him as she jabbed her braid up inside the crown. At least that way she could see out, though barely, and no one else would ever be able to make out her face in the shadow. From habit he held out his hand to help her from the boat to the wharf, but instead she bounded up ahead of him, her coattails swinging defiantly in his face.

With an oath he followed, his mood growing blacker with every step. He was angry with her, but more furious and disgusted with himself. He was a man, he was older, and he was a captain, a gentleman of responsibility and experience. Yet somehow this ignorant little fisherman's daughter could box him in so completely with her cock-a-hoop arguments that he'd stopped being reasonable himself, reacting without pausing first to think, and he hated himself for that, too. What was it about Polly Bray that made him behave like this? He felt moody and unsettled, entirely at odds with his own notion of himself. There'd been a time when he'd thought her witless, but Jesus, if anyone were mad now, it must be him.

There was no question of continuing the evening as he'd originally planned. Dressed as she was, he couldn't take her to the genteel inn he'd planned for supper, any more than he'd be able to give her the necklace. With her hair hidden beneath the hat, she looked more like a boy than ever, a wretched, willful, paint-daubed boy, that no decent house would welcome.

He glanced ahead to where she was waiting for him beside a pyramid of stacked barrels, her hands thrust into the pockets of her coat as she idly rubbed one stockinged foot against the back calf of her other leg. The wharf was full of men coming and going, none of them paying any attention to her at all, but Samson's gaze was riveted to that idle, sliding foot and the round calf in the coarse knitted stocking, his mind churning with a wealth of wicked thoughts that the simple, seductive movement set free.

He swallowed hard as she innocently tucked her foot back into her shoe. She'd been right about one thing: he didn't know what he expected from her, and the realization did nothing to improve his temper.

"Where are we going?" she asked, her small round chin raised in defiance as he took her by her upper arm.

"Supper," he said curtly, looking over her head. "But no place that will challenge you to be other than what you are."

Uneasily Polly glanced up at him. She knew she'd provoked him by not wearing the clothes he'd bought her, and the things that she'd said in the boat, though they'd needed saying, were likely nothing he'd wished to hear. They seemed to be always like this, at constant sixes and sevens, so much so that she'd come to expect it as part of the odd tangle that bound them together.

But there was a different quality in his voice now, a new hardness to it that made her wonder if she'd pushed him too far, if perhaps her Jonah's ill luck had finally swung around toward her alone.

"You will not tell me the name of this place, Samson?" she asked, trying to twist her arm from his grasp to take his hand instead. "Surely it must have one."

"The sign above the door is of a blue goat with yellow horns and grapes," he said carelessly, his fingers easily denying her efforts to escape. "I've never bothered to learn any name beyond that, nor will any of the others inside care, either."

A yellow-horned goat did not sound promising,

not the way a rampant lion or a king's head might, nor did she care for the way Samson had said it. He was holding her so tightly now that she had to concentrate on matching her pace to his, or stumble. She shoved the oversized hat back from her forehead, trying to will him to look at her again. She couldn't read his mood tonight at all, and fervently she wished that he'd decided to return to the ship after all, where at least she'd have Zach to turn to.

Yet as he hurried her from the long wharf to the streets alongside the waterfront, she found herself grateful for the way he held her close at his side. She had always heard that Charles Towne was a lovely, elegant city, one of the most beautiful in the colonies, but there was nothing elegant or beautiful about the places they were seeing now.

The bright flowers and French gaiety of Martinique had been left far behind with the warmer south, and a sour November wind from the river chilled Polly through her worn linen coat. The streets were narrow and unpaved save for a sticky, packed mud, and here near the water most of the buildings seemed to be either shops, shuttered and dark for the night, or looming brick warehouses with padlocked doors. Dramshops, taverns, and boardinghouses that catered to sailors crowded together as drunkenly as their patrons, their windows and doors thrown open to the street.

Raucous laughter and bellowed excuses for singing, a shrill song played on a fiddle or flute, and the sounds of inevitable quarrels drifted into the night, while men and women continued their entertainment outdoors against the warehouse walls with an enthusiastic openness that made Polly flush and swiftly look away, miserably ashamed to have seen such sights in Samson's company. Not that he seemed to notice; he might have been walking along an empty beach for all the effect his surroundings had on his expression, and she uneasily realized again how little she really knew of him or his past.

Finally he guided Polly toward a large brick tavern angled into the corner of two streets, and as they passed through the doorway Polly looked up at the signboard overhead; by lanternlight the yellow-horned goat was the most lascivious creature she'd ever seen, its leering eyes nearly crossed, while a misshapen bunch of wine grapes dangled suggestively from its mouth.

She did not want to be here. She wished desperately that she were back in her snug little cabin aboard the *Morning Star* or, better yet, aboard her poor lost *Dove*. Yet as awful as this evening was becoming, she couldn't complain to Samson. She was the one who hadn't wished to play at being genteel, a sham lady, and now, Lord help her, he was treating her exactly as she'd wished.

In the hallway they were stopped as much as greeted by the keeper, a one-legged man who introduced himself as McCall, perched on a tall stool and flanked by a pair of thick-armed black men in incongruous white wigs. The keeper bowed grandly from his stubby waist, even as he shrewdly appraised them from head to toe, deciding whether they were worthy of admission. His eyes narrowed suspiciously over Polly's appearance, then considered Samson's well-cut coat and polished buttons with more approval. Finally McCall nodded, a signal to the two guards to let them pass, and with a tobacco-stained grin he waved his hand toward the noisy room to the left.

"You are most welcome to my house, good sirs,

welcome indeed," he boomed over the mingled
sounds of pewter tankards and crockery thumped
and scraped on bare board tables, laughter and voices
grown raucous with drink. "The company's the best
to be found in Charles Towne this night, sirs, and the
entertainment's choice, most choice. The lasses are
young and fresh, er, ah—"

He broke off with a sudden cough, staring so
pointedly at Polly's face in the shadow of her hat's
brim that she flushed as he continued. "Master De
Lancey's brought his best emerald cockerel from the
country to take on all comers, good sirs, in the pit
directly to the back. A quarter hour hence, but time
enough to fill your glass and lay down your bets.
They say this cockerel's a most cunning bird. Good
sport, sirs, and a pleasant evening!"

"That man may be a rogue," she said to Samson as
they moved along to make room for other newcom-
ers, "but at least he had the decency not to insult me
to my face. 'Fresh lasses,' ha!"

"McCall didn't give a damn about insulting you,"
said Samson. "He thinks I'm your keeper and I've no
interest in any lasses, fresh or otherwise."

Polly frowned, not understanding. "My keeper?"

"A pederast. A man who prefers the charms of
pretty young boys to those of women."

"Oh," said Polly, suddenly understanding far more
than she wished. "*Oh.*"

"But I shouldn't worry," continued Samson as he
scanned the crowded room before them through the
haze of tobacco smoke. "Given the company here at
the Blue Goat, you won't be mistaken for a lady,
either."

One quick glance proved how right he was. These
women in their bright satin gowns and pinchbeck

jewels, their cheeks and chins patched with black spots and their necklines so low that more of their tight-laced breasts were bared than covered, were most definitely not ladies. Nor were they either fresh or young, as promised, but bold and shrill and terrifyingly confident of their effect on the men around them.

Unconsciously Polly shrank closer to Samson's side. She thought of all the times she'd defended herself as a good decent woman, no slattern, yet she'd done it without any real notion of what a true slattern was. She glanced up at Samson, and her heart sank as she saw how intently he was watching a saucy blond woman with a trilling laugh and an astounding bosom who was dealing cards to a fascinated table of men. Was this the kind of woman he preferred, then? She could never be any more like that than she could become a grand lady, and her heart sank even lower.

"What shall you have to drink?" asked Samson as a barmaid hovered before them. "We won't get our supper until we can get a table to ourselves, after the cockfight. There's wine and rum, punch, flips, toddies, and port, of course, but the Goat's best known for its persimmon beer."

"Persimmon beer," she said in a small voice. "If you please."

From habit Samson ordered rum for himself, his gaze not leaving Polly. Earlier this visit to the Goat had seemed such a good idea, to prove to her that she wasn't nearly as tough-minded and independent as she thought she was. What better way to teach her a lesson than to show her a glimpse of the harder, rougher side of common life that didn't exist in a place like Ninnishibutt?

God knows the Blue Goat wasn't the lowest place

in Charles Towne. By comparison to some it was
downright genteel, but still he'd guessed that the
leering, one-legged keep would be enough to make
Polly turn tail and run, straight into his own waiting
arms. He'd been willing to be gracious and forgiving,
and he expected the same, with a dash of meekness,
from her. At the time he'd been angry enough for it
all to make perfect sense.

But she hadn't bolted the way he'd expected, and
even now, in a room full of drunkards and harlots,
she stubbornly held her ground, with them and with
him. Not even being mistaken for a sailor's catamite
had made her do more than blink. Damnation, how
was he going to shock some sense into her if she
continued like this?

He heard the girl at the card table laugh again,
shrill enough to make him grind his teeth. She called
herself Belinda, and last spring it had taken a good
five guineas to separate Zach from her enthusiastic
embrace. He was surprised to see her still here at the
Goat; young and pretty as she was, he'd assumed by
now she would have charmed some poor idiot into
keeping her, or even into marriage. Women like her
were the reason he'd been driven to hurl that bottle
into the bay at Bridgetown in the first place.

He frowned absently to himself, and Belinda
slipped from his thoughts. Since Polly had come into
his life and he and Zach had made that damned
wager, he'd wanted to forget all about the bottle and
the wish for an ideal wife that he'd thrust inside.

What the Devil was it about Zach's weaknesses
that made *him* commit such rash, impulsive gestures?
He was not superstitious—no question of that—yet
since he'd thrown that bottle, his life had lost all of its
tidy, predictable order, and these last few days, with

Hidaldgo reappearing and the strange, unnatural storm, and popping his shoulder, had been among the most oddly eventful of his life.

And at the core of everything was Polly.

Uneasily he glanced down at her now, her face nearly hidden beneath that ridiculous oversized hat. He longed to throw that hat away the same way that he had her knitted cap, but he didn't want the rest of these rogues and rascals to discover her for the beauty she truly was. "Fresh," that was the word that the tavernkeeper had used to describe the painted and powdered hussies here in his bar parlor; if he'd seen Polly, he'd understand what "fresh" could really mean in a woman.

He could tell from the way she was standing—as close as she could without actually touching him— that she was unhappy and intensely uncomfortable. He couldn't blame her; he wasn't particularly enjoying himself either. All she needed to do to end their combined misery was to admit that she wished to go. That was all: she wouldn't even have to say that he'd been right, or admit that she really preferred that pretty little supper place with the tall window in St. Pierre. A handful of words to describe her unhappiness, and they'd leave.

But instead she was taking the tankard of persimmon beer from the barmaid's tray as easily as if she'd a lifetime of tippling behind her. She took a deep swallow and barely managed to turn a choking sound into a cough.

"'Tis—'tis very good," she gasped out, her eyes teary, as she wiped the crest of foam from her upper lip with her sleeve. "Though a bit tart."

He wanted to tell her to stop being so damned stubborn when a tumultuous cry rose from the next room, and people began swarming excitedly toward the doorway.

"The cockfight," said Polly over the din. "We should be going, too, shouldn't we?"

He winced as someone jostled against his shoulder. He hated cockfighting, the bloody spectacle of two crazed birds ripping one another apart while the crowd alternately cheered and cursed over the enormous sums they'd lost or won over some poor dead rooster whose body would be tossed on the offal pile. He was certain that Polly would feel the same if she'd ever seen such a fight.

But obviously, from the anticipation on her face, she hadn't.

"Come along, Samson," she coaxed, for the first time daring to take his sleeve. "Mr. McCall promised it would be fine entertainment. Wouldn't you like to see how Master De Lancey's country-bred emerald fares?"

He would not; but already they were being swept with the others toward the back yard, a small court before the stable and enclosed by tall brick walls. Hanging from the walls were cressets, like openwork iron cradles, filled with bright-burning pine knots to light the fight. The small space was packed with men and a scattering of women, all of them crowding and elbowing one another or climbing on benches to find the best view. In the center, marked by a low square fence, was the pit, or ring, in which the birds would fight.

Evidently a number of fights were planned for the evening: to one side stood a long row of the tall, closed wicker baskets holding the cocks until their matches. But there was no mistaking who would be first—the celebrated emerald—nor was there any question as to who Master De Lancey himself was. A stout gentleman with a long wig, sleepy eyes, and a bright green velvet coat to match his bird, he leaned upon a silver-headed cane while his slave held the bird up in two hands, high in the air for all to see. Coins and drafts passed back and forth as the wagers grew, the shouted odds shifting by the second.

"Ohh, what a lovely rooster!" said Polly, craning her neck to see better. "No wonder he's called the emerald, with a fine ruff of feathers like that! But what are those long silver things tied to his legs, I wonder?"

"His spurs," said Samson. "Clearly De Lancey's gentleman enough to wish his bird to have every advantage, even sterling fighting spurs from London."

Polly frowned, not understanding, and with a sigh he continued to explain. "True sportsmen believe the birds will fight better if they're armed, much like men. Those long spurs are sharp as swords, and they'll make short work of the other lackless bird if he's not careful. See how his comb and wattles have been cut and his tail feathers cropped, too, to give his opponent less to grab or bite. It's all part of the match."

"Final wagers, gentlemen," roared the starter. "Final wagers!"

Eagerly Polly stood up on her toes to look over the others, one arm against Samson for support. Cockfights had never been in fashion in Massachusetts—there chickens were thriftily bred for laying and the stewpot, not the ring—but of course she'd heard of fights as a great sport of the gentry, and who knew when she'd have the chance to see one again?

She could see the second cockerel now, a dull black

bird with a scrawny, overlong neck, no challenge to the emerald for being her favorite. The black bird wore spurs as well, though made from brass instead of silver, just as his owner wore plain broadcloth instead of velvet.

"I'll take the emerald," she said excitedly to Samson. "Look at how bright his eyes are! Mr. McCall was right: he's far too cunning to lose."

"You won't get me to argue one way or the other," said Samson dryly. "I've had my fill of wagers for now."

With a roar of anticipation from the onlookers, the two birds were simultaneously dropped into the center of the ring. For one brief moment they spiked out their feathers and thrust out their necks, drumming their wings against their bodies as they taunted each other with rasping screeches. Then the emerald flew at the black, driving his long silver spurs into the other bird's back as the crowd shouted its encouragement. Together the two birds fought, twisting and turning, biting and stabbing over and over so fast that they merged into a single tangle of feathers and yellow legs, their unearthly shrieks of challenge and pain nearly lost in the fevered oaths and shouts.

On some cue that Polly missed, the slave suddenly dived in between the two birds, separating them with a flat-bladed shovel to give them each a rest. Swiftly he raised De Lancey's bird into the air to display it again to the surging, feverish roar of the audience, and Polly gasped with horror. The emerald's yellow legs still flailed in the air, the firelight glinting off the cruel silver spurs dripping with crimson, while his head jerked oddly to one side. He twisted again, still proud, and showed the bloody place where his black eye had shown so bright.

"Oh, dear God, Samson, look!" she cried, sickened. "They'll stop the fight now, won't they?"

But Samson's expression didn't change, his face hard and emotionless as he watched the twitching, half-blinded rooster held high in the air.

"Not until one of them is dead, and the other close to it," he said over the blood-crazed din of the others. "Like men as well, that's how the game is played."

Her stomach lurched ominously. The sight of the beautiful bird so brutally disfigured, the near-hysterical crowd that would be satisfied only with a death that would make half of them richer, half poorer, the coolly impassive way that Samson was watching—she couldn't bear to be a part of it any longer. She turned and pushed her way between two apprentices, squeezing a zigzagging path through the jostling sea of people, back toward the tavern. If Samson was hardhearted enough to wish to stay, then he was welcome to, but she wasn't about to remain there with him.

"*Cochino torpe!*" growled one man, shoving her aside so roughly that she stumbled.

"Aye, and pardon yourself, too, you great clumsy noddy!" She turned back to glare at him, a burly, menacing man with a dark curling beard and thick gold rings in each ear, and as she did, he raised his balled fist to cuff her.

"*Bastardo estupi—*"

"*Fernando!*" barked another man impatiently. "*No es para tanto!*"

The bearded man's fist dropped reluctantly to his side, though he snarled one final threat.

But Polly wasn't listening; instead she was staring past him at the other who'd ordered him to stop. She was certain she'd recognized his voice, the coiled tension that came through even in the foreign words. In the shifting, raucous crowd, she couldn't at first be sure who had spoken, or so she tried to tell herself as her heart raced and her palms grew damp with dread. She could be wrong, she could be mistaken. This part of the world must be full of Spanish men.

Then a thickset man ahead of her turned gallantly to greet a barmaid with two pitchers of ale. He lifted his hat to the girl, smiling while he murmured some bit of flattery that made her laugh. The light from the burning cresset overhead washed over the the rich red velvet on his broad shoulders, the glittering golden braid that flowed down the front of his coat and around his cuffs. His gaze wandered over Polly without any interest or recognition before it returned, avidly, to the barmaid. As the girl tried to pass him, he reached out to run his open hand possessively along her back, finally bunching her petticoats to caress her bottom.

"Ah, *cara*," he said, laughing again as the girl deftly defended herself with a well-flung elbow. "You do not like my loving, eh?"

Polly looked away, hiding beneath her hat, her heart pounding with terror, and hoped the man's memory was shorter than her own.

Hidaldgo was here, and he'd come for Samson.

Ten

*P*olly turned and let herself sink back into the crowd, praying that Hidaldgo wouldn't realize who she was. As much as she wished to run, she knew she couldn't dare risk attracting attention to herself that way, and instead she forced herself to move slowly, the same as anyone else attempting to make their way through the press of people. She heard the Spaniard laugh once—she'd never forget his laugh, not after St. Pierre—but when she glanced back over her shoulder, he was gone, lost too among the others, and she allowed herself a tiny sigh of relief that, dressed as she was, he hadn't recognized her.

But that smidgen of relief was by necessity short-lived. She had to find Samson and warn him at once. They had to return to the ship and slip away again, just as they had in St. Pierre. Then it had been easy. This time would be different, for this time they'd lost all the advantage of surprise. This time, Hidaldgo was deliberately hunting them, and unlike Samson, Polly didn't share his constant belief that luck would always shine the English way.

She paused at the doorway to the tavern, searching

back across the sea of heads for Samson. He was so
tall that he usually stood out, but now he'd disappeared behind the men and boys who had climbed
on benches or barrels for a better view of the cockfight. She remembered where she'd left him, near the
front of the crowd, and if she could circle around
through the inn's second doorway and back into the
courtyard, then perhaps she could reach him before
Hidaldgo did.

She hurried back into the now nearly empty parlor,
past the tables with half-finished meals and playing
cards dropped in the middle of games. She caught a
glimpse of herself in a looking glass, her hair beginning to trail down in straggling pieces from beneath
the hat, ready to betray her gender. Impatiently she
paused to shove it back into the hat's crown, when
suddenly another face appeared beside her own in
the looking glass.

"Zach!" she gasped, barely stopping herself from
throwing her arms around his shoulders with a
gratitude no decent boy would show. "Oh, Zach,
Zach, I'm so glad that you've—"

"Where's Sam?" His customary grin was missing,
and instead his mouth was drawn into a tight bow of
anxiety. "I have to talk to him now."

"So do I." She took a deep breath before she
lowered her voice to an urgent whisper. "Hidaldgo's
here, Zach, in this place, and you know as well as—"

"Here? In this tavern?"

Polly nodded, and Zach swore and struck his fist
against the table beside her.

"That's why I've come," he said bitterly. "I saw
Hidaldgo's ship, and I wanted to warn him, but
now—now I'm too bleeding *late.*"

"Nay, don't say that!" whispered Polly fiercely.

"We have to find him before Hidaldgo does, that's all!"

"Not 'we,' Polly," he said firmly. "*I* do. Plunkett and Isaac are outside in the street. You go to them, and they'll see you safe back to the ship, the way Sam would want."

"He would not!" she said indignantly. "He would—"

"Oh, dearest sir, it *is* you!" cried the young blond woman whom Polly had noticed earlier at the card table. She snaked her hands around Zach's waist in a proprietary manner, resting her cheek against his shoulder and leaving a large circle of white face powder on his coat. "You cannot know how I have suffered since you sailed away!"

"Ah, good evening, Belinda," said Zach as he tried to wriggle free. Polly had never seen a man look more wretchedly ill at ease, or a woman more persistent. "But I've no time now, sweet."

"You are deucedly cruel." She pouted, her voice buttery as she thrust her breasts as close as she could to his face. "That you would cast me off so roughly, my own darling!"

"Zach," said Polly, already beginning to inch away. "I'm going back, whether with you or without."

Belinda frowned at Polly, her eyes losing all of their sweetness as her gaze raked her from head to feet, perceiving everything female that men seemed willing to miss.

"*You* are not a boy," she said scornfully, "though certainly plain enough to pass for one. My dearest Richard is already spoken for—we were practically betrothed last autumn before his bastard of a cousin came meddling—and I'll thank you to take your nasty self elsewhere."

There wasn't much sweetness left in Polly, either, not after hearing Samson described like that. "How joyful for you and Richard," she said tartly, "but how much more fortunate for *dearest* Zach. Now hurry, Zach, hurry now, you dawdling clodpate!"

"'Richard'?" repeated Zach indignantly. "'*Richard*'?"

"Just stow it, Zach," said Polly as she grabbed his hand and yanked him along with her. "Stow it now! You're every bit as bad as Samson says. Don't you care about all the good things he's done for you? Does that empty-headed little tart mean more to you than Samson's life?"

"It wasn't the way you think it is!"

"Oh, nay, surely not," she said with breathless disgust. "Likely it's a great deal worse."

They ran through the hallway and into the kitchen, which, like the bar parlor, had been left deserted by the cockfight. The second door to the court was blocked by the sizable cook and her maidservants, but the high, wide-open window had only two small boys perched on the sill. Swiftly Zach clambered up beside them, hauling Polly after him, and together they paused, crouched on the sill as they searched for Samson.

That was how Samson saw them from the far side of the courtyard: sitting cheek to jowl, her hand in his, for all the world like a pair of lovebirds on a branch. Here he'd been torturing himself over how his foul temper must have driven Polly away, his dread growing each moment he'd spent combing the crowd for her, when she'd disappeared from his side only to reappear at his cousin's.

And what the Devil was Zach doing *here,* anyway, let alone holding Polly's hand? Why wasn't he still on board the *Morning Star*, where he was supposed to be? God only knows his cousin was weak where women were concerned, notoriously weak, but could he be so infatuated with Polly Bray that he'd abandon his post and his responsibilities for her? And could Polly, surely the most sensible and seaworthy woman he'd ever met, expect him to make such a sacrifice for her?

He watched them there together, unable to force himself to look away. He should be angry, furious, raging at them both; but instead he felt an exhausting sadness, strangely empty and oddly abandoned. They were two of the people he cared most for in the world—he could admit that to himself, if to neither of them—yet seemingly they'd found a part of that same world that excluded him. It was not their fault, neither of them, but his, the result of his own inability to tell them what he thought or believed or, God help him, what he *felt*, deep in the muffled darkness of his heart.

Yet even as he watched them, even as he wrestled with his own feelings, a marvelous thing happened. Clear across the courtyard, over a score of shifting heads and shoulders, Polly lifted her face and looked directly at him, as neatly as if she'd been told where he stood.

She looked, and she smiled, her whole face glowing with joy beneath the black-brimmed hat, and he knew that joy was for him alone. For *him*: the rest of the world, including Zach, ceased to matter, or even exist, and when he stepped forward from the wall and grinned in return, he didn't give a damn who saw. He felt as if she'd been gone for weeks, not minutes, and so he meant to tell her as soon as he could.

As if sliding into water Polly dropped effortlessly

from the sill, while belatedly Zach reached for her, his hand this time empty. Samson lost sight of her then, but he wasn't about to lose her twice. He plunged into the crowd himself, impatient to reach her, and reach her he did. He caught her hand and pulled her close, ignoring her startled little yelp to lift her off her feet and into his arms. He held her, just held her, while she wriggled a bit and tried to scold him. He laughed, and she cuffed his ear, and he laughed again at the peculiar glances of the others around him before he finally set her back down.

"What in blazes are you *doing*?" she demanded, flustered and sputtering, her cheeks bright pink in the flickering light. "Of all the ridiculous, rampaging—"

"I thought I'd lost you," he said. "I'm glad to have you back."

She scowled. "Faith, how would I have become lost? I wished to get away from that wretched cock-fight, that was all."

His smile widened. Strange how she'd become utterly charming to him this way, whenever she turned all rosy and squawky and indignant over nothing. "Your bird won, you know."

But still she scowled, shaking her head, too, for extra emphasis. "Mind me, Samson! There's no more time for this dimwitted foolishness! We must leave now, at once—oh, *oh*, bother!"

A red-faced tradesman's exuberant elbow had knocked her hat askew, and when she reached up to catch it she managed instead to tip it completely off the back of her head. Her unraveling braid flopped down her back and the stray wisps fell over her face, and a ripple of surprised chuckles and exclamations around them marked the end of her disguise, even among drunkards at night. With an exasperated snort that almost tempted Samson unwisely to laugh again, Polly glared at them all as she bent to retrieve her hat.

And then, over her back, not a dozen paces away in the crowd, Samson saw Hidaldgo. By some optical trick or of the flickering light, the Spaniard had not yet seen him in return, but there was no doubt in Samson's mind that he'd seen Polly, his gaze intent upon her as she straightened and stuffed her hair back under her hat, his mouth curved in a delighted smile of recognition and triumph as he beckoned to another man beside him.

Hidaldgo in Charles Towne, farther north than he'd ever come before. Hidaldgo here, for no other reason than to come after me. And after Polly: the Spaniard's grinning jackal's face proved that. Jesus, how have I let myself grow so careless?

An animal roar rose from the crowd as another cockfight ended, and as the winning, bloodied bird was hoisted into the air as the victor, the men and boys once again surged forward with excitement, blocking Hidaldgo from sight. Instantly Samson grabbed Polly's hand and began to run, pushing a path through the others for them. To his surprise she didn't try to argue with him or demand to know his reasons but ran along with him, her fingers holding tight to his.

He didn't go back through the tavern, choosing instead the less obvious way through the stable. Their footsteps muffled by straw, they ran past the box stalls, past the nodding noses of curious horses, past a startled cat that drew back and hissed at them. To Samson's relief, they met no grooms or stablemen, all apparently in the courtyard instead of at their posts; no horse, however observant, would be able to betray them to Hidaldgo the way a groom would.

At the far wall they stopped, breathing hard, while Samson climbed a narrow ladder to unlatch the single high door, used for delivering fresh straw from wagons in the street outside.

"Hurry, oh, *hurry!*" whispered Polly, an unnecessary urging if ever there was one.

"Hush." With both hands Samson wrenched at the door, the wood swollen tight in the damp night air. "You haven't even asked why we're in such a blessèd hurry."

"Why should I?" She looked up at him strangely, her hands on her hips. "*I'm* the one who came to warn you, and considering—"

His hand jerked up to silence her as he heard the footsteps, running as their own had been. Swiftly he drew the pistol from inside his coat and cocked it. He didn't look when Polly gasped, trusting her to keep silent after that, and she did. Damnation, he *did* trust her, in this and in everything else—a startling realization he'd have to consider later. A horse whinnied, but there was no other sound except the hammering of his own heart and the footsteps coming closer. He prayed the gunpowder was dry. There wasn't time to check it.

He didn't want to have to kill anyone. Not tonight, not when he'd felt happier than he had in years, and especially not in front of Polly. But he didn't want to die, either, and for exactly the same reasons.

The footsteps were closer now, and he steadied his nerves as he steadied the gun in his hand. The footsteps paused: was it hesitation, or was their pursuer checking his gun as well? What was—

"Jesus, Sam!" sputtered Zach as he came around the last stall. "Do you want to kill me outright?"

"Give me another half reason, and I will," growled

Samson as he uncocked the pistol and thrust it back into his belt. "Now stop creeping about like a thief and help me with this blasted door."

Polly held the ladder as Zach climbed up, too. "It would have been your own fault if he'd shot you, you know," she said accusingly. "He was *ready*. I could see it in his eyes."

Zach ignored her. "Sam, Hidaldgo's here in Charles Towne. We sighted the *San Miguel* in the river right after you shoved off."

"You knew *then*?" Samson twisted about, appalled. "So why the Devil didn't you take Polly back to the ship directly, where she'd be safe, instead of sitting there in the window playing patty-hands?"

"Because *I* wouldn't go," said Polly with an exasperated sigh. "Zach tried to make me, but I wouldn't leave you behind. Now will you two open that infernal door or must I come up and do it for you?"

As if that were threat enough, the door suddenly gave way beneath Samson's forcing, swinging outward with a groan.

"You go first, Sam," said Zach, standing lower on the ladder. "I'll help Polly."

"The hell you will! As if I'd ever trust her with you after—"

"I don't need a fig's worth of help from either one of you!" hissed Polly. "Now go, both of you!"

She was right, as she was far too often, and reluctantly Samson went first through the door, dropping to the street with a grunt and immediately sliding back into the shadows along the wall as he scanned the surrounding streets and alleys. Clear enough so far, but there were no guarantees that Hidaldgo and his men wouldn't appear beyond the next corner.

Zach dropped heavily beside him, turning at once to hold his arms up toward Polly.

"Here, lass, I'll catch you!" he called gallantly as she pulled herself into the door.

Samson glanced at him with pity. He knew perfectly well what would come next, and he was surprised Zach didn't, too.

Surprised, but not displeased. As easily as if she were sliding from her bed, Polly dropped from the window to the street without squandering so much as a single look for Zach and his helpfully outstretched arms.

"Scrod," she said with a scornful sniff as she took Samson's hand, and without another word the three of them began to run through the streets toward the water.

She ran well, as fast as a boy in her boy's clothing, fast enough to make him and Zach work to keep up. In St. Pierre she hadn't been nearly as swift—in fact he recalled having to half carry her the last way to the boat—but then she'd been dressed as she should be, as a woman. Could her arguments against suitable clothing really have that much truth to them? Glancing down at her now, he rather hoped they didn't; she was still Polly, of course, regardless of what she wore, but what use would her ragamuffin self ever find for his coral beads and cameo?

At the beginning of the wharf he pulled them up short against the wall of a shuttered shop, purposefully thrusting aside for now all thoughts of appropriate dress for women.

"Any notion of where the Spanish boat would be?" he asked Zach softly. He could make out their own, still tied peacefully enough to the end of the wharf where they'd left it. He recognized Plunkett's hatless head, too, there by the light of a lantern, and he guessed—no, he prayed—the others were nearby as well.

Zach nodded. "The *San Miguel* is moored farther downriver, so I'd say their boat is there, too."

Samson groaned. "Meaning that the *San Miguel* lies between the *Morning Star* and the sea?"

"Aye-aye, sir," said Zach, turning deferential with the unhappiness of this news. "Though with the new canvas, we're bound to be faster than they."

"Oh, yes, and pigs can fly, too, if they wish hard enough." He'd almost forgotten that he still held Polly's hand until he felt the pressure of her fingers against his, a small, secret squeeze of comfort shared as she stared out along the wharf the same way as he and Zach. For her sake he hoped she wasn't considering their future with the same bleak misgivings that he was himself.

He sighed and awkwardly patted her hand in return. "High time, then, for these pigs to fly as best they can. If we can set sail before Hidaldgo does, we might have a chance, eh?"

"I'll go first," said Zach as he quickly pushed away from the safety of the shadows and headed along the wharf toward the boat before Samson could wish him well.

Brave, foolish puppy, thought Samson as he anxiously watched his cousin's back. If Hidaldgo's men were watching the *Morning Star*'s boat—which, if they'd any sense, they would be—then Zach would be their first target.

But the wharf remained quiet, empty except for a handful of the usual idlers and sailors from other vessels, and as soon as Zach reached the boat the oarsmen gathered, too, swiftly settling into their places on the benches. Zach waved once, a noncommittal wave that, if observed, could just as easily be intended for another boat in the harbor as for Samson and Polly.

Samson smiled to himself, proud as any father of his first mate's foresight; he was turning out well, his young cousin. If God saw fit to let them all survive this night, he'd see the boy got a command of his own for his next voyage.

"Our turn now, lass," he said softly to Polly. "As fast as you can without running."

She tipped back the brim of the oversized hat and smiled, her face flushed from running and wisps of hair clinging damply to her forehead. "Cheerily, cheerily?"

"Cheerily it is," he declared with as much conviction as he could muster. The wind was freshening, from the west, giving them more of a chance. Yet as they hurried down the wharf Samson still studied the faces of the few men they passed for danger, every barrel they passed, every stacked box, for a lurking Spaniard, while Polly effected an almost jaunty swagger, swinging her arms and whistling tunelessly as if she'd not a care under Heaven. Perhaps, being Polly, she didn't.

"All clear, lads?" he asked when they'd finally reached the waiting boat. He couldn't share Polly's nonchalance, for he knew what she didn't: that the worst was still before them. But his men did, and for their sake he made his voice as hearty and confident as he could, even reaching down to clap the nearest on the shoulder. "Ready to pull for the ship, and for home?"

"All clear, Sam," answered Zach. "But where's Polly?"

Samson's head whipped around. Only a second ago she'd been here beside him, whistling happily as a little sparrow. Now she was gone, vanished as completely as if that sparrow had flown away. Frantic, he began striding back down the wharf. Damnation, why hadn't he kept her hand—and the rest of her—when he'd had it? Why had he let her go, even for that moment?

Suddenly he heard a low cry of pain and surprise, followed by a dulled splash. He raced to where the sound had come, from behind a stack of hogsheads full of indigo. She was there, alone, standing on the edge of the wharf with her back to him and Plunkett's hat in one hand. Though the unspoken prayer of thanks he sent heavenward came straight from his heart, he still realized uneasily that something in the way her shoulders sagged and how she was staring at the water was not quite right.

"Polly, sweet, here," he called softly, not wishing to startle her into tumbling into the water herself. "The boat's waiting."

"I had to save Plunkett's hat," she said plaintively, without turning. "The wind took it straight from my head and down the wharf. But I couldn't let it go, Samson. I know what it's like to lose a good hat."

"I'll buy you and Plunkett both all the hats you want," said Samson carefully. "Now come, lass, come with me."

She nodded and turned, and then he saw the dark blood spattered across the front of her jacket and the knife, her knife, still clutched tight in her fingers.

"I caught the hat, and the—the man caught me," she continued, her voice trembling. "And oh, Samson, I know you told me not to fight back, but I couldn't help it. He called me a—something wicked that wasn't English.''

''Was it Spanish?'' He would have wagered his soul it was, but he needed to be sure.

She nodded. ''He was one of Hidaldgo's men, I know it. He tried to hit me, Samson, and that made me so angry that I—I drew my knife. And I—I used it, and he fell backward into the water, and I think . . . I'm afraid that he's . . .''

He held his arms out to her, but she shook her head. ''I'm not going to cry, Samson,'' she said unsteadily. ''I'm going to be brave instead.''

''You already are,'' he said softly. ''Now why don't you come with me so you can give Plunkett back his hat.''

This time she agreed, coming to rest her head against his shoulder with a tired little sigh. He knew what was hurting her. He'd suffered the same way himself, and it never grew any easier to bear.

But as overjoyed as he was that the blood on her clothes wasn't hers, he knew they shouldn't linger here. If he'd heard the man's cry, then others would have as well, and the last thing he and Polly needed now was to have to answer some watchman's over-particular questions. As swiftly as he could, he guided her back to the boat, onto her seat beside him in the sternsheets. On every face he saw the same worry and question about the blood on her jacket; for her sake, for now, he left it unanswered.

Gently he prised the knife from her fingers and dipped it over the side to clean away the blood from the blade. He wiped it dry and handed it back to her. She silently ran her fingertip along the steel blade, nodded once, and slipped it back into the sheath at her waist.

"If he's dead, it's likely the fall that killed him, not you," said Samson quietly, for her ears alone. "He was alive when he fell. I heard him. Likely he struck his head on a rock or piling."

"I know." She glanced up at him, her eyes full of sorrow in the moonlight. "I only cut his arm. But I'd never done that before, Samson. Never. Father taught me how to fight for myself like that, but he didn't tell me how hard it would be to—to *win*."

"If he was lucky, your father never found that out for himself." He rested his hand over hers, trying not to think of how close he'd come to really losing her. "But you *were* brave."

"Nay, I was only mad, madder than blazes," she said wistfully. "That's not the same thing at all."

"Maybe not, but you'd be surprised how often the one passes for the other."

"Then I'd rather not be surprised like that again." She sighed and took Plunkett's hat from her knee. She leaned forward to where he was pulling on the first oar, and with both hands she settled it upon the startled sailor's head.

"I thank you for the loan of your hat, sir, indeed I do," she said loudly. "And for your trouble, your captain has offered to buy you another, as fine as you wish. I heard him myself, for he's offered a new one to me, too."

Plunkett beamed, too dumbstruck to answer, as his companions chuckled and guffawed around him. Samson smiled, too, though for other reasons. Polly'd just won the loyalty, and the hearts, of every other man in this boat. As if she needed any more in her collection, he thought wryly. But she could make all the denials she wished: she *was* brave, not only for a woman but among men as well, and that would earn a sailor's devotion for life.

Leastways it seemed to be doing so for *him*. Strange how he'd never accounted bravery a great virtue in a woman. Now, thanks to Polly, he'd rank it near the top of desirable qualities. But his greatest hope was that he could squeak her home free from Charles Towne without her having to test that bravery again.

"Wind's changing, Sam," said Zach. He'd come to shore in a hired boat before and now sat squeezed in among the sailors. "In our favor, too, I'd say."

Samson didn't answer. The changing wind would only matter if they could set their sails before Hidaldgo's men. In an out-and-out race, the *Morning Star* would always win. She'd been built for speed, lean and narrow and light, while the *San Miguel* was large and sturdy in the Spanish fashion, her broad beam designed both to withstand the hurricanes that plagued her Caribbean home waters and to carry the large crew necessary for capturing smugglers. But if the *Morning Star* wasn't able to reach the open water, speed wouldn't matter. They'd be trapped.

"What I don't understand is why we have to run at all," said Polly innocently. "Carolina is an English colony, and we are English. Won't they take our side against Hidaldgo if we chose to stay here instead?"

The look that Zach flashed Samson's way said a great deal that first mates weren't supposed to say to their captains, and none of it was flattering.

"It's, ah, not that easy, Polly," began Sam, every bit as uncomfortable as Zach had suspected he'd be. "I told you before that our trade isn't, ah, isn't exactly as His Majesty might wish. Given the choice between a squabble with the King of Spain or saving our lowly hides, I'm afraid he'd choose his kingly brother and toss us right back to Hidaldgo and a prison in Havana, if not into his own gaol right here in Charles Towne. So, as for looking for help from that fine English fort out there near the bar, on Sullivan's Island—no, lass, I do believe we'll fare better looking after ourselves."

But though he braced himself for the righteous outburst from Polly that he was sure would follow, this time it didn't come. Instead she merely twisted her mouth to one side and scowled absently, thinking.

"Does Hidaldgo have cannon on his ship?" she asked finally.

"Oh, at least a score," said Zach gloomily. "And the men to use them."

"Which means you do not wish to fall into firing range," said Polly. "Nay, don't deny it, Samson. For all that you've guns of your own on deck, I've never once seen any of you practice firing them, which I know must be done daily to have any accuracy at all. You might not even have an ounce of gunpowder on board, let alone shot. Those guns of yours might not even fire."

"Of course they fire," said Samson defensively. Bravery was all well and good in a woman, but this alarming degree of perception was something else. "And they scare away most meddlers. But generally I'd rather leave fancy practiced gunnery to the navy men who don't mind dying for the sake of glory."

"Or to Hidaldgo?"

"Or to Hidaldgo, yes," he said, his exasperation spilling over into open irritation. "And so, yes, we will turn our shirking, cowardly tails and scamper away as fast as we can. Is that what you wish me to say?"

"Aye, near enough." She blinked and flipped her straggling braid over her shoulder. "And I wasn't playing patty-hands with Zach in the window at the Blue Goat. He'd helped me climb there, and was being deuced slow about letting my hand go, but that's not patty-hands, and you're not a coward. Are you happy now?"

He stared at her, speechless, while Zach discovered something irresistibly fascinating to ponder on the sole of his shoe.

She stared back and sighed with a fulsome resignation that was nearly smugness. "Very well, then. You'll be happy enough when you remember the neap falls tonight, or close enough to tonight to benefit you."

"Damnation, Polly," he said slowly, letting the entire, welcome significance of what she'd said settle comfortably around them. The neap tide ran only once in the moon's cycle, between the first and third quarters, and its run marked the shallowest difference between high and low tides. Most months this wouldn't matter to him, but this night a neap tide could mean the shallow-drafted *Morning Star* being able to float across the sandy bar that guarded the harbor's entrance and the broader-beamed *San Miguel* being forced to wait or risk being stranded aground on the bar.

"Double damn, Polly," he said again, with fresh delight. "You are *right*."

"Most times, aye. Especially about a neap, since it makes the cod act peculiar. Even the scrod," she said, then winked slyly. "*Especially* the scrod."

The boat bumped against the ship's side, and

Samson was saved from answering as they swiftly boarded and prepared to sail. This time no one suggested a bosun's chair for Polly, nor did she need one. Instead, as one of the first on the deck, Samson handed her his own long spyglass and asked her to tell what she could about the *San Miguel* in the distance.

To Polly the *San Miguel* looked like any other large ship, except for the brightly colored paintwork, as bright as a gypsy's wagon, and the long mustaches favored by the few crew visible in light from the ship's lanterns. And, of course, for the cannon, the gleaming long guns that Hidaldgo had none of Samson's hesitation against firing. Polly's gaze did not linger on those guns, and she prayed she'd have no other contact with them, too. Though she hadn't confessed it to Samson, she didn't think him cowardly but supremely sensible. She would much rather have him alive for company than any ghostly heroic memory.

But as the *Morning Star* began to drift underway toward the open sea, Polly finally saw something that made her whoop with excitement.

"Samson, look!" she said, running over to where he'd taken the ship's wheel himself. Nearly hopping with glee, she handed him the glass. "Look for yourself, there, between the *San Miguel* and that little fishing smack! It's their boat, Samson, the *San Miguel*'s blessèd boat, and it's only now coming back from town!"

The *Morning Star* was already under sail, gliding across the harbor with a west wind to puff her canvas, while Hidaldgo was still not even aboard his own vessel. From this distance Samson could make out the men bending double with each pull at their oars, striving to make their boat, and their captain, fly across the water. But it was not even close: the *Morning Star* was now passing the Spanish ship at her anchor, the *Star*'s rigging filled with jeering, taunting English sailors confident that they'd won again.

"You will not celebrate, too, Samson?" demanded Polly as she skipped a little jig of joy beside the wheel. "Faith, Hidaldgo must have stayed for every last cockfight. How much did he win in wagers on the birds, I wonder?"

"He won't be the only one to gamble this night." Unhappily Samson gazed up at the sails, and then at the sky and the stars that glittered so brightly across it. "I don't much like putting my fate in the hands of a wind as fitful as this. Look at it puff, then sputter. Not a thimbleful of breath to brag about there."

He didn't like it—he didn't like it at all—and with a single bark of an order he silenced the men in the rigging. They had nothing to celebrate until they were safely over the bar, into open waters, and out of sight of Hidaldgo entirely. A great deal to expect from a wind this weak, and his hands tightened on the spokes of the wheel.

"You'll find a way," said Polly softly, reaching out to give his hand a shy pat. "I know that you will."

He shook his head, unconvinced. "I'm not so sure, lass. I haven't yet found a way to make the winds obey me."

"If anyone can, Samson, you will," she declared with a confidence that made him wish he could move the ocean as well as the wind for her. "You *will*."

He didn't doubt for a moment that she believed in him so, and he couldn't remember the last time someone had. Perhaps never. Otherwise he surely would have remembered this rare, wonderful feeling of well-being that her words had brought to him, and the sense that he could truly accomplish whatever he set his mind to. Yet as much as he wished to tell her, to thank her, his feelings seemed too scrambled and disjointed to express. She did that to him, too—one more thing he'd have to sort out when he had the time. For now all he did was smile, and marvel at how her crooked little smile in return could make his chest and heart swell so much it almost ached.

"Mind your steering, Captain," she said with mock severity as she tapped the brass star inlaid on the wheel's kingspoke. "We're almost at the bar, and I've no wish to run aground now."

Neither did he, and he thrust aside his thoughts of Polly to concentrate on the task before him. The passage over the bar was not an easy one, the sandy bottom shifting and changing constantly, but in their haste to leave Charles Towne, Samson had decided to do without the guidance of a hired pilot and handle the conning himself. Finding the channel across the bar was a bit like blindly seeking a path through a darkened room full of furniture: feeling how the water held the ship, sensing every subtle change in the rudder and the wheel in his hands, listening to the sounding calls from the leadsman as he tested the ever-changing depths.

Carefully, carefully, the ship crept along. Yet even so Samson misjudged and she grazed the bottom with a shuddering lurch that made every man—and the one woman—hold their breath together. With a muttered oath Samson fought the instinctive urge to throw the wheel the opposite way, instead correcting it only a fraction, and was rewarded by feeling the ship lift free, rising up like a great bird on the crest of the waves that broke over the bar. Free, too, of the narrow channel, and of the bar itself, for suddenly they were alive again, racing across the dark, open sea.

"A handsome piece of work," shouted Polly into the wind, her hair whipping across her grin, "for a scrod."

"Save your compliments for later," he answered. "We're not home free yet."

He turned the wheel over to one of the men and went to stand at the stern to look back into the harbor. In the time they'd taken to cross the bar, the Spanish ship had weighed her anchor and set all the sail her crew dared. She was close to them now, with only the bar as an invisible fence between them. Close enough to see the faces of the men in the glow of the binnacle light, close enough for Samson to recognize Hidaldgo himself standing not at the wheel but almost on the bowsprit, leaning with his whole body toward the *Morning Star* like a hunting dog quivering after his quarry.

And as that quarry, Samson could understand Hidaldgo's eagerness, and his frustration, too. For five—or was it six by now? —years he'd managed to keep ahead of the *guardacostas*, and the bounty in Havana for his capture must be a steep one by now. He could almost feel sorry for Hidaldgo and the moment he realized that Samson had slipped free again.

"They'll never cross the bar," said Polly confidently. She was standing so close beside him, almost begging him to abandon his captain's responsibilities and put his arms around her. Not that he didn't want to hold her, and hear her chuckle against his chest when she called him a scrod, and then kiss her, and take her below to his cabin and—

Not *now*, he told himself sternly. Jesus, what was it about Polly that made him think like this?

"Most likely they won't clear it, no," he said evenly, as if his imagination wasn't conjuring a score of different, wicked things he wished to do with her on his bunk. "Not with their size, or without a pilot. God bless your neap tide, eh?"

She grinned, her face turned up merrily toward his. "Then I'd say I was—"

"Damnation, they're jettisoning their guns." He wouldn't have believed it if he wasn't seeing it for himself. One by one, Hidaldgo's men were unleashing one, two, three, *four* of the heavy gun carriages and pushing them through the ports and into the sea. Eight hundred pounds a gun, thirty-two hundred pounds lighter that the *San Miguel* would become. And more: twin sprays of water gushing from either side of the ship showed Hidaldgo had ordered the freshwater casks pumped dry, too, pounds and pounds of heavy water gone.

"Merciful Heaven," whispered Polly, her hand creeping into his for reassurance. "They'll be light enough to cross the bar now, won't they?"

They *were* crossing, the big ship easing over the bar more swiftly than the *Morning Star* herself had.

"We'll outrun them, lass," said Samson firmly. "We always do."

But to Samson's horror, they weren't, not this time. He felt the change on his skin even before he gazed up at the sails. The huge sheets of canvas hung horribly slack, barely rippling as the uneven wind that had brought them this far deserted them at last.

They were becalmed, still, the worst feeling in the world for any sailor.

Yet that same freakish wind that had abandoned them still filled the *San Miguel*'s sails, narrowing the gap between them at a perilous rate, bringing capture, prison, ruin to the *Morning Star*.

God in Heaven, thought Samson desperately, could it all really end like *this*?

Roughly he grabbed Polly's shoulders. "Mind me now, for there isn't much time," he ordered. "I'll have the boat lowered, and you'll make for shore as fast as you can, then scatter and run. Run fast."

"Nay!" she cried with anguish. "I'm not a coward, Samson, and I'm not leaving!"

"Yes, you *are*," he said as firmly as he could. There was so much he'd rather be saying to her now, but there wasn't time. "Besides, it's me Hidaldgo wants, not you. I want you safe, Polly, on shore. Tell whoever you meet that you were wrecked, or a castaway. They'll always believe that of a woman."

"I don't care because I'm not going!" she shouted, fighting him with all her might, pounding her fists against his chest. "I'm not going to leave you, Samson, and nothing you do or say will make me!"

"You *will* go, Polly!"

"Nay." She gulped, and abruptly the fight drained from her body. She stepped away from him, folding her arms across her chest, and for the first time he could remember she was openly crying, weeping the tears she'd always kept back, tears that now she didn't try to hide, tears that were for *him*. "I—I won't go, Samson."

He'd never in his life felt so completely helpless. He looked from Polly to the slack, empty sails, to the Spanish ship fast on their heels. He should go aft to be with his crew and prepare for the grim formality of being captured. Any second now they'd be in range to fire a warning shot across the bows of the *Morning Star*. There was no time left to save her now, no time left for anything.

Except, perhaps, for this.

"I wish to blazes this all were different, Polly. I wish I could tell you, show you that I—I—oh, blast it all!" He dug his hand into the pocket of his coat, searching for the leather box with the coral necklace. But instead of the necklace, his fingers first touched the dried rose, and though he didn't entirely understand why, the rose was what he drew from his pocket now and held out to her.

"I kept this, lass," he said, his voice hoarse with urgency. "Because you gave it to me after we kissed, and that—that made it special and dear to me. Because it was yours, lass, and because I—"

The warning shot came then, the deep, terrifying thunder of gunpowder, yet all he cared for now were the tears streaming over the cheeks of the girl before him as she stared at the faded rose in his hand.

"Oh, Samson," she whispered, her voice breaking with his heart. "I wish, I wish—oh, I wish so much were different now!"

She plunged her hands into her own pockets, her fingers twisting unhappily inside the worn linen. "I've nothing to give you in return, Samson, nothing but rubbish, but oh, what I most wish I could give you now would be wind, enough wind to save your crew and your ship and—and you and me together!"

Only Polly would wish for something so practical yet so achingly impossible. He began to reach for her, meaning to hold her for what might be the last time, then froze.

The loose curls around her tear-streaked face were beginning to quiver, tossing gently over her forehead. He could suddenly smell not only the salty scent of the sea around them but also the earthiness of the land to the west borne on the air, and beneath his feet the ship was coming to life again, stirring like some great animal beginning to wake. He looked up, high over Polly's head, and saw the canvas stretch and fill and grow into taut white billows.

Wind.

Damnation. She'd gotten her wish.

And so, in a way, had he.

Eleven

⟨⟩

*P*olly stood close to Samson, her back against the
broad wall of his chest and his arm around her, the
way they'd been together on the quarterdeck ever
since the wind had risen last night. It was past dawn
now, the yellow glow through the clouds to the east
the first sign of the new day. They were far enough
north that November meant winter, and not the
balmy warmth of Martinique. Sometime during the
night she'd been brought a woolen coat and a knitted
hat and mittens, and she'd accepted them gratefully,
without questioning from whose sea chest they'd
come. Her fingers and toes were numb from the cold,
her face stung from the lashing of the wind and
saltspray, and beneath her chilled, sodden clothes her
body was stiff and sore from exhaustion, but still she
would not go below to her cabin because she would
not leave Samson.

What had begun as a breath of wind had rapidly
swelled to a gale, the seas churning and white-
flecked. The crew had hauled in the cloud of canvas
overhead one sail at a time, until they were scudding
beneath only a scrap of canvas, yet still the ship

seemed to fly over the water at a pace faster than Polly dreamed possible. They'd lost sight of land in the first hour, and seen the last of the Spanish ship before the second watch was done, but Samson had refused to slow the pace, glorying in the speed, letting the ship have her head as they raced to the north. And the faster they ran, the higher the waves, the more terrified Polly became.

It was not the gale alone that frightened her, though the memory of how she'd been swept over the side of the *Dove* haunted her still. Nay, worse, far worse, was knowing that this wind, this storm, was her doing. Somehow, in an unfathomable way, she had called it into being, and the certainty of it made her blood run colder than the sea around them.

This wasn't the first time she'd done it, either. She realized that now. The facts were too close for common coincidence. Once before, when things had gone so wrong between her and Samson in St. Pierre, she'd wished for another evening on land with him. That same night the *Morning Star* had been struck with a wild, inexplicable storm, another wind of such sudden force that even the oldest sailors on board had shaken their heads in wonder.

The ship had limped into Charles Towne's harbor, and her wish had been answered. Yet in that same wind Samson had been hurt in an accident that could have claimed his life, a wish that she'd never make, but one that must be her fault as well, and once again she struggled to swallow her panic and fear.

But hadn't the same thing happened when she'd been swept over the side of the *Dove?* That storm had risen from nowhere, too, black and wicked, though then she'd been the one who had nearly died. She hadn't been able to remember much about that day, but now, in the hours she'd stood beside Samson in the same sort of storm, fragments of it had come back to her like an old dream.

She'd been alone in the little boat. She'd had to work hard to pull in the nets by herself, but her catch had been a good one. Tangled in the net, beneath the wriggling fish, had been a small rum bottle, which she'd shoved into her pocket instead of throwing back over the side. Then had come the storm, powerful enough somehow to carry her hundreds of miles from home to land on Samson's deck.

With the bottle in her pocket, just as it had been beneath her pillow the night in Martinique, just as it was in her pocket again now.

Merciful Heaven, however could an old bottle with a scrap of smudged paper come to have such power?

Fearfully she looked up at Samson, his angular, weather-worn face turned to challenge the wind and the sea, and his black hair streaming behind him the same as did hers. All he knew was the joy of having escaped the Spanish ship. But what would he say if he learned the unquestionable *truth* of how it had happened?

She burrowed closer against him, into the comforting shelter of his arm as she tried to make sense of her confusing secret. Maybe they'd all been right about her from the beginning. Maybe she *was* mad. But she'd never intended any harm, truly, and the wishes she'd made had been as much for Samson's sake—nay, even more!—than for her own.

Because she loved him.

That was the truth, and another secret that she carried close and tight within her. Even before she'd known he'd kept her faded rose and the memory of a kiss, before he'd said things to her so fine and dear that she'd wept, she'd known it in her heart. She loved him: in spite of the mysterious bottle, strange winds and storms, wagers and cockfights and Spaniards, she loved him. And before she'd made her last wish and realized what she'd done, she'd dared to hope he might care for her in return, too.

Lord, Lord, why couldn't she find the courage to throw the wretched bottle *away*, to hurl it far into the sea without another fearful thought for what would happen next?

"Time for the next watch," said Samson, bending close to her ear so the words wouldn't be lost in the wind. The ship's bell had just been struck to mark the hour—once, eight o'clock, the beginning of the forenoon watch—the sound of its usual ringing brass *clang* blown away over the waves. "Past time you went below, lass. I should never have kept you with me as long as I have."

"Nay!" she cried anxiously, twisting to face him. Who knew what disaster would befall him if she left his side now? "If you stay, Samson, then so shall I!"

He frowned, not understanding why she would protest so. "But I'm not staying, Polly. Double watch in this weather is enough for any man. Or woman. Come, I'll see you to your cabin."

Of course he'd be exhausted. While she'd been worrying over her own troubles, taking comfort from him, he'd been the one responsible for sailing the entire ship, seeing that they all were safe. She could see it in the heaviness of his eyes and in the lines of weariness etched deep on either side of his mouth. How selfish he must think her!

Contritely she let him lead her to the companionway. She was thankful for his arm across the rocking deck and down the narrow steps; she hadn't realized exactly how stiff and ungainly her muscles had grown with the wet cold until she tried to walk. Yet at the bottom of the steps, when he began to guide her toward her own quarters, she stopped beneath the glassed-in lantern, bracing herself against the bulkhead for support and keeping her hand as far from her pocket, and from the bottle, as she possibly could.

"Could we breakfast?" she pleaded with far more desperation than such a question merited. "You must be as hungry as I. Couldn't we eat together?"

"I'm hungry, aye." He sighed wearily, lifting his hat long enough to wipe the spray from his face with his handkerchief. "But there won't be anything hot since there's no fire in the cookstove, not in these seas, and I don't know what else would—"

"Please, Samson," she said so softly that her voice was barely audible. "I know most likely you're tired and wish to be by yourself more than anything, but I'm—I'm not ready to be alone yet."

Samson looked at her sharply. That plaintive, pleading note was as uncharacteristic for her as tears. The flame from the lantern's single candle cast uneasy shadows over her face, and by its shifting light her nose and cheeks were blotched, red and white, by the cold, and dark rings of exhaustion pooled beneath her eyes. That much he could understand; he doubted he looked one whit better himself, and likely a good deal worse.

But what had pulled him up short was the expression in her eyes, something that in anyone else he'd label outright terror. God knows she'd no reason to feel fear like that now, when they were as safe as anyone at sea was, but Samson had seen this before, men who'd been perfect heroes in battle dissolving into quaking tears once they had the leisure to consider what they'd survived.

After everything Polly had been through these last days—no, ever since she'd been fished from the sea—she was certainly entitled to her share of fearful second thoughts, and he could understand, too, why she'd no wish to suffer them by herself. He remembered all too well the nights in his past when he'd stayed on deck among the others simply to keep at bay the ghosts waiting for him in his solitary cabin.

He reached for her hand, linking his fingers into hers, and smiled. "You're right, lass. Breakfast would not be amiss, though mind you, it won't be more than dry biscuit and jam."

She nodded wearily in silence, looking down at their joined hands, and he knew he'd done the right thing. He understood her, just as she seemed so often to be able to understand him. In some ways he truly regretted she wasn't a man, for she could have become the best friend he'd ever had.

In his cabin he was quick to light the candles in the gimbal'd lantern, the soft glow reflecting off the polished brass and washing over the hewn beams overhead to warm the early morning gloom. Though the sun had risen, he'd had the wooden deadlights hung over the long stern window to protect the glass in the storm, and the cabin was as dark as if it were night, and nearly as cold as it had been on the open deck.

"Here you are, lass," said Samson, striving to be the cheerful, hearty host, as he held his own armchair out from the table for Polly. "I'll call for Joseph to see what he can beg from the galley."

"Nay, Samson," she murmured, "though I thank you."

He wasn't sure if she were refusing breakfast or the chair. Either way she remained standing, anxiously rubbing her hand along her other arm as she glanced at the boarded window as if she could still see through it.

"Then at least take off that wet coat." He shrugged out of his own by example, hanging it and his hat to dry on the peg on the door. He pulled the coverlet from his bunk and held it out for her. "Here. I'll grant you it's not as elegant as anything in that mantua-maker's shop, but at least it will be dry, and warm."

She nodded solemnly, first kicking off her shoes and peeling off her soaked stockings and cap, before she unbuttoned the long coat to hand to him. Beneath it her own linen jacket was wet, too, so wet that the stains of the Spaniard's blood had blotched and spread and faded into a grisly patchwork across the front. Without a word she unbuttoned this as well and let it drop from her shoulders to the deck.

Samson could understand that, too. Of course she'd wish to shed such a reminder, and he left it where it fell. He'd understand if she never wanted to let it touch her body again.

But it did surprise him—even stunned him—to see that she hadn't worn her waistcoat. The crumpled linen of her shirt was pale enough, and damp enough, that the high, round shape of her breasts was clear, the darker crests taut with the cold, and it took all his will to look away, back to her face.

Strange how he wasn't feeling cold any longer, or tired, either.

Quickly he opened the coverlet and swung it

around her like a cloak. "That's good, Poll," he said, clearing his throat now that such temptation was safely hidden. "You'll be snug and warm now."

She gathered the coverlet tightly around her arms and raised her chin to meet his gaze. She still was pale, still frightened, but in her eyes he could see that she'd resolved, one more time, to be brave. He wasn't sure what would come next, if she didn't wish to eat. But he found out soon enough.

"Samson," she said. She paused, her mouth twisting, and began again. "Captain Fairbourne. I have something most important to say to you. I've given it much thought, but still 'tis not easy."

He gazed down into her small frightened face, and he understood, and yet with a cowardice of his own that shamed him to his soul, he felt the bottom drop from his heart.

So it had come to this, then, to "Captain Fairbourne" and important words to say. Why, he thought in silent despair, why hadn't he guessed it for himself? Before they'd been rescued by the wind, he'd said things to her that he'd never said to any other woman, let alone meant them, and she'd answered in a way that he'd wanted to believe so much that the wild new joy of it was almost painful.

But then had come her wished-for wind, and their frantic race away from the *San Miguel*, and though she'd stayed with him on deck throughout the long night, there had been no more wishes, or promises, or even a comfortably shared "we" in conversation. He'd wanted to celebrate their escape, or at least to discuss the sailorly details of how they'd done it, the way she was usually so eager to do. He'd even dared hope that there'd be another opportunity to kiss her, to prove how clear a memory the dried rose, now once again in his pocket for safekeeping, had kept alive.

Most of all, he'd wanted to finish telling her he loved her. If the wind hadn't come up, he would have done it there, near the Charles Towne bar, while urgency had given him the necessary nerve and a voice to match. Without it, he'd spent the long night rehearsing the words in his head and praying for another perfect moment.

But that moment had never come. To make it worse, Polly had turned silent, withdrawn and lost in her own thoughts, and in return Samson found that doubt and uncertainty had gnawed away at his new-found joy. Despite her admirable knowledge of ropes and sails and seas, she was still a woman, and women saw things differently than men. He couldn't forget that, not even about Polly.

Especially not about Polly.

She stood there now, still waiting for him to answer before she continued herself, the uneasy silence stretching longer and longer between them. How long could it take her to find a way to unsay things she regretted saying, anyway? Didn't women do that all the time? Samson himself had pitifully little firsthand experience in such situations, and for the first time in his life he regretted it. He wanted to comfort her however she needed comforting, but he didn't want to hear she'd changed her mind. He didn't want to hear that at all.

"Polly," he said at last. "I already know what you're going to say, and damnation, you don't have to say it for my benefit."

"You do?" Startled, her brows rose. "I don't?"

"Yes, I do, and no, you don't." He took a deep, noble breath. "I understand it all. What's done is done, and let that be an end to it."

"Nay, but it's not nearly as simple as that!" she cried, her eyes wide with determined indignation. "You can't possibly know what I was going to say!"

He folded his arms over his chest. "Do you wish me to tell you?"

"Nay, because I shall tell *you* first!" She waved her hand toward the boarded stern window, the coverlet flapping from her arm like a wing. "I know you will think I've lost my wits all over again, but I swear that this is true: this wind, the one that's blowing now, is all my fault. Aye, it *is* true! I wished for it, and it came!"

"I know you wished for it," he said patiently. "I was there beside you, mind?"

"Not wishing like that, you great ninny! I mean that I *made* that wind blow! And the other times, too, in St. Pierre and clear back in Ninnishibutt, when I was washed over the side! Oh, I'm not explaining it well, Samson, but I swear to you it's true, all of it!"

He stared at her, completely at a loss. He knew he should be relieved that she wasn't trying to dismiss him, as he feared she would, but this—this was something he'd never expected. She was making as little sense now as when they'd first rescued her from the sea. But the difference now was that he cared for her, and even if she'd become mad as a March hare, she would still remain impossibly dear to him.

"You're tired, that is all," he said carefully. "You've suffered a great deal, Polly, a great deal. Once you've rested, you'll see how wrong—"

"So you do think I'm daft," she said, letting her coverlet-wings droop forlornly from her shoulders to her delicately pink bare toes. "*Again.* Oh, Samson, I worried so much over whether to tell you or not, from fear you would judge me so!"

That touched him, though it didn't change his mind. "I'm not judging you now, lass. All I'm saying is that no one, woman or man, has the power to beckon the wind with a wish."

"But I don't have power like that, leastways not by myself. I have help." She sank to her knees on the deck, searching through the pockets of her discarded jacket. "It's a sort of lucky piece, and when I touch it, I have whatever I wish."

"No." He was at her side in an instant, taking her arm and lifting her up to her feet. "I don't want to see your 'lucky piece' because there's no such thing."

"But there is, Samson!" she cried, trying to twist back toward her jacket. "I know you'd call it rubbish, and I thought so, too, when I found it, but I swear—"

"No more swearing," he said firmly, "and no more 'lucky' rubbish, either. If wind and weather could be mastered by wishing on lucky pieces, wouldn't every shipmaster in the world do so?"

"Aye, but this—"

"I told you, Poll, no more." He gently pulled her around toward him, and with his fingertips he tipped her troubled face toward his. "There're many things in this world that don't make sense, and most of them happen at sea. But God wouldn't have given me a good head on my shoulders if He wished me to use it to concoct heathenish claptrap to explain away whatever wasn't in my mortal understanding. As soon as a man begins believing in superstitions, then he stops believing in his own power to change what he don't like about his life. That's why I won't have such nonsense in this ship, Polly, not even from you."

She sighed deeply and lowered her lashes to avoid his gaze. "I'm not by nature given to fancifying or tales, and if I could explain it otherwise myself, I would," she said in a miserable half whisper. "But there is no other reason for it, Samson. None."

"But why does it matter so much to you, lass?" he asked, genuinely puzzled. "Why do you care like this?"

"Because I care for you, Samson!" she cried softly, shaking away his fingers on her chin to come closer, pressing her hands on his chest as if to force him to understand. "Because I care for you, and I could not let you go on without knowing the risk, that I might make another wish that—that could harm you, or make you fall again, the way you did in the last storm. That was my fault, Samson, all my fault, and I will never forgive myself—never!"

"Polly, don't—"

"Nay, you must hear me out!" Her silver-gray eyes glowed bright, almost feverish, in the lanternlight as they searched his face. "Now that I've told you, you must decide what comes next. And I will understand, and agree, whatever choice you make, even if you decide I am too much a danger to your ship and put me ashore. I—I would accept that, Samson, if it kept you safe, though it would break my heart. I *would*."

"Oh, Polly," he said, smoothing her damp, tangled hair back from her forehead. "Do you truly think I'd cast you off as a witch?"

She gulped, a hiccuping cross between a sob and a gasp. "Not a witch. A Jonah. A Jonah with wrongful powers."

Wrongful powers: Jesus, at any other time, he would have laughed outright. But not here, not now, and not with Polly leaning close against him, her fingers splayed over his chest where he was sure she must feel the racing of his heart.

"No witch, nor Jonah either, but only my Polly," he said softly, slipping his hands inside the coverlet to find her waist and pull her against him. "And the only sure power you have is over me."

He meant to kiss her only once, and lightly at that, as a kind of reassurance for her. He would keep it quick and chaste, and not let himself be lost in the heady, hot temptation he'd discovered when he'd kissed her before. He didn't need a rose to remind him of *that*. A single kiss, that was all; she was too fragile and unsure of herself for anything more.

But while he'd planned to be so honorably restrained, he'd forgotten about Polly herself. As soon as his lips touched hers, her arms were around the back of his neck, drawing him down to her level. Her lips pressed and slipped over his, cool and soft and tasting faintly of salt-spray, then tipped to one side to part for him. There was nothing cool about her mouth, as warm and rich and sweet as he remembered, and he couldn't quite help himself from kissing her in return. It was quickly begun, yes, but not chaste, and not finished in an instant, either, the way he'd planned.

The coverlet slipped away into a wooley puddle around their feet, and her breasts with their thin linen covering crushed gently against his chest. Instinctively, against his own wiser and infinitely better judgment, his hands slid down over her hips. His thumbs caught the rough waistband of her breeches, and on some distant level he considered how odd it seemed, her undeniably female softness tucked inside the rough male clothing like some rare, surprising gift.

Odd—but oddly fascinating, too—without the usual whalebone cage of stays and yards of petticoats as protection. In the worn boy's clothing, her woman's body was more beguilingly approachable, her own shape and not that of fashion. Mindlessly he tugged her shirt free, easing her breeches lower, and found skin, bare, velvety, lovely-to-touch flesh that swelled over her hips to fill his work-roughened palms, then narrowed at her waist, all the while drinking in the heady intoxication of her kiss.

He would stop. She didn't understand what they were doing, though God knows he did. He must stop, now, while he was still able to heed such cautionary warnings.

But he wasn't thinking, at least not with the brains that were in his head. He was tasting, and touching, and discovering, and savoring every marvelous bit of her. It had been a long time since he'd been with a woman, any woman—far longer than Zach would have dreamed humanly possible—and he'd never been with one who'd so thoroughly bewitched him like Polly Bray.

And she was the one who finally drew back, her breathing ragged and shallow and her eyes heavy-lidded, her arms still curled over his shoulders.

"Oh, my, Samson," she murmured, her crookedly uncertain smile bewildered. "So that is power?"

"Over me, yes," he admitted, his voice hoarse, his hand sliding farther into the back of her breeches, far enough to grasp her bottom. She gasped, and tensed with surprise, but she did not pull away as his fingers spread to caress her. The breeches slid the rest of the way down her legs, leaving her bare beneath her long shirttails, and Samson's senses reeling.

"It is—it is very nice," she stammered, her hands sliding down tentatively to his waist for support. "It is . . . *nice*."

It was considerably better than "nice," thought Samson with a desperation that was growing in direct proportion to his desire. His mouth was dry with longing, his blood hammering in his ears as if he'd just climbed to the top of the mainmast. It didn't help in the least that she'd pulled his shirt free, too, and was now sliding her hands up his back, her fingers exploring him the same way as he did her. He groaned and heard her chuckle with wonder.

Sauce for the goose, sauce for the gander; but he'd bet his life she was a virgin, and that she'd no notion of what she was doing to him, none at all. If he'd any morsel of honor left, that alone should have sobered him enough to stop. Instead it had the opposite effect: she could be truly his, his Polly, and he'd become the only man in the world who could ever say that.

He kissed her again, featherweight kisses of genuine sweetness, while his hand eased gently beneath her shirt to her belly, to the tangle of chestnut curls, and lower, to steal into the honey-sweet place between her thighs. She shuddered as he touched her, stroking with infinite, tantalizing care, and then she gasped again, breaking away from his kiss to squeeze her eyes shut and press her cheek into his shoulder. Her fingers clutched convulsively at his waistcoat, the fact that he remained decently dressed the last barrier to open disaster.

"Oh, Samson," she whispered hoarsely as she moved awkwardly against him, her rhythm, like her pleasure, too new and unpracticed to have any grace. "I—*oh!*"

She was so tight around his finger, small enough to make his guess about her inexperience a certainty. Small and tight and trusting and hot, all enough to make him want to howl with frustration. And there, too, in that sweet, narrow cleft, he found the proof that she wanted him as much as he wanted her.

"My God, Polly," he muttered, the beginning and likely the end of his vocabulary under the circumstances. "My God."

"I—I think I've lost my sea legs," she whispered as she swayed into him. "I can't seem—I shouldn't— oh, Samson, please, *ohh!*"

He was in perilous danger of losing more than merely his sea legs, and before they toppled over together to the unforgiving deck, he guided her the two steps to his bunk. She giggled as she fell backward onto the wool-stuffed mattress and rolled away to the head of the bunk when he tried to join her.

Before he could pull her back, she grabbed the hem of her shirt and yanked it over her head. She balled the shirt in her hands and threw it across the cabin, then sat back on her heels beside the pillow. She met his gaze evenly, almost challenging him to look at her, her breasts rising and falling rapidly with her breathing and her cheeks flushed as she tossed her hair back over her bare shoulders.

"Once you said I was the bravest woman you'd ever known," she said quickly, as if afraid of losing her nerve. "Well, I *am.*"

"Jesus, Polly." She was brave and bold, and he loved her for it. How could she dare think otherwise, especially now? He'd imagined her so many times without her clothes, but the vivid reality made his dreams seem poor and faded. Her skin glowed ivory pale in the lanternlight, her hair tangled chestnut around her face and a darker, burnished color in the tangled triangle below her belly. Her breasts sat high and round on her chest, with dark red crests that begged for his caress, and her lips, too, were dark and swollen from his kisses.

"You don't agree?" she said, her words still rushed. She shook her hair back again, her breasts bobbing like small ripe fruit as she swayed on her knees with the rocking of the ship. "That—that I am being brave?"

"Yes," he managed to croak. If she happened to glance downward to the front of his breeches, she'd know she might need every bit of that damned courage.

She smiled, her mouth ruddy and inviting, the way he'd made it. "Then let me see you, too. If you're brave enough, that is."

Yet still he hesitated, even as his whole body throbbed with need. She *was* daring him, blast her, and this time it wasn't merely another race up the mainmast that she was proposing. It didn't have much to do with courage, either. He wasn't even sure if she knew what she was asking for. How much had that old father of hers told her about men, anyway? Did she know the consequences she risked of losing her maidenhead to him, of taking his seed into her body? What, for that matter, would he do if he got her with child? He wasn't like a score of other carelessly single-minded men he could name. He *thought* about these things, double damn him for a fool, especially with Polly.

But Polly herself could know none of this. Too late he realized that all she could see was the doubt that must be painted like a signboard across his face, and in return he watched that brave invitation begin to falter and fade. She pulled the pillow from behind her and clutched it in her arms over her breasts.

"You're going to leave again, aren't you, Samson?" she said, her voice flat with a shame she'd no right to feel. "Just like you did when we kissed before. You're going to turn and leave, and that will be that."

She gave her shoulders a sad little shrug for emphasis, as if to prove she didn't care, even as she bowed her head and dug her fingers into the pillow to keep from crying. She was, after all, the bravest woman he'd ever known, and far too brave for that.

And it was that, then, that decided him. To leave her now would crush her, and he wouldn't do that. He *couldn't*. He knew he loved her, didn't he? Wasn't that enough?

And his conscience could just damned well go to blazes where it belonged, and where he could retrieve it later.

"No, Poll, I'm not leaving," he said hoarsely as he began to tear away his clothes, a wayward button skittering across the deck. "And I promise I never will again."

She didn't answer but looked and watched as he undressed, her silvery eyes intent on him as she hugged the pillow. He wasn't ashamed of what she saw. He was a well-made man, like all the Fairbournes, and proud of it. Yet as he unfastened the fall of his breeches and shoved them down his legs, he didn't miss her stifled gasp—of fear? surprise? approval? —and when he looked up her cheeks flamed.

"I am not frightened," she whispered fiercely. "Nay, I am not, so do not even think that."

"Then you won't need that to strike me," he said as he took the pillow from her hands and lay beside her.

"Though I'll grant you, as weapons go, goose feathers are more agreeable than a knife."

"As if I would do that to you, Samson." She laughed, a little trill of nervousness as he traced the long sweep of her hip and waist with his hand. "But if you can kiss me again and—and touch me the way you did before, then I won't even have to consider it."

"Striking me, or being afraid?" He kissed her gently, wooing her to put to rest the fears she swore she didn't have, and pulled her closer against him, letting her grow accustomed to the feel of his body beside hers. He didn't want to hurt her, though he couldn't forget how small and tight she was.

"Either one," she breathed, nearly forgetting to answer as he began to touch her again the way she wanted, and the way he wanted, too. "I told you I am very brave."

"And I've never doubted it," he said. "My own dear Polly."

Gently he nudged her knees apart, and she could feel him, all of him, hard and insistent against the inside of her thigh. She'd overheard enough whispered gossip to know what would happen next, even if she wasn't exactly sure how. She would trust that to Samson, just as she'd come to trust him in so many ways. With any other man such folly would mean she'd be ruined, but not with Samson. He wasn't *taking* her maidenhead, or making a male trophy of her inexperience. She was giving it freely, making a gift to him of the one single valuable thing she had to offer.

But as he touched her again, she forgot everything else but her desire for more, more of the strange, agonizing, wonderful tension that he was building inside her body. She ached for him in a way she'd never thought possible, and wouldn't be, if she hadn't loved him as much as she did. She pushed her hips forward, seeking more, her breath coming in short gulps as she clung to his shoulders.

"Be brave now," he said, his voice taut, and distantly she wondered why she needed to be brave at all.

Then he moved over her, that part of him that had seemed so alarmingly large probing where his fingers had teased her. Instinctively she fluttered against him, realizing too late that this would *hurt.* Too late, and he was driving deep within her, forcing her open, and she couldn't any more stifle her cry than she could get away.

"There now, Polly, it's done," he whispered, though from his grimace he didn't seem to be enjoying it any more than she was. "It will be better now, I promise."

She swallowed hard and nodded. She must trust him in this, too, as she had in so much else, for what other choice did she have?

But to her amazement, as he began to move within her, the searing pain she'd first felt began to fade, and in its place came the same sort of enjoyable tension she'd felt before, gathering and growing low in her belly. Tentatively she began to move with Samson, and he groaned in response, the kind of animal sound he'd made when she'd rubbed his sore shoulder. She liked being able to do that to him, giving him the same sort of pleasure that he was giving her, but the strange part was that the more she tried to give to him, the more she, too, seemed to gain for herself.

She arched her back to meet his thrusts, bracing herself against his sweat-sheened shoulders. This felt good, very good, and as she closed her eyes she realized the groans were now her own. Yet still the pleasure built, rising higher and sweeping her with it like the wind and white-capped waves were carrying the ship, carrying her, higher and farther until she feared she couldn't bear it anymore, and then, with wonderful, staggering abruptness, she was falling into the most beautifully blissful, calm sea, floating weightless in a safe harbor of purest joy.

And with her was Samson, holding her as they lay tangled together, soothing her, murmuring little non-sensical endearments as he kissed away her tears. Lord, how much she loved him, and how much she wished she could stop her life right now, at this perfect moment.

"Ah, sweet Polly," he whispered, and she shivered with delight as the words brushed against her ear. "Now you're truly mine, lass, mine alone to keep forever and ever."

And the perfect moment shattered into a million tiny shards.

Hidaldgo leaned over the charts spread across his desk, tracing his finger along the bumpy outline of the English coast. He frowned as he tried to sound out the names of the unfamiliar English rivers and towns, harsh, clumsy words given to cold, ugly places. He had never ventured so far from the Carib-bean, away from the sun and the islands that were always green, and he shivered now as he rested his feet on the small tin box full of hot coals. Its feeble glow was a poor replacement for the long, sweet afternoons he'd left behind, any more than the two coats he wore layered over a quilted waistcoat could take the chill from his bones. *Madre de Dios,* would he ever be warm again?

"And you say we must go where, Capitán?" asked Fernando anxiously as he, too, leaned over the charts, his hands tucked inside his sleeves. "How much farther before we can catch the Englishman?"

Hidaldgo's gaze was as icy as the air in his cabin. "You have lost heart for the chase?" he demanded. "You would turn back now, with your tail between your legs like an unmanned cur?"

"Not I, Capitán!" cried Fernando gallantly, but with more dread than real conviction. "But there are others who doubt, who fear that sailing so far to the north from Havana is not right. This cold, Capitán, *Jesu*, it is the Devil's handiwork, it gnaws at the bones like a wolf, an English wolf."

Impatiently Hidaldgo drummed his knuckles on the chart, somewhere off the coast of the colony of Virginia. Doubts, fa! Those who doubted would never find glory or gold. He did not know he'd such weak and muling cowards among his own people. They had not seen the English ship for seven days, and they might not see it again for another seven after that. The Fairbourne bastard was like that, full of cunning and deceit. Over and over he had wriggled free, like a worm from a hook in the instant before he is gobbled, but not again. This time must be the last, and this time the hook would not budge from the worm's fleshy side.

"If they are cold, tell them to warm themselves," he said to Fernando. "Shorten their watches, if you must. But whoever doubts will forfeit his share when we take the Englishman and his gold."

"Then there will be gold?" asked Fernando eagerly, greed warming him with new spirit.

"Would we have journeyed this far if there were not?" said Hidaldgo with a grand sweep of his arm, though secretly he doubted there'd be such treasure in the *Morning Star*'s hold. It was not in the way of the English to smuggle specie; more realistically he was counting on a profit from the sale of the ship itself and her cargo, combined with the bounty and ransoms for the English crew he would draw from the King. There was more risk, too, for so far into English waters meant they could run afoul of a British warship.

But all of that paled beside capturing Fairbourne and his woman. That alone was what was driving him north: revenge, pure and sweet, a violent, agonizing, shameful end to the man who had dared, again and again, to make such a fool of Don Diego Hidaldgo. And if to do it he needed to prime the greed of his crew with tales of gold coins, so be it.

He jabbed his thick-knuckled finger at the curving arc of land near the top of the chart.

"There," he said, "there is the Englishman's destination—we heard it so in Charles Towne, from one of his own men—and there we will trap him without mercy."

Fernando squinted at the chart, struggling to make out the word beneath his captain's finger. "Ap-lee-dor-aay?" he asked. "The gold will be there, too?"

"All we could desire, Nando," said Hidaldgo softly. "*All.*"

Twelve

The first thing that Samson did when he woke was reach for Polly beside him in the bunk.

The second thing he did was swear because she wasn't there.

Groggy, he rolled onto his stomach, laying his palm on the hollow her body had left in the mattress. Cold: she'd been gone awhile. Her clothes were gone from the deck, too. With another muttered oath, he let himself fall facedown on the place where she'd been, breathing the womanly scent of her that still clung to the sheet.

She'd no right to go wandering off like this. After what they'd done last night—no, it had only been this morning; storms blurred time like that—she belonged here with him. How could she misunderstand that? Here they'd shared one of the most astounding encounters between a man and woman in the history of the world, and she'd demonstrated her appreciation by disappearing. How could he tell her how much he loved her if she wasn't here to listen?

He missed her. He was lonely. He wanted to hear her chuckle happily as she snuggled herself in a cozy nest against him; he wanted to pull her close and kiss that special soft place on the side of her throat and fill his hands with her breasts and make her slick and hot and ready to take him all over again.

Hell. He was ready for her again now.

With a groan he leaned from the bunk to grab his breeches from the floor where he'd dropped them, pulling his watch from the pocket. The wind had quieted, and the creaks and groans of the ship's protesting timbers with it. With the deadlights still in place over the windows, he hadn't the faintest notion of the time. After standing double watch through the night, Zach would have seen to it that, with a captain's prerogative, Samson had slept undisturbed as long as he wished, though from long habit that generally meant no more than a seaman's usual four hours.

Four hours would have been gone in a flash if Polly had stayed here to help him pass it, and with frustration and general ill humor he swore again as he fumbled with the cover of his watch. Only one candle remained lit in the lantern, the others having long ago guttered out, and he tipped the watch's face toward the feeble light. Half past noon, and there, as if he needed another reminder, he heard the bell overhead clang the half hour. Past time to rise and get on with the day, as if nothing and everything had changed in his life.

He called for hot water for shaving and black coffee to clear his head, and resisted the maddening temptation to ask the boy who'd brought them for news of Miss Bray. As he stood before the mirror with his razor in hand, he kept glancing back over his shoulder, certain he'd heard her return, but certain only to be disappointed. He willingly invented a score of excuses for her absence—that she'd gone back to her own quarters to wash, to sleep, to change her clothes; that she'd gone up on deck for fresh air or to let him sleep in peace; that she was hungry, restless, or shy—and tried hard to believe them all. Besides, there was only so far she could go on board a ship at sea.

He pulled on his newly brushed coat over a clean shirt and patted the pocket to reassure himself that the coral necklace was still safely inside. He was glad that he hadn't given it to Polly earlier. Now, when he told her he loved her, he'd have it to offer as a token, a pledge. Women liked sentimental gestures like that, and so, where Polly was concerned, did he.

With his hat tucked beneath his arm, he went to stand before the door to her cabin. He cleared his throat before knocking, not wanting to croak like a bullfrog in heat.

If bullfrogs even went into heat. Jesus, what was making him fuss over something like *that?*

He pounded enthusiastically on the door, loud enough to rattle the hinges and echo the thumping of his heart.

No answer came, but he tried again, just to be sure.

"Miss Bray's topsides, sir," said Joseph, his face studiously impassive as he edged past Samson toward the galley with the empty water pitcher. "Talkin' with Mr. Fairbourne, she is, sir."

"I know," said Samson automatically, then silently damned himself for a righteous fool. The boy would be telling that one to anyone who'd listen, no mistake, and Samson couldn't say he'd blame him. With what little remained of his tattered pride, he thumped his hat onto his head and fled up the steps to the deck.

The day was clear and snapping cold, with the first bite of winter already in the air. Though the wind had fallen off from the earlier wild gale, they were still making a good pace of it, and he wondered if Polly and her vaunted "wrongful powers" were taking the credit.

If she were, she hadn't lingered to view her handiwork. There was no sign of Polly anywhere on the deck, though his cousin was standing on the leeside, watching the two men who were streaming the log to measure their speed. Samson came to stand beside him, waiting patiently until the half-minute glass was empty and the log reel was stopped.

Zach nodded at the men, then grinned at Samson. "You should have joined the wagering for our landing date when you could have, Sam. I told you we'd make record time, but our dear friend Don Hidaldgo put an extra skip in our step. By my reckoning we'll be even with the mouth of the Chesapeake by nightfall, and I don't think there's another ship afloat who can match that kind of run."

Samson nodded, too, though his thoughts were far from the voyage home. "So when does your reckoning say we'll mark the Cape?"

Zach's grin widened. To every sailor on board, "the Cape" meant only their own Cape Cod. "By the end of the week for certain, if this wind holds."

Of all the voyages he'd made in his life, he thought with glum despair, this *would* be the one to set a record for speed. Once they'd reached Appledore, he'd have no reason to keep Polly with him unless she herself chose to stay. Uneasily he clasped and unclasped his hands behind his back, trying to put such ideas from his mind while the coral necklace weighed heavily in his pocket. The way she'd hidden herself away now, he wasn't altogether sure that she would decide in his favor.

He sighed deeply. "The end of the week."

"Aye-aye, Captain," said Zach heartily for the benefit of the others, then he edged closer to Samson. "I've one more matter to report, Sam. Miss Bray is not happy with you."

Samson looked at him sharply. "You've seen her, then?"

"Seen her," declared Zach with far more cheerfulness than Samson thought appropriate, "and seen enough to tell you've fallen in great disfavor. Didn't speak a word, but she made her feelings clear enough."

"Did she now." This was not what he'd expected, nor did it make *him* particularly happy with Polly. "Did she also make it clear where she's been hiding?"

For an answer Zach leaned his head back and gazed upward. Reluctantly Samson did the same, though he'd already guessed what he'd find.

For there, a good forty feet above them in the foretop with her legs dangling over the wooden platform, sat Polly.

"What the Devil are you doing here?" he demanded as soon as he'd reached her, half out of breath from anger and from the climb. "Didn't I order you never to risk your neck like this again?"

She glared at him with all the subtlety of a vengeful angel. "Aye, you ordered me, but I'm not obeying. And I'm not marrying you either, Samson Fairbourne, so you can just hie yourself back down and leave me in peace."

He stared at her, strangled and stunned. "Who the hell said anything about marriage?"

"*You* did," she said vehemently. "This morning you said I was now yours forever and ever. Maybe you thought I didn't hear that, but I did, and if that doesn't sound like marriage, then I don't know what does. And I'm not going to marry you, Samson."

"Why the Devil not?" He hadn't climbed up here with any intention of asking her more than why she'd run away from him, but her determined refusal to a proposal he hadn't offered somehow made it perversely possible, even desirable. If she didn't want to marry him, then by God, he wanted to marry her, and he'd do it, too. "Do you think you're too fine for me?"

"Don't talk like that to me, Samson," she warned, the threat in her voice clear. "I'm not one of your crew, and I'm not your wife, either. I told you before that I answer to myself and no one else, and I'm not going to change now. Fineness has naught to do with it. Just because I spread my legs for you doesn't mean I'm your property, any more than it meant I was your whore."

"You're not a whore," he said sharply. "Don't talk like one."

"Oh, aye, now *that's* a comfort." Pointedly she turned her face away from his, choosing the wide-open sea over him. But he'd still had time to glimpse the bitterness in her eyes, the unhappiness hiding behind the protection of her anger.

He wished to hell he knew what he'd done wrong. Every other woman he'd known would be searching for a minister by now instead of treating his offer like the gravest insult in all Christendom. He wished they were somewhere else more private and less dangerous, so he could take her into his arms and improve things between them that way.

"Listen to me, Poll," he began again, barely remembering to soften his command. "Please."

She didn't turn, but she did sweep her wind-tossed hair around her ear to show that she was listening.

"This isn't only about you and me any longer, lass. What if you're with child?"

She flushed nearly purple. "We only did it the once!"

"The world's full of bastards gotten in less," he countered, not caring if he shocked her. "What would they say in Ninnishibutt if you returned with your belly swelling with my babe?"

"I wouldn't care what they said," she said swiftly. "I've never cared before, have I? I'd raise my child myself, the way my father did for me."

"Except that your mother bothered to marry your father," he said. "Who would take care of your boat when you grew too thick and clumsy to pull in your nets? You'd have to stop pretending you were a boy then. You'd have no choice. And who would come care for you when your time came?"

"I have friends," she said in a way that convinced him that she didn't. "I wouldn't be alone."

"That's because I won't let it happen, not to my child. Because that boy would be mine, as much my son as yours, Polly, and I—"

"Or daughter!" she shouted unhappily. "It could just as soon be a daughter, like me, and for me to keep!"

"Very well then, if it's a daughter like you, she'll still be half mine," he continued. He wished he'd remembered how she'd been born a disappointing female to her own father; he wished he had indeed, before he'd spoken to her like that. "Daughter or son,

I've still no intention of letting her—or him—suffer any want or shame on account of your pig-headed pride."

Strange how he was convincing himself as he tried to do the same with her, and stranger still how logical and agreeable marrying her would be. Surely she'd realized by now how attached he'd grown to her. He loved her; he'd showed her, even if he hadn't quite told her yet. But Polly was such an eminently sensible creature that she wouldn't expect a long, tedious, dawdling courtship. What mattered was that he wanted her always there, like the part of him that she'd become, and marrying her would be the best way in the world to do so, and to keep her safe from harm.

And it was time he built a house on shore, and time, too, for him to sire a few sons. Polly would make a first-rate mother to sailors, loving the water the same way he did himself, and she wouldn't get weepy and cling when the boys were ready to come to sea with him. She could have all the girls she wished, too. He'd never quarrel with her on that, as long as they turned out as well as she had. He didn't doubt but that she'd keep their house shipshape, and she'd be a royal pleasure to come home to after a long voyage. This morning had been most convincing on that score.

It all made perfect sense.

To him, that is, but alas, not to her.

"Nay, Samson, we would never suit!" she cried vehemently. "I have nothing, and you have—you have *everything!* You would expect me to be meek and obedient, and I could not do that, not even for you. I *won't* do it. I've been captain of my own vessel, same as you, and I like to give orders, not take them. However could we agree on anything, the way husbands and wives must?"

"We don't agree on much now," he countered, "and yet we still get on tolerably. Better than tolerably, most times. Why should that change?"

"I'm the one who can't change, Samson," she said firmly. "Have you learned nothing from this wretched wager of yours, or do you believe that Zach's the only one to learn from me?"

Samson frowned. "We're done with the wager, mind?"

She let her head drop back against the mast with a sigh of unguarded despair. "We'll never be clear of it, Samson, because it's the only reason I'm even *here*."

"Listen to me, Polly—"

"Nay, Samson, for once you'd do better to listen to me. I would make the most wretched excuse for a wife for you. All I know is sailing and fishing. I couldn't do a single one of the huswifely things you'd wish of me."

"You could rub my back," he suggested, with more honesty than wisdom, "and warm my bunk. That would be enough to start, and you could learn the rest."

Her eyes narrowed, suddenly murderous. "You truly *are* a scrod, Samson. Over and over I let myself begin to think otherwise, then *hah!* You say or do something that's so blessèd scrod-ish that I feel like a perfect ninny for ever having trusted you."

He'd misstepped again, misstepped badly. "Damnation, Polly, I trust you, don't I?"

"I don't know if you do or not. I truly don't." She sighed deeply and looked down at her hands. "Even now I'm thinking this foolishness about you wanting to marry me is just one more thing that will have you and Zach roaring and slapping at each other the minute I turn my back."

Not the bottle, he thought desperately. *If Zach has said one word of that to her, I am as good as dead.*

He swallowed his fear and reached out to cover her hand with his. "I don't know how I can convince you how wrong you are about—wait, hold now, I do. I can prove it to you right now."

He dug into his coat pocket, searching for the leather box with the necklace. Perched on the narrow wooden platform of the foretop mast, swinging high in the wind like this was a reckless place to make such a gift, but he needed all the help the little cameo mermaid could offer.

"Here, Polly," he said, putting the box carefully into her fingers. "Here's proof of how much you mean to me."

She looked at him uncertainly before she dropped her gaze to the box in her hand, clasping it tightly in her fingers without opening it.

"Go on, lass," he urged, anticipating her joy. "Open it."

Carefully she unhooked the lid and flipped it up. But her expression didn't change, the uncertainty still there in place of the excitement he'd expected.

"The mermaid reminded me of you," he said finally. "Her smile, and the way her hair's blown about by the wind."

Polly stared at the necklace, her heart in turmoil. It was lovely, the most beautiful gift she'd ever been handed. She could hardly imagine placing something so fine around her own neck, to fall there in the open collar of her worn old shirt. But how lovely it would look with her new lady-clothes, the tiny grinning mermaid nestled in the hollow of her throat! She longed to wear it, longed to stand before a mirror and fasten the gold clasp for herself and feel the cool polished beads against her skin. And yet just as she'd never marry Samson, she could never wear his necklace, and she gently closed the lid over it.

"When did you buy this for me?" she asked softly, sadly, for she already knew this answer and the next with it.

"In Charles Towne," he answered without hesitation. "In a Frenchman's shop, near the water."

She looked at him there beside her and felt the tears sting her eyes. She loved him so much it hurt; he'd said his gift would be proof of how much she meant to him, but instead it only proved how wrong she'd been to fall in love with him.

"You'd already decided then, hadn't you?" she said, each word pulled like a thorn from deep in her soul. "That you'd seduce me, and then reward me with a pretty trinket? Oh, aye, Samson, you did. You *did*; and who's the whore now?"

To his credit, his mouth dropped open with disbelief. "Damnation, Polly, that's not what the necklace is *for!*"

Swiftly, before she lost her resolve, she shoved the box with the necklace back into his hands.

"I gave myself to you because it pleased me, and because I wished to please you, too. That was all. I didn't want or expect anything else in return. You can't change me, Samson, and you can't buy or own me. And no matter what you say, I will never be your wife."

She grabbed the nearest rope and swung herself

into the shrouds, racing down the ratlines as fast as she dared. She needed to be alone, to think and gather her defenses away from him. He was so large, so strong and so aggressively male and accustomed to getting his own way, that beside him she wouldn't have a chance otherwise. She had to have time to remember who she *was*, or she'd be lost, swallowed up by him as completely as a minnow by a whale.

She didn't doubt that he'd follow because he hated for her—for anyone—to have the last say, but she was counting on her smaller size and agility to outrace him. Sure enough, when her feet touched the deck, he was still high above her, though gaining fast. If she could reach her own cabin first and latch the door, she'd be safe. No matter how angry Samson was, she knew he wouldn't lose his temper so openly on his ship as to batter down the door.

At least she hoped he wouldn't, and as she turned to run toward the hatch she looked up once again. Looked up, and not ahead, and pitched headlong and hard into Zach's chest.

"Let me go, Zach!" she cried as he steadied her, holding her fast by her shoulders. She needed to slip away by herself, not be held in great shameful spectacle on the open deck. "I must get free, to get away from Samson!"

But Zach didn't release her, his young face taut with concern. "What's Sam done to you, Polly?" he demanded. "By God, if he's hurt you in any way—"

"Good, Zach, you've stopped her!" said Samson as he reached them. "Bolted like a wild deer, she did, running off before I—"

"What the Devil have you done to her, Sam?" said Zach sharply. "Look at her! She's so scared of you she's trembling."

Samson did look, though his exasperated response was hardly as sympathetic as his cousin's.

"Hell, Polly's not frightened. She's not frightened of anything," he said, glaring at her to prove it. "But she *has* refused to marry me, and that's God's own truth."

Now it was Zach's turn to be stunned. "Refused?" he said, incredulous. "Outright?"

"Aye, outright," said Polly with as much breathless dignity as she could muster in the circumstances, "and with blessèd fine reasons, too, if your lunkhead cousin would only pause to consider them."

"But you did ask her, Sam?"

"Of course he did," said Polly. "I would not fancify about something as serious as that."

Then, to her uneasiness, she saw the expression on Zach's face change, from a champion's outrage to a gadfly's delight.

"Don't be so hasty, Polly," he said with a grin, still holding her fast by the shoulders. "Sam's considered a prize bachelor among the ladies on the Cape and in Boston, you know. I'd wait until after we've visited Appledore before you decline him proper."

"Appledore?" she said, perplexed. "I've no wish to go to Appledore."

"You've no choice, for that's where we're bound first," said Samson impatiently. "Unless you decide you'd rather swim somewhere else by yourself again."

"You'll like Appledore, Poll," said Zach, his relish at their discomfort bordering on glee. "It's the prettiest spot in Barnstable County, and a great deal more agreeable than Ninnishibutt. If you're fortunate, you'll make the acquaintance of Mistress Anabelle Fairbourne, my other cousin's wife and the most refined lady in the colony. Why, you might even be able to introduce her to Sam!"

Whatever courage Polly had left was shrinking fast. She'd rather face the Spanish captain and all his guns again than make the acquaintance of the most refined lady in Barnstable County.

"You just shut your damned mouth, Zach, or I'll shut it for you," growled Samson before he returned his attention to Polly instead. "It will only be for a day or two, I swear. I've no desire myself to idle in the place."

"But she might like it, Sam," suggested Zach, ignoring his cousin's threatening suggestion. "It might help her decide if she wants us Fairbournes as kin by marriage, especially if she sees you've more to your name than this little peapod of a ship."

"To *your* name, Samson?" repeated Polly, appalled that he'd keep such a monumental fact from her. "You don't mean you *own* the *Morning Star,* do you?"

He frowned, as contrite as if she'd caught him in some heinous act. "She's mine, yes," he finally admitted. "But that shouldn't alter anything between us."

"Oh, aye, it won't because there's nothing between us to alter!" she cried, helpless tears catching in her throat. As the captain of a ship like this he'd already been far, far above her station in wealth and power, but to learn he was the *Morning Star*'s owner, too, made the distance between them loom vast and uncrossable. No wonder he believed he could buy her; he could, a score of times over, with no more than the coins in his pocket.

"I believed you had owners in Boston, like most other captains!" she said bitterly as she finally tore herself free from Zach. "You let me think we were nigh equals, that we could be friends first, that we—that we—oh, blast you, Samson, for all the false-hoods you let me believe!"

"Hold now, Polly, wait!" Samson grabbed for her as she darted for the companionway, but as he did, Zach, too, turned, tripping him, and the two cousins hurled to the deck together in an unwieldy heap of arms and legs.

"Damnation, Zach, you clumsy, meddling little clodpate!" said Samson through gritted teeth as he scrambled back to his feet. "I should break you for this, see if I don't!"

"Upon my word, Sam, I don't see the sin in telling Polly you're not a pauper," said Zach defensively, still on his knees as he squashed his hat back onto his head. "Aren't you the one always spouting off to me about how women look at the fortune before the man?"

"Polly doesn't." With an impatient sigh Samson gave his hand to his cousin to pull him back upright. "If you'd half a brain in that cockle-shelled skull of yours, you'd have figured that out for yourself by now."

Zach tipped his head to one side, his brows lifted in outright skepticism. "You don't truly mean to marry her, do you?"

"If she'll have me, aye." Grimly Samson started toward the companionway where Polly had fled. He wanted her, wanted her badly, and all this cat-and-mouse foolishness of hers hadn't lessened that one bit, nor had it improved his temper.

"Sam," called Zach, and reluctantly Samson turned back to find the younger man studying him with an uneasy smile on his face.

"You've changed, Sam," he said, making sure that none of the men would overhear. "I know the whole game was to make Polly change, but she's stayed the same and you're the one who's different."

"The Devil take your impertinence," growled Samson, and he turned his back without answering more. Changed, hell. He hadn't changed one whit, except to have his pride twisted and turned into a thousand agonizing knots by Polly Bray, and the more he thought about it, the more outrageous her treatment seemed. All he'd done was to offer her his name, his fortune, and his heart, and an exceptionally nice necklace into the bargain, too, and she'd tossed every bit of it back in his face with a stream of illogical reasons he couldn't begin to sort out.

But what he did understand as he reached her cabin door was this: that he and Polly Bray belonged together like no other two people in all creation, and he'd be damned if he'd let her stubbornness keep them apart.

"Open the damned door, Polly," he said, thumping his fist against the thin pine for good measure. "We're not done yet, you and I. Open it *now*."

"Clear off, Samson," she said, her voice muffled by the closed door. "I don't have anything left to say to you."

"Oh, yes you do," he growled. She might feel protected by the door between them, but Samson knew this particular door too well for that, knew from Zach's complaints when the cabin had been his that the latch and lock were faulty. He put his shoulder to the door to shove it higher against the hinges, then struck the wood once, directly above the lock. When he heard the gentle *ping* from the other side he knew the bolt had sprung clear. Before she could notice he threw open the door and stepped into the tiny cabin.

She'd been standing in her shirtsleeves with her back to him and the door, her fists clenched at her sides. She spun around when she heard the door open and gasped when she saw him, then lunged for the knife in the sheath that hung on the same peg as her coat. She was fast, remarkably fast, but his knowing now what to expect from her made him faster still, and he pinned her back against the edge of the bunk with both of her wrists clasped firmly in his hands on either side of her body.

"No more, Polly," he said, his voice low and rough as he held her, trapped. "No more knives, or bad-luck charms, or whatever else you were hoping to fetch from your pocket. And no more running away. We're done with all of that between us, mind?"

"I won't promise you anything." Her eyes were enormous, dark and luminous with the defiance and the excitement she didn't want to admit. "Not until you stop giving me orders."

"Very well," he countered, "no more orders, and no promises, either. But if you won't listen to me, Polly Bray, then listen to yourself. We belong together, lass. *Together.*"

Her breathing had gone shallow, rough little pants through parted lips, as he leaned closer, pressing his hips into hers.

"You said I was yours," she whispered as she broke her gaze away from his to look down, somewhere toward his chest. "Like property you'd claimed."

"Not like property, you little goose," he said, his lips so close to her cheek that she felt the heat of his words on her skin. "Like my wife. If you belong to me, then like it or not, I belong to you, too. Like a husband. Damnation, like *your* husband."

She'd closed her eyes even before he began to kiss her. His mouth was demanding, possessive, with none of the tenderness he'd shown earlier. He was too desperate to be careful now, and that she could understand, his mouth hard against hers as he urged her lips to part for him.

Desperation: oh, aye, she understood desperation. What better way to define the jumble of her feelings, how she must leave him but how she must have him, have *this*, too? She'd never wanted to be anyone's wife, let alone the wife of a man like Samson Fairbourne. She'd always tried to be her own woman, her own self, Polly Bray of Ninnishibutt. But was independence only a finer word for loneliness? Was she willing to trade all the pleasure and joy and friendship and cussedly charming male contrariness and love—*love!*—that she'd found with Samson for the cold sake of saying she had?

His unshaven cheek was rough against hers, his tongue hot and fierce as it swept against hers. She didn't want to give this up, and with a sob that was lost in their mouths she kissed him back. This *was* desperation, then: what else could she call it? Mindlessly she struggled to free her hands from his grasp, and instead he lifted them to settle around the back of his neck. Swiftly he jerked her shirt free, bunching the linen upward as he slid his hand along the arch of her ribcage to the high, round flesh of her breast.

She gasped as his fingers teased her, her nipple hard and taut. Her body was turning traitor on her, growing soft and willing and malleable to his wishes in a way she now understood all too well. His mouth burned a wet, hot trail down her throat to find her breast, suckling hard enough to make her cry out from the wicked sweet agony of wanting.

"Oh, Samson," she whimpered as her fingers tangled in the coarse black silk of his hair. "Oh, I— oh, I don't know, Samson!"

"Yes, you do," he said fiercely as he shoved her breeches over her hips and lifted her onto the edge of the bunk. "Tell me you don't want me as much as I want you. Kiss me, and tell me we don't belong together."

She couldn't tell him, because she did, and because kissing him the hungry way she was now made her unable to think enough to put the words together. Their breathing was harsh in the small cabin, the air filled with the heady scent of their own bodies, and as he smoothed his hands along her inner thighs, she trembled with anticipation, and from need, as raw and uncompromising as his own.

"I—I cannot promise," she gasped, a last helpless protest by her conscience.

"Don't promise me anything," he ordered as he pulled her forward to meet him. "Damnation, just feel."

Some foolish fragment of her brain noted that he'd ordered her again, but the rest of her didn't, and didn't care, either. She cried out as he filled her, a wordless, keening welcome torn straight from the depths of her body. He slipped his arms beneath her knees and she arched her back to draw him deeper, and made him swear. With each thrust she felt her body tightening around him, the heat of it scorching her with its urgency. He dragged her closer, nearly sliding her off the bunk, and she gasped and shuddered at the difference it made, her fingers digging deep into his hard, sweat-slicked shoulders. He'd ordered her to feel, and now she could do nothing else, and with a brilliance that rivaled all the stars in the heavens her pleasure broke and his followed, rushing over her like a cresting wave of pure joy and happiness.

Exhausted, she let her head drop forward, resting her cheek against his shoulder as her thundering heart began to slow. She felt limp and drained, as helplessly weak as if she'd been cast away by another storm, but this time upon a beach of rare peace.

"Oh, Samson," she whispered, the catch in her voice betraying the tears that were puddling in the corners of her eyes. "However can I tell you—"

"Hush," he said, his voice at once rough and tender, his warm breath upon her ear sending little shivers down her neck. His arms tightened possessively around her waist, their bodies still so intimately joined. "Hush, and be still."

She smiled, drowsy and content. "You great silly scrod," she whispered fondly. "Why won't you let me tell you--"

"No, not a word," he said sternly, almost as if he feared what she'd say. "I won't hear it from you now, mind? You must be sure, with time to consider. Wait until—until after Appledore."

She sighed wearily, the warm glow of her happiness turning chill, and closed her eyes. She'd only wanted to tell him how much she loved him, the same as she wished he'd say to her. She told herself that he'd asked her to marry him, that such an offer, matched by his ardency, should be assurance enough. Yet somehow it wasn't, and to wait until after Appledore meant he still believed she could be swayed more by his worth than simply who he was.

But she wouldn't quarrel about it now, not again,

and a slow tear slid along the curve of her cheek to
fall onto her arm.

"Until Appledore, then," she said softly. "Until
Appledore."

Even to himself Samson always pretended that
he'd forgotten the day he'd last sailed from the place
where he'd been born. It was safer that way, easier,
and nothing that anyone questioned. There'd been no
great fanfare to mark the date when he'd left, nor, for
that matter, had there been any infamous scandal—
an outraged, cuckolded husband, say, or a violent
quarrel with a friend—to hurry him on his voyage, as
was often the way with sailors. He had simply
boarded a ship and left, on the fifth sunny morning in
a May nearly four years past.

From here in the harbor, the town looked exactly as
he'd remembered, both awake and in his dreams: a
small town that had begun low near the water and
then crept higher up the sloping hillside, neat gray-
shingled and clapboarded houses and shops centered
by the sharp, white spire of the meetinghouse. On
one side, to the east, lay the pale sweep of the
marshes and the silvery sheen of Merriminac Pond; to
the west, frostbitten pastures and farmland criss-
crossed with wobbling stone fences; while on the
highest point of the hill sat old Rodger's windmill, its
blades spinning like a whirligig as it ground last
summer's corn. The two arms of land still curved
around the harbor to hold it in a loose embrace, and
Samson knew that if he could see farther, beyond the
hilly pastures, he'd find the rocky shore of Cranberry
Point, and the tiny cottage where he and his sister
and two brothers had been born.

It was all the same, yet all different, too. He'd heard

Appledore had prospered, changed, and everywhere he looked he could see it. Those gray-shingled houses and shops had multiplied, nesting farther up the hill along new streets and paths like so many brooding hens keeping close against the cold. The meeting-house spire was now crowned by a gilded globe and a cockerel weathervane to crow the Second Coming. Three wharfs jutted out into the harbor where there had been but one before, with gambrel-roofed ware-houses waiting to be filled with goods from home-coming vessels. The muddy fenced common where everyone had kept their milch cow was gone, and in its place rose a brick markethouse with formal white-washed trimming, imposing and elegant enough to stand in Boston or Philadelphia.

And on the best lot on the hillside, aloof and apart from the other houses, sat a handsome four-square house with tall twin chimneys and glossy black shutters. His brother's house: no one else in Apple-dore would build such a gentleman's house, just as no other man would have gone clear to London to steal away some duke's granddaughter for his bride. Joshua's elopement with his Anabelle had been the talk of all New England for months.

No wonder that here in this town full of sailors, when people spoke of "the Captain," it was under-stood that they meant only one captain in particular, and only one of the Fairbourne captains at that. Unconsciously Samson's jaw tightened. Joshua was like that, determined to stand out wherever he went. His unmistakable mark was everywhere in Apple-dore, not only on his own grand new home but on all the other improvements in the town as well.

For the hundredth time Samson smoothed his hair back and resettled his hat on his head, then fussed with the lawn ruffles on the cuffs of his best shirt. Once he'd decided to come back to Appledore, he'd been determined to make a show of it himself. He'd had Zach work the crew extra hard to make every brass shine and every bit of paintwork on the *Morning Star* gleam, and he was secretly glad that he'd had to buy that fresh new set of sails in Charles Towne. He wasn't going to hang back and moor in the harbor like a poor relation, either. He'd already given orders for a gaudy bit of seamanship, to bring the ship alongside the Fairbourne wharf where even Joshua wouldn't be able to ignore them.

For many of the crew, this was an unexpected homecoming, and every man who wasn't actively involved with the ship's progress stood at the rail, eager for the first glimpse of his wife or sweetheart. They'd been noticed on shore by now, of course, and as word spread through the town more and more distant figures were beginning to gather on the dock. Indulgently Samson let the crew chatter among themselves, for he could understand their excitement even if he didn't share it. Besides, with all the fuss, no one was paying much heed to him and Polly, which was how he liked it.

He cleared his throat and glanced down at her beside him. He'd given her his spyglass to study the town as they drew closer, and her silence as she'd done so had been pointedly complete.

"Well now, Poll," he said with a great show of heartiness. "What do you make of Appledore?"

Slowly she lowered the glass from her eye and handed it back to him. "It looks to be as fine a town as Zach said," she said carefully. "Much finer than Ninnishibutt."

"Appledore's been here longer, that's all," he said,

not wanting her to feel ashamed of her own hometown, though God knew she'd a right to, considering. "And we've gone in for trading instead of fishing."

"I warrant you're right," she said without much enthusiasm, her gaze still on the town.

Samson frowned with concern. She looked pale to him this morning, almost fragile, and while everyone else on board was wearing his best shore-going clothes, to Samson's surprise she'd once again chosen her old boy's breeches, jacket, and likely her mysterious lucky piece in the pocket, too, with a borrowed coat that hung from her shoulders and over her hands like a scarecrow's. She'd been quiet all morning, now that he thought about it, even though he'd taken extra care to make her feel appreciated in his bunk before breakfast. Perhaps he'd been too enthusiastic in his lovemaking. Perhaps, he worried, he should have let her sleep late instead, and when he reached out to take her hand, she immediately curled her fingers into his for reassurance, the way a child might.

"You're not ill, Polly, are you?" he asked uneasily. "With all this chattering crowd about, would you rather go back below and rest until we've docked?"

She shook her head, still staring out at the town. "Which house is yours?"

"None," he said, silently cursing Zach and his misinformed opinions yet again. If Zach hadn't made it sound as if he owned half of the colony, then Polly wouldn't be disappointed now. Damnation, he should have gotten her to accept his proposal before this, when he'd still had a chance she'd agree, instead of acting like such an infernal coward and fearing she'd say no. Hell, he still hadn't found the right time to tell her he loved her, and now, by waiting, he'd only made things worse. Once Polly had met Joshua, God only knew what she'd decide.

"No house at all?" she repeated, sounding oddly hopeful.

"None," he said firmly, determined to be honest now, no matter what it might cost him. "But that grand one there on the hill belongs to my oldest brother."

"That is Joshua's? And Anabelle's, too?"

He nodded glumly. Joshua had been overbearing and lordly enough before he'd married a duke's granddaughter. What must he be like now, with such a prize on his arm?

He looked down at his dear Polly, with her boy's clothes and sunbrowned cheeks and hair that wisped from her braid, and with sickening dread he thought of how she'd appear in Joshua's eyes, side by side with his own extravagantly, exquisitely garbed wife.

God help him, if Josh dared say one word against Polly, if he breathed so much as a single unkind whisper in her direction, then he'd have to—

"Oh, Samson, I cannot do it," cried Polly in a rush, her doleful silence broken in a tumult of anxiety. "Look at me, *look* at me! I will shame you, I *know* it, and I'd never wish to do that before your family, before your own brother and his lady-wife!"

"None of that now, Polly," he said fiercely, appalled that he'd somehow transferred his misgivings to her. "None of that! You'll come with me, where you belong, and where you'll never shame me. Never, mind?"

But she shook her head, her silver eyes managing to be at once both defiant and miserable. "Nay,

Samson, best I stay on board, here, and hide myself away where I can cause you no disgrace!"

"And how little you must think of me, even to speak such!" he growled, more wounded than he wanted to admit. "A right faithless bastard, that's how you've painted me."

She sighed and seemed to wilt as he watched. "Nay, never that," she said unhappily. "Not you, Samson."

"Then come here, you little noddy." He drew her into his arms, grateful again for the excitement of the others that made him and Polly unnoticed as he held her tight against his chest. "How could you believe I'd tire of you because you aren't a twin to my brother's wife?"

"I didn't," she confessed, her arms wrapped tight around his waist. "I couldn't. But oh, Samson, this all scares me, scares me nigh to death!"

"Not you, Polly," he said as he gently stroked her hair. "Better to be my own brave lass, and not give a tinker's dam for what others think."

She sniffed and nodded her head against his chest, but she didn't pull away and he didn't let her go. Brave words, he thought, brave words indeed.

What a wretched pity he couldn't make himself believe them as well.

Thirteen

~⋘⋙~

*F*ew things made Polly feel so utterly alone than the safe return of a homebound ship. Whether the crew had been away for only a day after codfish, seven months on a deep-water voyage to London and back, or two years hunting whales off Greenland, the joyful family welcomes were always the same, celebrations of thanksgiving and happiness on wharfs or beaches that made her achingly aware of how she'd no one to care whether she returned or not.

Even now with Samson beside her at the wheel, she'd felt the same dull, too-familiar pain as the *Morning Star* had docked. Men had begun jumping from her side to the wharf even before the ship had been properly laid aside, while others waited until the gangplank had been lowered and their families and friends could rush aboard to meet them. The *Morning Star* had sailed from Boston two months ago, and Appledore men had been away from home at least another fortnight beyond that, long enough for wives to weep with relief at their return and children to become shy with fathers or older brothers they'd forgotten. The tale of how they'd all miraculously escaped the Spaniards was already being told with rich embellishment. Even Zach seemed to have yet another sweetheart in this port, a rosy-cheeked girl with glossy black hair who was clinging to him as tightly as a mussel to a rock.

"You've done a good thing, Samson, coming back to Appledore like this," said Polly softly, running her fingers along the polished spokes of the steering wheel. She'd rather have held *him,* but once the wheel had been lashed into place he'd been too preoccupied to take her hand again, and among so many strangers she'd been too shy to reach for his in turn. "You've made a great many people happy this day."

"I suppose I have, yes," said Samson with a shrug that was meant to be careless. But Polly knew that while he smiled, he was still searching the crowd of well-wishers for family of his own, and the reality of her own isolation struck her yet again. "That's worth a farthing or two, isn't it?"

"Oh, aye, indeed it is," she said as she tried to smile, too, and at least to appear as if she shared in the gaiety around her. "And I'd warrant it's worth a king's ransom to that girl with Zach."

Samson winced. "One of the Cullen daughters, though I can't guess which. When I sent him here from Boston to recruit Appledore men for the *Morning Star*'s crew, I didn't believe I'd left him time to consider the women as well."

She wrinkled her nose with feigned dismay. "I'd thought you wiser than that, Samson."

"Not too wise, but too trusting." He shook his head as he watched the younger man slide his arm

familiarly around the girl's waist. "But Cousin Zachariah had better watch himself with that one, unless he
wishes to meet the wrong end of William Cullen's
musket. Oh, blast, there's Captain Merrihew. I must
go to him, Poll. He's the harbormaster, and since I've
docked without his permission, I'll have to bow and
scrape for his forgiveness."

"Wait, and I'll come, too," she said hurriedly, but
Samson was already forging a path for himself
through the crowd, grinning and greeting well-
wishers as he went. With a forlorn sigh Polly let her
forehead rest against the tall wheel, her fingers tight
around the spokes. The snug, private world that she
and Samson had fashioned for themselves in his
cabin this last week, a blissful world of shared meals
and confidences and lovemaking, had evaporated
before her eyes in the pale November sunshine, and
she'd no notion of what would take its place. She
didn't belong among these happy, laughing people,
or in their tidy and prosperous town. Worst of all, as
she watched Samson moving farther and farther away
from her, she wasn't sure she even belonged any
longer with him.

"Pray, could you help me, lad?" asked a woman's
voice behind her, and Polly turned reluctantly to face
her.

She was younger than Polly would have guessed
from the breathless huskiness of her voice, most
likely younger than Polly herself, and so much shorter that she had to turn her round little face up toward
Polly's as she spoke. She wore a dark royal cloak that
made the blue of her eyes all the more startling, just
as the golden-brown fur that lined the cloak's hood
emphasized the perfect ivory of her skin, now only

slightly tinged with rose from the cold. On her small, plump hands were yellow kid gloves, edged with the same golden fur, and in her arms, bundled in a trailing, embroidered blanket, slept a baby with his bonneted head nestled into her shoulder.

"Why, you're not a boy at all!" exclaimed the woman. "How vastly stupid of me not to notice! Pray forgive me, if ever you can, though I am not sure if *I* would, in a similar predicament."

It was, decided Polly, a predicament this particular woman would never encounter. If she ever found a pair of breeches to fit her, she was so voluptuously, unmistakably female that not even a blind man would confuse her with a boy. Beside her Polly knew she must look gawky and brown and angular, but because the young woman's smile was so cheerfully warm she discovered that, for once, she didn't care.

"You are forgiven, ma'am," she said shyly, grateful to have someone to speak with. "'Tis a common enough mistake."

"Common or not, it's a monstrously ill-bred mistake for me to have made." She clucked her tongue as if to scold herself, and as she did the baby stirred in her arms, lifting his head heavily from her shoulder to rub his sleepy fist against his cheek. "Oh, no, no, my darling, it's not time to wake and squawk just yet. I know you must think me foolish not to give him to a nursemaid's keeping, but he's so dear to me I cannot do it. Hush, hush, little love, and back to sleep you go."

The baby opened one groggy eye halfway to consider Polly, then let it fall shut with a little sigh of contentment, oblivious to the crowds around him. He was a beautiful baby, his cheeks as round and well fed as his mother's, and much loved by her, too, from the way she kissed his drowsy forehead and from the care she'd lavished on his elaborately embroidered woolen cap, the silk ribbons tied in an extravagant if lopsided bow beneath his chubby chins. He would, decided Polly with a wistful yearning, be exactly the kind of baby she'd wish for herself, if she were ever so fortunate to become a mother. There was even something about his sweet baby face that reminded her of Samson, enough that he could be his son.

"How proud you must be of him, ma'am," she murmured, wishing she could touch his velvety skin. She'd spent so little time in the company of other women that babies remained a mystery to her. "He's a beautiful babe."

The woman grinned, her cheeks dimpling. "Oh, I'll grant you he's beautiful enough now, an angel when he's asleep, but he's a perfect little tyrant when he's awake and cross, shaking his fists and demanding instant obedience. No wonder his papa spoils him so; they are cut from the same ell of cloth entirely. Entirely!"

She laughed merrily, her gold ear-bobs dancing in the sunlight. Polly laughed, too, but the mention of the baby's father made her realize guiltily how long she'd monopolized the woman's time, time she'd doubtless rather be spending with her newly returned husband.

"Are you here to find your husband, ma'am?" she asked, mentally running down the *Morning Star*'s crew as she puzzled over who among them would have such a young woman for a wife. "I can go look for him, if you wish."

"You'd have quite a hunt, if you went searching for

my husband," the woman answered. "He's gone across the county for the court sessions, and *that's* such sport to him that I haven't a notion when he'll return home. Tomorrow at the earliest, if they don't decide to hang anyone."

She leaned forward, inviting Polly's confidence as she lowered her voice to a conspirator's whisper. "It is just as well that he is away, for I do not think he would consider my being here entirely proper. I'm here, you see, to meet another gentleman."

Polly's mouth fell open with surprise as once again she considered who among the crewmen would make such an assignation. "Another gentleman, ma'am? On board the *Morning Star?*"

"La, yes!" The woman winked gleefully. "And the wickedest part is that I have never once laid eyes upon this gentleman, let alone any other part of my person, and I—oh, oh, that *must* be him!"

She scurried around Polly, carefully supporting the baby's head while her own hood flopped backward onto her shoulders. She hurried around the open hatch, wriggled between two dockmen with a smile as an excuse, and then, to Polly's shock, stopped directly before Samson as he was coming back to the quarterdeck.

"Samson Fairbourne!" she exclaimed as heads all around her turned to watch. "My most prodigal and mysterious brother Samson! For so you must be, you know, since I am Anabelle, Anabelle Fairbourne, and your own brother's wife. But you have guessed that already, haven't you? It is so vastly fine to have met you at last!"

She thrust out her hand with the wrist cocked downward, expecting Samson to kiss it. But Samson was too stunned for such niceties, staring at Anabelle as if she'd been a hideous sea serpent cast up on his deck instead of his brother's wife.

"Anabelle?" he said at last with a self-consciously awkward sharpness that would have made the sailors beneath him quake with dread. His expression was grim and fixed, his scowl of a gaze directed somewhere above her head. "Anabelle. Your—ah, your servant, ma'am."

He neither lifted his hat to her nor bowed. Anabelle's small, yellow-gloved hand remained hanging in the air, unnoticed, unkissed. Her baby began to cry.

It was enough to make Polly forget her own shyness and rush to the rescue of all three.

"Samson," she said as she came to stand beside Anabelle. "Samson, isn't it fine that Mistress Fairbourne has come to welcome us to Appledore? Your brother is away, but she came expressly to greet you. And their baby, too. This is your brother's *son*, Samson, your own nephew."

"Alexander," said Anabelle helpfully, and helpfully, too, she removed her hand from the fray, settling it instead upon her fussing son's back.

"Alexander?" repeated Samson incredulously, staring down at the baby. "Now that's a damned peculiar name for Josh to give his son."

"He didn't," said Anabelle, so unperturbed that Polly guessed the two brothers must share a gift for tactlessness. "I did. Alexander Fitzgerald Fairbourne. I had him baptized for Alexander the Great, the Macedonian king. It suits him, being imperious, and besides, it sounds vastly fine and antique. The Fitzgerald's for *my* brother, who's Alexander's godfather."

"Alexander Fitzgerald Fairbourne," said Samson with patent disbelief. "Jesus, what a mouthful."

" 'Tis no more unwieldy than 'Samson,' " said Polly, determined to defend such a lovely baby. "And you must love him regardless, for he is your kin."

Anabelle turned and beamed at Polly. "And who, pray, is this wise and charming lady, Samson? She had been most helpful to me, and it would be so agreeable to be able to thank her by her own Christian name."

Samson looked at Polly, his eyes bleak with the same open despair he would have shown if he'd been drowning.

Which, Polly suddenly realized, in a way he was. Being without any family herself, she'd simply assumed that he would be eager to return to see the siblings he'd been blessed with—which, clearly, for whatever reason, wasn't the case. She'd always assumed, too, that he hadn't returned to Appledore because of the demands of his voyages, but it seemed more likely now that he'd stayed away from choice instead. Poor, poor Samson! It wasn't mere churlishness that was making him behave so badly with Anabelle Fairbourne, but such genuine reluctance to trust his brother's wife that it bordered on fear.

He frowned, concentrating, and cleared his throat with such determination that Polly longed to be able to take him aside and ask what had happened, what was wrong, what she could do to make it right for him. If he was drowning, then she wanted to be the one to pull him back to shore.

"This, Mistress Fairbourne," he began, "that is, ah, Anabelle, this is Miss Polly Ann Bray, of Ninnishibutt River. Miss Bray has been my, ah, my special guest on the *Morning Star* since Bridgetown."

"A special guest": so that was how Polly was to be introduced to his family. Fair enough, she decided, considering how awkward the truth could be.

But with only a single arched brow and the slightest twist to her mouth, Anabelle managed to convey how scandalously improper such a well-meant arrangement sounded and how vastly interesting, too.

"Samson—that is, Captain Fairbourne—he rescued me," said Polly hastily. "I'd been swept over the side of my boat, and he saved me from drowning and offered to bring me home."

"Oh, my poor Miss Bray!" cried Anabelle with more genuine sympathy than Polly would have expected. "To be cast away into the sea, to face your end by drowning, is a terrible thing—most terrible! And to lose all your belongings, your clothes, everything! But, oh, how very fortunate for you that Samson sailed into your life at the perfect moment! One marvels at the workings of Fate when such disasters are so tidily resolved."

Polly didn't dare look at Samson. The workings of Fate, whatever they were, couldn't have half the influence over their lives as did the little bottle carefully tucked deep in her pocket.

"But Fate has done quite enough," continued Anabelle, "and now it is up to me to follow in her footsteps. Is Fate a her, I wonder, or a he? I disremember myself. Yes, yes, I'm quite resolved, so do not try to dissuade me. You must come with me now, Miss Bray, and stay with us on dry land as long as you please. Surely you are ready to trade that wretched hard bunk for a decent featherbed, aren't you?"

"Polly isn't going anywhere," said Samson, falling back into his usual manner of a captain who expected to be obeyed. "Damnation, Anabelle, she's been my guest this long, and there's no reason for her to up and become Joshua's now."

But obeying captains, even Fairbourne captains, didn't seem to be something that Anabelle did.

"There most certainly is a reason, Samson," she said without hesitation as she smoothed Alexander's cap back from where it had slipped over his eyes. "While it was perfectly gallant of you to have her as your guest whilst you were at sea and there were no other lodgings available, to keep her here on your ship with only you and your men for companionship—la, that is hardly a credit to Miss Bray's virtue, is it?"

Polly flushed with silent misery. How could either she or Samson quarrel with an argument like this? What had been acceptable at sea would never be so on land, at least not in this colony. While the *Morning Star*'s crew, even Zach, had politely pretended not to see what had blossomed between their captain and the castaway, they would certainly be telling their friends and family about it around the hearthfires tonight. How could they not? If Polly insisted on staying with Samson now, the way she desperately wished, then Anabelle and the rest of Samson's town would call her his whore.

Only she knew he'd asked her to be his wife. Only she knew she'd turned him down.

Anabelle smiled at her warmly over the baby's head, already assuming her hospitality would be welcomed. No matter how much deep-water captains expected to be obeyed, decided Polly unhappily, granddaughters of dukes expected it even more.

"We'll find some decent clothing for you, too, Miss Bray," said Anabelle. "No need for you to be mistaken for a boy again. La, however could I have done that, with you so pretty and all?"

Polly's flush deepened. She knew Anabelle was simply being kind, just as she knew she wasn't pretty, especially not in the way that Anabelle herself was.

"Polly looks fine the way she is," said Samson. "More than fine, even, since that's how she wants to dress. She's not like that puling baby of yours, you know. She can decide for herself."

Polly stared at him, her amazement mingled with an unquestioning rush of love. When had he come to understand her so well?

"Besides, I have other clothes of my own, too," she said proudly, so happy that she was unable to take her gaze away. He *was* hers, this great, growling, handsome man with his blue eyes squinting just a little against the sun and his sister-in-law. "Beautiful lady-clothes. Samson bought them for me, in St. Pierre, at the same shop where your husband has bought things for you."

Samson made an odd little rumble in his throat that could only have lodged there from embarrassment. "That was part of the wager, Poll, mind? I had to let that Frenchwoman have her way with you, else Zach would never learn to keep away from strumpets."

Anabelle blinked, and as her smile widened with glee, Polly's heart sank. Even staying under the roof of Captain Joshua Fairbourne wasn't going to redeem her virtue as long as the captain's wife was waiting to gather up all the tempting, disreputable details with such undisguised relish.

"Wagers and strumpets and Madame LaFontaine, too!" crowed the smaller woman. "What a vastly amusing voyage you must have had! You must tell me all, Miss Bray, and then Samson can tell his version tonight when we all dine together. *En famille*, which means Serena and Duckie as well."

"Duckie?" repeated Samson. "What sorry creature has my sister taken in now?"

"Only her husband," said Anabelle blithely. "His real name is Gerald, of course, but because he is my dearest brother and I have called him 'Duckie' for so long, I cannot change now. I shall expect you no later than seven by the clock, Samson, but of course you may show yourself earlier, howsoever you please. Now come with me, Miss Bray, and let us leave the captain to whatever it is that sailors always find needs doing about their ships."

She turned toward the gangway without pausing to see if Polly followed or not.

But Polly didn't budge. She knew exactly what sailors found to do on board their ships, and she'd rather stay here doing them with Samson than anything else in the world. From the way he was smiling at her—or, more precisely, half smiling and half grimacing—she knew he'd prefer to keep her here, too.

"Miss Bray?" called Anabelle expectantly from the gangway. The baby was awake now, snuffling and twisting awkwardly in her arms. "You are coming? I can't tarry much longer. Alexander needs to return home, as you can see for yourself. Or rather, perhaps you can see, but I can smell his urgency."

Yet still Polly hesitated, torn between what she wished to do and what she should. She smiled

uncertainly toward Anabelle, and as she did she felt
Samson's hand come to rest upon her shoulder,
strong and sure, his thumb rubbing gently at the side
of her neck.

"Go with her, lass," he said softly, for her ears
alone. " 'Tis right. But take care you don't forget me
before supper, eh?"

Polly perched on the very edge of the tall-backed
armchair and cautiously sipped her tea. She could not
imagine which would be worse: to allow the fragile
porcelain dish, so fine the firelight glowed through it,
to slip through her clumsy fingers and shatter on the
floor, or to let her rough, unsteady hand slop the hot,
dark tea from the dish onto the yellow and pink
chintz flowers that covered the feather-filled cushions
of the armchair. She'd barely survived pouring the
tea from the long-spouted silver pot and setting it
back down on its unsteady little feet without disaster,
and then carrying the too-full dish of tea back to her
chair without stumbling. Who would have guessed
that drinking tea with Anabelle Fairbourne would be
so fraught with endless peril?

And it wasn't the tea-drinking alone. When she'd
followed Anabelle beneath the tall pedimented doorway, she'd entered a rare new world, full of beautiful
things as well as dangers. Even here in the corner
bedchamber that Anabelle shared with Joshua, there
was more to wonder at than in any one shop in
Boston, from colored drawings as real as life, framed
and hung behind glass, to gaily painted porcelain
figures that seemed to dance along the chimney shelf.
The chamber's paneled walls were painted a deep,

rich green, the same color as the new ferns in the woods near the river at home. What must it be like to awaken each morning in a room where it was always spring, and as warm as spring, too, thanks to the fire that burned so brightly, without a thought for the heady cost of firewood? And what, too, would it be like to sleep in a bedstead piled so high with feather-beds and coverlets that it needed a little three-step ladder to climb into it, or one with curtains and a rich canopy that could be drawn closed and snug against chills and drafts? She had spent so much of her life being wet and cold that the idea of drifting to sleep warm, safe, and dry was, for her, beyond imagining.

Beyond imagining, too, was possessing the kind of easy, inborn grace that Anabelle had even as she rocked gently back and forth, nursing Alexander, or the elegance and the confidence to live among so many beautiful objects as if she'd always done so. Which, of course, as a grand noble lady, she had.

But was this what Samson expected of her, too? Is this why he'd decided to let her come with Anabelle, that she might observe and learn these graces that were expected for a Fairbourne captain's wife? She was willing to do a great many things for him, but there were others that were completely impossible, no matter how much she loved him.

At least that was what she steadfastly told herself, trying to remember all the good and useful skills she already could claim, such as splicing a rope stronger than it had first been made, or sighting and identifying another ship far away on the horizon. And hadn't Samson defended her wearing her breeches, as shabby and worn as they were by comparison to the chintz-covered cushion beneath them?

"There now, Alexander, you small and voracious person, that should satisfy you for at least a quarter of an hour," Anabelle was saying as with one hand she deftly laced the top of her bodice closed again. In reply Alexander released a large and satisfied burp over her shoulder and rubbed his face against the cloth his mother was using to protect her clothes. "And now, of course, you'll wish to sleep again, which means you'll be chirping like my own tiny sparrow come midnight. You smile now, Miss Bray, but you won't be half as happy when he rouses you tonight."

"Perhaps he's only practicing for when he'll keep watch on his father's ship," suggested Polly as Anabelle carried the baby to his cradle. She was sorry to see him go to sleep again so soon. Now that she knew he was a Fairbourne, too, she saw even more of the family's resemblance in miniature, and she liked the chance to picture how Samson might have looked as a baby, and how in turn his own son might appear. "Four hours awake, four hours asleep."

"Then that is entirely Joshua's fault, giving his son such nonsensical ideas of behavior," said Anabelle as she bent to draw the coverlet over the baby. "Or perhaps it is mine, for setting him to sleep in such an outsized boat of a cradle."

" 'Tis very large," ventured Polly, hoping that that would be sufficient comment. She'd never seen such an enormous cradle, nor one so awkwardly unappealing. She guessed it was old, for the wood had darkened with time to nearly black, with countless scratches and gouges that could have come only with long and hard use. If it were a boat, as Anabelle said, then it was an ungainly, bluff-bowed boat, with thick turned spindles to keep the baby from tumbling overboard. The only frivolous thing about the entire cradle was the sweet-faced angel carved into the bonnet, eager to smile her grace upon any baby sleeping below.

"Very large, and rather ugly," said Anabelle with a frankness that made Polly wish she'd said something less guarded, if untrue. "You don't have to pretend otherwise. I did not make Joshua haul it clear from London because it was beautiful. No. But it was my poor mother's before she died, and her mother's before, and goodness knows how many others of my blood, which to me makes it supremely beautiful."

Lightly Anabelle touched her fingertip to the angel's smile, and her own smile, full of memories both happy and bittersweet, made it clear that, in a room full of costly treasures, the ungainly cradle was the greatest treasure of all to her, and the one, too, that Polly could truly envy. Her own mother had died the same day she'd been born, and she'd nothing at all of her beyond the handful of memories that her heartbroken father had shared. How she wished she'd something like this cradle to connect herself to the past and the mother she'd never known!

"No wonder you care for it so," she said softly. "How could you not, if it was your mother's?"

"Ah, but it has more story than that, you see," said Anabelle with a grin that was hardly maternal. "When I met Joshua, I was quite promised to another man, and so Joshua had to steal me off, right from under my grandmother's nose, which was vastly scandalous—I vow I would be pelted with rubbish if I dared show my face in London again in this life! Joshua brought me here on his ship, but on our way he and I were washed over the side in a great storm, and only by hanging to this cradle were we saved. So I am doubly thankful that it is so old and large, since it's rather our ark, too. If we hadn't been washed overboard, and then clung to the cradle, and *then* been castaway on that little island with only each other for amusement, why then, Alexander wouldn't be here now at all. Well, at least not quite so soon as he did appear."

"Nay," said Polly weakly, the only thing she could say to such an astounding confidence. In Ninnishi-butt, families could live side by side for generations and not exchange above a hundred words. But in London society, it seemed, there were no conversational constraints at all.

Anabelle touched the wooden angel's smile again as she gazed happily down at her sleeping son. "That is what I meant earlier about the workings of Fate. I cannot explain how or why, but I do believe that through this cradle my mother kept Joshua and me safe through that terrible storm, just as Samson was somehow brought to you, for that same purpose. It is all vastly strange and wonderful, isn't it?"

It was, thought Polly. But besides being vastly strange and wonderful it was also vastly unsettling and outright scary, too, when she remembered the power of the bottle in her pocket. And as much as she might wish for a memento from her unknown mother, she hoped it would be something more auspicious than an empty rum bottle with a smudged scrap of paper corked inside.

"But here I am, prattling on and on and *on*, as I always do," said Anabelle as she settled in the chair across the table from Polly's, arranging her petticoats about her with a well-practiced sweep. "I've barely left you space to breathe, let alone to tell me the fascinating story of your voyage."

Self-consciously Polly set the tea dish down on the table. "There's not that much of a story to tell."

"Oh." Anabelle's mouth drew into a moue of acute disappointment. "That is what people say when there is in fact a great deal of story, none of which they are inclined to share. But I shall not beg you, nor pry. You are my guest, and I will respect your privacy."

Polly looked down at her empty dish, thoroughly unhappy with herself. She liked Anabelle, liked her enough to want to trust her with the "story" of how she and Samson had found one another and everything else since. But speaking about herself didn't come easily, the way it did with Anabelle, and besides, there were so many things about her and Samson and that wretched bottle that she couldn't explain to herself, let alone to a woman she'd met only that morning.

Anabelle sighed with polite resignation, straightening the rings she wore on three of her fingers. "We shall speak of other matters, then. As Joshua will doubtless tell you, I can speak of nigh anything, or nothing, or them both together by the hour. But now I have a most specific something to ask of you, a great mystery that has plagued me since I heard the *Morning Star* was at the point. Why has Samson decided to return to Appledore now?"

Polly smiled with relief. This was easy to answer. "Madame LaFontaine asked him to deliver gowns to you, and because Appledore is near to Boston, he agreed."

"Oh, bah," scoffed Anabelle, her plump hand slicing through the air in dismissal. "That is nonsense. No male, at least no Fairbourne male, would order their ship and a score of men out of their way to deliver a bundle of bespoke petticoats. Especially not after he has kept away for years and years."

Polly's smile faded with uncertainty. "He wished to see his brother and sister?"

"Now you do disappoint me, Miss Bray, truly you do." Anabelle leaned forward, resting her chin on her linked hands, her elbows propped on the table's piecrust edge. "You need spend only a very little time with any of this family to see that the men have great difficulty getting along with one another."

"Samson scarce speaks of his family at all," said Polly softly. "When I first heard of you, from the mantua-maker, I thought you were his—his wife."

Anabelle laughed, deep in her throat. "More likely his *mistress*," she said with an accuracy that horrified Polly, "and some grasping little baggage at that. But I will tell you this much, Miss Bray. Oh, bother, but that sounds clumsy! May I call you Polly instead, and you call me Anabelle, or Nan?"

Polly nodded swiftly. She hadn't been calling the other woman anything.

"I will tell you this much, Polly," Anabelle began again. "I love my husband more than the world, and I will do most anything to make him happy. He has me, and Alexander, and his ships, and oh, a thousand other things that help. But there are dark places in his past, in his soul, that I cannot touch. What Joshua needs next is to see his family as one again, and not scattered all over God's creation. And now you, dearest Polly, have brought Samson home."

"I didn't bring him!" exclaimed Polly. "No one could make Samson do that if he didn't wish it!"

"Of course not, for he is both Fairbourne and male,

which makes him close kin to donkeys in degrees of stubbornness." Anabelle narrowed her eyes with mock sagacity and pointed one bejeweled finger at Polly. "But even if neither of you realize how it has happened, he *is* here in Appledore, and it *is* your doing, though you shall never hear it again outside of this chamber."

"But I never did—"

"You did, and I refuse to quarrel with you over it otherwise." Her merriment faded, her face turning serious. "I know nothing of you, dear Polly, and less of your people. But with precious few exceptions, the family into which I was born is wicked and deceitful enough to shame a pack of jackals. The Fairbournes may not be perfection incarnate, but they are infinitely better than the Crosbies, and for the sake of my husband and my son, I mean to do my best for them the same as they've done for me. Does that make any sense to you at all?"

Once again Polly could only nod, but this time her silence came from being so dangerously close to weeping. How could what Anabelle said leave her untouched? Her poor, careworn father had done everything he could for her, and though each night she blessed him in her prayers for it, he had never been able to make up for the warmth and security of a mother and brothers and sisters. No wonder Anabelle longed to see the Fairbourne brothers reconciled.

And could she herself wish any less for Samson? The same dark corners that Anabelle sensed in Joshua lurked there in Samson, too. She knew he'd never admit it, but perhaps he had come back to Appledore to try to find the answers to the shadows in his past before he could find a future with her, and the love she needed to go with it. It was a bold, daring hope to consider, but it was possible. It was *possible*.

"There now, I've prattled on too long," said Anabelle softly, reaching out to pat Polly's hand. "After all you've suffered, you must surely be exhausted, yet still I burden you with my own worries instead. La, what a sorry hostess I make!"

She laughed then, but now the bright cheer was missing, and they both knew it. With a sigh, she shook her head and rose, leading Polly toward the hall, and the bedchamber that would be hers.

Yet at the doorway, she paused, impulsively standing on her toes to give Polly a swift, fierce hug. "I am so vastly glad you're here, Polly Bray! Your coming is a great, good thing to this house. I can feel it tingling to the tips of my toes, and my toes do not lie."

Polly smiled as Anabelle lifted her hem to show her feet, and she silently prayed those toes in their red-heeled mules were tingling true for her.

"There were times on board the *Morning Star* when I didn't believe in good luck at all," she admitted, and she fought the urge to touch the bottle in her pocket. "Faith, I was certain I was a Jonah."

"A Jonah?" repeated Anabelle, mystified.

"A Jonah." Polly gave her shoulders a little restless shrug. "At sea a Jonah's a bearer of ill fortune. A Jonah can be an animal, a pet cat kept by the cook, or even a parrot in the wardroom, but most often it's a person that is the Jonah and brings bad luck to the ship and crew with him. Or her."

"Then you are no Jonah, Polly," said Anabelle firmly. "With you, I feel sure that only the very best of luck for us all is on its way."

* * *

Just as from the water Appledore had looked as
Samson had pictured it, this scene, too, was one he'd
seen countless times in his mind's eye, a version of
home that was every bit as idealized, and every bit as
seductive.

A long table still spread with the remnants of a
good supper, the rich aromas of roasted beef, pota-
toes, and Madeira sauce still lingering. The glow of
the candles reflected in the matched mirrors on the
walls and in the silver platters and serving spoons
and, more muted, in the well-polished mahogany of
the table. Another bottle of wine had been uncorked
to fill the glasses one more time, and the warmth of
the laughter and conversation matched the comfortable heat from the fire that crackled and popped in
the hearth, and kept the cold November night outdoors where it belonged.

In the chair beside him sat sister Serena, her hand
resting lightly on his sleeve as if to reassure herself
that he truly was there. She'd grown more beautiful
than he'd remembered, or maybe it was happiness
that made her seem so, her hair gleaming like burnished gold in the candlelight and her cheeks full and
rosy as ripe peaches in summer.

Happiness, and love, the love that beamed from
her face each time she looked across the table to the
handsome man who'd become her husband. Gerald
Crosbie was witty and charming, with a quickness
that made Samson vaguely uneasy, just as the heavy
silver embroidery and fur trimmings on Gerald's
velvet coat struck Samson as more appropriate for an
empty-headed courtier than a man wed to his only
sister. But there was no questioning his devotion to
Serena, or the gentleness with which he treated her
now that she was so large with their coming child.

There was no questioning Anabelle's devotion to Joshua, either, not from the way she'd glance wistfully to his empty place at the head of the table whenever his name was mentioned. How Joshua had so captivated a woman like Anabelle was a puzzle to Samson. She was every bit the delightful, flirtatious beauty that Joshua had sworn she was, but what would make such a lighthearted young woman run away with his grim, overbearing older brother? For himself, Samson suspected he'd soon tire of her almost giddy high spirits, her beauty notwithstanding; and following her convoluted conversations, especially those with Gerald, seemed as exhausting and fruitless as chasing a wispy trail of woodsmoke.

Besides, for himself, there was only one woman he'd never tire of, and she was now sitting across the table from him. At most he'd been apart from Polly six hours, but after the endless proximity of their voyage that six hours had been among the longest of his life to bear. He had missed her, missed her more than he'd dreamed would be possible, yet to have her now an arm's length away and not be able to touch her, to hold her, to kiss her, was nearly worse than not seeing her at all.

To his surprise, she wore one of the gowns he'd bought her in St. Pierre. He'd told her to wear the old boy's clothing she preferred, and he couldn't decide if she'd changed because he had, or in spite of it, or if she'd done so simply to be more like Anabelle.

In his eyes, there was no contest between the two women. Polly's gown was pale green silk that emphasized her sun-browned skin rather than trying to make it seem more fashionably lighter, the style simply cut close to her body. It still startled him to see how small her waist became when laced in by stays, and how round and high her breasts. Doubtless with Anabelle's help, she had twined the black lace scarf around her throat and into the front of her bodice with Madame LaFontaine's artful elegance, but she'd worn her hair down, loose over her shoulders the way he liked. As little as he knew of ladies' fashions, he did understand this to be decidedly unstylish, but he understood, too, that she'd done it for him, which mattered infinitely more.

Yet as beautiful, as desirable, as she looked to him now, what he'd missed the most in those interminable six hours had been her company. How many times in the day had he longed to ask her opinion, or to show her something unusual about the ship? She seemed to be enjoying herself—they had yet to be left alone together so he could ask for sure—with Anabelle, and while he acknowledged that this was a good thing, the right thing, in his heart he believed her true place was back on the *Morning Star*, not here in his brother's house.

Damnation, he thought with despair, her true place was with *him*. What in blazes was it going to take for her to realize it, too?

"I said, Samson, that surely you will grant us that much?" Anabelle sipped her wine, waiting for his reply, and by the hint of an edge to her voice he wondered how many times she'd already asked him the same question. "It's only a pittance, even for the captain of the *Morning Star*."

He frowned and tapped his finger against the side of his glass, considering how much of his profits from this voyage he would offer to learn whatever it was that Anabelle had asked.

"You told me you couldn't remain in Appledore above two or three days," said Polly. "On account of the countinghouse men in Boston."

He could tell from the way she blinked at him above her smile that she'd seen his dilemma, and for that alone he would have married her that moment, before the cheese and brandy, if only she'd agree.

"True enough," he said firmly. "Two or three days at the most."

And perhaps, if fortune really shined upon him, they'd slip away before that, and before Joshua returned as well.

"Two or three days, you say." Polly's smile faded, her gaze slipping away from his. "And then I shall be home in Ninnishibutt."

Hell, was she having that fine a time here that she wished to linger forever? Or was she that eager to return home, and be rid of me for good?

"But that is more than time enough to make the arrangements!" exclaimed Anabelle gaily as she clapped her hands. "La, I can do it in a single hour! A party in your honor, a right, royal frolic, with music and dancing and a supper at midnight!"

"Hang the supper, Nan," said Gerald amiably. "All a first-rate hostess need supply is plenty of strong drink for the gentlemen, and plenty of candles for the ladies, the better to show off their gowns and figures whilst dancing."

"Dancing?" repeated Samson, stunned. This was Massachusetts. This was Joshua's *house*. "And music?"

"Yes, yes, yes," said Anabelle, clearly unaware of how rare such an event would be in Appledore, or at least the Appledore that Samson remembered. "I've found fiddlers in the ships that would make you believe you were back in Dublin itself! And as for the supper, why—oh, hush, and listen!''

Even though she'd been the one talking, they all sat obediently still, listening with her. The creak of the key turning in the heavy box-lock, the heavy front door swinging open with a rush of the wind and closing with a *thump*, the footsteps in the hall, footsteps that Anabelle recognized at once as she rose from her chair, her face aglow with anticipation.

Footsteps, too, that Samson himself would have known anywhere, but without anticipation, without rejoicing, without anything more than the dull weight of dread in his belly that he never seemed to outgrow.

"Samson," said Joshua Fairbourne as he filled the doorway. "God help us all, it is you."

Fourteen

～

$\mathcal{N}$ot having brothers of her own, Polly couldn't say for sure that this was an ill-humored way for Joshua to greet Samson. Men could be odd with each other like that. But one quick glance across the table toward Samson, one instant to see how tightly his fingers were gripping the wineglass as he fought to keep his face impassive, and she knew her first guess had been right.

"How fine it is to see you, too, Joshua," he said, clearly striving to sound as if he didn't care. "Though I recall you depending more upon aid from the Devil than the Almighty."

"Indeed." Joshua's face remained coldly impassive while Polly held her breath for Samson's sake. The resemblance between the two brothers was striking—they both shared the same dark hair and blue eyes, the same ability to fill a room with the force of their presence alone—but though there was at most three years between them, Joshua seemed far older. He was still a handsome man; those first strands of silver in his dark hair added character, and the deeply etched lines that radiated from the corners of his eyes could be found on anyone who followed the sea.

But there was something in those eyes that made her believe he'd seen things he wished he hadn't, a deep, hidden sorrow that had tested and hardened him, and she remembered what Anabelle had said about the dark shadows in his soul. They were there, those shadows, in his soul and written bold upon his face in a way that almost made Polly shiver. His first words had been to ask God for help, but she'd wager that help should go first to whatever man dared cross Joshua Fairbourne.

Then, with the same abruptness as the sun breaking through a winter's sky, he smiled. "Time hasn't gentled you, has it, little brother?" he asked softly. "But at least you've seen fit to come home to meet my bride."

With a chuckle of happiness, Anabelle held up her arms to welcome him home, the soft lace at her cuffs turning back over her wrists. Clearly she was his shelter, his safe harbor from whatever had carved those lines into his face. His embrace was so eager that he lifted her from her chair, one arm curled around her waist and the other hand trailing gently down her throat to her breast, and they kissed with such open ardor that Polly looked down at her plate in embarrassment. If Joshua and Anabelle were this way after a year of marriage, what must they have been like when he'd carried her off from London?

"There now, love, you sit," said Anabelle when they separated at last. Flushed by the passion of her husband's kiss, she seemed to glow with the sheer joy of having him back. "I'll have your food warmed and brought out while you chat with Samson."

"Oh, aye, my dear brother Samson," he said, as he slowly circled the long table, unfastening the pewter clasp on his long, black boat-cloak. "Samson the prodigal, Samson the Boston-man, Samson who's grown too fine to sail from Appledore."

"Stop it, Josh," said Serena quickly. "I don't want to hear you two squabbling again, not tonight. Sam's done nothing you didn't do yourself, and nothing at all to deserve your name-calling."

Samson's smile in return was tight and guarded. "Serena's right, Joshua. Everything I've done I've learned from you, just as you wanted it."

"And so now my sins have come back to roost in my own house." With a sigh Joshua dropped heavily into his chair, reaching for the bottle of wine. "I suppose I should be grateful that you've come back at all, eh?"

"Joshua, love," said Anabelle, rapping her knuckles impatiently on the table. "Behave yourself, or you shall have no dinner."

"I've already eaten. I stopped at the Swan on my way," said Joshua. "But for your sake alone, sweetheart, I promise to behave."

The silence around the table, little more than a truce between the two brothers, yawned uncomfortably while Joshua swirled the wine in his glass. Granted, it *was* his house, but for Samson's sake, Polly did wish he had stayed at that tavern just a little longer.

"All the talk in Barnstable was of a strange Spanish ship that every sot in the county has sworn he's seen," he said almost pensively. "Who would have guessed the rogue would turn out to be Sam?"

And with that, Polly's patience as a guest snapped.

"Samson is not a rogue," she declared, "and there is absolutely nothing about the lines of the *Morning Star* that could make anyone confuse it with a Spanish ship."

Samson's fist slammed down on the table, hard enough to make the forks rattle. "Damnation, Poll, listen to what he's saying! A Spanish ship, here, and—"

"And exactly who *are* you, young woman?" asked Joshua, ignoring his brother to turn toward Polly.

"Polly Ann Bray of Ninnishibutt River." She had the distinct feeling that he'd only just noticed her at the table, and while most times she knew she wasn't particularly noticeable, tonight, in the gown that Samson had given her, such a slight stung her pride. "And you are wicked wrong about the *Morning Star.* To be Spanish she'd need her quarterdeck raised and her bows blunted. Even a Barnstable *sot* could see the difference."

"Miss Bray is my guest, Joshua," said Anabelle quickly. "*Our* guest. She was cast away from her ship into the sea, just as we were, before Samson rescued her."

But Joshua's expression didn't change, his attention still riveted to Polly and that single word *sot,* the glass with the wine in his hand going pointedly untouched. "You seem to know a great deal about Spanish ships, Miss Bray."

"I know about one in particular, Captain Fairbourne." She would not flinch from his gaze, nor be the first to look away. "The *San Miguel,* which belongs to a filthy rogue of a *guardacosta* named Hidaldgo who has tried to take us prisoner, oh, about a dozen times, but we always got clear."

"This is what I've been trying to say!" said Samson excitedly. "If Hidaldgo has followed us this far, if he's here in our own waters, then—"

"No shoptalk of ships, Samson, I warn you," said Anabelle, rapping her knuckles on the table for emphasis. "You, too, Polly. I have few rules at my table, but that is one of them, and I expect it to be obeyed. I suggest we return to discussing the party. Joshua, love, we are hosting a small frolic tomorrow night to welcome Samson and Miss Bray to Appledore."

But for once Joshua didn't seem to hear her. "Hidaldgo here, Sam?" he said, one skeptical brow raised. "I cannot believe the devil has the ballocks to do it."

"Joshua, love," murmured Anabelle mildly, "you forget yourself. Again."

"Forgive me, sweetheart," he answered with affectionate contrition. "But Don Hidaldgo's enough to make me forget my own name. I'll call for volunteers and outfit an armed sloop to search for him tomorrow. I suppose I must send word to the admiral in Boston, too, and to—"

"This is my business, Joshua," said Samson curtly. "And I'll tend to it my way."

Joshua swept his hand through the air, dismissing Samson's objections. "You've brought Hidaldgo here to Appledore, true, but by doing so you've made it my business as well. I can't afford to sit back and let some Spaniard come plunder my home while you decide how to 'tend' to him."

"And you wonder why I stayed away," said Samson bitterly. "Or have you forgotten that once Appledore was my home, too, before you claimed it all for yourself?"

"You never could abide taking orders from me, could you, Sam?" said Joshua. "No wonder you went off to Boston instead of sailing for me, as was right for brothers. No loyalty to this family, not from you. Instead you always wanted to be master yourself, whether you were fit for it or not."

"I'd still be waiting if I'd left it for you to decide!"

"I would have made you a captain when you were ready," said Joshua, his eyes turning flinty. "Do you think I would have risked a ship and a cargo and crew otherwise, let alone your own damned fool neck?"

Furiously Samson shoved his chair back from the table to rise to his feet. "Mark the order you put that in, with me dead last, and then say no more of loyalty."

Automatically Joshua rose, too, the two tall, angry men looming over the table. "Damn it, Sam, you could not be trusted to act alone! You were too blasted headstrong to be a master! Hell, to hear you now, you still are!"

"What I hear, Joshua," said Samson, "is that nothing has changed between us, and never shall."

He turned and bowed curtly to Anabelle. "I thank you for your hospitality, ma'am, and I wish you a good night. Serena, Gerald, until tomorrow. And Polly . . ."

In the half second his gaze met hers, she could glimpse the bottomless pain that fueled his anger to such white-hot fury, the hurt like a child's that cried out for understanding and comfort. She began to slide back her chair, meaning to go to him, but before she could he'd shuttered the pain away again, his face again the stony shield he'd showed to his brother.

"Polly, lass, good night," he said with another rigidly formal bow. "Good night, and sleep well."

And then, before anyone could stop him, he was gone.

Polly had wondered what sleeping on a featherbed would be like, but though she lay deep in the warm burrow of the bed in the Fairbournes' spare chamber, she still didn't know. Sleep was impossible with the argument between Samson and Joshua echoing in her ears, and she felt her heart begin to beat faster all over again from the memory alone. It wasn't just the ugly anger of their words that haunted her but the sad conviction that, no matter what they'd said, each brother at heart still cared very much what became of the other.

She took a deep breath and tried to calm herself, to relax, but she couldn't. She felt lonely and inexplicably frightened, for both Samson and herself, and no matter how luxurious and warm this huge bed might be, she longed for the bunk in the captain's cabin on board the *Morning Star*, and the captain himself to share it.

From the parlor downstairs she heard the tall case clock chime the hour: twelve bells—midnight in landsman's time. Then she heard another sound, this one nearer, a loud, cheerful crow for attention in the quiet house, and in spite of everything else Polly smiled at the thought of Alexander as happily wide awake as his mother had predicted.

She thought she heard the murmur of Anabelle's voice trying unsuccessfully to hush him. She must have dozed herself, for the next sound she heard was a tentative scratching at her own door, accompanied by Alexander's chirping. Swiftly she hopped from the big bed and padded in her bare feet to open the door.

"I was hoping you'd be awake, too," said Anabelle

with a sigh as she entered the room, the baby propped against one shoulder and a shaded candlestick in the other. "Alexander does like his company. Dear Lord, but it is cold!"

Together they scurried back to the warmth of the bed, drawing the curtains shut to make the space a cozy small room within the larger chamber. While Polly carefully hung the candlestick on the hook at the head of the bedstead, Anabelle settled Alexander between them, sitting him squarely on his clouted bottom so he could watch them both while he gurgled and played with the silver bells on his coral-tipped rattle.

"When I was little I was always being punished for bringing a candlestick into bed," said Anabelle as she drew the coverlet up over her knees. "But because I was also always afraid of the dragons I felt sure were in the curtains with me, I kept doing it. Of course now I know how dangerous it must have been—to think that my innocent small hand could have burned down the entire ancient house of Kilmarsh!—but I still have nights when I fear those dragons."

"Like this one?" asked Polly uneasily.

"Exactly like this one." Anabelle linked her fingers behind her head and sank back against the bolster. "Have you ever seen two such fire-spitting dragons as that pair of brothers at supper?"

Polly sighed unhappily, pleating the edge of the sheet between her fingers to avoid the other woman's eye. "I knew how unhappy Samson was, yet still I do believe Joshua spoke as he did from love for him. And though you would not guess it, Samson does care for Joshua, too, else he would not try so desperately to earn his praise."

"Oh, I guessed it at once," said Anabelle. "I have

three brothers of my own, you know, and they are every bit as pig-headed in such matters."

Polly shook her head. "But I should never have spoken that way to your husband. I only made things worse, trying to help Samson."

"La, don't blame yourself. You couldn't help it, and neither could he, or Samson, for that matter," said Anabelle comfortably. She looked younger in the ruffled nightcap, the ribbons tied beneath her chin in much the same way as Alexander's. "Besides, though you'd never guess it, Joshua is much taken with women who speak back to him, most likely because so few do. You made a vastly splendid impression upon him, and he asked me far more questions about you than I could ever hope to answer."

"Hah," said Polly glumly. "No doubt he asked what I am doing with his brother."

"No, no, not in the least! If anything I believe he thinks you are too fine to waste yourself on Samson, but that is another tangle altogether. No, Alexander, I do not want your dreadful rattle." Anabelle wrinkled her nose as she pushed the sticky rattle away from her face, and the baby gurgled with amusement.

Gently Polly dared to trail her finger along the back of Alexander's neck, tracing the downy whorls of his dark hair. "How lucky you are to have him."

Anabelle twisted her mouth wryly to one side as she tickled Alexander's cheek with the trailing end of the ribbon from her nightcap. "How lucky, too, that he is being so charming at present, for it will make what I must say next more agreeable. I'm going to be meddlesome, you see; it is one of the few prerogatives granted to old wives and mothers like myself."

"Oh, aye," scoffed Polly good-naturedly as she

looked at the other woman's merry, beruffled face. "You're so blessèd old!"

"I am nearly eighteen," said Anabelle solemnly, "which makes me vastly ancient indeed. But that is of no matter now. No. What I wish to know now is exactly how attached you are to Samson."

Polly stiffened. "I don't know what you mean."

"Oh, yes you do, so don't pretend otherwise, not with me. I have eyes, don't I? This morning on the ship I could see at once that you were not merely Samson's guest. A *guest*, for all love! But after tonight, when I watched how you jumped to defend him against Joshua, I decided there was something more. Am I not right?"

Polly didn't answer, staring down instead at the little fan she'd made of the edge of the bedsheet as her cheeks grew hot.

"Oh, Polly, you needn't try to hide it from me," said Anabelle with a sigh, taking Polly's guilty flush for the answer it was. "I know all too well how tempting these Fairbourne men can be, especially at sea, when there's just the two of you and that cozy little bunk waiting for you to tumble back upon it. Isn't my darling Alexander proof enough of that? But it was not well done of Samson, to rescue you one day and seduce you the next. Heroes are not supposed to behave like that."

"But he didn't force me!" exclaimed Polly indignantly. "I gave myself to him freely, of my own will."

"Gave yourself into your own ruin is what you mean." Anabelle clucked her tongue with dismay as she tried to make her expression stern. "I've no notion of how wise you are in these matters, dear Polly, or what your mother has told you about the consequences of such delicious dalliances."

"My mother died when I was born," said Polly softly.

"Ah," said Anabelle sadly. "Mine died long ago as well."

"Then you know," said Polly simply, and she knew that Anabelle did. "And my father—my father would never speak of such things."

It was not that she was being willfully stupid about—about *this*. She didn't need Anabelle or anyone else to tell her the risk she was running, how dangerously close she was to ruining her life in all the ways that mattered. Yet still somehow she refused to believe that she could already be carrying Samson's child deep within her body, just as she could not truly believe he meant to sail for Ninnishibutt in two days and leave her, and all of this would be over.

Over.

Anabelle's brows pinched together with anxious concern. "But you do know that babies—even the dear, charming ones like Alexander—that babies do result from lying with a man? Faith, you've only to look at Serena and me to see that the Fairbournes make vastly accomplished breeding stock."

If Polly had put her face to the candle her cheeks could not have grown any hotter. "That's what Samson himself said when he asked me to marry him."

"Hah, there now, I have misjudged the poor man!" cried Anabelle, clapping her hands together with relief. "Come, let me kiss you as a sister should, by way of congratulations. We shall use my little party tomorrow to announce your betrothal, and then we must begin planning your wedding. We must be quick about it, of course, to spoil the gossips' finger-counting, but that's no reason for—"

"He asked," interrupted Polly slowly, "but I did not accept. It is so hard to explain."

"Oh, I doubt that," said Anabelle. "Do you love him?"

"Aye, but—"

"Hush, I'll hear nothing beyond that 'aye,' for nothing else matters," said Anabelle firmly. "If you love Samson, truly love him, and he loves you, then everything else will follow of its own."

"But you don't understand!" wailed Polly miserably. "If I marry him, I will lose everything that I *am!*"

"And will he lose nothing in return?" Anabelle waggled her fingers in the air beside her face to signify the ease with which such sacrifices could be made. "Consider how Samson has already offered to abandon his bachelorhood—the dearest possession among many men, beside which our maidenheads are nothing—for you. He has taken you into the sanctity of his cabin, no small shakes among shipmasters."

"But Anabelle—"

"No, you shall hear me out! By bringing you with him back to Appledore, he has shared with you some of the deepest secrets of his past. I'd only to look at him to see that he's already given you his heart, holding it out to you in his very hands. I do not know what else you expect of the poor man, indeed I do not!"

Polly hung her head forlornly, overwhelmed by Anabelle's tidy reasoning. How was it that all of her own deepest worries about marrying Samson sounded so shallow in Anabelle's voice? Had all the time she'd spent watching after herself really made her so incapable of thinking of anyone else, even of Samson?

"Oh, Anabelle," she said miserably. "How selfish I must sound to you!"

Anabelle patted her hand. "Not selfish," she said kindly. "Careful. Cautious. And these are good things, of course. But you must also learn to trust the man you love, which is even better."

Polly shook her head. "But I can't begin—"

"No more of this *I can* or *I can't*," said Anabelle firmly. "It's past time you began thinking of *we*. Yes, you must give up a part of yourself when you marry. But what you and Samson will find together to replace what you'll each lose will be ten times—a hundred times!—better for you both."

Alexander toppled forward, fussing wearily as he tried to reach for the front of his mother's lace-trimmed nightrail, and with a half-stifled yawn of her own she scooped him up into her arms.

"There now, little love, you're proof enough that I've droned on far too long," she said as she slipped her legs through the opening in the curtains and over the side of the bedstead. "Back to our own beds, pet, and we'll leave Polly to her own."

"Wait, Anabelle," said Polly as she hurried to unhook the candlestick. She wished Anabelle would stay; she'd enjoyed the rare company of another woman, and besides, her own thoughts were racing so that she doubted she'd fall asleep at all before dawn.

With a sleepy smile, Anabelle paused to take the candlestick from her with her free hand.

"And mind, don't forget this, either." Carefully Polly tucked Alexander's rattle into his sticky grasp. "You might want it later."

"More than you shall, anyway." She winked wickedly. "I'd wager you'd like something of more substance to keep you company."

Polly smiled shyly and leaned forward first to kiss Alexander's forehead, then Anabelle's cheek. "Good night," she said softly. "And thank you, for everything."

"Good night to you as well," whispered Anabelle over her drowsing son's head. "Trust Samson, and trust your own heart, and the rest will take care of itself."

Trust Samson, and trust your own heart. . . .

There could not be simpler advice in all the world, decided Polly, and none harder for her to take.

Throughout the night she listened to the clock count away the hours until five, when she decided she'd had enough of trying to sleep. She shivered as she slid from the warm bed, but because she wasn't going to linger, she didn't bother poking the coals in the grate back to life.

Instead she broke the ice in the bowl and washed her face swiftly, then dressed as fast as she could in her old clothes. She worked a second pair of stockings over the first to help take the chill from her toes and wrapped the thick woolen shawl that Anabelle had lent her over her waistcoat and tied the ends in a knot at her waist. Once she'd buttoned up both her jacket and the borrowed coat, she looked as stout as a barrel, but at least she'd have a better chance of keeping warm. She tiptoed her way through the still-sleeping house and down the back stairs and let herself out by the kitchen door.

She didn't take a candle or lantern, for with two hours left before winter dawn, the three-quarter moon still hung low on the horizon, bright enough to shine her way to the water. She thought of that and smiled as she hurried through the empty streets: no matter where she was her path always took her back to the water. To the water, and now, to Samson.

The first fires were already being lit in the kitchens of the taverns near the dock, gray smoke curling from the chimneys into the cold dark air and gold slivers of firelight showing from between the shutters. Polly tucked her mittened hands beneath her arms, puffing her frozen breath into a pale cloud before her face. It was cold enough to make most people reluctant to leave their beds, burrowing down for one more minute before they'd have to rise. Only mad, lovesick fools like herself would be about so early, she thought wryly, and she tugged her cap lower over her forehead as she paused to admire the *Morning Star* at the wharf before her.

With sails furled tight for port and only a single lantern lit, the ship was ghostly in the moonlight, unreal, her masts and spars like bare silver trees. She wondered if Samson was still asleep, there behind the stern windows. She rather hoped he was, if only because she'd spent a good part of this sleepless night imagining inventive and pleasurable ways to wake him.

She was imagining them still when she felt a man's hand come to rest upon her shoulder. With a gasp, she jerked away and turned to face him, her knife ready in her hand.

Samson sighed, his face turning toward the shadows where she could see nothing of his face. "I'd wager a guinea that Anabelle doesn't know you've left her keeping."

"No more wagers." She wanted to throw her arms

around him, to hold him close and tell him all the things she'd considered and decided alone in the big featherbed. But there was an undercurrent of wariness in his manner that made her hang back, a sense that he'd yet to shed all of the hostility that had radiated from him at the supper table.

Instead she slipped her knife away and hugged herself, shifting from leg to leg with the cold. "What are you doing here, anyway?"

"Making sure you come to no harm," he said gruffly. "All that nattering about Hidaldgo—and most likely it is nattering, mind?—all that made me worry over you like an old hen. Though I shouldn't tell you how much of this night I've passed staring up at my brother's house, trying to decide which window was yours."

"Oh, Samson," she said with a breathy little catch of surprise. "Oh, that was so nice of you!"

"More harebrained than anything," he said, clearly disgusted with himself. "I'm sorry, Poll. Mind, I shouldn't have put you through that misery last night, but I did, and, damnation, now I'm—I'm sorry."

"You needn't apologize to me," she said softly, her conversation with Anabelle still fresh in her thoughts. "But you and Joshua—"

"You stop right there," he ordered. "What's done is done between Joshua and me, and it all has naught to do with you and me."

"But if you two could only—"

"I said it's done, Polly," he said with a harsh finality that even she could not ignore. "Now will you come with me, or would you rather go back to my brother's house?"

"Faith, Samson, 'tis not *me* that's crossed you," she

answered indignantly. Being a peacemaker was one thing, but she wasn't going to let him bite her head off in the process. Maybe Anabelle could do that, but she couldn't. "Am I allowed to ask where we would go if I were to come with you, or is that too bold a question as well?"

He sighed impatiently. "A place I wish to see. A place I wish to show you. Is that answer enough?"

She considered for a moment. "Only if breakfast comes with it."

Breakfast did, in the form of slices of ham and yellow cheese, stuffed into bread so fresh from the tavern's oven that the small round loaves steamed in the cold morning air as they walked. The town was slowly beginning to waken as the sky grew gray with dawn: heavy-eyed apprentices with buckets on their way to the well in the square for water, a stray dog snuffling through the rubbish behind the tavern for his breakfast, wagons driven by bundled farmers on their way to the new markethouse.

"Will you look at that jumped-up market shed," said Samson contemptuously as they paused to watch the farmers arranging their stalls beneath the brick arches by the light of tin lanterns. "Tell me if it's not as ugly and out of place as a jackass in the middle of the ocean!"

Polly studied the building as she chewed a piece of cheese. "It's a great deal more handsome than a jackass anywhere, as you know perfectly well. You just don't like it because it's your brother's jackass."

"My brother never knows when to leave well enough alone. He won't be content until Appledore's as big as Boston itself, with all the troubles that go with it."

"But towns must change to improve themselves,"

reasoned Polly. "Otherwise we'd all still be living in the same little Indian huts covered in tree bark that our great-grandfathers did when they first came here. And would you wish to trade the *Morning Star* for a hollowed-out log and a paddle?"

As she spoke, she suddenly realized that what made sense for towns made sense for people as well, and she thought again of what Anabelle had told her. She frowned and looked up at Samson, trying to think of a way to explain it to him, too.

"It's not just tree bark huts and markethouses and a hundred years' difference," she said, choosing her words with care. "Look at me. I'm not the same as I was when I left Ninnishibutt."

"What blather is this?" asked Samson suspiciously. "Of course you're the same. If you weren't, then I would have won the wager instead of Zach."

"That was because you were both looking for the kinds of changing that show on the outside." She balled up a few crumbs of bread and tossed them to a seagull hovering greedily before them. "Dressing me up like a doll-baby wouldn't change anything about me except my clothes, and that's easy enough to put back. I mean I've changed inside, where I'm just me. And so, I think, have you."

"You're daft," he said instantly.

"Maybe about other things, aye, but not now." She smiled beatifically, knowing she'd both bested him and given him something to consider in the process. "*You're* daft if you don't accept it."

"Well, I don't, and I'm not daft, either." He hurled the heel of his bread directly at the gull, hard enough to make the bird squawk in protest. "Now are you coming with me or not?"

It did not take long for them to leave the town

behind, for despite Samson's concerns about its growing size, Appledore remained small and close-packed. Soon the street dwindled to a rutted path barely wide enough for a one-horse cart, and the houses and shops were replaced by stubbled fields glistening with frost. Dividing the fields were low fences made of piled stones, mute testimony of the toil of earlier generations of settlers. No wonder so many of them had turned to the sea, thought Polly; no storm could possibly be worse than spending day after day clearing stumps and piling rocks.

She glanced curiously up at Samson, wondering if his grandfathers had been among the rock-pilers, here on this narrowing point of land. He'd said nothing more since they'd left the markethouse, and this seemed a harmless enough question to break his silence. Besides, he spoke so seldom about his family that she knew next to nothing about them.

"Did your family come here as landsmen," she asked, "or have they always been mariners?"

"Eh?" He looked startled, as if she'd awakened him after all, and she asked again.

"Oh, they were mariners, Poll," he answered absently, "nothing else. Do you see that great rock there, at the point of the fences? Danny and I used to climb upon it and pretend it was our crow's nest, spying on other ships. Lookout Rock, we called it. Most times we were the first in Appledore to spot the Boston packet, too, before it came in the harbor. Here, give me your hand, and I'll show you."

She let him help her up the high, smooth side of the stone, even though she could have done it readily enough by herself. "Danny is your other brother?"

"The poor rascal caught in the middle," he said,

steadying her with his hands at her waist. "There! Have you ever seen such a view from the land?"

She hadn't, not like this. Until she'd climbed on top of the rock, she hadn't realized that it rested on the crest of a hill, with the meadow on the other side of it sloping off sharply to the water's edge. Here near the end of the point, it seemed the entire sea lay spread before them, the sun rising pale red into the clouds on the horizon, a snow sky if ever there was one.

But the sight that took her breath away was closer, here by her side. As Samson stared out over the water, he'd somehow become that long-ago boy on the rock again, the sorrows of his life slipping away before the same eager excitement that he'd felt then. The black stubble on his jaw didn't matter, nor did the lines the sun had marked into his face. From the way his eyes shone he *was* a boy once more, spying on pirates with his brother.

"How old were you when you and Danny came here, Samson?" she asked.

"Oh, not very. It had to be before I was five." His eyes darkened briefly, a cloud passing over the blue, then he laughed. "Danny and I were such clumsy little sprats that by the time we reached the top, we'd have to lie flat on our backs, gasping until we could find our wind again. Yet still we meant to challenge all those pirate kings to the very death!"

He laughed again and so did she, from the sheer pleasure of seeing him so happy. So this was what he wished to show her, this rare, special part of himself that he'd kept locked away from everyone else. Wasn't sharing like this close to trusting, and trusting close to love?

Trust your own heart, and the rest will take care of itself.

"Do you see the smoke rising there, beyond that hill?" he asked, turning her so she could better see. "That's from our chimney, our house, though how the trees have grown around it! As long as I could see that smoke, I'd know I'd be safe, for I was still near enough to home that Mam could hear me if I yelled and come to my rescue."

"Did she do it often?" She didn't say anything about how the past and present were blurring, and she wouldn't.

"More than I'll tell you," he said, chuckling. "But Mam never told Father, not once. To him we were always brave as punch. Come, we'll go there now."

He clambered down the rock and turned to hold his hands up to her. "Be brave, Poll," he teased. "It's far to the ground, I know, but I promise I'll save you if you slip."

"But Samson," she said softly. "You can't go—we can't—oh, Samson, you lived in that house a long time ago."

"I know that." His grin widened, and he winked broadly. "I told you before I wasn't daft, didn't I? Serena lives in our house now, and has for years. But everything looks just as it did when Mam kept it, down to the way the honeysuckle curls up the shingles every June."

"Samson Fairbourne, you are *bad*," she declared soundly, and as proof of her displeasure she ignored his offered help as she hopped down the rock herself.

"Exactly as bad as you," he said as he reached for her mittened hand. "That's why we get on so well, isn't it?"

She swatted his hand away. "Or perhaps why we

don't get along at all," she said. "How much farther is it to your house?"

"I showed you. It's just beyond that hill, on the tip of Cranberry Point." His teasing grin began to fade, and when he reached for her hand again, she let him take it. "It's not much to see, Poll. I should tell you that. One great room with a loft over it, a chimney that smokes more than it should, shingles that have never seen a lick of paint. My father built it himself with two friends the summer before he wed my mother. But there's nothing to the house half so grand as Joshua's."

"And do you think I care?" she asked as they began to walk together. "I'm not Anabelle, Samson."

"Thank God for that," he said so fervently she giggled. She loved this moment, loved it nearly as much as she loved him. So why, then, couldn't she just tell him so?

"No palace, our house," he was saying, "but it is the one place I've thought of as home. There's always a bed waiting for me—and for Daniel and Joshua, too, if they wish it—in the loft, and Serena will make whatever I wish for my first supper ashore."

"Then it *is* home," she said wistfully, thinking how she'd no such place waiting for her.

"Aye, lass, it is," he said firmly. "It is."

He kissed her then, swift and sweet, a kiss that was more about promises than passion, and when he smiled as their lips parted, she saw again that long-lost boy of Lookout Rock. She'd never seen him so relaxed and happy, nor had she felt the bond between them to be as strong as it was now. She wished she could make this moment last for him, a gift from her of this kind of happiness whenever he wished it.

But maybe she could. The idea came to her at once, with a speed and seductive possibility that was terrifying, and her fingers trembled as they slipped into her pocket to seek the bottle. Oh, God forgive her for such heathen thoughts, for believing in things that couldn't possibly be right or real! Yet hadn't every wish she'd made come true as long as she touched the bottle first? And wasn't this wish for another's sake, for Samson, not some selfish whimsy for her own benefit?

Playfully he touched a fingertip to her nose, his smile wide and easy, and before she changed her mind she curled her fingers tight around the bottle in her pocket and made her wish.

Let Samson find whatever he needs to always be happy like this. Whatever he needs, may it always be his.

Samson tightened his fingers into Polly's through the wooliness of her mittens, drawing her along the path to his parents' house. Beneath the knitted cuff of her hat her nose and cheeks were red from the cold, her hair sticking out in stray wisps like straw from a scarecrow, and from the lumpy shape of her coat, she must have worn enough clothes to outfit a scarecrow, too. But when she laughed with him, she was the most beautiful woman in the world, and he'd never hear anyone say otherwise.

He couldn't say what impulse had made him bring her here, but now he knew it was the best, most perfect idea he'd ever had. Here, in his parents' small shingled house overlooking the bay, she would be able to know what mattered about his family—the important things, not the extravagant displays that Joshua so relished.

He would show her the knife-nicks in the doorway where his father had proudly marked the height of his three growing sons, the darkened bricks in the hearth that showed where his mother had baked the best cornbread in Barnstable County, the opening in the loft by the ladder worn smooth by the three young brothers' endless comings and goings, even the odd triangular patch near one window where his seagoing father's carpentry skills had faltered.

He would never be able to bring Polly to his parents as his new bride, to see his mother welcome her with tears of joy in her eyes or hear his father declare her the prettiest girl in the colony, but he could still show her all the things that had made this house his home and the people who'd lived in it his family; and, because Polly was Polly, his Polly, she'd understand everything.

And when he finally told her how much he loved her, how infinitely dear she was to him, she'd understand that, too.

And this time, when he asked her again to marry him, she would say yes.

"Only a little farther, lass," he said as they neared the crest of the last little hill. "In a moment, you'll see it."

But she wouldn't and neither would he, for when he reached the top of the hill, to his horror there was nothing left to see. The house that his father had built nearly thirty years before had vanished, and Samson felt the loss as keenly as if he'd been struck, struck hard, in the chest near to his heart. It would have been bad enough if the little house had burned or been swept away by a storm. Such tragedies happened, particularly to those who chose to build so far from town. But this tragedy had been wrought by man, and from the look of it, Samson knew exactly which man must be responsible.

For on the plot where his parents' cottage had once stood now rose a raw new house, still half covered with carpenters' scaffolding, two stories tall beneath a flaring hip roof. Six windows were spaced across the front, all double hung and sashed in the latest fashion; and in fashion, too, was the swooping curve of the carved pediment over the front door, crowned by a gilded pineapple for hospitality.

In elegance and proportion, it reminded Samson of the markethouse in town, but even more it reminded him of his brother's house, an opulent house meant to impress visitors more than welcome them. This, then, was why his brother had bought the old cottage for himself—not for Serena to keep but to knock it down and build a fine country seat away from town, the way the London gentry did.

Jesus, how could Joshua have done this? To the house, to the memory of our parents? How could he have done it to me?

"Oh, Samson," murmured Polly sadly beside him. "This isn't what you expected, is it?"

He felt devastated, betrayed, too bereft to be as angry as he should. Sickened, he turned his back on his brother's handiwork and where had stood his last fragile connection with the past; and with Polly at his side, he silently began the long walk back to town.

Fifteen

"He's late." Polly peered through the window into the night, seeing little in the darkness beyond the swirl of snowflakes. "He should have been here an hour ago."

"And what's an hour to one of my brothers when there's a beloved ship to cosset and coax?" asked Serena lightly. "You know that with this snow, Samson had to take the *Morning Star* to a mooring out in the harbor to be safe, away from the wharf. But he'll be here soon, Polly. He's not going to forget us, not tonight. Likely he's on his way already."

Polly turned from the window, impatiently kicking aside her gown's full silk skirts to keep them from tangling around her legs. She wasn't nearly as confident as Serena that Samson would decide to appear at the party, but then Serena hadn't seen her brother's face that morning when he'd seen that his parents' house was gone. No amount of coaxing would make him speak of it, or for that matter speak at all, during their long walk back to town.

But the empty, desolate look on his face had said enough, shutting her out of his anguish as completely

as one of those endless stone walls. He had left her at
Joshua's house with scarcely a word of farewell, let
alone of explanation, and though at the door she had
lifted her face to kiss him he hadn't noticed—or,
worse, pretended not to. His whole manner had been
more fit for a funeral than for a party, and if he
decided to stay away, she would be hurt and lonely,
but she would understand. Oh, aye, she'd understand, just as she understood now that the bottle—
the same bottle that from habit she'd shifted from her
jacket pocket to the lady's pocket tied beneath her
petticoats—was no more than any other piece of
rubbish when it came to making wishes to make
Samson happy.

"And won't he be pleased to see you when he does
come," said Serena from her chair beside the fire.
They'd both come here to Anabelle's bedchamber to
dress—or, rather, to *be* dressed, under Anabelle's
supervision—for the frolic. While Polly wore one of
the gowns Samson had bought for her on Martinique,
Anabelle had added flounced lawn cuffs to the
sleeves and an extra pink ribbon bow at the top of the
bodice. "That pale green silk is so lovely on you,
Polly, and how your hair is dressed—oh my! There's
no one else like Anabelle for turning us plainspoken
Massachusetts lasses into duchesses, is there?"

"I'm not so certain about being a duchess," said
Polly wryly. "But that sow's ear does come to mind,
aye."

"You are too hard upon yourself," said Serena
gently, "and you would never say that if you saw how
Samson looks at you."

Polly shrugged, uncomfortable with such a compliment, and glanced again out the window. She'd trade
all the silk in China to have Samson here with her

now, and the entire country itself to see him smile again in the lighthearted way he had this morning.

"I hope Samson will bring you to see me before you must leave," said Serena, her dark gold hair gleaming in the firelight as she reached from her chair to ruffle the fur of the large black dog, Abel, beside her. Polly had quickly learned that Abel was Serena's constant and loyal companion, and despite his size, he was welcomed with her everywhere she went. "It's not that far to Cranberry Point, but you'll need him to show you the way the first time."

Polly glanced at her curiously. "We were there, this very morning, but he—Samson, that is—he didn't think you lived there still."

"Well, wherever else would Gerald and I live?" asked Serena with equal curiosity. "I wish Samson had stopped, so I could have shown him all the improvements that Gerald has made. He's very clever that way, always drawing new schemes and plans for houses and such. By now you must have seen the markethouse—that's his doing, too."

"Then it wasn't Joshua who tore down your parents' house," said Polly as she slowly began to fit together the pieces of this latest Fairbourne puzzle, "but you and Gerald?"

"Tore it down!" exclaimed Serena, aghast. "I— we—would never do such a thing! I know from the path it doesn't quite show, but the old house is behind the new wing, joined to it through the west wall. Otherwise it's just as it was, facing out to the sea. However could Samson believe we'd torn it down?"

"Not you," said Polly. "But he thought Joshua had, to build another house for himself."

Serena screwed up her face. "As if Joshua needed

more than one!" she scoffed. "But poor Samson! That little house is so special to him. How it must have grieved him to believe it gone!"

"It did," said Polly sadly, remembering the horrified shock she'd seen on his face as they'd stood on the hill. "But I suppose that after having lived there most of his life, since he was born—"

"But he didn't," said Serena, clearly surprised that Samson had told Polly so little. "None of us did. I was only a baby when Father died and Mam had to sell the house to pay his debts. Then she died, too, not half a year later. Joshua was eight, so Daniel must have been six and Samson five. After that, because we were orphans, wards of the parish, we were all put to board with different families until we were old enough to work for ourselves."

"You were separated?" asked Polly, shocked. If she'd been blessed with a brother or sister, she would never have let them be parted.

Serena smiled sadly. "What choice do children have in such matters? I suppose we were fortunate we weren't left to starve. But you can certainly see why, as soon as he'd earned enough, Joshua bought the house back for all of us."

What Polly could see was Samson as a grief-stricken little boy who'd lost both his parents and his home as well, clinging to the memory of a golden childhood that had ended before he was six. No wonder the house had meant so much to him: it was the single connection he had to that time, and, in a way, to his parents as well, and her heart went out to him all over again to think of how he'd suffered.

"I think, being sailors, the house means even more to my brothers," continued Serena wistfully. "They could journey wherever they pleased but always knew that home was waiting for them there on Cranberry Point. I'm certain that's why Sam brought you there, Polly. Even after so many years, it's still home. I only pray that some day Daniel will come back home to us, too, just as Samson has with you."

Once again Polly stared at the snowflakes in the night, trying hard to fight back her tears for the little black-haired boy standing on Lookout Rock. How much Samson had suffered in his life, and how hard he'd fought to keep that suffering locked up inside, where he'd thought it couldn't hurt him! And yet he had wanted to trust her with that secret, to share it with her; he had tried this morning, and had come heartbreakingly close.

Behind her she heard the door swing open, and she turned eagerly, hoping it was Samson.

"You two have hidden yourselves above stairs long enough," scolded Anabelle, patting the plume-shaped brooch of diamonds pinned into her hair as she bustled through the doorway. "You must come down directly, else I'll begin sending people up here to you instead."

With a sigh Serena pushed herself up from her chair, one hand over her belly. "She means it, too, Polly," she warned. "Anabelle thinks nothing of receiving company right here in her bedchamber, before she's even dressed."

"Before I've even had my *tea*," said Anabelle with a wicked grin. "But here, Polly, a boy brought this for you, and I'd wager my life it's from your darling Samson. Oh, hurry, hurry, open it! Those little leather jeweler's boxes always hold the best treasures!"

"It must have been Joseph." Reluctantly Polly took the box, recognizing it and remembering the last time Samson had given it to her.

"Go *ahead*, Polly!" urged Anabelle, crowding close. "You know whatever it is you must wear it tonight. Pray it's pearls. Pearls would do vastly well with your gown."

There was no help for it, not before Anabelle and Serena. She would have to open the box, and with a deep breath, she did.

"Oh, la, that's *extraordinary!*" cried Anabelle. "What admirable taste Samson has in his gifts! And a mermaid is so very perfect, considering how you met!"

Serena leaned over Polly's arm to admire the necklace as well. "The mermaid rather looks like you, Polly," she said with amusement. "No wonder Sam could not resist! But he should have been more careful before he sent it to you—what is that in there, too? An old leaf? Here, brush it away before it dirties the coral."

"Nay, don't!" cried Polly, cupping her hand to shield the box. "That is, it's not an old leaf. It's—it's a rose petal, from the rose I was wearing when we—when we first kissed. I didn't think he still had it."

Anabelle's eyes grew huge. "Ohh, Polly, that is so vastly romantic of him! If you do not marry him directly, why, you shall be the most foolish woman in the world, as well as the most careless, to let such a divine man slip through your fingers. Now come, turn about, and I will fasten the clasp for you."

Obediently Polly turned and dipped so Anabelle could reach the back of her neck, still clutching the box with the wizened rose petal locked safely inside. She thought again of the first time he'd tried to offer the necklace to her and thought, too, of how much had happened and changed between them, enough to make all the reasons she'd had for refusing it then now evaporate into the air as surely as a snowflake falling on the hearth. That single rose petal had told her more of how he felt than a score of poets could. He loved her. He *loved* her.

And as for herself, aye, she loved him, too. She loved him, and she trusted him, exactly as Anabelle had said, and how very ready she was for the rest to follow!

Smiling to herself, she stared at her reflection in the looking glass. The coral beads lay cool and smooth around her neck, the cameo resting at the base of her throat with an unfamiliar weight. Lightly she touched her fingertips to the carved profile of the mermaid, her wispy hair and little grin, and thought of how much better this would be for luck instead of the old bottle.

"There now, my dear," said Anabelle with a little pat to Polly's shoulder. "You can see how much the necklace becomes you. And when Samson sees it around your throat, he will know what's in your heart. He will *know*. Now come, let's go to the parlor and see how exactly right and wise I am."

Her heart pounding with anticipation, Polly began searching through the guests for Samson while she was still on the stairs. The front parlor had been cleared for dancing, with the chairs from the dining table set along the walls, and already the two fiddlers were tuning their instruments and testing their strings. Supper had been set in the smaller parlor behind it, with rum and wine and a spiced punch served in a huge bowl dotted with floating, sliced lemons. White paper chains draped across the mantels, over boughs of greenery that Anabelle had had cut and brought that afternoon, and scores of candles turned night into day.

Already the rooms were crowded, voices and laughter growing louder, with each new guest arriving accompanied by a gust of snow from the opening door. Polly had never seen so many people gathered into one house at one time, more people than it seemed possible lived in Appledore.

And she didn't know a single one of them.

Both Serena and Anabelle had been swept away by friends and swallowed into the crush, and with growing panic Polly hung back on the last step and gripped the newel post, wishing over and over that Samson would come through the door to rescue her.

"Pretty Polly!" cried Zach exuberantly as he pushed his way toward her. "Ah, what a wondrous fair vision you are this night!"

"Zach!" She grinned with relief and with pleasure at seeing him as he gallantly kissed the air over the back of her hand. And if Zach were here, then Samson must have finished with the ship and would be here soon, too. Perhaps he already was, and she eagerly searched the faces behind the younger man. "Where is he, Zach?"

"Sam?" Zach's ebullience faded a fraction as he, too, looked back toward the parlor. "He should be here by now. We were on the dock together at least half an hour ago."

"Oh." Half an hour: that meant that the same boat that had brought Joseph with the necklace to shore had also brought Samson. So why hadn't he come himself? Why wasn't he here, now, with her? Lightly she touched the mermaid cameo at her throat. Had she so misread that wordless message of the rose petal?

"How was he when you saw him last, Zach?" she asked uneasily. "Was he happy, or—or otherwise?"

Zach patted her hand, which he'd somehow conveniently forgotten to release. "Don't fret over him, Polly. He was his usual broody-moody self, but all rigged out in his best finery for your sake. He'll be here soon enough. Besides, what ill could befall him here? You must not believe those drunkards' tales about Hidaldgo. They're not true. They *can't* be. This is Appledore, not Charles Towne."

She took a deep breath and squeezed his hand in return. "I thank you, Zach. For everything."

"Oh, yes, everything." His smile twisted oddly. "Do you know how many times I've wondered what would have happened if you'd wakened to see my face first?"

"Oh, Zach." From the first she'd liked Zach, but she'd never once thought of him in the way he apparently thought of her. "Though you don't wish to hear it from me, you will find someone else."

"Not like you," he said glumly. "There aren't any other girls like that."

"True enough." She smiled, touched, even though she wasn't quite sure if that was a compliment or not. "But you're bound to find one who's even more perfect. You're certainly looking enough, aren't you?" she said, trying to tease him into a better humor. "You'll find her, Zach, a young woman who's sweet in temper and without vanity, modest and truthful in words and manner, perhaps even obedient, though I rather doubt that. And beautiful, too, to match you."

But instead of laughing or even teasing her in return, the way she'd hoped, Zach's face abruptly turned so guarded that his expression could almost be mistaken for fear.

"Where the Devil did you hear that, Polly?" he demanded uneasily. "From Sam?"

"Nay, of course not. Can you ever imagine him saying such nonsense?" She shrugged carelessly. "The words just came into my head, that is all."

"That's not possible," he said quickly. He *was* frightened, and Polly couldn't begin to guess what she'd done. "Not when you—"

"Off with you now, you young rogue," ordered Joshua Fairbourne as he suddenly appeared at Zach's side with a scowl that reminded Polly so clearly of Samson. Some families cultivated their smiles, but with the Fairbournes, it seemed to be a challenge among the brothers over who could muster the blackest frowns. "Shove off, and let the lady have her peace."

Automatically Zach ducked his head and backed away, bowing, though the fear still remained on his face. "Aye-aye, sir. Captain Fairbourne, sir. Miss Bray, your servant."

Polly watched him go, still puzzled. Perhaps Samson could explain it to her later, and with a sigh she turned to the older man.

"Captain Fairbourne," she said. "I should thank you, too. For having this party, I mean."

"That's Anabelle's doing, not mine," he said, and though he managed to keep his voice gruff, at the mention of his wife's name his scowl softened into something much more mild, almost sunny. "Besides, what choice did I have? Whether it pleases me or not, Anabelle will do what she wishes."

She narrowed her eyes, appraising him. Most likely Anabelle was right about the number of women—or men—ever daring to challenge him. Such a grim, forbidding face, and the height and shoulders to support it, would intimidate most people. Fortunately, she'd grown so accustomed to Samson that she wasn't intimidated at all.

"Don't blame this upon Anabelle," she said evenly. Because she still stood on the bottom step, they were very nearly eye to eye, and because everyone else seemed determined to keep a respectful distance from Joshua, she felt free enough to speak plainly. "You're as pleased as she that Samson's come home, just as you're not half as mean-spirited as you wish the world to believe."

"Ha," said Joshua. "You've never served on any of my crews."

"If I had," she answered, "I certainly wouldn't have mistaken the *Morning Star* for a *guardacosta*."

His eyes might have twinkled with a spark of amusement, though she could not swear to it. "No, Miss Bray, I'd warrant you would not. But you do believe I'm too hard on my brother."

"That's because you are." She hadn't expected him to be so direct.

"I had to be," he said, with more reluctance, too, than she'd thought she'd hear from him. "By the time I was eight, Miss Bray, I was supporting my mother, my brothers, and my sister. I was the one sent to sea, and though I hated every damned minute of that first voyage, I did it because they needed me. But Sam— Sam was Mam's baby, and she coddled him like a pet. We all did, doing whatever foolishness we could until we made him laugh outright, and then we'd laugh, too, until we fair ruined him for anything useful. Mam's dying hit him the worst, so much we feared we'd lose him, too."

"But he was only a little boy!" cried Polly plaintively, remembering the rare happiness on Samson's face that morning when he'd stood on the rock, and remembering, too, how contented little Alexander was being spoiled in exactly the same way.

"We were all of us young," said Joshua sadly, "and we each—Samson, Daniel, and I—knew what life Father and Mam wished for us. We had no choice, not really. We had to work and learn then to be shipmasters like our father, and his father before that. There's no place for weakness in a captain, and that's been hardest for Sam, too. You judge me too severe with him, but he needed to learn. If a captain turns soft before his men, even once, then they'll never again respect him enough to obey."

"Yet look at all he has done since then! He is a captain himself, and he has prospered enough to own the *Morning Star* outright!"

"Ha," said Joshua with disgust. "I'll wager he paid double what it was worth, too. He'd no business going to those North Shore shipyards when I could have gotten him a better vessel here on the Cape for less coin."

"But you didn't," she said gently. "He had to go and prove to himself that he could succeed out of your shadow. And he has. Even you must see that."

Stubbornly he shook his head. "So far, aye, he hasn't failed outright," he admitted, and it wasn't much of an admission at that. "Even with the addle-pated notion that he alone could fight a score of Spanish cutthroats with one hand behind his back. That is, he would *if* there were a Spanish ship about, and I don't believe there is. But I worried about Sam when he was a boy, Miss Bray, and I still do."

"Because you love him," she said, the reality of that simple statement so infinitely complicated between these two men.

"Because he is my brother." Joshua looked away purposefully, toward the parlor where the fiddlers had begun to play in earnest. "Would you like to dance, Miss Bray?"

Sadly Polly sighed. She'd be willing to wager that Joshua Fairbourne had once been every bit as merry a little boy as Samson, long before those self-imposed captain's lessons had stifled his spirits. No wonder he loved Anabelle and her open, spontaneous gaiety and joy, for it gave him permission to feel his own.

She shook her head politely. "Thank you, but I do not dance."

"Because you don't wish to?" he challenged. "Or because you fear what Sam will say if he finds you dancing with me?"

"Faith, no!" she said indignantly. Samson would not be particularly pleased to see her with his brother, but she didn't want Joshua to think he'd won, even in so trivial a contest. It was simply not in her nature to back down. "I'm not dancing because I never learned how."

"I never did either, until my wife insisted I learn to stumble about." He waved his hand toward the parlor, encompassing the fiddlers, the guests, and everything else to do with the party. "You know what Anabelle's truly about with this, don't you? She's trying to make us all celebrate Christmas time as if she were still back in heathen old Ireland, at Kilmarsh, instead of here in Massachusetts. Last year it was little gifts and a fancy pudding, now it's a frolic for half the town and cut-branches on the chimney-pieces. Inch by inch, that's how Anabelle works to get her way. She denies it, of course, but in another year or two, we'll be having Maypoles on the lawn, see if we don't!"

He was trying to look as gloomy and stern as the Massachusetts men of a hundred years before, but there was something about his expression that proved how secretly pleased he was with Anabelle's "work." He could preach all he wished about being hard, but where his young wife was concerned, he was as soft and yielding as one of the featherbeds upstairs.

It was love that made Joshua behave this way, thought Polly wistfully, love pure and simple. But would Samson ever come to feel this way about her? For that matter, would he ever even come to this house tonight?

"Here, Miss Bray," said Joshua as he led her to the parlor. "We'll blunder our way together."

The two rows of dancers took another sideways step to allow them to join them, the two fiddlers waiting expectantly for the nod from Joshua to begin again. Reluctantly Polly joined the line of women and strived to stand with her back straight and her hands curved at her sides the way the others did.

Fleetingly she imagined what her father would say to see her here, a fine lady in a silk gown dancing with a deep-water captain in a house worth more than all the buildings in Ninnishibutt combined. Whenever she and Father had sat together on board the *Dove*, waiting for the fish to bite, he'd spin tales of how someday she'd be a lady, though secretly she'd never believed it herself. How proud he'd be to see his tales had come true, if only for a night, and how she wished he'd lived long enough to see it and to meet Samson. Father would like Samson, she was sure, though he'd be tongue-tied and shy in the beginning. But after a time, she was sure—

The fiddlers began with a flourish, and Polly hastily focused her thoughts on the music. She didn't hope to be graceful, only to keep from tripping over her petticoats and landing in a disgraceful heap on the floor. But as the tune progressed she realized that most of the other dancers were equally inexperienced or simply had already drunk too much punch. Making some sort of step in time to the fiddlers seemed to be the most that was required, and before long she was out of breath and laughing like everyone else as they bounced and jostled along with the quick-paced music.

"Handsomely now, Miss Bray, handsomely!" called Joshua over the din, and she grinned as he turned her in a lopsided circle before him.

As she spun the faces of other guests blurred past her, laughing and clapping and shouting encouragement to spur them on. But even in the blur, one face stood out, one guest who neither laughed nor clapped nor shouted, but stood in stony, appalled silence near the doorway.

"Samson!" she cried happily, pulling free of Joshua's hand and of the other dancers. She was dizzy from the dance, unsteady on her feet, but still she hurried toward him. She was so relieved to see him that she willingly overlooked his own lack of greeting, instead seizing his hands in hers and turning her face up to him. "Oh, Samson, how glad I am to see you at last!"

But he didn't draw her close, the way she'd expected, let alone kiss her. Instead he took her by the arm and pulled her away from the dancing, from the parlor, and down the hallway.

"We must talk, Samson," she said breathlessly. She wished he would smile; she wished it very much. "I have so much to tell you!"

"I'm sure you do, Polly," he said curtly as he shoved open the last door and pulled her inside with him. "And I've plenty to tell you as well."

He let her go as he turned to pull the door closed, and she backed away, rubbing her arm where he'd gripped it. The chamber was small and cold, without a fire in the hearth or any candles, and the only light came secondhand, filtering in through the unshuttered windows from the lanterns outside the kitchen door. Here behind the closed door, the merriment of the party was no more than a distant murmur, far away and forgotten.

By the half-light Polly could see the room must serve as Joshua's office, with a desk, a table spread neatly with maps, and tall shelves full of ledgers and wooden boxes marked with the names of ships, but most of all she could see the frozen impassivity on Samson's face. He stood beside the desk, one hand curled in a tight fist on its lid.

"You wish to talk, Polly," he said, snapping off each brittle word as if it were an icicle. "Now talk."

He frightened her when he was like this, not from fear of what he'd do to her but of the damage he could do to himself.

"It's about this morning, Samson," she began, working hard to keep her voice steady. Unconsciously she touched the mermaid cameo, her fingers searching for whatever reassurance the necklace he'd given her in a warmer moment might bring to her now. "I've learned that your brother's done nothing to your parents' house, that it—"

"*Damn* this morning!" he thundered, striking his fist so hard against the top of the desk that the ink bottle rattled. "For this last hour I've been standing out there in the road, in the damned *snow*, trying to decide what I should say to you, while you—you were simpering snug here inside, letting my brother make a damned *fool* of you!"

"It wasn't like that, Samson, not at all!" she cried. "We were talking of you, of what you—"

With a single furious sweep of his arm he cleared the top of the desk, the ink bottle crashing to the floor followed by his brother's pens and letterbooks.

"*Damn* your talk! Do you think I care what he says to you, what he says about me?" He raked his fingers back through his hair, the little drops of melted snowflakes winking in the half-light. "Jesus, Polly, what kind of idiot do you take me for?"

"I never said—"

"You never, and he never, and I never." His laugh was sharp with bitterness as he once again struck the desk. "Do you know that when I try to remember my father, all I can see is Joshua's face in place of his?"

"Oh, Samson," she said softly, daring to take one step toward him. "Please, sweet, do not do this to yourself."

"Yes, plead with me as if it's all my fault, and none of Joshua's. It never is, is it? But I won't let him take you from me, Polly. You're the one thing that's mine, and he's not going to—"

"I love you."

He did not move, and neither did she, the moment stretching endless between them.

"Don't mock me, Poll," he said finally, his voice choked hoarse with emotion. "If this is some womanly game, some way of yours to taunt me, why then—"

"I love you," she said again, the words ringing clear and pure from her heart though her smile was unsteady. "I've waited so blessèd long for you to speak first though you were such a wretched scrod that you never did and now I've had to do it first instead and I—I—oh, I *do* love you, Samson!"

He came to her then, sweeping her into his arms with such force that he lifted her from her feet and against the edge of the table. He kissed her with a desperate urgency, a hunger that she recognized in herself as well as she closed her eyes and threaded her fingers through his hair to hold his head steady, to make this kiss go on and on and on.

"I love you, Poll," he rasped, his breath hot on her ear. "And I loved you first, mind?"

"First, ha, you foolish scrod," she murmured, but she didn't argue beyond that and let him believe he was right because she loved him so much. She could drown in him, all of him, and when she felt him feverishly dragging her petticoats up over her legs, she helped him, her fingers clumsy with desire as she tore at the buttons of his breeches. She wanted this and she wanted him, recklessly, desperately, hot and ready and forever and always, and as she curled her legs around his waist and he thrust into her she could have wept from the joy of being marked this way, of being completely his.

She gasped and sank back as she arched her hips against him, charts fluttering around them like drifts of paper snow, and if she hadn't opened her eyes to watch him moving over her, she wouldn't have seen the light from the hallway angle across the ceiling as the door began to swing open.

"Samson," she gasped, but this time from shock and shame, not pleasure. "Oh, God, *no!*"

She wriggled backward, feeling Samson slip free as he twisted around to shield her as best he could. With a whimper of panic she shoved her skirts back down over her bare thighs with one hand while she pulled her bodice back up over her breasts with another. Not that it mattered now. There was nothing more left of her slatternly self for Joshua Fairbourne to see, and she had never been more shamed in all her life. How could she ever face him after this? Not even love could help her now. Her legs were weak as she stumbled forward, her body ached wickedly from unfulfillment, yet her one thought was to flee.

"Don't go, Polly," said Samson raggedly as he reached to stop her. "Damnation, wait!"

He squinted at the light from the hall as his brother entered, slamming the door shut as he came.

"Cover yourself," ordered Joshua as he glanced with disgust at Samson's untucked shirt and open breeches. "There are ladies in this house."

"To hell with you, Joshua," muttered Samson as he buttoned his breeches and began to push past his brother. He had to find Polly. That was all that mattered now.

But Joshua blocked the door with his arm. "You *will* marry her, Sam."

Samson met his brother's gaze without flinching. "I will marry her the moment she'll have me," he said softly, "but she won't. God help me, she won't. And as many things as you've bent to your will, Joshua, Polly Bray won't be one of them."

All she wanted was to be alone.

Down this hall would be the party, with scores of curious eyes to follow her. But if she tried to retreat upstairs she'd run the risk of meeting Anabelle or Serena, both women far too good for her as she was now.

"Pardon me, miss," said the red-faced cook, puffing as she squeezed past Polly with her two hired maidservants in tow, each of them bearing the first heavy dishes like prizes for the supper table. With them heading toward the second parlor, the kitchen would be empty, and before they returned Polly darted back down the hall. A half-dozen cloaks and coats of all sizes hung on pegs beside the door. Polly grabbed the nearest, a worn green hooded cloak, flung it over her shoulders, and slipped from the door into the yard outside.

The snowflakes swirled, stinging against her face, and crunched, dry and hard, beneath her shoes. She'd be alone enough here, no doubt of that. She hugged the cloak around her shoulders, clutching the rough wool in her fingers. She didn't want to feel anything but the cold and the snow, and with a shuddering sigh she closed her eyes and tipped her head back as she leaned against the clapboard wall.

She should not have run away and left Samson to face his brother alone, especially after all he'd gone through today. How could she love him and do something like that? She was not only a slattern but a coward as well, and she couldn't say which she despised more.

Yet curling up through her disgrace like a new green shoot through ashes was the knowledge, the wondrous certainty, that Samson loved her. He'd said it himself, and showed her, too, and she'd never doubt either.

He loves me. . . .

She heard the crack of a dry branch, the sound magnified by the silence of cold night air, and she didn't bother to look. A cat come for scraps at the kitchen door, a skunk, even a frozen branch giving way beneath its own weight.

He loved her, and she smiled foolishly at the memory, touching her lips with her fingertips.

He loved her, and this time her eyes stayed closed too long, and when the greasy scarf came down over her face and tightened around her neck, silencing her, choking her, stealing her consciousness away with her breath, she could do nothing but struggle weakly and tumble down into the darkness.

He loved her, and now he was too late.

Sixteen

Dios mío, but it was cold, as cold as death, as ice, as the black empty place where a whore's heart should be. The spray that broke over the prow of the small boat was like a thousand needles when it struck his skin, and though Hidaldgo had heard tales of snow, he'd never imagined the cruel reality of tiny, flying pieces of ice flailing him in the night. He had no feeling left in his feet or his hands, nor would he ever again be able to ease the frozen grimace from his face. He could sit in the middle of a heretic's pyre and still not be warm enough.

But when he looked down at the woman lying so still at his feet, a bundle of rough green wool dusted with snow, he knew both his prayers and his suffering had been rewarded. Striving to be unnoticed, he had landed in the town with but two men at the oars of the boat, and he and Fernando had gone to Fairbourne's house intending to leave a message, a challenge that would lure the Engishman back to his ship. But instead the saints had granted him a true gift: Fairbourne's gray-eyed woman alone behind the house, a single blossom waiting to be plucked and stolen away.

Now the rest would be easy. Guided by his lust, Fairbourne would follow, out to the ship that he'd so graciously moved within Hidaldgo's reach. That had been another gift, another sign that his cause was blessed. The *Morning Star* would have only a handful of men on board for harbor watch, maybe even fewer on account of the storm, and likely no officers, who would all be with Fairbourne himself at his brother's house.

In their home ports, Englishmen always grew lazy and careless, and Hidaldgo meant to take every advantage their carelessness offered. By his reckoning, the ship should have already been captured by his own men. Once he'd joined them, they would only have to wait long enough for Fairbourne to come after his woman, and into Hidaldgo's own hands. By the time these fat, foolish Englishmen realized the *Morning Star* and her captain had disappeared from the harbor, Hidaldgo would be well on his way back to Havana, and sunshine, and a prodigious bounty in honor of their bravery from the grateful royal governor himself.

Hidaldgo prodded the unconscious woman with the toe of his shoe. He had told Fernando to be gentle with her, but she still had not wakened. It would be a pity if she perished—he had anticipated the entertainment she'd provide on the long voyage home, there in Fairbourne's own cabin—but alive or dead, she'd still served her purpose in destroying her lover.

Hidaldgo smiled. The pleasure of such revenge would be sweet indeed, and suddenly the snow seemed no torment at all.

* * *

"Where is Polly?" repeated Anabelle as she sipped her little glass of punch. "La, Samson, you should take better care of her. She should not be mislaid like a stray stocking."

"She is not mislaid, ma'am," said Samson curtly. "I cannot find her, that is all."

Anabelle moved closer, her diamond plume winking by the candlelight and her voice lowering in confidence. "If Joshua is to be believed, you found her readily enough earlier. Oh, hush, no one else knows, but that was not well done, Samson, not well done in the least. No lady wishes to be treated with such flagrant disrespect, you know. If you care for her at all, you truly must learn to lock doors."

Samson grumbled with exasperation. He had gone over the entire house twice and found not one trace of Polly. No one had seen her since she'd stopped dancing with Joshua. In her bedchamber her coat was still hanging from its peg, her battered old knife still sitting in its sheath on the chest of drawers, so he knew she hadn't run away. Wherever she was, she would be safe enough under Joshua's roof. But where could she have hidden herself with the house so full of witnesses?

But Polly didn't play games like this, especially not something as childish as hide and seek, and uneasiness pricked at his conscience. As startled and ashamed as she'd been, he should not have let her go, not with so much left unfinished between them. He should have insisted on keeping her there with him. She was the woman he loved, and he would never let her go again.

"I'd venture that Polly merely wished a bit of quiet to herself," suggested Anabelle, giving him a sisterly wink. "The way you Fairbourne men bluster and

stomp about like the bull on the village green can
make any woman feel weakish, and to be confronted
by two of you in such a situation—well, I should
wish a bit of peace after that myself."

"Ah, Sam, here you are at last!" said Zach as he
elbowed his way to Samson's side. "That is, good
evening, Captain, sir, I—oh, hang it, Sam, I have to
talk to you, right now."

He was clearly so agitated that at once Samson
rested a steadying hand on the younger man's
shoulder.

"What is it, lad?" he asked with concern. "Have
you word from the ship? Is there some sort of
trouble?"

He took so deep a breath he seemed to draw it from
the toes of his buckled dress shoes. "It's Polly."

"Polly." So his misgivings, his fears, his uneasiness, were all founded in fact. Blast it all, if she'd
come to any harm . . .

"Aye, Polly." Zach took another deep breath. "She
knows about your oath, Sam. *All* about the oath, clear
to the bottle and the paper that you stuffed inside it."

Whatever Samson had expected, this wasn't it.
"How the Devil could she know that? And how do
you know she knows?"

"She told me herself, clear as daybreak. She pretended she was describing the perfect wife for me, but
I'm not a halfwit. 'Sweet in temper and without
vanity, modest and truthful in words and manner,
beautiful and obedient'—she had it all, Sam, every
word of it, even though she swore you hadn't told
her." Anxiously he searched Samson's face. "But you
did, Sam, didn't you? Didn't you?"

"Oh, la, now this is *vastly* intriguing!" said Anabelle as her eyes lit with keen interest. "An oath from

Samson and a perfect wife for Zachariah, and Polly somehow stirred into the thick of it!"

"It's nothing," said Samson quickly, and he prayed it wasn't. He had enough on his mind concerning Polly without adding that infernal oath to the mix. "Nothing, mind?"

Anabelle laughed and poked his sleeve with her furled fan. "What I mind, Samson, is that your 'nothing' is most certainly something. You gentlemen do believe that we ladies have no—oh, stay a moment, here comes Joshua!"

"Damnation, I won't see him," said Samson, pointedly turning his back in the direction that his brother must come. "I'm sorry for your sake, Anabelle, but I can't—"

"Hush," said Anabelle, all her customary merriment draining from her face as she looked toward her husband. "You *will* see him, and now, for he has news of Polly."

Samson turned back immediately, and his uneasiness mushroomed into heartsick foreboding. In one of Joshua's hands he held a crumpled paper, while in the other was a too-familiar strand of coral beads, swinging gently with the weight of the mermaid cameo.

"Here," he said as he thrust the paper into Samson's hand. "I do not know how, but that bastard Hidaldgo has Polly."

It took only an instant for Samson to scan the nearly illegible scrawl to understand the message: if he wished to see Polly alive, he must come at once, unarmed and unaccompanied save for the men to row his boat, to the *Morning Star*. With the curious abstraction of a nightmare, he stared at the one neatly written word on the page, Hidaldgo's own signature, penned with a clerk's tidy precision. Strange how in all the years they'd danced circles around one another in the Caribbean, he'd never once seen it before.

"John Rodgers found the note when he arrived," continued Joshua bitterly, "tucked into the knocker on the front door. I would not believe it to be real except that Miss Bray's beads were wrapped around it. The snow by the kitchen door's all churned, too, and the cook swears her cloak's been stolen. That Spanish devil knows his trade well enough."

Silently Samson nodded as he took the beads from his brother, looping them around his fingers as if they still held the warmth of Polly's skin. He hadn't been sure she'd accept them tonight, either, and he'd been so proud to see the carved mermaid finally resting in the hollow of Polly's pretty throat. And in silence, too, he slipped the beads into his pocket and began to head toward the door.

"It's you Hidaldgo wants, Samson," said Joshua, his voice effortlessly rising to fill the space between them. The other guests stood mute and still, watching the two brothers like players in a private tragedy. "You know this is a trap to catch you."

Samson paused but didn't turn. "He has Polly."

"You go alone, and you're as good as dead," said Joshua. "What the hell use will you be to her then?"

"He's not going alone." Zach came to stand beside Samson, holding his head high so he was nearly the same height as his cousin, while from the back of the parlor rose a small, mournful wail of disappointment from the girl he'd danced with last. "I'm coming with you, Sam. For you, and for Polly."

"Hell, do you think I'd send him off by himself?"

Joshua crossed the room in three strides to clap his hand on Samson's shoulder. "You tell me what you need and it's yours."

"I'm not asking for anything from you, Joshua," said Samson warily.

"And all I'm doing is offering," said Joshua. "You don't have to take a blasted thing more from me if you don't want it. But you're still my little brother, and, like it or not, you're still a Fairbourne."

Slowly Samson forced himself to turn and meet his brother's eye. He'd never dreamed he'd hear such words from Joshua, or that he'd actually sound as if he meant them. It wasn't quite a reconciliation, but it was definitely the first step toward one. He only wished it hadn't taken Polly's capture to make it happen.

"Fairbournes, aye," he said slowly, not trusting himself to give in to everything just yet. "Meaning Zach, too."

Yet to his surprise Joshua nodded, including Zach in a way that made the younger man beam with pleasure.

"Here, Sam," said Serena breathlessly as she, too, joined them, leading her dog with her fingers looped through his rope collar. "Take Abel with you. There's a chance they haven't left the land, and he'll track any scent, even in the snow."

Anabelle darted forward, tugging Samson down to her level long enough to kiss him on the cheek.

"You *will* bring Polly back," she said fiercely. "Whatever it is that has brought you two together is not about to let you stay apart now. You are too vastly perfect for one another for it to be any other way! So you *will* bring Polly back to us, Samson, back to

Appledore. Yes, yes, that is it: go now, and bring her back home."

How many times had Polly awakened in a boat like this, how many times beyond counting?

Her head hurt too much to open her eyes, and she was stiff and cold from lying in the same damp place for too long, but the gentle rocking of the boat moving over and through the swells, the squeak of the oars in their oarlocks, even the muffled sound of the water beneath her ear, under the hull of the boat, were all so familiar and comforting that she could have drifted back to sleep and forgotten the ache in her head and the cold and the awkward bend in her back.

But then she heard the man speak, the words soft and full of sounds that made no sense to her ear. She'd heard this man speak before, and though she could not understand his language, she knew him, and all thought of peace and sleep vanished.

It had been so easy to slide back toward unconsciousness, but now that she needed to pretend it to save herself, it seemed almost impossible. With her eyes still closed, she tried to force her other senses to work instead. She lay in the bottom of an open boat—that was certain—and in the boat with her, God help her, was Hidaldgo.

If she concentrated, she could just remember standing in the yard near the kitchen door, the details blurring as if through a grimy window. Somehow the Spaniard must have made her his prisoner then and brought her to this boat. She remembered how he'd treated her in St. Pierre, the enjoyment he'd found in making her suffer, and her heart plummeted with fear and dread of what he'd do now.

He would have kidnapped her like this only to hurt Samson. He would kill her, and then, if he could, he would kill Samson as well, and oh, she did not want to die, not when the promise of Samson's love hung there so brightly before her!

Yet she knew, too, that if she'd any hope of escape, she must not panic. Aye, she must use her wits, and seek out what in this grim situation might be used to her own advantage.

First there was the boat itself. If they were still in a boat, then she was most likely still in the harbor at Appledore, which was good. If they were still in the harbor, then she was not so very far from the *Morning Star* and her crew, which was even better.

But there was more in her favor as well. From the sounds of the oars, she guessed there were only two men rowing, plus Hidaldgo himself—three men at most. Not good odds, but better than if there'd been eight or ten, the usual number in a ship's boat.

And last, but far from the least consequential, was the fact that Hidaldgo had once again dismissed her as another silly, helpless woman. Her wrists and ankles had been left unbound, her mouth ungagged, and if she'd bothered to wear her knife under her silk petticoats—which, to her sorrow, she hadn't, on account of dressing with Anabelle—she didn't doubt that that would have been left untouched, too.

The boat was slowing at Hildaldgo's command, the men at the oars in response maneuvering the boat to some unknown destination. Whatever was going to happen to her next would happen soon, as well as what she decided to do in return, and once again she fought to tamp down her panic and fear. She had to survive, and she had to escape, for Samson's sake as well as her own.

But oh, Samson, she prayed in silent desperation, *whatever else may happen, know that I love you. . . .*

Hidaldgo studied the English ship before him. He'd never had the chance to see it this close before, and he could already count what so fine a vessel, in such good repair, would bring at the prize auctions in Havana. A clean capture by stealth like this would mean he wouldn't even have to make allowances for repairs, the way he would if he'd taken the *Morning Star* by force.

"*Capitán*," said Fernando uneasily as he looked over his shoulder at the ship ahead. "The signal, the flag—it is not there, *Capitán*."

Belatedly Hidaldgo shifted his gaze upward, to the place on the mainmast where the ship's ensign should be. Once his men from the *San Miguel* had boarded and taken possession of the *Morning Star*, they were supposed to change the flag from the English ensign with the St. George cross to Hidaldgo's own, a red banner with a single yellow bar. But the flag that hung there limply was white, not yellow, and he cursed his men's forgetfulness.

Fernando shook his head, his expression bleak beneath his knitted cap. "They did not come, *Capitán*. If there is no flag, then they did not come."

"Of course they have come, Nando!" said Hidaldgo angrily. "They had their orders! To steal this ship would be as easy as taking eggs from an old woman's market basket! More likely they are below, filling their worthless bellies with Fairbourne's rum!"

"Ahoy there!" came the call in English from the bow of the English ship. "What boat?"

"There, *Capitán*, there is the proof of your order," said Fernando as he spat contemptuously over the side while the man at the other oar, Juan, crossed himself and began to mumble prayers for his own salvation. "Our men are not within a league of this place. They have gone, *Capitán*, sailed back to Havana, and abandoned us to our fate in this English hell of ice and snow."

Hidaldgo swung his fist and struck Fernando hard across his bearded cheek. "I'll hear none of that traitorous talk! You may wish to betray me, but I tell you the others do not."

Fernando sneered, shaking off the blow as if it had been no more than a tap. "That is because you have been as a deaf man, and refused to hear while I have listened. They know your promises of gold are lies. They have only to look at this barren coast to see there is no fortune to be found here. In the fo'c'sle they whispered that you were possessed by demons, that you live for nothing beyond catching this Fairbourne. You may live for that, Hidaldgo, but they will not die for it."

"You will die now like a dog if you do not obey." Swiftly Hidaldgo drew his knife, pressing the tip of the long blade to the other man's chest. "Cross me again, Nando, and you will see how possessed I am."

The mate began to rise to his feet, lifting his hand to shove the knife away, but before he could do so Hidaldgo flicked the blade upward and into Fernando's exposed throat below his beard, twisting it once as the mate gurgled blood. As Juan recoiled and swore, Hidaldgo shoved the dying man over the side of the boat.

"Ahoy there, in the boat," called the man again from the rail of the *Morning Star*. Another sailor now stood beside him, a lantern raised high in his hand to cast light upon the boat below. "Have you trouble there?"

Roughly Hidaldgo grabbed Polly by the shoulder. "Time to wake, pretty pigeon," he ordered, pulling her upright with him, her back to his chest as he held her with one arm clamped tight below her shoulders. "Time to greet your admirers, eh?"

Polly struggled, hating the feel of his body against hers, but the long cloak only tangled more around her arms and legs. With her eyes squeezed shut she'd heard the two Spaniards fighting over her head, though she'd understood not a word of their quarrel, and heard the splash, but it was only now she saw that one was gone from the boat. Suddenly the light from the *Morning Star*'s lantern swept over them, and to her horror she saw the blood, so much blood, spilled over the bench and the oar and the side and her own cloak, too, and the black shadow of the dead man's body bobbing in the water, his dangling oar drifting in a clumsy circle from the lock.

Oh, Samson, save me, save us both. . . .

"So you were not asleep at all, *dulce*, were you?" said Hidaldgo softly into her ear, jerking her arm tighter. "Then you will know that I expect obedience."

She felt the blade of his knife, sticky with the dead man's blood, press close to the side of her neck, and she whimpered with terror.

"Ahoy, *Morning Star*," called Hidaldgo, and the lantern's light held steady. "We have a lady who wishes to board. You will recognize her, *sí*?"

"Miss Bray!" called the man at the rail, and though his voice was taut with shock, she could recognize it as belonging to Plunkett. "Miss Bray, can you hear me?"

"Answer him," ordered Hidaldgo, "or die."

"Let—let us come aboard," she called hoarsely, her throat twitching convulsively where the knife pressed into it. "Please, Mr. Plunkett. Please!"

"Aye-aye, miss, whatever you wish," he said, hurrying with the lantern to the break in the rail near the boarding steps to toss down the guide ropes. "That's—ah, that's not the cap'n with you, is it?"

"Do not tell him who I am," hissed Hidaldgo. "He will learn his new master's name soon enough."

"Nay, Mr. Plunkett," she called faintly. "It is not Captain Fairbourne with me."

But how desperately, how dearly, I wish it were!

The boat nudged against the ship's side. "You will go first, pigeon," said Hidaldgo, taking the knife from her throat as he sat back down on the bench, "and Juan will follow close, to keep you from falling. But no plans of escaping, eh? For you see, I have another way of punishing you if you do."

With a flourish he drew a long-barreled pistol from the front of his coat, the steel beautifully engraved with swirling vines and flowers in the Spanish manner. Mutely Polly nodded, her panic growing. She doubted the pistol's powder would flash in the snow and so near the water, but that was a gamble she wasn't willing to take.

"Up with you now, *dulce.*" Hidaldgo motioned toward the shallow, carved steps with the pistol. "Dawdling like this unsettles me."

"A moment, pray," she said quickly. "If I'm to make such a perilous climb, then for decency I must make certain, ah, adjustments to my dress."

Not only did she not find such a climb particularly perilous, but she'd never spoken in that kind of lady-talk in her life. But she did have the beginnings of a

plan, and lady-talk and lady-decency were a part of
it, even if she were smeared with a dead man's blood.
She forced herself to smile, and Hidaldgo preened.

"One moment, then," he conceded, though he
kept the pistol aimed at her. "But that is all."

Quickly Polly pulled one corner of her blood-
spattered cloak frontward, between her legs, and tied
it to the other corner, modestly looping her petticoats
into a bunch between her legs. But her legs, in a pair
of fancy yellow silk stockings with knitted roses that
had been borrowed from Anabelle, were very much
on display, nearly to the tops of her garters. Both
Spaniards were staring, as she'd hoped they would,
and the sight gave her the courage she needed.

"Do you be needin' any help, Miss Bray?" called
down Plunkett anxiously as he peered over the side.
Behind him Polly could just make out several other
men, the rest of the small harbor crew, and she
prayed they would all be clever enough to follow her
cue, and that at least one of them was armed himself.
"Do you be needin' us to rig the bosun's chair
again?"

"Nay, Mr. Plunkett," she called as she took hold of
the guide ropes and waited for the next swell to lift
the boat closer to the ship. The shallow steps were
slicked with ice, and she didn't want to misstep; the
water tonight would be cold enough to kill. "I'll be
well enough on my own."

"Juan will be right behind you," warned Hidaldgo
in her ear, "and I will be watching you both."

It was a warning she didn't need, or want. She took
a deep breath and made the small leap across the
water to the footholds. She made her way slowly up
the side, not wanting to get too far ahead of Juan. She
could hear him puffing along on the steps behind her,

more out of breath than any sailor had a right to be. But she was counting on that; if he'd been less stout and more agile, her plan wouldn't work.

When her eyes were level with the deck, she hesitated a minute, giving him time to nearly overtake her, and also giving him a closer view of her yellow stockings. Then she kicked her heel back as hard as she could into his chest. For an endless moment the man seemed to hang there, caught upon her shoe, and then he was gone, arcing backward, away from Polly and farther from the ship, with a startled bellow that ended only with the splash when he hit the icy water.

Not that Polly waited to watch. Swiftly she scampered up the last few steps and flung herself onto the slippery, snow-covered deck, sliding on her stomach past the astonished Plunkett with a shuddering gulp of relief.

She'd escaped, and she hadn't been shot. She'd be safe here now among Samson's crew, until he could—

She shrieked with pain when the weight of Hidaldgo's body slammed on top of hers, crushing her against the hard planking. Yet almost immediately he had rolled onto his back, taking her with him, and then he was on his knees, holding her, gasping, before him like a shield with the knife again pressed tight against her throat. The five men from the crew stared at them, their faces frozen into masks of shock, horror, and bewilderment.

"What kind of fool do you think I am?" he demanded, his breath coming in short, hard spurts. "You are lucky I do not slit your throat now instead of later, when your lover can watch."

"Plunkett!" came the distant call from the water. "Plunkett, ahoy! Where the Devil are you, man?"

She'd know Samson's voice anywhere, even now, and with a shudder of a sob, she closed her eyes. As much as she wished to be saved, she didn't want him here, now, on the other side of Hidaldgo's gun.

"Don't consider it, *dulce*," warned Hidaldgo as he pushed her stumbling clumsily across the snow-covered deck to the rail. If she slipped, she'd fall into the blade of the knife at her throat, and she struggled to keep her footing. But Hidaldgo was careful, too, careful always to keep her between himself and the other men who might try to help her.

"Fairbourne!" he shouted down at the water. "Fairbourne, can you see who I have with me? Come, pigeon, show yourself now."

Through the snow and the darkness she could just make out Samson's upturned face as he gazed up not at Hidaldgo but at her. There were four other men in the boat with him, two she knew were *Morning Star* men and two others she didn't recognize, not with their hats pulled low against the snow.

"Would you be so good as to come aboard now, eh, *Capitán?*" jeered Hidaldgo. "Is my invitation good enough for you?"

Without answering Samson reached for the ropes and began to climb aboard.

"Nay, Samson, don't!" cried Polly before the Spaniard jerked her back from the rail.

"I have told you to obey me," he said sharply, "and obey me you will, or *he* will be the first to suffer, here before your eyes. You recall that my pistol still carries its ball. How pleasant it would be to use it upon your captain!"

"Nay," she sobbed as Samson himself climbed over the side, as easily and as confidently as if he were still in complete command of the ship. He was almost unbearably handsome to her, there with his face so somber and the snow dusting the shoulders of his dark coat, and unbearably dear as well. "Oh, nay, Samson, don't come, please!"

But Hidaldgo only smiled, gently running the knife over her throat in a gruesome mockery of a caress. "She is most sensible, your woman, and when the time comes for her to die, I shall almost miss her. But that is because she has seen how angry I become when crossed, and you, *Capitán* Fairbourne, have crossed me too many times."

"Let Polly go," said Samson with great care, striving not to upset Hidaldgo as long as he held the knife. "She's done nothing. You can send her back now with the others to town."

"Oh, but I cannot, Fairbourne," said Hidaldgo with relish. "I cannot, for she is my passage back to Havana, and yours, too. I am only one on this ship of yours, you know. If I were to let her go, what assurance would I have that you would come with me? Your worthless English word? An oath sworn upon your Testament? No, no, *Capitán*, this lady stays with me, for so, then, will you."

"Then for Polly's sake," said Samson quietly, "I will stay. You tell me what you wish, and you shall have it, as long as Polly is unharmed."

For the first time since he'd come on deck Samson turned toward her, and the look they exchanged was so eloquent that she felt her heart breaking all over again. How could he be this calm when their life together could be ending before it had begun? He might believe Hidaldgo's promises, but she could not, not when she wore the blood of another who'd dared question him. Whenever he tired of her or this game, whether in an hour or a day or a week, he would kill her.

She had never felt as helpless or as useless, and tears of fear and pain blurred her eyes as she thought of everything that she and Samson might now never share: the voyages to other ports, the babies that might look like little Alexander, the laughter and the lovemaking and the *love* that made what they'd found so special.

She clenched her hands into fists, determined to keep from crying openly. As she did her hand brushed against her skirts, and something hard beneath: the bottle, her supposed good luck charm that had been so worthless when she and Samson had gone to Cranberry Point. After that, she wasn't ready to believe it could influence anyone's fortune, for good or ill, but right now she was desperate enough to try it.

Carefully, so that Hidaldgo wouldn't notice, she eased her hand inside her pocket and held the bottle tightly in her fingers. She closed her eyes and blotted out everything but her wish.

Please, please make Hidaldgo set me free so I can tell Samson how much I love him, how I always will.

"You must guarantee me safe passage to Havana," Hidaldgo was saying. "This ship, this crew. We must sail this night, now, before you can call to your miserable little town for help and before my hand grows weary and lets this knife slip."

Please, please . . .

The first whisper of the wind was so faint that she thought she'd imagined it, the merest ruffling of her skirts. But then it began to build, undeniable, driving the snow hard against her face and making others around them on the deck grab for a line or rail to steady themselves. She saw Samson's gaze flicker to her hand in her pocket, then the mixture of incredulity and triumph light his eyes as the wind tossed his black hair.

"*Dios mío*, such a wind!" Hidaldgo laughed with joy and turned his face to shout at the sky. "What a rare blessing to guide our voyage!"

But this was not weather that any wise mariner would wish for a voyage. The night sky seemed to turn darker still, low and menacing, while the harbor grew restless with white-capped billows. Then the wind struck hard, sweeping down and striking the ship like a giant, unseen fist. The deck pitched at a crazy angle. Polly felt her feet begin to slide out from under her, and she flailed to keep her balance. Catching himself, Hidaldgo grabbed for the rail with the hand that had held the knife to her throat. But now he held her trapped against the canting rail with only his body, the two of them awkwardly leaning far out over the churning waves below. Polly gasped, clawing against Hidaldgo to pull herself back as the deck slanted more and more steeply beneath the force of the wind.

"Not like this!" roared Hidaldgo furiously, his words whipped away by the storm as he struggled to keep them both from falling backward over the side. "*Maldición!* It is Fairbourne who must die, not me! I am not ready to die like this!"

To Polly's horror he pulled his hand from the railing and lifted the knife to plunge it into her. Without thinking she put both her hands on his chest and shoved as hard as she could. He grabbed at her, trying to regain his balance, but the force of the wind had already caught him, sweeping him over the railing with a last wild roar. Frantically Polly grabbed at the railing, dropping to her knees to huddle against it. With shaking fingers she reached in her pocket for the bottle, the precious bottle that had done its job and saved her one more time.

"Polly!" roared Samson, using the guide ropes to fight his way across the deck toward her. "Hold on, lass!"

But abruptly the wind shifted, slanting the deck in the opposite direction. Polly's frozen fingers lost their grip on the rail, and she felt herself sliding again, downward toward the other rail. Her fingers flew open, and the bottle popped free, rolling ahead of her in a bumpy path over the snow-covered deck.

"Nay, come back!" she cried breathlessly, scrambling to reach it as she slipped and slid toward the other rail. "I cannot lose you now!"

"Polly!" She felt herself jerked back as Samson stopped her fall, his hands tight around her waist as he hauled her back. Holding her close to his chest with one arm while his other held tight to a guideline, he fought his way up the slanting, rocking deck to brace them both against the thick trunk of the mainmast.

"Polly, love, tell me you're not harmed," he demanded urgently as he pushed her wet hair back from her face. "Jesus, when I saw you there—"

"I love you, Samson!" she gasped, the only answer that mattered. "I love you, and—"

"Then marry me."

She looked up at him in wonder, her lashes dotted with snowflakes and her smile wobbling through her tears. "Oh, yes, you great wonderful scrod! Yes, yes, yes, I *will* marry you!"

He kissed her then, and while her head was spinning in the usual delicious way it did when they kissed, she noticed that the wind had died away as dramatically as it had risen, leaving the deck once again peacefully level beneath their feet. The snow had stopped, too, and the black night clouds were beginning to shred and drift away.

She broke their kiss and pushed her way back a bit in his embrace. "Look, Samson," she said breathlessly, holding the bottle up between them for him to see. "It saved us again!"

"So this is your famous lucky piece," he said, his voice fondly teasing, "your one sure—my God, Polly, how did you come by this?"

He snatched the bottle from her, holding it up to the light from the binnacle lantern, his face full of wonder and, perhaps, a smidgen of fear.

"I don't know," she confessed. "That is, I cannot remember. But it was in the pocket of my coat that first morning I woke on your deck, after I nearly drowned, and it has been good luck to me—to both of us, really—ever since."

"It cannot be," he muttered. His fingers were shaking as he worked the cork from the neck of the bottle and fished the paper from inside. "Jesus, it cannot *be*."

"Oh, that's nothing but rubbish," she said as he unrolled the scrap of curled paper. "Someone's supper bill, from the look of it, but I didn't dare toss it away for fear it was part of the luck."

"Thank God you're unharmed, Polly," said Zach fervently as he hurried to join them. "Joshua and I were in the boat with pistols waiting for a chance to shoot that bastard Hidaldgo when—holy hell, Sam, that can't be—"

"Don't say it, Zach," said Samson hoarsely as they both stared at the bottle. "Don't even *think* it."

Polly shrugged, embarrassed now, especially by the shock that showed on Samson's face as he turned the paper over and over between his fingers.

"I know you think I'm a silly noddy for believing in such things, Samson," she said sheepishly, touching her fingers over his. "I know you're so brave and strong that you don't need to believe in Jonahs and lucky bottles at all, but I'm afraid I'm not, and I do, and now that I'm going to be your wife--"

"Your *wife?*" repeated Zach with an enormous, incredulous grin. "He's finally asked you to marry him? Then it worked, Sam, just as you—"

"Not one word, Zach," warned Samson as he stuffed the scrap of paper back into the bottle and corked the neck. "Not now, not ever."

Polly frowned. "You're neither of you making any sense."

"That's because I've given up trying," said Samson, taking her by the hand to lead her to the stern rail, where the full moon was finally beginning to peek through the clouds. He put the bottle firmly into her hands. "Here, take this, lass. Now I want you to make one last wish for us both."

"Oh, Samson, I don't know," she said uneasily. "Whenever I do so at sea, such wicked grand things seem to happen."

"You must trust me, Poll," he said firmly. "If you love me, you must trust me, and do exactly as I say."

Trust Samson, and trust your own heart. . . .

"Very well," she said, "though I cannot promise I will always be so obedient and accommodating when we're wed."

She took a deep breath, closed her eyes, and made

her wish. "I wish for us to be happy together for-ever!"

"Now throw it, Polly!"

She opened her eyes. "Throw it away? Into the water?"

"Throw it *now!*"

She looked down at the bottle, and then up at him, and she smiled. What need did she have for good luck tokens when she had Samson?

Without looking, she tossed the bottle over the side and slipped into the embrace that she never wished to leave again.

And as they kissed, the last clouds disappeared from the sky, and the moon shined bright as day on Appledore harbor.

Miranda Jarrett

The Captain's Bride

The Dazzling Fairbourne Family Saga Begins!

"Miranda Jarrett can always be counted on for
the very best in romantic adventure!"
—Kathe Robin, *Romantic Times*

Now available from Pocket Star Books

POCKET
STAR
BOOKS